BLOOD OF THE SOUTH

BLOOD OF THE SOUTH

An Aelf Fen Mystery

Alys Clare

severn
House

This first world edition published 2014
in Great Britain and 2015 in the USA by
SEVERN HOUSE PUBLISHERS LTD of
19 Cedar Road, Sutton, Surrey, England, SM2 5DA.
Trade paperback edition first published
in Great Britain and the USA 2015 by
SEVERN HOUSE PUBLISHERS LTD.

British Library Cataloguing in Publication Data

Clare, Alys author.
  Blood of the South.
  1. Murder–Investigation–Fiction. 2. Great Britain–
  History–Norman period, 1066–1154–Fiction. 3. Detective
  and mystery stories.
  I. Title
  823.9'14-dc23

ISBN-13: 978-0-7278-8432-9 (cased)
ISBN-13: 978-1-84751-541-4 (trade paper)
ISBN-13: 978-1-78010-585-7 (e-book)

All Severn House titles are printed on acid-free paper.

Severn House Publishers support the Forest Stewardship Council™ [FSC™],
the leading international forest certification organisation. All our titles that
are printed on FSC certified paper carry the FSC logo.

MIX
Paper from
responsible sources
FSC   FSC® C013056
www.fsc.org

Typeset by Palimpsest Book Production Ltd.,
Falkirk, Stirlingshire, Scotland.
Printed and bound in Great Britain by
TJ International, Padstow, Cornwall.

For my beloved son Jonathan,
who also goes down to the sea in ships.

Lassair's Family Tree

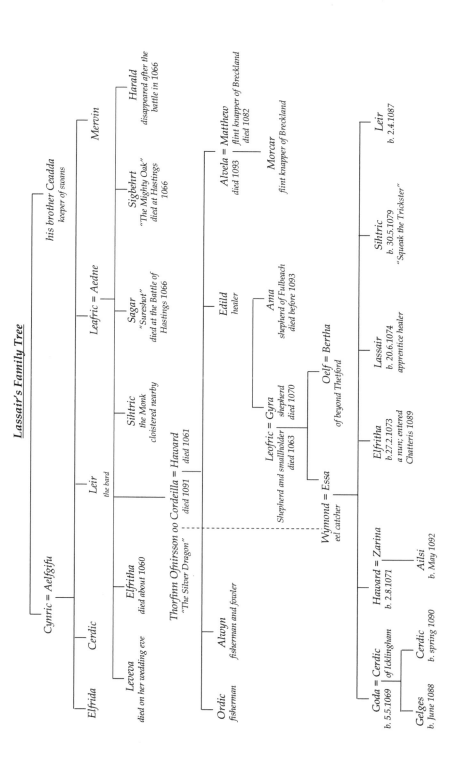

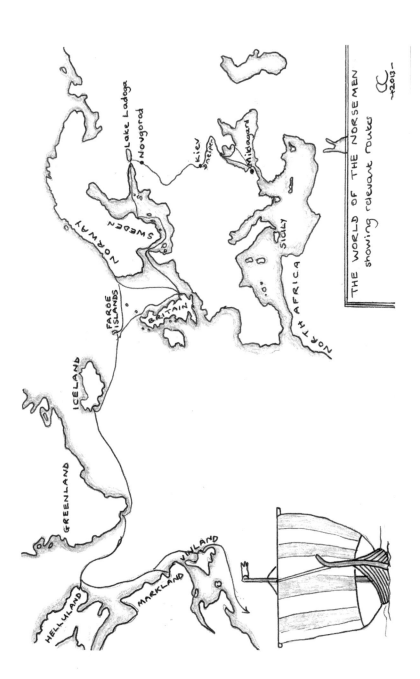

THE WORLD OF THE NORSEMEN
showing relevant routes

HELLULAND

MARKLAND

VINLAND

GREENLAND

ICELAND

FAROE ISLANDS

NORWAY

SWEDEN

BRITAIN

Lake Ladoga

Novgorod

Kiev

Dneiper

Miklagard

SICILY

NORTH AFRICA

CC
—2013—

ONE

There is a collective evil that comes over a crowd of people intent on bullying someone. Faces that are habitually genial twist and distort; mouths made for smiling turn down into scowls of anger, dislike and even hatred. It is as if, given a strong lead by the man who first singles out the victim – and I'm afraid it usually seems to be a man – other, kinder souls feel compelled to follow. Then the whole thing gathers an awful sort of impetus, and before you know it, someone gets hurt.

That September morning, as Gurdyman and I stood on the Cambridge quayside in the thin, early sunshine, the victim was a young woman. From her garments, her voluminous veil and what I could see of her face, she was not local. She had a baby with her: in that first glance, I could make out no details, merely noticing the wrapped shape placed on the ground beside her, the swaddling blankets folded too tightly to allow anything to emerge from the bundle except high-pitched, piercing screams. The woman was not trying to soothe her child; she wasn't even cuddling it. She had both hands up in front of her face in frantic, terrified self-defence, because someone had just chucked a lump of smelly mud at her.

Gurdyman and I, latecomers on the scene, were right at the back of the thronging people. We had intended to be on the quay early, since Gurdyman was expecting the arrival of a cargo from far away and he wanted to ensure first choice of the exotic, mysterious goods. Intentions often go astray, however. I had overslept, Gurdyman had forgotten that today was the day the boat was due to arrive, and, by the time we finally arrived puffing and panting on the path by the river – well, Gurdyman was puffing, but then he is many years my senior, twice my girth and he doesn't go out much – the port was already heaving. We had been steadily making our way through the crowd to where our boat was likely to tie up, when the loud, braying voices caught our attention.

'Filthy foreigner!' someone screamed. A woman; it is not only men who bully.

'You're not welcome here, you lying, cheating cow!' A man's voice, deep, furious. And he didn't say *cow*.

'Send her back where she came from!' someone else chimed in. 'We've got cheats and thieves enough of our own, without importing more!'

The voices were getting louder and angrier. The woman tried to say something – from the gesture of her clasped hands, I thought it might be an appeal for mercy – but this only served to further antagonize her persecutors. Another big lump of mud flew over the heads of the crowd, this one hitting the woman on the arm. She gave a sharp cry of pain. The mud had been packed round a stone.

The missile had been thrown from somewhere just behind us. I spun round and saw a fat, red-faced man stooping down to prepare another. Before Gurdyman could stop me – before I had time to think about it, and perhaps stop myself – I leapt on the fat man, knocking him to the ground and falling on top of him. *'That's enough!'* I screeched. 'She's got a baby with her!'

The fat man lurched to his knees, shoving me away with sufficient force to make me sit down hard on my backside. 'What's it to you?' he demanded, struggling up and looming over me, his small eyes turned to narrow slits of fury. 'Mind your own bloody business!'

'It *is* my business if you hurt either the woman or her child!' I cried. 'I'm a healer!'

I was just getting to my feet, but he grabbed me by the shoulders and sat me back down again. 'Heal your own bruised bum, then!' he leered.

I'm not sure what would have happened next. In all likelihood, he'd have gathered up another fistful of mud, I'd have tried to stop him hurling it at the woman, he'd have hit me, Gurdyman would have had to step in and a tussle would have rapidly become a free-for-all. Without a doubt, there was enough violence in the air for punches and glancing blows to have escalated into knife-thrusts and serious injuries. Just at that moment, however, there came the sound of several pairs of booted feet marching in step, and a strong, carrying voice that held a distinct note of authority demanded to know what was going on.

The forces of law and order had arrived.

As the sheriff's men went about dispersing the crowd – not without one or two blows of their cudgels, if the occasional cry of pain was any indication – one of the senior deputies came over to where Gurdyman was helping me to my feet and brushing the dust from my skirts. 'You're that healer girl, aren't you?' the deputy demanded.

'Yes, I am,' I said reluctantly. I was cross, in pain, and humiliated by having Gurdyman repeatedly beat his hand on my bottom. Surely I wasn't that dirty.

'You're wanted,' the deputy said shortly. 'Over there.' He jerked his head towards the place where the woman was cowering. A bareheaded, broad-shouldered man in a leather jerkin – the sheriff, I presumed – was bending over her.

Impatiently I pushed Gurdyman's hand away. 'Is the baby hurt?' I asked anxiously, hurrying off in the deputy's wake. Oh, if that wretched fat man had inflicted some awful injury . . .

'Don't know about that,' the deputy said, turning briefly to look at me. Again, he nodded towards the sheriff. 'Him over there, he just said to fetch you.'

I glanced back to see if Gurdyman was following. He caught my eye, and gave an all but imperceptible shake of the head. Then, swiftly, he pointed to his eyes.

I understood. Gurdyman is wisest of the wise; my teacher, my mentor, my companion and my friend. In addition, he is a wizard – although he himself never uses the word except in ironic self-mockery – and he loves nothing better than to conduct extraordinary and sometimes terrifying experiments in the crypt hidden deep beneath his house. He is a practitioner of alchemy; he is trying to make a map of all the known lands of the world; he makes mysterious potions that on occasion almost choke him with their noxious fumes; he knows so much that often I wonder how it can all be contained within his round, bald head with its fringe of perfectly white hair. He is, I am convinced, a powerful magician.

All of which are reasons why he does not court attention. In those two small gestures – the infinitesimal shake of the head and the finger pointing to his eyes – he was telling me that he wouldn't accompany me as I answered the sheriff's summons, but that he would keep his eyes open to see what transpired.

My breath catching in my throat, I skidded to a stop in front of the woman and her baby. The sheriff looked up at me briefly and said, rather calmly, I thought, under the circumstances, 'They may have been hurt. Will you check them for injuries?'

I nodded. The child, its screaming now reduced to a pitiful sobbing, still lay where the woman had placed it. She had sat, or perhaps collapsed, down beside it, her back straight, the folds of her long, voluminous, high-collared cloak pooling round her feet. She was trembling. She wore a headdress consisting of generous folds of deep blue silk, wrapped round and round her head, concealing her hair and her forehead. The headdress was fringed with small black beads and tiny gold bells that tinkled softly when she moved. Beneath the headdress, entirely covering her nose and the lower part of her face, she wore a heavy veil. The sheriff was standing over her, and he opened his mouth to say something to me. I shook my head. I didn't want to talk; my instinct, both as a healer and simply as a human being, was to gather up the child, then crouch down beside the woman and give her a hug. She had, after all, just been through a horrifying ordeal. The sheriff seemed to understand. He nodded.

I got as far as scooping up the baby. Then, as I went to approach its mother, she turned and stared at me.

The look in her near-black, slanting eyes stopped me dead.

I felt as if some invisible force was holding me back. Confused, I muttered something, covering my embarrassment by looking down at the baby in my arms. It had stopped sobbing, and was now staring up at me with wide blue eyes. It was quite heavy, and I was just thinking that it was older than I had first thought – too old, surely, to be swaddled so tightly? – when, as if in response to my thought, it gave a powerful wriggle and kicked an arm and a foot out from within the blankets. The heel of the little foot caught me in the stomach; the fisted hand just missed my nose.

I'd had enough.

'Your child appears none the worse for its fright,' I said to the woman, staring at her as fiercely as she had just been staring at me. I had the advantage of height; she was still sitting on the ground. 'Won't you take it?' I went on. 'There are no one's arms better equipped for soothing a baby than those of its mother.'

For a moment, she didn't respond. Beside me, I sensed the sheriff move, and I guessed he was about to intervene. I went on looking down at the woman. Finally, with a sort of sigh, she nodded. Kneeling down in front of her, carefully I placed the squirming bundle on her lap. She didn't seem to know what to do next – undoubtedly she was in shock – and so, gently taking hold of her hands, I put one behind the baby's head and the other under its hips.

'We need to move her away from here,' the sheriff said quietly. He had bent down so that he could speak right in my ear. 'The mood's very ugly. We'll get to the bottom of it, but I'd be happier if that lot –' he cast a frowning glance over his shoulder – 'weren't still hovering around her.'

'I agree,' I replied. 'But first I need to check if either of them has been wounded.' If you move someone with a broken bone or a head injury, you can make a bad matter ten times worse. The sheriff appeared to know this, for he nodded, muttering something inaudible. 'Can't your men hold the crowd back?' I demanded. 'They appeared to be only too willing to crack a few heads just now, when you all burst on to the quay.'

'I have a dozen men with me, and the mob numbers maybe four, five times that,' the sheriff remarked. You could understand his point.

'I'd better be quick, then,' I muttered.

It seemed unlikely, but I was sure I heard the sheriff give a short laugh.

While the child lay across the woman's lap, I unwound the blanket and folded back the little garments. The blanket was of fine, soft wool, and the baby's robe was of silk. Whoever the woman was, she wasn't poor. Quickly, for the morning air was chilly, I checked over the baby for signs of injury. It – he – was a boy; he must have inherited his light blue eyes and fair hair from his father, but his skin – a beautiful, deep golden-brown colour – was like his mother's. He was clearly well-fed. He was, I judged, about six months old. He had been circumcised. His flesh was clean and sweet-smelling, and he had clearly been put in fresh linen a short time previously, for the wrappings were still dry and unsoiled. As far as I could tell, he had suffered nothing worse at the hands of the mob than a nasty fright.

I turned my attention to his mother.

I had not expected that she would permit me to examine her, and I was right. She drew herself away, one hand going to her veil as if she feared I was about to tear it off.

I nodded my understanding. 'I was not proposing to inspect you as I have just done your son,' I said. 'But I must ask if you are hurt? Did any of those stones or lumps of mud hit you, especially on the head or face? Such blows can cause concussion, and that carries grave risks.'

'I am not injured,' the woman whispered.

It was, I realized, the first time she had spoken. Although not as dramatic in its effect on me as her original intent stare, nevertheless her voice was a surprise. It was immediately clear that the common language was not her mother tongue, although her manner of dress, her veil and her dark eyes had already informed me that she was a stranger, just as they presumably had told the screeching fishwife who had yelled out, *Filthy foreigner!* No: it wasn't her accent so much as the husky timbre of her voice that was so startling. She sounded . . . it was odd, but she almost sounded like someone with a naturally deep voice who was trying to make it higher in pitch. It was totally absurd, but just for a heartbeat I wondered if the veiled woman was really a man.

'We must go,' the sheriff said, and now his tone had a definite sense of urgency. Two brawny-looking men had been talking to him while I dealt with the baby and his mother, and one of them raised his voice in repeated accusation: the veiled woman, it appeared, had tried to take two small loaves of bread when she had only paid for one. It seemed a small enough crime to warrant all this fuss, but then times were hard. Bakers have to earn their living like everyone else, and it's true that nobody likes thieves and cheats. The fact that, being a foreigner, the veiled woman had simply made a mistake seemed a distinct possibility, but I didn't think now was the time to mention it.

Between us, the sheriff and I got the woman to her feet. She seemed to be unsure how to carry the baby – I thought once more that she was probably still in shock – and she tried to hold him across her outstretched arms, so that his head lolled backwards and he shrieked in alarm.

'Dear Jesus, she's going to drop it!' the sheriff hissed. 'That's all we need. Take it from her!'

'*Him*. He's a boy,' I said, before I could remind myself that being pert with sheriffs is not in general a wise course of action. The sheriff, however, accepted the reprimand with a grin, and said softly under his breath, 'Take *him*, then.'

I did as he said, holding the baby up against my chest and wrapping my arms round him. Either he was comforted by being held so firmly, or else his crying had exhausted him; the important thing was, he stopped yelling. Then he gave a huge yawn, his eyelids fluttered down and he went to sleep.

The sheriff's men had formed up into a double line, standing two abreast, and they held back the crowd while the sheriff led the woman and me away from the quayside. The aggrieved baker and his companion stomped along behind. More deputies had arrived, and the mood of the mob seemed all at once to go off the boil. There was a lot of muttering, some name-calling, and I thought I heard the screeching woman again, still protesting about filthy foreigners. It was deeply unpleasant and unsettling, but I no longer felt in danger of actual harm, either to myself or to the veiled woman and her child. Soon, the river, the quay and the humming activity of the town's port were left behind us.

I wondered if we were heading for the small stone-built house by the Great Bridge. It was the place where the port officials were to be found, and I knew of it because I had occasionally been there on errands for Gurdyman, when goods he had ordered and paid for were temporarily impounded: Gurdyman's list of necessities contains some quite unusual items. Thinking of him made me wonder where he was, and if he had succeeded in keeping the promised eye on me. I glanced around, but the streets were busy and I could not see whether or not he was following. You would think that Gurdyman, being short, rotund and habitually dressed in a brightly coloured shawl which he drapes over his sombre gown, would have been easy to spot. In fact, when he wants to, he manages to blend in with his surroundings remarkably well.

The sheriff, the veiled woman, the baker and his friend and I strode on, past the port officials' house and over the Great Bridge. Once or twice the woman stumbled – she didn't seem much better at walking than she was at holding her baby – and each time the nearest deputy reached out a hand to steady her. I noticed that she didn't thank him.

Suddenly I knew what was the matter with her. The costly blanket and garments in which the baby was wrapped should have given me a hint, and, now that I had belatedly realized, her own cloak and richly decorated headdress supported my conclusion. I glanced down at her feet: she was wearing soft little boots in a gorgeous purplish-blue shade, the leather so shiny and supple that it looked like a second skin.

She was, of course, a rich woman. Rich woman weren't called upon to do much for themselves; other people set out their clothes, helped them into the garments, fetched horses or carriages to transport them, tended and carried their babies. For some reason, the veiled woman was here alone with her child, separated by some mischance from husband, kin and servants. No wonder she seemed so ill-equipped for managing the world on her own; usually, she never had to.

Smiling to myself, proud of my astute summing-up of the situation, I followed the sheriff, the veiled woman and the more senior of the deputies as we walked on. We passed the large plot where a vast gang of men were busy building the new priory, and then turned to stride up Castle Hill to the intimidating wooden structure crowning its summit. Our little procession made its way up a steep, narrow walkway made of stout planks that led to the castle's first-floor entrance, and, my heart in my mouth, I stepped from the sunshine into the chilly, dimly lit interior. The baker and his companion shuffled in behind us, and the last of the deputies slammed the door.

We were in a stone-walled anteroom. It looked as if it was the sort of place where lesser men filter callers, dealing with minor matters themselves so that the man at the top isn't constantly bothered by trivialities. The veiled woman settled herself elegantly on the only seat: a bench set against the wall opposite the door. She spread the wide skirts of her cloak around her so that anyone else wishing to sit down would have had to move them out of the way. She made no move to take her son from me, so I held on to him. He was sleeping soundly now, and it would have been a shame to risk waking him by transferring him to those inept, inexpert arms.

The sheriff ran his hands through his light brown close-cropped hair – some of the mud thrown at the veiled woman had missed its mark – and then opened a solid-looking door studded with iron, disappearing under a low arch that presumably led through to his inner sanctum. I heard voices: his, and another; the other man sounded at first irritated, then downright cross. Finally he yelled, 'Christ's bones, Chevestrier, *you* deal with it! It's what I pay you for! It's only a matter of one fucking bun!'

Instantly I realized my mistake. *Of course.* If I'd stopped to think about it, I would have known full well that the man on the quayside wasn't the sheriff of Cambridge. He was too young, for one thing; only a handful of years older than me; and, for another, the sheriff was hardly likely to have abandoned the cosy shelter of his private quarters to hurry outside on a chilly morning to attend to a minor rumpus over the alleged theft of a small loaf. No. Picot – for that was the sheriff's name – was a self-serving, sly and reputedly deeply corrupt man, who our local monks referred to variously as a hungry lion, a prowling wolf, a dog without shame and a filthy swine: to a man, the monks did not approve of Picot. It was said – mainly by the monks – that he deprived the local populace of their rights to some of the common pasture, which he had appropriated for himself. Such actions do not win a man approbation, when so many go hungry to their beds at night. Assuming they *have* a bed . . .

The man I had believed to be the sheriff, and whom I now knew to be called Chevestrier, returned to the anteroom. He must have been aware that we'd all overheard Picot shouting at him, but, far from being disconcerted, he was smiling to himself. He closed the heavy wooden door with exaggerated care, as if intent on saving Picot any further interruption, then turned to the rest of us and said, 'The sheriff sends his apologies, but he is busy on important matters of state. He has entrusted this business to me.' He added something under his breath; I wasn't sure, but it sounded like, *One fucking bun ought to be within my competence.*

From the quirk that twisted his well-shaped mouth, I guessed he was suppressing a chuckle.

He turned to the baker. 'Now, will you tell me what this woman stole from you?'

The baker looked at the veiled woman, posed on the rough bench as if she were a queen on a throne and staring at the baker with cold eyes as if she would like to condemn him to the deepest dungeon. 'Er—' he faltered. His companion gave him a nudge, hissing something in his ear. 'That's right!' he said pugnaciously, recovering a bit of his original umbrage. 'I told her how much them little loaves cost, and she paid me for a single piece, then bugger me if she didn't pick up a second one!' He nodded for emphasis, glaring round at the assembled company. One or two of the deputies were grinning. Chevestrier, however, seemed to have conquered his amusement.

He stared at the baker. His eyes, I noticed, were a bright, clear shade of green, untouched by blue or brown. He frowned in thought, then said, 'She picked up a second loaf, you said?'

'Yes, that's right!' the baker said, indignant all over again. 'Blatant-like, with no attempt at all to cover it up!'

Chevestrier nodded, as if something had just been proved to his satisfaction. 'Is that how thieves normally operate?' he asked quietly.

I began to see what he was doing. The baker, however, did not. 'No, it's not!' he replied hotly. 'Normally they sneak things off my stall when my back's turned, or they get some guttersnipe accomplice to attract my attention, and often I only realize I've been robbed when I stop to count up at the end of . . . Oh.'

Realization, it seemed, had struck.

'I think,' Chevestrier said kindly to the baker, 'that you may have acted a little hastily. Which is quite understandable,' he added swiftly, as the baker's face began to redden with angry embarrassment. 'My lady –' he spun round to face the veiled woman – 'will you give your word that you made a genuine mistake? That you believed you had paid for two loaves, when you had in fact only paid for one?'

The veiled woman twitched her head to one side, as if she was heartily sick of the matter. She gave a graceful shrug. 'It is as you say,' she said dismissively.

'And are you now prepared to pay for the second loaf?' Chevestrier went on.

She shrugged again, then, reaching under her cloak to a beautiful, bejewelled little leather purse that hung from her belt, she shook out a couple of coins and flung them at the baker's feet.

It was a disdainful, insulting action.

Chevestrier clearly thought so too. 'And maybe,' he said silkily, 'if you were to add a small consideration for the good baker's inconvenience, he might be persuaded not to press charges against you and let this unfortunate business drop.'

It might have sounded like a mild suggestion rather than an order, but I don't think anyone was fooled. The veiled woman certainly wasn't; she shot Chevestrier a look from those dark eyes that would have sent a superstitious man grabbing for his rosary. But then she extracted another coin, and this time, with Chevestrier still watching her, she got up and placed it in the baker's hand.

The baker muttered something that it was probably better I didn't hear, then he turned, nodded his thanks to Chevestrier, spun on his heel and, flinging the door open, marched off down the walkway, his companion at his side. Chevestrier spoke quietly to one of his deputies, leading him and the others outside. The veiled woman, the baby and I were momentarily alone in the room.

She sat gazing at the wall opposite to her. Not by word, gesture or glance did she acknowledge my presence. She might have been temporarily parted by some distressing circumstance from her own kin and attendants, but, as far as servants were concerned, she seemed quite willing for me to step up as replacement.

For my own part, I wasn't so sure. It was tempting to dump the baby in her lap and quietly slip away, but, on the other hand, I was intrigued by this veiled foreigner with her rich garments and her husky voice.

I stood there, gently rocking to and fro – the baby was beginning to wake up – and waited to see what would happen next.

The ensuing events lacked the high drama of what had just occurred. Chevestrier came back into the anteroom, and the

expression on his face suggested something had just been
arranged to his satisfaction.

'My lady,' he said, standing before the veiled woman and
giving a quick bow, 'have you somewhere to go? People who
await you?'

She stared at him for a moment. Then she shook her head. 'I
am – alone,' she murmured.

'So I assumed, since nobody stepped forward in your defence
out on the quay,' Chevestrier said, more to himself than to her.
'What is your business in Cambridge?'

'In Cambridge?' She looked surprised, although surely she
must have been aware of the name of the port in which she had
that morning arrived. Unless, of course, something else had gone
amiss with her; something in addition to apparently losing every
last one of her travelling companions and her servants. Was she
ill? Had she lost her memory? Her mind?

'This town is Cambridge,' Chevestrier said gently. 'In the
country of England,' he added. Perhaps he too was wondering
if the veiled woman had parted from her wits.

'I am aware of the country,' she said loftily. 'I seek a place,
but the name is not Cambridge . . .'

Chevestrier waited. I waited. Finally he prompted her: 'Yes?'

'I seek kin in *Fen*,' she said at last. 'Perhaps, *Fens*.'

Chevestrier muttered under his breath. 'The fens are over
there.' He waved an arm roughly in an eastwards direction.
'But –' he shot a glance at me – 'the region is extensive, as this
young woman could tell you.' *He knows where I come from*, I
thought. I didn't know if to be intrigued or afraid. 'If you want
my help,' Chevestrier went on, 'you'll have to be more specific.'

She fixed her slanting, dark eyes on him. It was hard to tell,
with her lower face covered, but I had a good idea she was
scowling. 'I have not asked for your help.'

He sighed. It was hardly surprising; most men would have run
out of patience with her ages ago. 'Have you somewhere to stay?'
he repeated. His tone was definitely less kindly now.

She gave that eloquent shrug again. 'I must find my kinsman's
dwelling, but I do not know where it is. For now, there are inns
on the quayside . . .'

'I would not recommend them to a woman of means,'

Chevestrier replied. 'But one of my men has a sister who works in a better class of tavern.' The veiled woman looked as if she was about to protest, but he did not give her the chance. 'A room is being made available, and I will take you there now.'

Abruptly she stood up, the movement accompanied by the swishing sound of her cloak, her gown and what sounded like several layers of silk underskirts. 'Do so,' she commanded. She jerked her head towards me. 'She will bring the infant.'

I was about to protest, the angry words lining up, but Chevestrier did it for me. 'I think it would be more polite to ask,' he said with icy courtesy. He turned to me, giving me the exact same bow he had earlier given to the veiled lady. 'I'm sorry, but I don't know your name. I'm aware of your reputation as a fine healer and I know you by sight, but not how to address you.'

'Lassair,' I said.

'Lassair,' he repeated. Then: 'We have taken up a good part of your morning, and I am sure you have your own affairs to attend to. However, it would be very helpful if you could accompany us over to the tavern. There will undoubtedly be practical tasks to be done for the baby, and—' He stopped, spinning back to look at the lady.

And I don't think she'll have the first idea how to start was, I imagined, what he'd been about to say. I grinned. I quite agreed with him. 'I'll come,' I said.

He bowed again. 'Thank you.'

Just then, the door to the inner room was flung open, and a short, pot-bellied, red-faced man stood glaring out at us from close-set eyes. This, I guessed, was Sheriff Picot. His gaze fixed on Chevestrier. 'Christ's holy bones, are you still here?' he demanded, spittle flecking his thin lips. 'I told you to—'

He had spotted the veiled lady. With the quick intelligence of his kind – it's said that the Conqueror chose for the office of sheriff men who shared his ruthless ambition and determined self-advancement – he ran his sharp, assessing eyes over her. The furious scowl changed to an ingratiating smile; no doubt the expression he habitually adopted before the wealthy and powerful.

'My lady,' he said, making a low bow – I noticed he'd carefully arranged his thinning, gingery hair across a big bald patch

– 'I am Sheriff Picot, and I am at your disposal.' He straightened up, and his expectant grin suggested he was hoping for more than the lady's look of cold disdain. Discomfited – you could hardly blame him – he spun back to Chevestrier. 'Get on with it, you indolent sod!' he yelled. 'Don't keep her standing here – help the lady!'

I watched Chevestrier's face. There was an instant when I thought he was going to give in to temptation and give the response that Picot deserved, but then it was gone. An expression of bland serenity ironed out the fury, and Chevestrier said calmly, 'As you wish, sir.'

Then he spun round and led the way out into the sunshine.

TWO

The tavern was not far from the market square, on one of the main streets that run through the centre of the town and close to St Benet's church. I had never been inside, but I understood it to be a well-run, clean and decent place where ruffians intent on theft and trouble-making were unlikely to gain admittance. In acknowledgement of the old ways, a bundle of brushwood hung above the wide entrance into the courtyard: the ancient symbol for an inn.

Chevestrier led the way inside, where a plump woman in a white apron, her hair covered in spotless white linen, was waiting. Our little procession was shown along the passage to a tiny, dark room, in which there was a bed, a three-legged stool, a table with a ewer of hot water set beside a basin and a worn but clean cloth for hand-wiping. 'There's the communal room, of course,' the plump woman was saying nervously, 'only I thought as how a *lady* would like a bit of privacy.' The veiled woman looked around, gave a disdainful sniff, and then removed her cloak and flung it on the bed. Chevestrier thanked the plump woman and dismissed her.

I barely noticed. My eyes were on the veiled woman's gown, revealed in full now that she had taken off her cloak. The gown was gorgeous: deep blue velvet with a purplish sheen, tight in the sleeves and over the hips, then spreading out in generous flares and gores that swirled around her ankles as she moved. It fitted her beautifully, except that it was a little loose in the bust: no doubt she had lost the fullness in her breasts that comes with pregnancy and childbirth, and had not yet had the chance of ordering a seamstress to take in the seams.

Breasts . . . That reminded me. I shifted the baby in my arms – he was winding up to cry, and already giving increasingly heart-rending little whimpers – and said, 'My lady, your son needs to be fed.'

She looked at me as if I was simple. 'He was fed before we left the boat.'

'I'm sure he was.' I held on to my temper. 'But now he's hungry again.'

She looked around, as if hoping that whoever it was that normally cared for her child might appear out of the wood panelling. 'Oh,' she said.

Chevestrier came to stand beside me. 'I don't suppose you know of a wet-nurse?' he asked quietly. There was a note of desperate optimism in his voice.

I smiled at him. 'I do.'

'Thank the Lord,' he muttered. 'Do you think she's likely to be available?'

I handed the baby over to him. After a moment's hesitation – he had much more of an idea how to hold a child than the baby's mother – he laid the increasingly noisy little bundle gently down on the bed.

'I'll go and find out,' I said.

I located the wet-nurse – a lovely, strong, sensible girl called Mattie, with three strapping young boys of her own and a delicate little daughter at the breast – and she was happy to provide her services for the lady in the inn. Understanding that her new charge was probably extremely hungry by now, she came straight away. I introduced her to Chevestrier and the veiled woman, and instantly she bent down to the baby, already unlacing her gown. Then I turned and left.

Chevestrier, clearly not wishing to witness the intimacy of

breastfeeding, hurried out after me. 'Thank you for your help,' he said.

I smiled. 'It was more for the baby's sake than hers.'

He smiled back. 'Quite.' Then he gave me a salute and strode away.

I had forgotten all about Gurdyman. When I got back to his wonderfully well-hidden house – you have to fiddle your way through the lanes behind the market square, doubling back on yourself, and when I first went to live there, it took me many attempts till I could do it without thinking – it was to find him already installed in his sunny little courtyard, waiting for me to tell him my side of the morning's events. 'I saw you go into the inn,' he said, 'and then hurry off to fetch Mattie.'

'Yes, she's just got herself another mouth to feed,' I replied. 'And her new mistress ought to be able to pay her well. You saw her, no doubt.' It wasn't even a question.

'Yes, I did.' Gurdyman paused. I thought he was going to say more, but he didn't. Instead he asked why she had been attacked, and what had occurred up at the castle, and, once I had told him, he appeared to be satisfied and allowed the conversation to lapse, closing his eyes and enjoying the soft warmth of the sun.

'She's heading for the fens,' I said.

'Oh, really?' Gurdyman seemed only mildly interested.

'She's looking for kin there.'

'Well, now!'

I knew him in this mood: he didn't want to discuss it, and nothing I could say would make him. 'Do you know of Chevestrier?' I asked instead.

Gurdyman opened his eyes. 'Jack Chevestrier is a better man by far than his master the sheriff,' he pronounced.

I smiled. 'Ah, but that could be said of virtually every man in Cambridge.'

Gurdyman acknowledged the truth of that. 'He is decent, honest and, as far as I am aware, capable,' he said after a moment. 'Norman blood, but he can't help that. Picot, of course, takes advantage of his man's efficiency, leaving him to do twice as much work as he should while Picot busies himself acquiring wealth and possessions to which he is not entitled.'

'You'd think Jack Chevestrier would notice, and do something to stop him,' I said.

Gurdyman shot me a look. 'No doubt he does, and, in time, he probably will.'

'But—'

'Enough, Lassair.' Gurdyman quite often does that: brings a topic to an abrupt end because he wants to raise another one. 'Now, go down to the crypt and bring me the little bundle wrapped in a piece of sacking that you will find on the end of my workbench.'

I did as he bade me, returning to put the parcel in his hands. He held it for a few moments – it seemed to me he was testing his reaction to it, which was, on the face of it, unlikely – then, to my surprise, he looked up and said, 'It arrived this morning. I collected it on the quayside from my merchant friend. Open it. It's for you.'

I unwrapped the sacking, revealing a lump of bright blue stone, about the size of the top joint of my thumb. I held it up to the light, and the sunshine caught golden glints among the blue. It was very beautiful: the colour was a distillation of summer skies in the late evening.

'Do you know what it is?' Gurdyman asked.

'I believe it's lapis lazuli.'

'It is indeed. Do you recall where it comes from?'

I remembered a morning when we pored over his map, and he pointed out a land that seemed impossibly far away to the east; on the edge of a huge range of mountains which, according to Gurdyman, scraped against the sky. 'It comes out of the east,' I said dreamily. 'Men hack it out of the ground, and they sell it to the traders who travel the vast distances of the Silk Road.'

'And what do we use it for?' Gurdyman prompted.

'It is used by painters to make the costly shade known as ultramarine.'

'Yes.' He hesitated, looking at the blue stone that I still held in my hand. 'There is another use to which it is put. Since you are not an artist, Lassair, it is this second use that I had in mind when I ordered your stone.'

I felt a shiver of apprehension. Gurdyman's voice had altered subtly. I was afraid of what he was going to say.

He nodded, as if he had picked up my fear. 'Do not worry,'

he said softly. 'I will be beside you. We shall experiment together.'
There was a pause. 'But not now,' he said in his normal tone.
'Put the lapis away, child, and fetch us something to eat.'

In the course of the next day, nothing more was said about the piece
of lapis lazuli. Gurdyman keeps a sack stuffed with odd bits of fabric
down in the crypt, and I selected a piece of silk and sewed a tiny
bag to hang from my belt, in which to keep my stone. Gurdyman
said I should keep it close, so that it picked up my essence.

Late that evening, after I had gone up to my little attic above
the kitchen, I heard Gurdyman step softly along the passage to
the door. I detected a faint rumble of voices, both of them male.
Very few people know where Gurdyman lives; he likes it that
way, being reclusive by nature and frequently engaged on tasks
that are better unwitnessed. One man, however, comes quite often.

I slipped out of bed, grabbed the lovely shawl which my sister
Elfritha made for me years ago and, wrapping myself in it, went
down the ladder and into the kitchen. Following the faint sound
of the voices, I padded down the passage, then turned to descend
the steps that lead to Gurdyman's crypt.

I would not have dreamt of spying on Gurdyman and his night
visitor. Apart from such an action being ill-mannered towards
the man who houses and teaches me, it would also have been
extremely dangerous, especially if the guest was who I thought
he was. So, without stopping to think, I jumped down the second
flight of steps and burst into the crypt with a cheery, 'It's me,
Lassair! I heard voices.'

The two men standing by the workbench turned to stare at
me. Gurdyman's face wore a mild smile, as if my uninvited
presence was a bit of a nuisance but nothing worse. The other
man, even now throwing back the deep hood of his heavy, dark
cloak, glared at me out of silvery eyes narrowed in irritation.

'Hello, Hrype,' I said timidly.

If I had to make a judgement, I'd probably say that, although
Hrype is the more scary-looking, it is undoubtedly Gurdyman
who is the more dangerous. Both men are powerful magicians;
capable, I'm sure, of feats far beyond anything I have yet experienced, but Gurdyman has the advantage of being many years
older, and thus more deeply steeped in his art.

Hrype, anyway, is my lovely aunt Edild's lover, although I'm one of the few people in on the secret. I wouldn't say that fact makes him treat me with any special consideration, but I think he'd probably stop short of doing me harm.

His icy expression seemed to have softened very slightly. Capitalizing on this, I hurried forward, grasped his hand in mine and demanded news of my aunt, my village and the rest of my family.

'Everyone is well,' Hrype said impatiently, dropping my hand after the briefest of squeezes. 'Nobody knows I'm here, so don't expect any fond messages. And,' he added with the hint of a smile, 'don't go imagining I'll be taking any back.'

'Of course not,' I muttered meekly.

There was an awkward pause, during which I reflected that my presence really wasn't welcome at this secret night-time meeting. Hrype glanced at Gurdyman, who gave a faint grimace and murmured, 'Well, she'll have to know, eventually.'

There was a brief, tense pause. Then Hrype sighed, turned to me and said, 'There *is* news, Lassair, although not of your family at Aelf Fen.' I opened my mouth to speak. 'And, before you ask, it does not concern either of your sisters living elsewhere.' That was a relief: I'm not that fond of my eldest sibling, Goda – although I wouldn't wish her ill – but Elfritha, the one who's a nun at Chatteris, I adore.

'Who does it concern?' I whispered.

Hrype said softly, 'Skuli.'

Skuli.

For an instant, the crypt seemed to grow even colder, and I felt a shudder run through me. I had every reason to fear the very name, since only a few months ago Skuli had been all set to kill me. He was my distant kinsman: my grandfather and Skuli's father were cousins.

The events of the spring still gave me bad dreams. They had also left me with an ache in my heart, for I had discovered a grandfather who I never suspected I had. Nobody but Hrype and Gurdyman knew about him; I had no idea how to reveal to my beloved father that his mother – my late and much-loved Granny Cordeilla – had had a brief and passionate liaison with a huge, bearded Norseman, and my father was the result. I was not at all sure how my father would receive the news that the mild, hard-working fisherman whom Cordeilla married, and with whom she conceived all her other children, had been temporarily usurped in her bed. Nor, indeed, how he'd feel on finding out his siblings were actually only half-siblings; neither are facts a daughter is usually called upon to explain to her father.

So there was news of Skuli. Well, Hrype could keep it to himself. I didn't want to know. Skuli had sailed off towards the sunrise in his slim and elegant craft, and he had been heading for Miklagard. With brutal ruthlessness, he had done everything in his power to take a precious family heirloom with him, but, although he didn't even stop short at murder, ultimately he'd failed.

That heirloom – the mystical, compelling shining stone – was now in my possession; put into my nervous hands by my grandfather.

I still missed him. I'd thought that the passage of time would ease the hurt. So far, it hadn't.

With a shudder, I brought myself out of my reverie. I looked at Hrype, then at Gurdyman. My mouth felt dry, but I swallowed a couple of times, and then said, 'I don't know why, but I think this has to do with the shining stone.'

And, not really to my surprise, Hrype nodded.

'Gurdyman and I believe that it is not in your best interests to postpone any further,' he said.

I had an awful feeling that I knew only too well what he meant.

'Er – you mean it's time I began to – to get to know it?' My voice wasn't quite steady.

Hrype looked at me and there was compassion in his eyes. 'The stone has come into your hands for a reason, Lassair,' he said softly. 'You know that.' I nodded. 'You will also know, I'm sure, that the intention was not simply for you to creep up to your attic room and unwrap the stone once in a while to gaze at it.' *How does he know I do that?* I wondered wildly. Sometimes, my curiosity overcame my fear of the magical object that was currently in my possession . . .

'We will be beside you, supporting you as best we can,' Gurdyman said quietly. 'It is an object of great power, and it is right that you are in awe of it, child.'

In awe was an understatement.

I looked at Hrype, then back at Gurdyman. They appeared to be waiting for something.

'You don't mean – surely you don't want to begin *now*?' I squeaked.

Gurdyman smiled encouragingly. 'No time like the present.'

By the time I returned to the crypt, my heart hammering from the combined effects of just having raced up to my little attic room and my increasing apprehension, Gurdyman had made his preparations. A piece of clean white linen had been spread over one end of the workbench, and smooth beeswax candles had been lit at the four corners. The seriousness of the moment struck home: beeswax candles are fearfully costly, and Gurdyman had just lit *four*. Somewhere close by, incense was burning; sniffing, I detected the strong, heady smell of frankincense; another very expensive commodity. In addition, I smelt cumin, dill and garlic.

All four substances are used for protection.

Gurdyman and Hrype stood like guardians, either side of the white expanse of linen. Hrype beckoned, and I stepped forward.

When it had first been put into my hands, the shining stone had been wrapped in a coarse length of old sacking. But, feeling that such a covering was unworthy of the stone, I had fashioned a bag out of a piece of soft dark brown leather, decorating it with a pattern of tiny glass beads sewn into a spiral. I had stitched a narrow hem in the top of the bag, through which I threaded a drawstring. I had collected fluffy pieces of sheep's wool from the hedgerows, and, once I had washed and dried them and combed out the burrs and the tangles, the resulting soft nest made a good protective lining to the leather bag.

Now, approaching the workbench, I loosened the drawstring and opened the bag. I drew the stone out of its wrappings. I can just hold it in one hand, and I usually find that it is my right hand that reaches for it.

'Put it on the cloth,' Hrype intoned.

I obeyed. The stone, a perfect sphere, made as if to roll to one side. Then it seemed to change its mind.

The three of us, Gurdyman, Hrype and I, stared down at the shining stone.

At first glance, it appears to be solid, unrelieved black, with a

brilliant sheen that repels the attempts of an onlooker to peer into
it. But there is more to it. It's as if the stone has light inside it;
light that seems to flow, as if in some strange way the centre is
liquid. You see a flash of gold, then a brief ribbon of deep green,
there and gone in an instant. I recalled what Gurdyman told me
of the stone's origin. He told me – and I still find it hard to believe
– that once it had been solid rock within the heart of a volcano,
heated to such a ferocious temperature that it turned molten and
then, when it encountered water and cooled, turned once more
into a solid, but of a very different kind. *Its nature is for ever
changed from what it was*, Gurdyman said. *Through the medium
of fire and water, rock is turned into glass.*

I had been sure when he told me, and I remain sure, that he
had been describing some sort of alchemy, of a kind I could not
even begin to imagine.

I took a breath, trying to steady my fast-beating heart.

'Have you your piece of lapis lazuli?' Gurdyman asked softly.

I started. 'Yes.' I took it from the pouch on my belt.

'Hold it in your left hand,' he said. 'It will help.'

There was utter silence in the crypt. Then, his voice soft,
hypnotic but also irresistible, Hrype said, 'Lassair, look into the
shining stone.'

Clutching the lapis tightly, I bent over the stone. Again, the
flash of gold, and the deep green ribbon, moving as if it was
water . . . a great river, perhaps. My eyes narrowed, and it seemed
as if a film of smoke was swirling inside the stone. I thought I
could make out faint images in the smoke: dark figures, moving
in a wide empty landscape; a long line of hunched men, engaged
on some arduous task; water again, as a river became a sea,
white-capped waves breaking on a far shore. Then, across those
vague, everyday images, suddenly something else: something
heard, or perhaps sensed, rather than seen, for it sounded like
the heavy hoof-falls of a fast-pressed horse . . . no, two horses.
I leaned closer to the shining stone, trying to make out the horses
and their riders, but now the smoke was swirling faster, and the
images I had seen – imagined – were gone. Then I saw a pair
of birds, jet-black against the pearly grey smoke, and instinctively
I drew back. In that swift instant before they disappeared, it had
looked as if they were flying right at me.

I took a deep breath, then looked into the stone again.

There was nothing. It was black once more; dense, impenetrable black.

My left hand eased out of its tight fist – I hadn't been aware of how hard I'd been clenching the piece of lapis, but now I realized it had dug painfully into the flesh of my palm. I opened and closed my fingers a few times to ease the discomfort, rolling my shoulders to get the tension out of my muscles.

As if he couldn't bear to wait another moment, Hrype said sharply, 'Well?'

I turned to him. 'Well what?'

'What did you see?' he hissed.

What *had* I seen? 'Smoke,' I said. 'Figures, moving about. Water.' I shook my head. 'It was very vague, and I'm pretty sure I was just imagining it.'

Hrype gave an impatient *tut*, turning away.

'It is all but impossible to determine where the imagination ends and true sight begins,' Gurdyman said quietly. 'Indeed, it is a matter hotly debated among the wise, for there are no easy answers.' He paused. 'Was there anything else, Lassair?'

I shook my head. 'No, nothing. I'm sorry, Gurdyman.'

He smiled, but I sensed it took some effort. I could feel his disappointment. 'Well, never mind. It was but your first attempt, after all.'

'Will I get better at it?' I hated to let him down.

'Of course you will!' he said robustly. 'And I shall help you.' Now the smile was unforced, and I sensed the affection behind it. 'I promised to do so, did I not?'

Indeed he had. I remembered vividly exactly what he'd said: *I will teach you all that I know, and we shall hope that would be enough.*

I'd found it distinctly alarming even then, all those months back. Now, when learning how to use the shining stone was no longer a distant prospect but right before me in the here and now, I was downright terrified.

But I wasn't going to admit it. Gurdyman, by my side, appeared to be waiting for some response. I said – and I could hear the shake in my voice – 'I'll do my best.'

*　*　*

Hrype left, and I went back to my bed. I was exhausted, as if I had been on a long, wearisome journey, or had been beset with worries and problems that it was up to me to resolve.

But, once I was snug up in my little attic room, warm beneath the bedclothes, scenes from the day kept playing before my closed eyes. I saw Hrype, throwing back his hood to stare at me. I saw Gurdyman, his face creased with concern as he asked if I had the piece of lapis lazuli. Then Gurdyman again, his face reflecting his acute disappointment as I confessed I'd seen no more than a blur of smoke and a few nondescript figures.

The scenes played again, and then again. At last, however, fatigue overcame me, and I felt my body and mind relax towards sleep.

On the point of a dream, two things leapt up to the forefront of my mind, hurling me back to wakefulness. The first was an image of those two black birds, flying out of the stone straight for me. Without a doubt – and I had no idea where the awareness came from – I knew they were ravens.

I could not for the life of me think how, when Gurdyman asked if I'd seen anything else, I'd forgotten about them . . .

The second thing was to do with my piece of lapis, and its use other than as a pigment with which to make blue paint. As every apprentice wizard could have explained, lapis lazuli is used to heighten psychic ability. To hold a piece in the left hand is to invite the spirits to emerge from the shadow world and into our own.

Gurdyman hadn't given me the lapis for protection. He'd given it purely and solely to heighten the chance that my first attempt to see inside the secrets of the shining stone would be successful.

And I hadn't told him how well it had worked.

THREE

The next day, Gurdyman tactfully refrained from mentioning the shining stone. Since I much preferred to put the whole worrying incident to the back of my mind, I tried to forget all about it. But I kept seeing those two ravens, flying like arrows towards me. Two ravens . . . now what did that make me think of? *I don't want to know!* I told myself.

It was easy to keep busy. Gurdyman takes his role as my teacher and mentor very seriously, and I do not have much time to retreat inside my own thoughts. He was currently instructing me in the art of mixing certain ingredients in precisely the right proportions to enhance their ultimate potency. I was already familiar with the concept, having been well taught by my healer aunt, Edild, when I first became her apprentice. Gurdyman, however, was not only a healer but a magician too, and, under his tutelage, I was beginning to learn the more arcane aspects of the art, such as the exact time that a plant must be picked and, perhaps most mystical and strange of all, the correct way to address the herbs before they are added to the mix.

We were preparing the Nine Herbs Charm: plantain, mugwort, lamb's cress, betony, chamomile, nettle, chervil, fennel and crab apple. Edild had taught me about many of those herbs: mugwort's sweet flowers are tied in bunches as an insect repellent, and it is also used to flavour beer; plantain heals cuts and sores, and you make a thick, syrupy infusion sweetened with honey to ease coughs, especially in children; fennel is used for stomach ailments and indigestion; crab apples ease constipation, and old lore maintains that the bitter, unripe apples drive out worms.

I knew of betony, since Edild occasionally uses it to treat diarrhoea and cystitis; she does not regularly keep it in her store room because she says it's overrated. I have since learned – from Gurdyman, of course – that it is a magical plant; this, I suspect, is why my aunt is wary of it. Edild tries not to rely on magic, and treats the superstitious fears of the Aelf Fen villagers with courteous but ruthless disdain.

Beside me at the workbench, Gurdyman was grinding ingredients with a pestle and mortar, muttering under his breath. He had taught me how to make a paste of ashes and water, which we would then boil up with fennel. We worked steadily, and I tried to copy the neat, economical movements of his hands.

Suddenly he turned to me and said, 'We have insufficient crab apples. Hurry and fetch more – a dozen will serve.'

I nodded, wiped my hands on my apron and leapt up the stone steps leading out of the crypt. I ran along to the kitchen to fetch a bag, then left the house and emerged on to the narrow lane outside. I knew where to go for crab apples: there is a tree on one of the tracks leading down to the river, and its fruits were already ripening, falling on to the path beneath its spreading branches. I was not entirely certain whose tree it was. It stood on common ground, but land rights are fiendishly complicated, and it probably belonged to somebody. I did not think he – or she – would miss twelve crab apples, particularly when much of the crop was being trodden underfoot and going to waste.

In the event, there was nobody about to witness as swiftly I bent down and thrust a dozen small red apples into my bag, checking them carefully for blemishes and the marks of insect infestation. Gurdyman is very strict about such things. Ingredients must be untainted, and his crypt – as I well know – must at all times be spotlessly clean. I often reflect, at the end of a long day, how many hours of my apprenticeship with Gurdyman I spend with my hands in a bucket of soapy water, washing down utensils, surfaces and floors.

I was on my way back – crossing the corner of the market square – when somebody called out to me. Turning quickly, impatient to take the crab apples to Gurdyman, I saw that it was Mattie.

'Oh, Lassair, I'm that glad to see you!' she panted as she hurried up to me. 'I'd have sought you out, only I don't know where you dwell.'

No, she didn't. I had made sure of it. Gurdyman is virtually a recluse, and, for reasons of his own safety, prefers not to broadcast the whereabouts of his twisty-turny house, hidden away in its maze of narrow alleyways. I understand his reasoning. Some of the things he gets up to down in his crypt would make his fellow townspeople's hair stand on end if they knew, and it's amazing how swift men can be to turn on the outsider, the one who is different, the person perceived as a threat. I always do my best to protect Gurdyman's privacy, although at times it makes my own life difficult. When, for example, a friendly soul like Mattie asked where I lived because she wanted to show me her baby – newly recovered, thanks to medicine I had prepared, from a nasty cough – and give me a basket of apples as a thank-you.

I looked into Mattie's plump, anxious face. 'What can I do for you?' I asked. I wasn't going to explain why I had to be so secretive about the whereabouts of my lodgings.

'It's that woman, the one with the veil,' she said, a note of indignation entering her voice.

I smiled. 'Hasn't she paid you?' I wouldn't have been surprised.

'Oh – yes, yes she has,' Mattie said. 'Eventually,' she muttered under her breath. 'It's not that – it's her baby, her little boy.' Now her face creased in distress.

'Is he ill?' Already I was calculating my next moves: back to Gurdyman with the crab apples, fetch my satchel, then straight to the veiled woman's inn.

But Mattie was shaking her head. 'He's not *ill*, not so far as I can make out, although you're the expert and it's not for me to say.'

'What, then?' Mattie hesitated. 'Oh, come on, Mattie!' I pressed her. 'I'm out on an urgent errand, and I'll get into trouble if I delay!'

'Yes, sorry,' she said hurriedly. 'The thing is, see, the baby's sad.'

That brought me up short. '*Sad?*'

'He suckles well, takes a decent feed, and his bowels function nicely, but when I've fed him, winded him, changed him and he's got no reason not to close his sweet little eyes and have a bit of a nap – because I can *see* he's sleepy – he just lies there, staring around, for all the world as if he's looking for something, and can't let himself drop off till he's spotted it. And the look on that dear child's face! Oh, it fair twists my heart.'

Kind, sentimental Mattie's eyes filled with tears, which rolled slowly down her plump cheeks.

'You'd like me to come and have a look at him.'

'Yes, I would.' She wiped the tears away. 'That Jack Chevestrier, he said to come and find you.'

'He did?' I was surprised. Having resolved the problem of the appropriated bread and found accommodation for the veiled woman, I'd have thought his involvement would have ended, although his fat little sheriff had commanded him to look after her . . .

'Yes. Seems he's been keeping an eye,' Mattie said darkly.

'Maybe he suspects she'll slip out and nick another loaf if he doesn't put in an appearance now and again, to remind her of the difference between right and wrong.'

I suppressed a grin. There spoke a totally honest woman. 'Of course I'll come,' I reassured her. 'I must first complete my errand, then I'll go straight to the inn.'

'Thank you,' Mattie breathed. 'I won't come with you. I've just come from there, and the little lad won't be needing me for a while.' She sighed, shaking her head.

Impulsively I leaned towards her and planted a kiss on her cheek. 'Go home to your own children,' I said. '*They* need you.' She looked at me doubtfully. 'Mattie, your own sons and daughter are your main responsibility. You've done your best for the veiled woman's baby. I will help, if I can. Go home,' I repeated.

She nodded. Then she squared her shoulders and strode off in the direction of her house.

I flew down the steps to the crypt and laid the crab apples on the workbench. Then I explained to Gurdyman what had just happened. I had half-thought he would command me to finish the preparation of our herbal charm, but he said, 'You must go, Lassair. I will finish this.'

'I'm sorry to abandon the lesson,' I said. 'Will we have to begin again, another time?'

He smiled. 'Yes. But it doesn't matter – preparing even something very special must take second place to tending to the living. Off you go.' He waved a shooing hand at me.

I ran back to the steps. Just as I was hurrying up them, he added, 'Oh, and Lassair, you might pick up something hot for our supper on your way home.'

As I swiftly picked up my leather satchel and once more left the house, I was grinning. My dear Gurdyman might be deep in the mystical process of murmuring magical words over a precise mixture of very particular ingredients, but, nevertheless, a part of his wide-ranging, capable and highly intelligent mind was on his stomach.

I reached the inn. The same white-coifed woman showed me along to the veiled lady's room. I knocked on the door. There were sounds of movement – I heard a sort of rustling – and a voice said, 'Enter.'

She was sitting on the stool, one elbow resting on the table beside her. She had been sewing; hemming her skirt, it seemed, for she was smoothing it down as I went in, her needle stuck into a little pincushion. Her headdress and veil were in place, and I wondered if the sounds I had heard were her movements as she adjusted them. I understood that women of the east, if that was where she came from, habitually wore veils, so that only their own close kin saw their faces. Above the veil, her black eyes stared fixedly at me, their impact almost overpowering in the small room. I wondered if she had enhanced their effect by the use of some sort of paint; her long lashes seemed to glisten, and the fine skin of her eyelids was very dark.

But the veiled woman was not my chief concern.

I looked towards the bed. The baby lay there, well wrapped, relaxed and calm, except for the steady, repetitive movement of his head. Mattie was right: he looked as if he was staring round the room, searching for something.

Or perhaps some*one*.

I had an idea who the someone might be.

I turned back to the veiled lady. 'Madam, I have been given to understand by concerned people that your baby may need my attention,' I said stiffly. Her steady, unblinking gaze was unnerving.

'*Concerned* people?' Her husky voice echoed and mocked my words, managing to make them sound risible. 'Who are these people? And why should *your* attention be required?' Again, she used emphasis with cruel efficiency, as if it was unbelievable that anyone in their right mind could think I could be of any help.

'I am a healer, madam,' I said coldly. 'As I believe you are aware.'

She sniffed, drawing herself up. 'I am not unwell.'

'Perhaps not.' I was holding on to my temper with difficulty. 'You, however, are not the only person here.'

She looked across at the narrow bed. 'He is in good health,' she pronounced. 'He feeds, he does not cry unduly.' She shrugged, as if to say, *So why are you here?*

'May I not look at him?' I asked. I tried to smile, but found that it was impossible.

She shrugged again. 'If you must.'

I went over to the bed, and the movement caught the baby's attention. The light blue eyes turned to me, and I was quite sure I saw expectation in them. Then he gave a sad little sigh and turned away.

I picked him up, holding him close to me. I murmured to him – silly nonsense, intended to soothe – and kissed the top of his head. He smelt sweet and clean; Mattie was doing a good job.

'It is not my embrace he needs, madam,' I said quietly. I glanced at her. 'He had, I imagine, a nurse?' For the life of me, I couldn't imagine the veiled lady ever having held her son in her arms. It was not her he pined for.

'He did.'

'And that nurse is no longer in your employ?'

'There is another one who comes.'

'Yes, I know.' *It was I who found her for you!* I wanted to yell. Dear Lord, was she still in shock? Had something so awful happened on the way here that her mind had been affected? I took a calming breath. It would not help either the veiled woman or her child if I became agitated. 'The new wet-nurse will not be familiar to your son,' I said, trying to speak kindly. 'It will take him a while to get used to her. She will smell different from the previous nurse, and her milk will not be quite the same.' The veiled woman gave a distinct shudder of revulsion. *She is a grand lady*, I told myself firmly. *It is not her fault that she has been brought up to believe such ordinary, human functions are not only beneath her but also slightly disgusting.* 'Madam, would you not hold him?' I suggested. 'In the absence of his old nurse, you are someone he knows and recognizes.' I stepped closer, ready to put the baby in her arms if she showed the slightest sign of being willing to receive him.

She turned away.

I went back to the bed, laid the child down and sat down beside him, gently stroking my fingers across his forehead. His skin was cool and smooth. As far as I could tell, he was indeed perfectly well.

He was just, as Mattie had so accurately said, *sad*.

I stared at the veiled woman, and, as if she felt my eyes on her, she turned to face me. 'What is his name?' I asked.

She glared at me. There was a long pause, and I was just deciding that she was going to refuse to tell me, and, moreover, order me out of her room for my presumption, when she spoke. 'Leafric.'

'Leafric,' I repeated under my breath. I was surprised, for it was a Saxon name; one of the old names that had been in use before the Normans came. There were Leafrics in my own ancestry. I had inherited the role of bard from my Granny Cordeilla, and one of my responsibilities was to memorize the long list of our forebears. I should have expected such a name, for the baby's light eyes and fair hair had already suggested to me that his other parent must have originated a lot further north than the veiled woman.

I risked another question, although I held out little hope that she would give me an answer. 'Your boy was named for his father, perhaps?'

Again, the long pause, while she fixed me with her dark-rimmed, black-eyed stare as if calculating how much to reveal to this brash and forward stranger sitting on her bed beside her son. 'Not his father.' Another pause. 'But, yes, an ancestor. Of my late husband,' she added.

She was a widow, then. That alone should have made me more compassionate. The baby was no more than six months old, so this poor woman's loss must have been quite recent. 'I am sorry,' I murmured.

'Sorry?'

'For the death of your husband.' Surely it was obvious?

'Oh.' The veiled woman lowered her head. Then – and it sounded as if she had to force out the words – 'Thank you.'

There was much more I wanted to know. My thoughts were whirling. Things that I had just been observing were reminding me of matters which Edild had touched on, as together we treated and, later, discussed the patients who beat a steady path to the door of her little house back in Aelf Fen.

I was tempted to begin asking questions there and then. As if she sensed it, the veiled woman said, with a note of cold command in her voice that expected instant obedience, 'And now you will leave. I wish to rest.'

*   *   *

I managed not to slam the door. There was the baby to consider. I strode off along the passage, the heavy satchel in which I carry the requirements of my craft banging painfully on my hip, and flung myself out of the inn, all the while muttering under my breath, calling the veiled woman the sort of names that would deeply have shocked my parents.

Out on the street, my failure to see beyond my own fury made me temporarily blind, and I marched right into a man coming the other way. I came off worse, for he was so stocky and hard-muscled that it was like walking into a stone wall. I lost my footing, and a strong hand caught my elbow, holding me upright.

'Thank you,' I said, 'I'm sorry, that was entirely my fault. I wasn't – Oh!'

I had just bumped into Jack Chevestrier.

'Are you hurt?' he asked, restoring the strap of my satchel to its place over my shoulder.

'No.'

'You appear to be cross about something.'

It seemed he'd heard my cursing. 'Er – yes.'

He nodded in the direction of the inn. 'I think I might be able to guess the cause of your anger.'

I smiled. 'You'd be right. She's not an easy woman to help.'

Sudden sharp interest flared in his eyes. 'You'd gone to help her?'

'Well, her baby more than her. Mattie sought me out – she said you'd told her to.'

'It wasn't a command, Lassair,' he said mildly. 'I said if she happened to see you, she might ask if you'd give your professional opinion concerning the baby.'

I studied him. To look at him – not over-tall, sturdily built, thick with muscle and habitually grave of expression – you'd take him for the sort of powerful, unsophisticated and boneheaded strongman with whom the great lords who uphold the law like to surround themselves. His apparel supported this, for he was armed with sword and knife, and the sleeveless jerkin, made of sturdy leather, was marked with what looked like the scuffs and scars of old fights. Yet I sensed there was far more to him than that. For one thing, his manner of speech was not that of a common thug – he had just made a courteous remark – and, for another, I had the feeling that there was a fine intelligence inside his round, close-cropped head.

He appeared to be waiting for me to speak. I brought myself back to the matter in hand. 'Mattie said the baby wasn't ill, but seemed sad,' I said. 'Now that I've seen him, I agree.'

'Can you—'

He was interrupted by a gaggle of women shoving their way along the street, laughing and chattering, making so much noise that he'd have had to shout to make himself heard. His face creased in impatience, and, once they had passed, he said, 'We'll go somewhere quieter. If you can spare the time?'

'Yes, I can.'

He led the way off up the street. We crossed the alley that runs to the west of the market place, threaded our way between two churches, then emerged on to the long, wide stretch of gently sloping grassland that borders the river. He stopped some distance short of the water; down there, it was only marginally less busy than the centre of the town.

Turning to me with a smile, he said, 'Now, tell me about the baby.'

I'd been assembling my thoughts as we walked. Jack Chevestrier was obeying orders and keeping a watchful eye on the veiled woman and her child. He'd been asking Mattie about her, and, just now when I'd walked into him, it was likely he'd been heading for the inn. Given what I'd concluded concerning his intelligence, I didn't think he'd be satisfied with anything but a full answer.

I took a breath, then said, 'To judge by her clothing and the fact that she has no idea how to nurse or even care for her child, the veiled lady is a noblewoman. Until very recently, she's had a wet-nurse for the baby, and, I imagine, other servants too. The baby is well-fed, dressed in costly garments, clean and, as far as I can tell, healthy. Her attire, too, is luxurious and in good condition. Someone's been polishing those fine leather boots, and her robe and cloak have been diligently maintained.'

I paused, thinking. 'She's a widow, and her bereavement must have been within the last fifteen months, because I don't think the baby is more than six months old. The baby's name is Leafric, and, although the veiled woman is a foreigner – originally from the south, perhaps, to judge by her very dark eyes and olive skin – her late husband must have been a northerner. There's the baby's name, for one thing – the woman told me he was named for a forebear of her husband's, and Leafric is a Saxon name – and also his colouring. Although he has her olive skin, his hair is fair and his eyes are light blue. Oh, and I think the woman may be a Saracen – for one thing, there's her veil, which I haven't yet seen her without, and I'm sure I heard her putting it on when I tapped on the door of her room just now. Also, her little boy's been circumcised, and that's not a custom we routinely practise here.'

Was she a Saracen? I wondered. Where had she come from? What did she—

Jack Chevestrier, I noticed, emerging from my intense concentration, was waiting.

'I think something frightening must have happened to her very recently,' I said. 'When we first encountered her, you asked if she had kin or servants with her, and she said she was alone. She also said she was making for the fens.'

'She did,' Jack Chevestrier murmured. 'I told her to be more specific.'

'She's had a shocking experience of some sort,' I went on, 'and it's very likely she's still suffering from the after-effects. That would account for her strange air of detachment, and—'

'And her failure to engage with the child?' he suggested.

'Oh, no, I think that has more to do with the level of society she comes from,' I said. 'It's usual for high-born ladies to hand the whole matter of raising their babies over to others. No: I think there was an accident of some sort, and somehow – although I've not the first idea how, for it seems so unlikely – the veiled lady became separated from her travelling companions and from her servants. Well, I can't swear that she had travelling companions, but, as I just explained, she must have had servants. Or, at least, a nursemaid and wet-nurse, or maybe it was the same person.'

Jack Chevestrier was silent for a while. I risked a quick look at him, and guessed from his expression that he was thinking hard. Finally, he turned to me. 'I don't suppose you'd like to come and work for the sheriff?'

He kept such a straight face that it took a moment for me to realize he was joking. And that he'd just paid me a pretty nice compliment.

The compliment had me confused. Looking down at my left boot, with which I was tracing semicircles in the grass, I said, rather more brusquely than I'd intended, 'It was nothing – just listening and observation.'

'That's what I keep telling my men,' he said with a sigh. 'You've no idea the problems I have getting them to use their eyes and ears, never mind their brains.' He fell silent again. Then, after a moment, said, 'She arrived on one of the trading boats that ply the fenland rivers. I spoke to its master, who told me she'd come on board at Lynn.' He glanced at me. 'Although I don't think either you or I believe her journey originated there.'

'No, I'm sure it didn't. Was she alone when she boarded? Other than the baby?'

'She was.'

'And did the boat's master report anything out of the ordinary happening at Lynn? Rumour of sickness on board another ship, or a fight?'

'You're trying to account for the missing companions and servants.' I nodded. 'No, he didn't. He—' Abruptly he stopped, then, taking my arm, said, 'Come and talk to him. His name's Alun, and his boat's called *The Maid of the Marsh*.'

I hurried along behind him. 'But surely he'll have left by now? It was –' how long had it been? – 'the day before yesterday that the veiled woman arrived.'

Jack Chevestrier turned briefly and gave me a swift grin. 'He's still here,' he said firmly. 'His boat's bows needed repair, and he's not sailing till tomorrow. Come on!'

FOUR

*T*he Maid of the Marsh was a typical river craft: long and narrow, not very big, with a wide space on her foredeck for cargo. There was a mast amidships and spaces down each side for oars. One of her crew had clearly

suffered a lapse of attention, allowing her to run into something hard, and at some speed. On the right hand side of her
bow, there was quite a large area of new planking, in the
seams of which a sailor was now splashing large amounts of
a thick, tarry substance. Hearing our footsteps, he looked up
and gave us a toothy grin.

'Is your master aboard?' Jack asked.

'Aye, that's him, back there.' He inclined his head towards
the stern.

'May we come on board and speak to him?'

The man waved his brush in an expansive gesture. 'Aye, help
yourself.'

I followed Jack along the plank that provided the only access
to the boat. It was several paces long, and it was just that: a plank,
with no handrails or even a rope to hold on to. I had a vision of
myself ending up in the water, but I managed to keep my feet.
We crossed the deck and edged along to what appeared to be the
master's own particular space. Not that there was much to distin-
guish it from the rest of the ship, being cramped, and hemmed
in with crates and sacks, neatly stowed.

The master sat on a narrow shelf, swinging his legs to and fro
as he watched us approach his domain. Recognizing Jack, he
greeted him cheerfully.

'Repairs nearly done, I see,' Jack said, having returned the
greeting.

'Aye, and I'm docking the cost from that stupid bastard's
wages,' the master said. 'That'll teach him to eye up pretty girls
when he should be keeping his mind on his work.' He was staring
at me. 'Talking of pretty girls . . .'

'This is Lassair, Alun.'

The master jumped down from his seat – he was a head shorter
than me – and gave me a bow. 'How d'ye do, Lassair,' he said with
a grin.

'Very well,' I responded, returning the smile. It was impossible
to resist his good cheer.

'That woman you picked up at Lynn,' Jack said. 'We have
some more questions.'

The master gave him a knowing look. 'Been stealing again,
has she?'

'Not as far as I know, and she insisted it wasn't theft the first time,' Jack replied.

The master gave a snort of laughter. 'Oh, she did, did she? Well, it looked like it to me.'

'She paid the baker both for the loaf and for his inconvenience,' Jack said. 'I decided to let that be an end to the matter.'

'Well, you know your own business,' the master said. 'She was a slippery one. We were all glad to see the back of her.'

I sensed Jack's suddenly heightened alertness. 'What makes you say that?'

'Arrogant, she was. Gave orders like a queen, and expected my crew to jump to it. Surly, too – when we tried to look after her, she acted like it was her due and never gave a smile or a thank you. Well, like I told you, she came on board at Lynn, wanting passage up to Cambridge. She wanted to get into the fens, but you can't just drop a passenger out in the middle of nowhere, and I reckoned this was the best place, and the nearest port to the fens. I mean –' his face creased in a frown – 'if I'd have put her ashore out in the watery wilds, likely she'd have lost her way and drowned, and that little baby along with her. She paid it no mind,' he added with sudden vehemence. 'Didn't seem to know how to look after it. Didn't even seem to *like* it, come to that.' His frown deepened. 'The mate found someone who knew how to get a bit of milk inside it, otherwise it'd have yelled its head off all the way.'

'It's a *he*,' I said. 'He's being tended by a wet-nurse, and he's doing all right.'

The master turned to me. 'I'm right glad to hear it.'

Encouraged, I said, 'It's obvious she's a noblewoman, and must somehow have become separated from the companions and servants she was travelling with. She seems to be in a state of shock, and I was wondering if, back in Lynn, you heard any talk of some incident that might have resulted in her being all alone? A ship having met with an accident, or illness aboard?'

The master shook his head. I saw his left hand make the sign against evil, no doubt in reaction to my mention of shipwrecks and sickness. 'No, I heard nothing.'

'Did she say where she had come from?' Jack asked.

'No. She offered no information at all.' The master thought

for a moment, then grinned. 'But I think I can tell you what ship she arrived in, because she'd underpaid the cost of her passage – see, told you she was a slippery one! – and one of the crew came after her to collect what she owed.'

'What was the ship?' Jack's eyes were narrowed like a cat's. 'And where had she come from?'

'She was *The Good Shepherd*,' the master said, 'out of Yarmouth.' He nodded, as if confident that he had answered all our questions. 'That's where that veiled woman came from – Yarmouth.'

Jack Chevestrier didn't say a word as we headed back over the Great Bridge into the heart of the town. I could understand his mood; it really had seemed that we'd been on the point of discovering something crucial about the veiled woman. Yarmouth, however, was no likelier a starting point for her voyage than Lynn.

I went over my earlier encounter with the lady. Something had occurred to me, pushed out of my mind by subsequent events, and now I returned to it.

There had been an aspect of her which recalled a matter I'd once discussed with my aunt Edild. It concerned a new mother in Aelf Fen who, for some inexplicable reason, had taken a dislike to her newborn daughter; a dislike so profound that she had, for a few terrible days, refused to feed, tend or in any way care for the child. The baby was not her first; there was just something about her that the mother couldn't tolerate. Edild said it sometimes seemed to happen – fortunately not with any frequency – that, following a birth, a mother became inexplicably miserable; unable to feel any joy in the new life she had brought into the world. Often it occurred when a birth had been particularly long or hard, as if the baby was a constant reminder of the pain and the distress its arrival had caused.

My wise aunt had succeeded in persuading the Aelf Fen woman to accept the baby. Observing the veiled lady, I'd wondered if Edild might be able to help her, too. And, after all, the lady wanted to locate her kinsman's dwelling in the fens.

I hurried to catch up with Jack. 'I've had an idea,' I panted.

He turned to look at me. 'Yes?'

'I should take the veiled woman and her child to my village.'
'Why?'

'First, because she'll have to go into the fens if she's to find
her kinsman's house, and that's where my village is.'

'I know,' Jack said. 'You are from Aelf Fen.'

'I didn't—' Then I remembered. When the veiled woman had
said she sought the fens, Jack Chevestrier had said it was an
extensive region, and he'd added, *as this young woman could
tell you.* He'd known I was a healer. He knew where I came
from. It was only surprising that he'd had to ask my name.

'So, why else do you want to take her to your village?' he
asked.

'My aunt Edild is a healer.'

'So are you,' he observed.

'Not like her!' I protested. 'She's my teacher, and she's had
years of experience. She's very knowledgeable, and full of compassion for people with problems. She helped a village woman who
couldn't love her new baby, and she's fine now; the woman, I
mean. Well, they both are, the woman and the baby, only she's
not a baby any more, and the woman's had another since and—'
I stopped gabbling. I could hear how stupid I sounded.

But Jack didn't seem to think so. He said, 'If you are the
healer you are because of your aunt's teaching, she is indeed a
fine woman.' Then, before I could even begin to deal with the
embarrassment his words had caused, he added, 'And we'd better
see about getting you, the veiled woman and her baby out to
your village as soon as we can.'

I dreaded telling Gurdyman I was leaving. For one thing, we
were in the middle of a new course of study. For another, I knew
how eager he was for me to have another attempt at looking into
the shining stone. He thought he was managing to disguise his
impatience, but he gave himself away with constant oblique
references to it. I didn't want to look into the stone. The thought
of peering into its smoky, murky depths frightened me, and I
kept seeing an image of those two dark birds. I was quite sure
they came from another world: the world of the spirits. Being
presented with an excellent reason for distancing myself from
my strange inheritance was like a gift from some beneficial god.

In the event, the anticipation was worse than the actuality. When I told Gurdyman where I was going, and why, he simply nodded and said, as he always does, 'May the good spirits guard your path.'

As I checked through my satchel and packed into it a few necessities for my journey, I congratulated myself on having neatly evaded something I dreaded doing. But, just as I was fastening my satchel straps, I heard heavy steps on the ladder up to my attic room, accompanied by the sound of Gurdyman's laboured breathing. His head appeared at the top of the ladder, and, with a smile, he said, 'Take the shining stone, child. It needs to stay close to you.'

My heart gave a leap of fright.

Had he said what I thought he said? Surely it must have been, *You need to stay close to the stone*?

I listened to the echo of his words. No: he had definitely said *the stone* needed to be close to *me*.

As if it had thoughts and emotions.

As if it were alive.

Without my volition, my hand went to the place beside the bed where I keep the shining stone. I watched myself pick it up – I noticed how reverently I handled it – and place it carefully inside my satchel.

Behind me I heard Gurdyman murmur, 'Well done.'

It was a vast relief to find myself outside in the bright, fresh air of early morning. It was the next day; Jack hadn't wasted any time. Putting the memory of that disturbing scene with Gurdyman right to the back of my mind, I strode off through the maze of lanes and emerged on to the wide street that leads up to the Great Bridge.

Jack was waiting on the far side. Beside him, the veiled woman sat on a beautiful bay palfrey. She had fastened her high-collared cloak tightly around her throat, and pulled its generous hood up over her headdress and veil. Her dark eyes seemed to be fixed on some point in the distance, as if she was determined to disassociate herself from the proceedings. Since those proceedings were entirely for her benefit, I thought this a little arrogant.

Jack was talking to a tall, slim man dressed in dark garments, a cloak slung back across his shoulders. Whether from choice or necessity, his head was bald. His lean face was pale, and his close-set, narrow dark eyes were shadowed by heavy brows drawn down in a thunderous frown. He was speaking rapidly, gesticulating, and seemed to be issuing orders. As I reached the group, he looked up and saw me. He leaned close to Jack to say something more, his mouth right up close to Jack's ear, then he spun round and, with a whirl that revealed the luxurious lining of his cloak, marched away. He turned briefly to spit on the ground and give Jack a final glare. I turned to Jack, about to ask who the man was, but Jack's expression was equally forbidding and I lost my nerve.

Mattie stood beside the lady's mount, the baby in her arms. I smiled at her. 'Are you coming with us, Mattie?'

'No,' Jack said curtly. Then, his expression softening, he added, 'Well, not if you're prepared to carry the baby.'

I'd carried heavier loads between Cambridge and Aelf Fen. 'I'll manage,' I said grumpily. Great lady or not, it seemed a bit hard that, although the veiled woman was mounted, it was going to be me, walking on my two feet, who would have to carry the child.

'. . . should be here very soon,' Jack was saying.

I came out of my sulk and asked, 'What was that?'

'I said, the other horses should be here soon,' he repeated.

'Other horses?'

'Yes,' he said. Then, as I still must have looked blank, he went on, 'Mine – he's having a new shoe fitted – and one from the sheriff's stables. For you,' he added.

'For me?'

He grinned. 'Of course. How do you usually get to your village?'

'I walk.'

'Well, you can't walk carrying a baby.'

My spirits rose. I love riding, and only wish that the chance to do so came my way more often. And today I was going to ride a horse from the sheriff's stables! We all knew Picot didn't stint himself, so this wasn't to be some sway-backed old nag not capable of more than a resentful trot.

Then something occurred to me. Whoever was bringing my

horse was also bringing Jack's. Was he coming with us? I had imagined that his involvement would end with explaining to the veiled woman what was planned for her, finding her a horse and sending us on our way. I hadn't thought he'd travel out to Aelf Fen with us; didn't he have duties that kept him in the town?

He was looking at me as if waiting for my thoughts to run their course. Then, leaning close and speaking quietly, he said, 'I am concerned about our mysterious veiled lady, and I sense that there is much going on that we do not know.' He paused. 'I may be wrong, but I will not risk your safety.'

'What about hers?' I whispered back.

His mouth twisted down in a wry grimace. 'Whatever trouble she may be in, she has probably brought it on herself. You, on the other hand, are involved purely because you wish to help.'

I'm not sure how I would have answered that. Fortunately, I didn't have to. There was a clatter of hooves on the road leading from the bridge, and one of Jack's deputies appeared, leading two horses. One was a grey gelding, its pale, silky mane and tail catching the light breeze, its wide, dark eyes eager and interested. It went straight to Jack, and he put his face to its nose, quietly murmuring its name, which sounded like Pegasus. It was clearly his horse; without doubt, he was its man.

My horse was a black mare. She was small and neatly made, with lines that suggested excellent blood. I stepped up to her and gently patted the graceful curve of her neck. She gave a low whicker.

'Her name's Isis,' Jack said. My delight must have been obvious, and he was smiling at me. 'Mount up, and Mattie can hand the child to you. Then –' he glanced up at the sky, where the clear light of morning was slowly being overtaken by gathering cloud – 'we'd better be on our way.'

We were lucky with the weather. September was marching on and we weren't far from the equinox, which so often brings violent storms. Although rain threatened for most of the journey, however, we didn't receive more than a brief shower, during which the veiled woman insisted we sheltered in a copse of fir trees. The lady didn't want to get her finery wet.

Jack Chevestrier had packed food and drink, and we stopped

when the sun was at its zenith to consume it. The baby – Leafric; I was trying to remember to whisper his name to him as I tended him – had been asleep in my arms, soothed by the smooth pace of my lovely horse, but woke hungry when we stopped. Mattie had fed him before we left, and had prepared soft bread sops soaked in her milk for the journey. Leafric was reluctant at first, but, driven by increasing desperation and catching the familiar smell of Mattie, finally ate. I cleaned him up as best I could, then put him back in the cradle I had fashioned for him from my shawl. He burped, blinked his eyes a few times, then fell asleep again.

By early afternoon, we were close to Aelf Fen. I was amazed at how much faster the journey was achieved on a good horse. We were taking the veiled lady to Lakehall, the residence of Lord Gilbert and his wife, Lady Emma; nowhere else in Aelf Fen was suitable for a noblewoman. Jack, apparently, knew of Lord Gilbert. I wondered if he was aware that, while a basically kind man, Lord Gilbert carries the fat of over-indulgence, is indolent and not very bright, and that the brains of the family rest, along with a good heart, with Lady Emma.

As my mind leapt ahead to riding up to Lakehall and presenting our foreign companion, I hissed to Jack, 'We don't know her name!'

Jack frowned. 'I've asked her, but she's reluctant.' As if making up his mind that he'd had enough of her nonsense, he drew rein, waited until the veiled woman came up beside him, then said firmly, 'Madam, we shall shortly arrive at the house of Lord Gilbert de Caudebec, who we hope will welcome you as his guest. Lord Gilbert will help you locate your kinsmen.'

She studied him with her usual cool-eyed stare, but made no reply.

'You have so far refused to reveal your name, and, out of courtesy to a stranger, I have not pressed you,' he went on. 'Now I must insist. You cannot be presented to Lord Gilbert as an anonymous foreigner, and, in addition, he will need to know your family name if he is to help you.' He paused, and I had the sense he was controlling rising irritation, if not anger. Then he said abruptly, 'Speak, please, madam.'

The veiled lady gave an over-dramatic sigh, and in a tone of resignation, as if she was being forced to accede to a totally unreasonable demand, said grandly, 'I am Rosaria Dalassena, widow of Hugo Guillaume Fensmanson.'

None of the names meant anything to me, although the family name Fensmanson supported the woman's claim to have kin hereabouts. Well, not her own kin; it was her late husband's family she sought. That seemed reasonable enough. Widowed, and left with no one to support her and her child, she had abandoned the faraway place where she had met and married her husband and made her way to England, to seek out his kin. You had to admire her courage. Perhaps she had been driven by desperation . . .

Jack was studying the woman with a frown. 'Dalassena?' he said softly. Her eyes shot to him, their expression hard and challenging, as if daring him to question her further. 'Let us ride on, then, Lady Rosaria.' His tone was carefully neutral. Nudging his heels into the grey's sides, he led the way on down the track.

We came into Aelf Fen from the south, having followed the road that curves round the lower limits of the fens. Lakehall was the first dwelling we came to. I pointed it out, and Jack stopped to study the place.

I have known it all my life, but I tried to see it as a newcomer would. The house had been built by Lord Gilbert's father, Ralf de Caudebec, who had fought with the Conqueror and been awarded the manor of Lakehall as reward. The estate rose up to the eastern side of the track, a mixture of arable land on the higher, drier ground, and waterlogged marsh – rich in eels – out on the fens. The house and its outbuildings were surrounded by a paling fence, and the house itself boasted a wide hall, a solar and extensive kitchen quarters. Lord Gilbert was very fond of his food.

We set off up the drive. 'The reeve will receive us,' I said to Jack. 'His name's Bermund. He's not exactly a cheerful, outgoing sort of man –' my younger brother Squeak had once said the reeve looked like an anxious rat – 'but he's fair.'

Jack nodded. 'Anything else I should know?'

'Lord Gilbert's lazy and not very quick-witted.' I lowered my voice. 'If you can enlist Lady Emma's sympathies, the job's done.'

He nodded again. 'Thank you.'

We clattered into the courtyard, our horses' hooves announcing our presence. A lad poked his head out of the arched entrance to the stables, and someone else ran up the flight of stone steps into the hall. Bermund appeared in the doorway.

He studied each of us, his eyes resting on me. 'You're the eel-catcher's daughter. The healer girl,' he said.

'I am,' I agreed.

His glance went back to Jack, then to Lady Rosaria. 'What do you want?' He fixed me with a stare. 'Who are these people?'

I opened my mouth to speak, but Jack forestalled me. 'My name is Jack Chevestrier,' he said, 'and I am an officer of the sheriff of Cambridge. This is the lady Rosaria Dalassena, widow of the late Hugo Guillaume Fensmanson, and she has come here to seek her husband's kinsfolk, bringing with her his child.'

Bermund's eyes narrowed suspiciously. 'What has this to do with Lord Gilbert?'

'The family whom Lady Rosaria seeks are fenland people,' Jack said firmly, 'and she needs help in finding them.'

Bermund looked as if he'd like nothing better than to shut the great door in our faces. But observance of the old rules of courtesy, hospitality and chivalry to ladies in distress goes deep. He said curtly, 'Wait there,' and disappeared inside the hall.

He reappeared a short time later. 'You're to come up.' He summoned the pair of stable boys who had been watching, wide-eyed, from the courtyard, and they hurried forward. Lady Rosaria, Jack and I dismounted, and the lads took our horses. Just then, the baby gave a start – the movement had woken him – and let out a shrill cry. The cry swiftly escalated to a steady scream of protest: Leafric was ravenous.

I made an apologetic face at Jack. 'He won't stop till he's fed, and there's no more of Mattie's bread sops,' I said above the yelling. 'I'll take him straight to Edild. She's bound to know of a wet-nurse, and, in the meantime, she'll feed him.'

I turned and, on foot since there was nowhere at Edild's house to care for a horse, set off back towards the track, all other thoughts and preoccupations dissolving in the face of Leafric's mounting distress. His little body had stiffened in outrage, his mouth formed a gaping square, and his face was screwed up and bright red. Jack called after me, 'Where will you be?'

'I'll stay at my aunt's house,' I called back. 'Go on towards the village, past the church, and it's the next house on the right.'

Then, clutching Leafric close, I broke into a jogtrot and hurried away.

FIVE

Edild exhibited no surprise at my sudden arrival with a screaming baby in my arms. Typically, it was his needs she addressed first, warming some milk over the hearth and dipping in some small pieces of bread. 'He is presumably in need of a wet-nurse,' she said in the sudden, blessed silence.

'Yes.'

Leafric was on her lap, gazing up at her as he sucked at the bread, his gummy jaws mumbling like an old man's. She glanced up at me over the top of his head. 'And are there the means to pay such a woman?'

I explained about Lady Rosaria. 'She paid the woman I found for her in Cambridge,' I concluded. Mattie, I recalled, had told me Jack Chevestrier made quite sure Lady Rosaria rewarded her adequately.

Edild nodded. 'The smith's wife had a baby two months ago,' she said. 'It's her fourth, and she has ample milk. I will ask her.'

I didn't answer. I was watching Leafric, and wishing that the woman who had given birth to him was a little more maternal. A little more loving. Well, that was how it was with rich noble-women, and nothing I thought or felt would make any difference. 'What is it?' Edild asked.

I remembered, then, the other reason for bringing Lady Rosaria to Aelf Fen. 'Do you remember the woman who took against her baby?' I asked. I'd lowered my voice, as if I didn't want poor little Leafric to overhear. Silly, really.

'Yes.'

'You helped her.'

Edild sighed. 'Time helped her, Lassair. As the days and weeks passed, she came to her senses and realized that her little girl needed her.'

'Then you can do the same with Lady Rosaria!' I exclaimed. 'You can do what you did before, and—'

But my aunt shook her head. 'It's not the same at all. The woman who bore this child hasn't been brought up to be a mother, except in the sense that she conceived, carried and gave birth to him. High-born ladies are not expected to have anything to do with their offspring. Child-rearing duties are put into the hands of others, paid for their services.'

'I know, but—'

'No, Lassair,' Edild said firmly. 'Where is Lady Rosaria now?'

'Up at Lakehall. She's trying to trace her late husband's kin. She says he was from a fenland family.'

'Then no doubt Lord Gilbert – or, more likely, Lady Emma in conjunction with that reeve of theirs – will help her, and, before we know it, Lady Rosaria and her son –' she looked down at the baby, one hand gently stroking his head – 'will be swept away into the bosom of her family, and that will be the last we'll ever see of her.' She looked up at me, her expression intent. 'Don't get involved, Lassair. She's not like us, and she lives in a very different world.'

'So you won't go and see her?'

'If Lord Gilbert sends for me because his guest requires my assistance, then yes, naturally I will. Otherwise, no.'

Then she picked Leafric up and put him against her shoulder, rhythmically rubbing his back. 'Now, I shall go and speak to the smith's wife. That bread and milk has satisfied him for the time being, but he'll be yelling again soon if we can't find him what he really wants.'

She stood up, and I knew the discussion had come to an end. I gazed down at my hands, folded in my lap. I felt very miserable suddenly.

As Edild passed me on her way to the door, she put her hand on the top of my head. 'Don't be sad,' she said softly. 'He'll be all right.' Then she was gone.

I sat there for some time. Yes, Leafric was going to be

well-fed and cared for – providing the smith's wife was willing – but that didn't necessarily mean he would be *all right*. His mother didn't love him: how *could* he be *all right*?

It's the same for all children born into nobility, I told myself. Why, then, was I so disturbed about this particular one? I didn't think it was personal – although, in truth, he was a very appealing baby – since I'd only known him a matter of days. Sitting there by Edild's hearth, I tried to analyse my feelings.

And, all at once, I knew what it was.

In my head, I heard Mattie's voice. *He's sad*, she said. *He just lies there, staring around, for all the world as if he's looking for something, and can't let himself drop off till he's spotted it. And the look on that dear child's face! Oh, it fair twists my heart.*

Yes. I knew exactly what she meant, and it twisted my heart, too.

What was troubling me so much was that, somehow, I *knew* this little boy had experienced love. Someone – presumably the nurse who had cared for him on the journey and who now appeared to have left Lady Rosaria's employ – had shown him what it was to be cared for with tenderness and consideration.

And, bless him, he missed it.

All at once my sorrow at the ways of the world overcame me. I dropped my face into my hands and wept.

I had managed to pull myself together by the time Edild returned. The smith's wife had agreed to care for Leafric while Lady Rosaria was in residence at Lakehall.

I got up. 'I'll go and tell her,' I said. I couldn't summon much enthusiasm for the task. 'I'll call by to see my parents before I come back,' I added, wrapping myself in my shawl. When I'm in the village, I live with Edild; besides the fact that I work with her and it's better to be on the spot, one less body in my family's home definitely eases the overcrowding.

'Very well,' Edild said calmly.

Even if Lady Rosaria appeared indifferent concerning the arrangements for her infant son, others at Lakehall were anxious to hear. Perhaps I did her an injustice; perhaps it was she who had dispatched Bermund to keep an eye out for my return. He ushered me inside the great hall, where Lady Emma sat peacefully sewing beside the fire. She looked up and gave me a smile.

'I would judge by the fact that you no longer bear a child in your arms, Lassair, that you have been successful?' she said.

I returned her smile. I like Lady Emma. 'Yes, my lady. My aunt Edild found a woman willing to act as wet-nurse, and Leafric is with her now.'

'She's welcome to come and live here while she is in Lady Rosaria's employ,' Lady Emma said. 'Lady Rosaria may wish to have the baby close.'

I gave a sort of snort of disbelief: it just burst out of me before I could stop it. Lady Emma studied me for a moment, and I thought I could guess what she was thinking. Tactfully, she made no comment. After a short pause, she said, 'Lord Gilbert and Jack Chevestrier are already thinking how to set about finding the lady's kinsmen. She is providing what information she can, although it appears to be rather sparse.'

'Where has she come from?' I asked. 'From her colouring and her style, she seems to be a woman of the south.'

Lady Emma gave a graceful shrug. 'I have no idea. I was not privy to the conversation.' Again, her eyes met mine, and, from their expression, I would have sworn that her absence from the discussions was entirely her own choice.

I can't say I blamed her for wanting as little to do with Lady Rosaria as possible.

I said quietly, 'I am sorry to have brought her here, my lady.'

Again, she shrugged. 'You had little choice, Lassair. She could scarcely have been left to fend for herself in a Cambridge inn.' She sighed. 'Let us hope that Lord Gilbert's enquiries will swiftly meet with success.'

Then she bent her head over her sewing once more, and I sensed myself dismissed.

I was setting out along the road into the village when I heard running footsteps. I stopped, turning round and saw Jack hurrying after me.

'You've found a wet-nurse, I hear,' he said. He'd just been running, quite hard, and yet he wasn't at all out of breath.

'My aunt did. And *I* hear that you and Lord Gilbert have been planning how to find the lady's relatives and dispatch her off to them as fast as you can.'

He grinned. 'Quite right, although I bet Lady Emma didn't phrase it exactly like that.'

I waited, not speaking. 'Well?' he said after a moment. 'What is it?'

'Isn't it obvious?' I said. 'I'm waiting for you to tell me all about her.'

He sighed, falling into step beside me. 'Not much to tell. She says her husband's father was a Saxon noble from a wealthy, landowning family, and he left England after the Conquest to set about restoring his fortunes. His name was Harald Fensman, which I suppose we could have surmised, given that her late husband was called Hugo Fensmanson.'

'It's the Norse way, to add *son* on to the father's family name,' I said. 'My—' I'd been about to tell him that the man I now knew to be my grandfather, Thorfinn Ofnirsson, had the same custom. But I held back; very few people knew that my Granny Cordeilla's husband had not fathered her third child, my father. Including my father . . .

'What?' Jack asked.

'Er – nothing. Did she reveal any more?'

'Not much. She said she's a widow, which we already knew, and that her husband died earlier this year.'

I gave an exclamation of impatience. 'If she wants to be helped, surely she needs to be more forthcoming?'

'I agree,' he said. 'So, I think, does Lord Gilbert, although courtesy to his guest prevents him from saying so.'

'What will you do now?'

I was afraid he'd say, *I'm heading straight back to Cambridge.* But he didn't: he said, 'I've offered to stay for a few days to help in the search for this Harald Fensman's kinsmen.'

'Why?'

'Because Sheriff Picot commanded me to look after her.'

'But surely—' I began. Surely he was needed back in Cambridge? Surely the sheriff hadn't intended his officer to go on taking care of Lady Rosaria until her family were found? I didn't utter either remark; it would have been stupid, when I'd been hoping so much he'd stay.

'But surely what?' he prompted. He was smiling.

'Oh, nothing.' Embarrassed, I cast around for something to say. Then, remembering something I'd meant to ask, I said, 'Who was the tall, bald-headed man you were arguing with as we set off?'

Jack's smile vanished. 'Gaspard Picot,' he said tersely.

'A relation?'

'Yes. He's the sheriff's nephew, and views himself as heir and natural successor to Picot's position. He's certainly evil enough,' he added in an angry mutter.

'He doesn't seem to like you very much,' I observed.

'He—' Jack hesitated. 'He resents the closeness he believes I have to his uncle. He thinks I'm a party to the schemes by which Picot makes himself rich and powerful, and considers I have usurped his rightful position.'

I recalled what Gurdyman had said: *Jack Chevestrier is a better man by far than his master the sheriff.* 'But you haven't,' I said quietly.

Jack shot me a quick look. 'No.' Then, as if he didn't want to say any more, he turned and strode away.

I headed on into the village. A cold, forceful east wind was rising, and it threatened rain. Although I couldn't yet see the moon in the early evening sky – and it would probably be concealed by the gathering clouds – I knew it would be full.

I increased my pace, a shiver of alarm running up my spine. The full moon, combined with the time of year, meant that the tide would be high tonight. If it combined with strong easterly winds – perhaps, judging by the steadily darkening clouds overhead, even a storm – then there would be flooding in the low-lying areas. The people of the fens and the bulge of coastal East Anglia have learned to dread such conditions, for at such times a great wall of water builds up and surges inland. You can't fight the sea, when it has made up its mind to flood over the land.

Edild and I spent a cosy evening in her neat little house. The rain had begun, beating down fast and furiously. We shut out the violence of the night and sat close to the hearth, and soon, my belly full, I felt my eyes beginning to close.

'Go to bed, Lassair,' ordered my aunt.

I needed no second telling. I had a cursory wash, removed my outer tunic and snuggled down under the bedclothes. I was vaguely aware of Edild, moving soft-footed around me as she tidied up and prepared for bed, then I fell asleep.

It was the wind that woke me. It was howling round the house like some desperate monster, and its cry ranged from a low, throbbing hum right up to a full-lunged scream. Back draft from the smoke hole in the roof had disturbed the embers of the fire in the hearth, and there was a mist of ash and smoke in the room. It was raining even harder, and there were regular thumps as objects were hurled against the stout walls. It sounded, in my shocked-awake state, as if the creature outside was trying to break its way in.

As my awareness grew, I realized there was another sound: the muttering of quiet voices. I pushed my humped bedding down a fraction and peered out.

The room was almost dark, lit only by the dying fire. Edild and Hrype sat close together on the far side of the hearth. Hrype's heavy cloak lay spread on the floor, steaming gently. He had removed his boots and folded back his hose, and his bare feet were towards the fire.

I was torn between pretending I was still asleep and giving them some rare privacy, or making it plain that they – or, rather, the storm – had just woken me up. If I chose the former, there was always the chance that their closeness might proceed to the sort of intimacy that I really didn't want to witness, even with my head under the covers. I faked a yawn, stretched and, feigning surprise, said, 'Hello, Hrype. What are you doing here?'

He looked at me, his strange silvery eyes glittering. 'You have the shining stone with you,' he said.

'Yes,' I admitted. He hadn't asked; he'd stated the fact. He'd presumably have been talking to Gurdyman.

'Then you must—'

Edild interrupted him, murmuring quietly into his ear. He listened, nodded curtly and began again. 'Lassair, it is very important that you begin to make appropriate use of the stone. Your—' This time, he stopped of his own volition. There was a pause, as if he was weighing his words, then he said, 'Please will you try once more to look into it? You have had it in your possession for many months now, and it will know you when you handle it.' I made myself ignore the shiver of fear that gripped me at the thought of the stone *knowing* me. 'You should not be apprehensive. If you approach it properly – and I am here to make sure that you do – it will be a powerful tool in your hands.'

I thought about that. The shining stone, or so I had been told, permitted anyone who stared into it to see the truth; more alarmingly, if you had the strength, apparently you could use it to search out and harness the forces of the spirit world. The very idea terrified me.

They'd persuaded me to try, Gurdyman and Hrype, that night in Gurdyman's crypt. Clutching my piece of lapis lazuli, I'd stared into the stone's dark depths. I could still recall all too vividly what I'd seen and heard. The straining figures, the waters of sea and river; the galloping horses; those two ravens, flying straight for me.

I had tried not to think about it, particularly the birds. Whenever the images had returned, I had swiftly dismissed them. Now, as I allowed them full rein, perhaps for the first time, something else occurred to me: something which I thought I had quite forgotten, except I couldn't have done because now it was the only thing in my mind . . .

When I went down to the crypt that night and found Gurdyman and Hrype closeted together, I'd asked Hrype if there was news of my family. Not of them, he had replied, but there was news of somebody else.

I looked at him now, filled with the firm resolution not to weaken. 'Hrype, what exactly is it you want me to find out for you?' I asked. 'When you and Gurdyman made me use the stone before, you'd just told me there was news of Skuli.'

I was studying him intently, watching his face in the dim light for any subtle change of expression. And, as I spoke Skuli's name, I saw it: a tiny flicker in his eyes. As if, just for an instant, some shadow had blocked out their brightness.

'That's it, isn't it?' I whispered. 'Somehow, word of what he's doing has reached you, and you want me to look in the stone and verify what you've learned.' I had no idea whether I was right – what I was suggesting sounded so unlikely – but Hrype's face remained impassive.

Then the absurdity of it hit me hard. 'I can't!' I cried. 'I'm a complete novice, and I haven't the first idea how to use the shining stone! If I'm very lucky, I might see some random, meaningless images, and yet you're asking me to look for one specific man, who's somewhere out in the wilds between here and Miklagard! Hrype, I can't do it!'

Slowly the echoes of my loud voice faded and died. There was nothing to hear but the fury of the storm outside. I waited for some reaction, from Hrype, from Edild – surely my aunt would come to my rescue? Couldn't she see as well as I could how impossible a task Hrype was demanding of me? – but neither spoke a word.

Finally, Hrype said, 'You won't know till you try.'

I don't know how it came about, but, not long afterwards, I was sitting cross-legged by the fire, the shining stone resting in my open hands and my little piece of lapis tucked inside my bodice, close to my heart.

I sat there for some time. The rising pitch of the storm seemed to recede, and I was only barely aware of the furious, driving rain beating weightily down on the roof. I seemed to have lost the last remaining residue of my own will. I did as Hrype bade me, and focused all my attention on the stone.

At first, I saw the same images I'd seen before. A wide river, winding away ahead into infinity. Then that picture of a team of men, working so hard that I could sense the strain as they pulled and heaved at long ropes and an unbearably heavy load. Now I perceived that there were oxen too: big, lumbering beasts that steamed with the sweat of effort. Fast water, broiling in high plumes of white spray over vicious black rocks. A shaped stone, marked with runes. Then the sea – I heard waves lapping on a shore – and a sense of calm as the wind filled a great square sail high above. A vast port, white buildings brilliant under a bright blue sky filled with sunshine. People, so many people, their garments, even their skin and hair, very different from any I'd ever known; voices raised in furious dispute. The water again, deep, deep blue . . .

Lulled, half-entranced, I let myself be led. I allowed my vigilance to drop. And then they came straight at me, those two dark, sinister birds. For a split-second I saw a very familiar face – what on earth was *he* doing there? – and then the ravens were upon me, their long, strong, cruel beaks wide, their claws spread out like a handful of knives. I cried out, dropped the stone and my hands flew up to cover my face. In that instant, I *knew*, the ravens had been on the point of going for my eyes.

For a few heartbeats, nothing happened except that, perhaps in response to the terrifying thing I'd just seen, the violence of the storm increased for a moment to screaming pitch. Then Hrype gave a deep sigh, and, as if that released Edild from some spell, she got up, hurried across to me and took me in her arms.

I could have stayed there, held close against her, hearing the steady beat of her heart, for a long time. But then Hrype said calmly, 'Lassair, the shining stone is loose on the floor. You must treat it with more respect.'

I disengaged myself from my aunt's embrace. Reaching out, I picked up the stone. It had felt quite hot before, probably from the warmth of my hands, but now it was cold. I wrapped it in the sheep's wool and put it back in the leather bag, pulling the drawstrings tight. Then I replaced the bag in the little recess behind the shelf where I store my bedding during the daytime. As soon as it was hidden away, the atmosphere in the room changed.

But I wasn't going to be allowed to forget what had just happened. Hrype said, 'Did you see him?'

'I didn't see Skuli, no.' I was going to keep to myself the identity of the man I *had* seen.

'What *did* you see?' Hrype persisted. 'What scared you so badly?'

I took a breath, trying to calm myself. 'I saw a river, and a place where men used oxen, and their own strength, to drag a long, slim ship over the land,' I said. 'I saw perilous rapids, and a stone carved with runes. I saw the sea, and then a busy port. Voices arguing, and the sea again. Then –' I faltered – 'then the birds came.'

'You saw Skuli's voyage,' Hrype said, and I could detect a note of triumph in his voice. 'You saw his journey down the long rivers that lead off to the east and the south, and the portage route where they transport the vessels overland. You saw the rapids, and—'

It was high time to rein him in. 'Hrype, all of that could have come from my imagination,' I told him firmly. 'I already knew about the journey to Miklagard –' my grandfather had described it, in great detail – 'and no doubt I just *thought* I saw those pictures in the shining stone. Probably,' I added, glaring at him, 'because you just put Skuli into my mind, and you've been pushing me so hard to succeed in spying on him.'

He considered this, and gave a curt nod. 'That's possible,' he acknowledged. 'Perhaps, in truth, you saw only what you expected to see.'

'What is this news of Skuli?' I demanded. 'And how do you even come to *have* news, when he's so far away?'

'The journey to Miklagard operates both ways,' he said. 'Men travel back north again, and they bring tidings from the south lands.'

Yes. That made sense. There was nothing mystical about a returning mariner bringing tales of what he had seen and experienced. I still didn't understand, though, how Hrype had come to hear these tales; perhaps he'd been visiting some port up on the coast. 'So what do they say, these tidings?'

Hrype watched me for a moment. Then he said, 'Merely that Skuli has arrived in Miklagard, and that the voyage passed without major incident.'

Such was the power of his presence that, in that moment, I accepted what he said.

Suddenly he got up, reaching for his still-wet cloak.

'You're going?' Edild said. He nodded, drawing on his boots. She gestured with one hand towards the roof, on to which the rain was hammering in a hard, steady, deafening beat. 'You can't go out in this!'

He smiled briefly. 'I am already wet. A little more will not hurt, and it is not far.' He bent and kissed her, pausing for a moment to rest a tender hand on her cheek. She bowed her head in acknowledgement.

He had the door open and closed again so swiftly that only a little rain came in. I watched my aunt staring after him. Briefly, all the pain of her situation was in her lovely face. She must surely know that she had Hrype's love and his heart; sometimes it probably wasn't enough.

She busied herself spreading out her bedding once more, then she lay down. The fire was dying, giving only a small amount of light. 'Try to sleep, Lassair,' she said. 'From the sound of it, this storm is a very bad one. We will have troubles enough to face in the morning, and will need our strength.'

I turned on my side, facing away from the hearth, and closed my eyes. But I knew I wouldn't sleep; not yet, anyway, for my mind was racing. Something was wrong, and now, in the darkness, I worked out what it was.

While his powerful, dynamic presence had still been in the little room, Hrype had easily persuaded me that the news of Skuli's arrival in Miklagard, following an uneventful journey, was nothing to get excited about. He'd wanted me to accept the news without question – without even stopping to think about it – and, Hrype being Hrype, that was exactly what I'd done.

But Hrype wasn't there any more.

As if it were an animal roused from sleep and instantly on the alert, I felt my curiosity wake up. I even had a swift image of my spirit creature, and I felt Fox's warm presence curled up beside me. It was a while since I'd been aware of him, and it felt good to have him back. He was, I'm sure, encouraging me.

A dozen thoughts and ideas flew through my head. I forced them into order, and, focusing all my attention inwards, this is what I finally concluded.

From the first time I'd heard about Skuli and the mission he felt compelled to fulfil, there had been the sense that I wasn't being told the full story. My grandfather had said Skuli was driven by powerful forces within him to succeed where his forefather had failed, and complete the journey to Miklagard. Thorfinn had implied that there was something deeply perilous about the voyage, which was why Skuli had tried so desperately and so ruthlessly to acquire the shining stone. Not only did he believe he was its true keeper; he was convinced he would not succeed without it. Out of the past, I seemed to hear my grandfather's voice: *He believes that the place where he is bound can only be reached with the aid of the spirits.*

I had understood – no, they had all *encouraged* me to understand, Thorfinn, Hrype, even Gurdyman – that the place Skuli
was bound was Miklagard. But now I saw very clearly two major
objections to that. The first was that, while the journey was
undoubtedly long, arduous and dangerous, it was regularly and
routinely travelled by many mariners, none of whom had the
aid of a magical stone. The second was this: if Skuli had reached
Miklagard safely, then that meant his mission was over. Why,
then, was Hrype still so very eager for me to go on trying to use
the shining stone to see what Skuli was up to?

In the darkness, I was smiling in triumph. I'd always *known*
there was more to this tale of Skuli's mysterious journey than
had been revealed to me. Now, in my own mind, I had proof.
What I was going to do with that proof, and, more importantly,
how I would react next time someone asked me to look into the
shining stone, I had yet to work out.

I could hear Edild's deep, regular breathing. She had gone to
sleep, and she had advised me to try to do the same. I knew she
was right, and that I needed my sleep. The storm was still howling
outside, and now its violence was intensifying. I must rest.
Deliberately, I visualized putting my excitement over my brand-
new discovery into a bag and stowing it away. Then I turned to
the vivid, violent images which the stone had put in my mind.
Slowly, one by one, finishing with those awful ravens, I banished
the pictures I'd seen.

One image, however, I allowed myself to see again. Although
he looked very different – he was in pale robes, with a headdress
that covered his blond hair, and his skin had been darkened,
either by the sun or by his own skill – I had recognized him
instantly. His presence among the visions I'd seen in the stone
was puzzling. What on earth *was* he doing there, somehow
involved with Skuli's voyage to the south? Even if I'd imagined
it all, why had my mind elected to place him there?

I had an explanation, although I shied from it. I tried to tell
myself it was nonsense, but it persisted, nudging at me until I
steeled myself to face it.

The explanation was this: what I had seen was an image of
Rollo Guiscard, who is my one and only lover; the man who
stays in my heart although he is usually far away and we are

together only rarely. We had made each other no promises, recognizing our love simply by a hand fasting and the exchange of gifts: I gave him a braided leather bracelet, and he gave me a heavy gold ring, which I wear on a chain around my neck. It was almost a year since I had seen him.

Had he appeared before my eyes in that flash of vision because a part of me wanted to make sure he was at the forefront of my thoughts? Was my heart issuing this timely reminder that Rollo was the man I loved; the man I was content to wait for, no matter how long, because our future was together? Hadn't I once had that brief, lovely image of the child I would one day have with him; the son who would be a mix of Rollo's Norman and my Saxon blood, a warrior to take on the whole world?

I squeezed my eyes tight shut, as if that would shut off my inner vision. It didn't. I wanted to cry my distress, and it took a big effort to hold back.

I knew why my conscience had pushed that image of Rollo out of the shining stone and before my eyes, and it had precious little to do with Skuli and his travels.

It was because Jack Chevestrier had entered my life.

Out at sea, huge waves were being driven hard by the howling wind. The full moon meant a high tide anyway, but, that night, an unremitting gale out of the east-north-east was pushing the waters yet higher. With nowhere for the piled-up waters to go, the Wash was overflowing.

Low-lying coastal villages received the punishment first. Small craft were beaten against the shore, some of them smashed to splinters on breakwaters and quays. Tracks became wet, sodden, then turned into streams. Dwellings of every sort flooded, from great manors to lowly hovels, for the elements are no respecters of a man's wealth and position. People gathered together, trying to help one another. Trying to protect their property. Trying to save lives.

Seawater began to flow up the fenland rivers. Fresh water gave before the onslaught, as huge and powerful wind-driven waves crashed inland. On the Ouse at Lynn, the lower reaches of the town were swiftly inundated. Boats moored at the quays clashed together, and the sound of smashing wood competed with the howls and screams of the gale. Still the water pushed on, and now it drove before it a tide of wreckage.

The waters of the river were still rising some ten miles inland to the south, and abnormally high waves drove repeatedly upstream. In many places, the water swiftly overcame the muddy, marshy fenland river banks, and the surrounding land was soon flooded. Occasionally, the headlong rush of the torrent and its piled debris met an obstacle. The broken planks of a wrecked boat caught against the underside of a small wooden bridge, and the resulting pile-up of water on the seaward side swiftly spread out into a widening pool.

Caught in the swirling current, the torn and shattered pieces of wood moved in swift circles. From time to time, one would be thrust right up out of the water, before once more being drawn down beneath the surface. Amid the wreckage, something white suddenly appeared, to flash briefly in the faint light of early dawn. It was swept under, then, after a while, it bobbed up again. This time, some random eddy in the hugely swollen river cast it up against the side of the little bridge, where it lodged.

It was pale, shimmering slightly under the pre-dawn sky. Perhaps the waters receded a little: for, slowly, more of it became visible above the flood line.

It was a body. It was naked, and lay face down. Its limbs were long and well-muscled; its hair was soaking wet and muddy but, where it was beginning to dry, could be seen to be fair.

The body was in the very early stages of decomposition. The eyes had gone, and small marine creatures had started to feast on the flesh. It stank.

Dawn broke.

The wind began to abate, and, at long last, the great mass of water that had been forced up the rivers and over the land stopped rising. Infinitesimally, it began to recede. The light grew and the new day began. In the ports, towns and villages where the devastation had hit, people began to clean up and count their losses. Several had been killed, and dozens wounded by water-borne debris they had failed to see in the darkness. Livestock had been carried away. Many dwellings had been damaged beyond repair. Crafts of all sizes had been driven from their moorings, many to be wrecked on the shore.

People began the slow trudge up the rivers, searching for swept-away items. Anything that might come in useful for the hundreds of repairs necessary would be eagerly dragged out of the water and carried home. Not long after dawn, a group of three men – a grandfather, his son and his grandson – came down from their village on the fen edge to inspect the wreckage around the little bridge.

On spotting the body, the grandson – he was just a lad – was sick. The grandfather sent his son to fetch help while he stood vigil.

And, as the morning broke, the man came hurrying into Aelf Fen, where he ran up the track to Lakehall and banged hard on the door.

SIX

The South, autumn 1093

Rollo Guiscard felt as if he'd been travelling for ever.

In the year since he had left England, he had crossed the mainland of Europe and finished up on the island of Sicily; his birthplace, and the area where his kin still lived. He had sailed on eastwards across the Mediterranean, planning to go to Constantinople. A violent storm had interfered with his plans. When at last the savage winds died down, his ship made landfall far to the south, and, rather than head back to Constantinople, he amended his plans and spent a couple of months travelling through Syria, making his way south to Palestine and his ultimate goal: Jerusalem.

He had kept out of sight of any but the poor and the powerless while he made his assessment of the land in which he found himself. Very soon it became clear that, unless you were an important lord, a wealthy merchant or a Christian pilgrim, you attracted little notice and people left you alone. Rollo adopted local dress and proceeded, unchallenged, on his way.

He had been unprepared for the sheer power and the beauty

of Jerusalem. He spent several days simply looking. Dressed as he was as a humble rural Turk making the longed-for visit to the Holy City, it was easy to blend in with the hundreds of men, women and children, all doing likewise and all overcome with the same awe. Rollo was moved almost to tears at his first sight of the Dome of the Rock, and his heart went out to the many whose emotions overcame them.

It was a populous city, its narrow streets humming with activity. Since the Turks had captured it in 1065 they had made its character their own, and the place was thriving. The necessities of life were readily available; food and drink were abundant and cheap, and hospitals tended to the sick and the injured. Craftsmen flourished, each trade having its own market. Men's souls were looked after too, both by the mosques, beautifully decorated with marble and brilliant mosaic, and by the many institutions dedicated to teaching. Intellectual activity was enthusiastically encouraged, and available to everyone.

But there was also a dark side to Jerusalem. Keeping to the shadows and avoiding confrontation, Rollo witnessed the city's ugly face. He observed with his own eyes the treatment meted out to those whose faith did not accord with that of the majority. That majority had newly adopted Islam, and they had the zeal of new converts. Some of them – the minority, Rollo hoped – were brutal in their mindless violence, and targeted anyone who was not of the same faith, whether or not they had the ability to fight back. There was, it appeared, only one god, and only one approach was deemed permissible.

When he felt he had seen enough, Rollo packed up his few belongings and left. As he set out on the long journey north, he found himself conducting an inner debate: overall, bearing in mind the undoubted benefits and the terrible penalties, was religion, as men currently chose to practise it, beneficial to the world or not?

Now, at last, he was on his way to Constantinople. Although he still had immeasurable miles to go before his mission would finally be completed, nevertheless it felt good to be nearly at the end of the first leg of the long journey.

As he crossed Anatolia and the distance to Constantinople

steadily lessened, he fought to suppress his impatience. The late summer sun shone brilliantly out of a clear sky, illuminating the wooded slopes around him. He had been happy to leave the burning temperatures of Syria behind; during all his time in the south, he had been uncomfortably hot. It had helped that the necessity for disguise had forced him to adopt local dress; the long, loose-fitting, pale-coloured robes allowed the air to circulate, keeping his skin relatively cool. The cloth wound round and round his head protected him from the sun, and it had been useful to be able to draw the loose end over his nose and mouth when, as so often happened, the wind suddenly howled and the hot air filled with tiny particles of sand. When, at last, he had brushed off the last of the desert dust as he began to climb up on to the Anatolian plateau, the relief had been enormous.

Rollo was weary, with a fatigue that went far beyond his tired body.

Now, as the long day of travelling neared its end, he was at the northern edge of the plateau, and the steep slopes leading down to the Black Sea were ahead. He looked up into the sky, noting the position of the sun. He could not hope to reach Constantinople today; he would not risk arriving after dark. The city was edgy, and all too aware of the aggressively warlike neighbours who dwelt to the south across the Bosphorus. The tough men who manned the walls were more likely to greet a solitary wanderer tapping on the gates by throwing him into a dungeon than by inviting him into some cosy guardroom to take food and drink, and soak his weary body in a scented bath.

When it was too dark to travel any further, Rollo would do as he had done on countless nights before: get off the road, find a safe place to shelter, eat, and, at last, sleep.

As he lay relaxed in his bed roll, staring up at the dazzling stars overhead, he thought about what he had found out; the answers to the questions which his king, all those long miles away in England, had sent him to investigate. He smiled, reflecting that, as usual, so much of King William's reasoning had been absolutely right. It was going to give Rollo some pleasure in eventually telling him so.

William Rufus, his agile and capable mind ever on the

lookout for ways in which to advance both his own fortunes and those of his kingdom, had noted with interest the way in which the Christians of the north had steadily managed to reverse the Muslim conquests of the preceding century. The Byzantines had taken Cyprus and Crete, and then the Normans, following eagerly and ruthlessly in their footsteps, had taken Malta and Sicily; the latter prize had fallen to Rollo's own kinsmen, the Guiscards.

William had wondered what other lands might be ripe for conquest by the apparently unstoppable forces of the west. As rumour began to filter northwards of a fierce nation of new converts, the Seljuk Turks, word spread of atrocities, particularly against Christians. For centuries, pilgrims had taken it for granted that they could visit the places where Jesus once walked the earth; now, William had been told, these precious sites were barred to them. And, moreover, barred with ferocious cruelty: Christian pilgrims, or so they said, were being attacked, beaten and tortured.

William had observed that it was impossible to say where the truth ended and the wild exaggeration of propaganda began. Not that this troubled him: as Rollo well knew, the king's interest in the matter was purely pragmatic. The rich and extensive lands that lay on the eastern shore of the Mediterranean were, in his mind, the natural successors to the long list of Christian conquests, and what a prize they would make for the land-grabbing lords of the north.

Nowhere in the king's planning was there any scheme to join in such a conquest himself. For one thing, he had not the necessary devotion to suffer the myriad hardships, expenses and dangers of a campaign whose sole aim was to free the Holy City from the infidel; he was far too realistic about its chances of success, and he just didn't care enough. His interest in the matter was for another reason: his brother and rival, Robert, Duke of Normandy, was just the sort of man who would respond to a call to free the Holy Land. Robert, however, was chronically and perpetually short of funds; if the moment came when his soul filled with religious zeal, he would instantly look round for someone from whom to borrow the necessary cash, and his eyes would light on his brother William, across the narrow seas. And what had he to offer as collateral on the loan? Only one thing: his dukedom.

If events were to roll out as King William suspected they might, then his brother, with his eyes shining and his heart high, would set off on the long and perilous road to Jerusalem. If he failed to return – and surely that was so likely as to be almost a certainty? – then Normandy would fall like a sweet, ripe fruit right into William's hands. He would have won the dukedom he wanted so badly without even having to lift his sword.

Rollo had been the king's eyes and ears in the Holy Land. He had observed, considered, judged, memorized; names, locations, strengths, weaknesses. He had ventured into dark and dangerous places, and paid dearly for information meant to be kept hidden. He had crawled under men's defences, winkled out their secrets. He had misled people, lied to them, bribed them, persuaded them to act against their conscience and bent them to his will. He was too good at his job; what he had learned went far beyond his king's remit. He had, he sensed, left behind in the Holy Land a part of his soul.

He knew exactly what he would say to his king; how he would summarize, in the succinct, brief statements which the chronically impatient king demanded, all that he had seen. Now, though, before he could set out for England, he must find a way to make some sort of contact with the mighty ruler of Constantinople.

His mind leapt ahead to what he must do when he arrived in the city. His prime mission was to discover how Alexius Comnenus viewed the enemy on his doorstep and what he proposed to do about his perilous situation. Besieged as he was by the Seljuk Turks, this race of ferociously devout men who, it appeared, would stop at nothing until the entire world believed exactly as they did, how was Alexius going to react? Would he, as William believed, send out to the kings and the great lords of the west, asking for their help in the inevitable confrontation that was coming? Once Rollo had found out all he could – and, so far, he had only the sketchiest notion of how he was to go about it – he must find the fastest ship heading back to north-west Europe. With luck, he might find a swift craft sailing all the way to England, although that was surely too much to ask.

It was going to be tricky, worming his way into a place where he could have some sort of open exchange with those who ruled the huge Byzantine Empire, but he had something with which to bargain. So recently arrived from the turbulent lands where the Turks were flexing their muscles, he was in possession of certain facts of which Alexius Comnenus was possibly unaware.

One fact in particular stood out; something Rollo knew to be more important than virtually anything else. He hoped it was going to be enough . . .

In the middle of the following morning, he stood on an elevation on the southern side of the Bosphorus, his eyes fixed on the Queen of Cities across the azure water. It was fortified by thick walls, interspersed at intervals by narrow gates manned with guards. Beyond the walls, on a series of steep hills, rose the buildings of Constantinople. Rollo had an impression of graceful towers and gilded domes, the bright morning light dazzling off stone, metal and paint so that the entire city shimmered.

The waterway dividing the Greek and Turkish halves of the city was hectic with traffic, and he watched ferries darting from north to south and back again, weaving a path among the slow, heavy merchant ships making their way up or down the Bosphorus. To his right, the narrow strait stretched on north-eastwards, towards its meeting with the Black Sea. Almost opposite to where he stood, the Golden Horn flowed out, its quays thick with vessels loading, unloading or waiting their turn to tie up. To his left, the Sea of Marmara opened up, and along its northern shore he saw the life of the city spread out.

He stood in silent thought for some time, then, with a decisive step, made his way down the steep track to the settlement spread out below.

He had at last made up his mind how best to make the approach to Alexius's inner circle that would enable him to find out what he needed to know. He had concluded that, as he was a foreigner in the city, the logical conduit to Alexius's ear was via other foreigners. These particular foreigners, indeed, had the additional bonus of being closer to the emperor than any men outside his own kin, for they formed his elite personal bodyguard.

They were men of the north: big, broad, brawny and blond, in a land where men were habitually lean, dark, short and slight.

Their loyalty and warrior prowess were beyond question, and far in excess of anything the emperor found among local recruits. The first look at them was enough to terrify lesser opponents, huge and well-equipped as they were, and they attacked with a rage so reckless that even the prospect of bloodshed and agonizing wounds did not appear to hold them back. They were, the whispered, horrified rumours said, the *berserkergang*, and they fought in a trance state that gave superhuman strength and the ability to be wounded and feel no pain.

They were known as the Varangian Guard, and Rollo knew quite a lot about them, for his Guiscard kin in Sicily had encountered them in force as these ferocious northern warriors fought to repel the Normans' advance and ultimate capture of the island. The Varangians might have lost that battle, but they had been more successful in the lower Balkans, where the Guiscards had definitely come off second best. Rollo detected a note of grudging admiration among his kinsmen; as his cousin, Count Roger Guiscard, had remarked, the Varangians were Northmen like themselves, and you knew where you were with a northerner.

Nevertheless, Rollo was aware that he should be cautious. Fellow Northmen the Varangians were, but they had been his kinsmen's enemy not many years ago, and, when it came to offering the hand of friendship to someone they had once battled against, undoubtedly they would have the long memories of fighting men.

As he stood on the deck of the ferry, watching the Greek half of Constantinople rise up before him, Rollo realized that it was time to change his appearance. The guise of a hard-working, impoverished Turkish merchant was not the way to gain admittance to the emperor's bodyguard. He needed a bath, haircut, shave, clean linen, fresh clothes. Then, presenting himself not as Rollo Guiscard, Norman adventurer, but instead simply as a lonely and homesick English traveller, he would try his luck in the huge barracks close to the Bucoleon Palace where the Varangian Guard were housed.

Rollo had not imagined he could simply walk into the Varangians' stronghold. Approaching its massive outer defences, he gazed up at the crenellated walls rising high above. Their solidity was broken by one single opening, where sturdy iron-bound gates were guarded by at least a dozen men.

When he was still some distance away, he stopped and took in his first sight of the emperor's personal guards. Everything he had heard concerning them was accurate; indeed, reality exceeded rumour. If these gate guards were typical, then the Varangians richly deserved their fearsome reputation. They were exceptionally tall, broad-shouldered, giants of men. They wore their hair long, some sporting elaborate plaits banded with cord and even small coins; in colouring, they were fair or red-headed. Beards appeared to be the norm, and, again, some of the men had woven their facial hair into thick, wiry braids. They were clad in short sleeveless corselets made of iron rings, under which they wore brightly coloured tunics. Perhaps in acknowledgement of local dress customs, some wore baggy, loose-fitting striped trousers tucked into their high boots.

All were armed. They carried the huge, heavy, long-handled axe; the terrifying weapon which was largely responsible for the Varangians' fame. Rollo stared at the axes. They were, he had been told, capable of splitting a man's head in two. If the death stroke was made by a particularly strong and skilled man and the axe was sufficiently sharp, the bisection of the victim had been known to extend right down to his breast bone.

As if the axe was not enough, each guard also wore a long sword and carried various knives and daggers attached to his belt. The men were watchful, clearly on high alert. Had something happened, to make them suspect an enemy at the gate?

I am not their enemy, Rollo told himself firmly.

Enemy or not, a brazen demand for admittance to the stronghold did not seem wise. Instead, Rollo found a place in the shade from which he could observe without it being too noticeable that he was doing so. Then he settled himself as comfortably as he could for a long wait.

It was not until late afternoon that he spotted what he was looking for. A group of six guards, talking loudly and laughing uproariously, were heading for the formidable gates. They had clearly been drinking, and were, presumably, going back to their barracks to sleep it off. Hurrying to catch them up, hoping

desperately that alcohol would have increased their sense of
bonhomie and lessened their suspicions, Rollo called out a
greeting and, when the huge men turned round, said quite
truthfully, in the language of the cold north, that he was a
traveller from England and, finding himself in Constantinople,
had decided to seek out fellow countrymen in the emperor's
guard. Several of the Varangians immediately responded,
greeting him like a long-lost brother, enveloping him in vast
hugs and slapping him on the back. Then, without Rollo
understanding exactly how it happened, he found himself being
escorted inside the fortress, up a narrow stone stair and into a
crowded guardroom.

'This man's from England!' bellowed one of the guards who
had dragged him inside. 'He brings news from the north, and he's
thirsty! Get him a mug of ale, Sibert!'

The guards greeted him enthusiastically, many leaping up
to shake his hand or give him a slap on the shoulder, and the
promised huge mug of ale was thrust into his fist. Questions
were hurled at him, but, since all the guard were speaking at
once, he could make out little of what they said. With a grin,
he shrugged and took a long pull of ale.

One of the men – an enormous redhead with a round stomach
bulging out over his beautifully tooled leather belt and a flagon
of wine in one hand – said, his blue eyes wet with emotion, 'Ah,
but it's good to see men from our homelands. We haunt the quays
where the longboats from the north tie up, you know, and very
often we encounter distant kin.'

'Like that wild-eyed madman who's there at the moment,'
another put in. 'Not that anyone here's related to him, or, if they
are, they've got the good sense not to admit it!'

Other men arrived, word apparently having spread of Rollo's
presence. They crowded round him, demanding to know if he
had ever come across Eilif of York, Harald One-Eye of Lincoln
or Sigurd the Smith who lived a few miles south of Norwich.

'Ah, England's a big place,' one of the English guards said
with a sigh when Rollo admitted that no, he hadn't actually met
any of the men. 'It's a shame, though. I'd have loved news of
old Sigurd. He was good to me. Like a father, you could say.'

'Just as well he was, Ottar,' one of the others said with a great

snort of laughter, 'given that your own father buggered off even
while your mother was still straightening her petticoats.'

Ottar aimed a good-tempered lunge at the man, then took
another giant slurp from his mug.

It was another aspect of the Varangians' reputation that was
proving accurate, Rollo reflected: their enormous capacity for
alcohol. He had heard them referred to as the emperor's wine
bags, and now he was seeing for himself just how accurate the
description was.

Something in the recent exchange had snagged at his attention,
and while, first with words and then with his fists, Ottar continued
to fend off increasingly ribald suggestions concerning his likely
paternity, he went back over the conversation.

Eilif of York . . . the smith who lived south of Norwich . . .
Harald. Yes, Harald: that was what had alerted him. Harald
One-Eye. Rollo knew of a man called Harald, who had once
fought beside his king and, when that king fell, had fled his
native land rather than bend his knee to the man who had felled
him. And the man called Harald was Lassair's great-uncle.

While the shouts and the yells of laughter – and quite frequently
of pain – carried on around him, Rollo seemed to enter a small
bubble of quiet. Lassair's face appeared in his mind, and he drank
in the grey-green eyes with their watchful expression, the wide,
well-formed mouth beneath the small, straight nose, the glorious
copper-coloured hair. He saw, too, the pale crescent-shaped scar
on her left cheek; the scar she had won when once she had fought
beside him.

A huge fist flying past his ear brought him back to the moment.
'Sorry, mate, I was aiming for him!' yelled an enormous man
clad in bright scarlet, the colour clashing violently with his brilliant ginger hair. With a grin, Rollo leaned back, out of his way.

Harald. It was a common enough name, and it seemed very
unlikely that this Harald One-Eye of Lincoln was Lassair's great-
uncle, since the family were firmly convinced that he had long
ago left England. But, if indeed he had made his way south to
join the Varangians, then might not one of Rollo's new friends
know of him?

There was only one way to find out.

When the wrangling finally subsided and the dozen men sitting around the long table in the guards' room had refilled their mugs – and Rollo's – he said, into a gap in the chatter, 'Someone I know in England has a long-lost kinsman. I'd love to be able to tell her I found out he joined the guard.'

'Is she pretty?' one of the men said, provoking a flood of further questions, largely concerned with intimacies which Rollo certainly wasn't going to discuss. Grinning, he held up a hand. 'She's extremely pretty,' he said, 'and that's all I'm prepared to share with you. It's her great-uncle who may have come here; her grandmother's youngest brother. He and his two older brothers were at the battle and fought beside the king –' there was no need to specify which king, or, indeed, which battle; not to these men – 'and the other two were killed. He left England, never to return.'

Abruptly the laughter and the joking ceased, and the atmosphere in the stark room turned sombre. For a moment, nobody spoke, and the men sat with bowed heads. It was as if, Rollo thought, each one was saying a silent prayer to the past and its griefs. Then Ottar said, with a sigh, 'Many of our men did the same. What's this great-uncle called?'

'Harald,' Rollo said.

Ottar gave a brief laugh. 'That's it? Just Harald?'

Rollo shrugged. 'It's all I know.'

'Well, there's any number of Haralds. What else d'you know about him?'

Rollo thought briefly. 'His family are fishermen and eel-catchers. They've lived in and around the same East Anglian village for generations, although for sure it hasn't made them rich.'

'No, not many of us come from wealthy families,' Ottar agreed.

'That's what we come here for,' one of the others put in with a belly laugh. 'Nobody cares what you have or haven't got when you arrive. If you do your job well, then you'll soon acquire riches.'

'Your imperial master values you, then?' Rollo remarked.

'We're his axe-bearing barbarians,' the man said with fierce pride. 'Of course he values us! Some of us have been here for generations, and loyalty to the emperors is a family tradition with us. We view it as a sacred trust.' He nodded emphatically. Then, scowling, he went on, 'We've been busy, over the weeks and months of this interminable summer, what with the rumours and the riots.' Rollo looked at him quizzically. 'The Turks!' he hissed. 'They grow closer each day, and their presence sparks off unrest among our own citizens. It's not right!' he burst out.

'In what way?' Rollo did his best to disguise his sudden flare of interest.

'It's not right because, until this new menace started to threaten us, men of many different faiths lived here together quite happily,' the man said angrily. 'Now, it's all changing. We've had riots, let me tell you; riots between Christian and Saracen, Turk and Jew, and all because people are afraid of what's to come. It makes them nervous, see.'

'That and the heat,' put in another man.

'Well, yes, I grant you there's always more trouble when it's hot,' the first man agreed. 'But not like we've had this summer! Men have been dragged out in the streets and killed, for no more reason than the manner in which they choose to worship God.'

His angry words echoed in the sudden silence. For some reason, Rollo observed, the other guards seemed uncomfortable at their colleague's outburst. 'In such an atmosphere, your emperor must have valued you even more than usual,' he remarked mildly.

'Oh, he did, he did,' Ottar said quickly, as if eager to move the talk on to safer ground. 'Our emperor knows we won't betray him. We're his personal guard, and we swear our oath of loyalty directly to him.'

'And, naturally, your loyalty is handsomely rewarded?'

'You've heard the talk, no doubt,' Ottar said.

'The talk?'

Ottar shifted on the bench, and his wide leather belt creaked as his great bulk strained against it. 'It's said among the locals that when an emperor dies, the Varangians are permitted to visit the imperial treasury and take away what gold and gems they can carry in their two hands.' He gazed down at his own hands, lying palm uppermost and huge on his knees. 'They call it palace-pillaging, but only because they're jealous.' He gave Rollo a wide smile. 'It's true, we do have that unique privilege, and it's not pillage because the emperor himself permits it.' Again, he glanced at his hands. 'You'll have observed, my friend, that most of us are built to a generous scale, and our hands hold a lot. As Bersi here was just saying, we acquire riches, right enough.'

'So, what of the Harald I was asking about?' Rollo said. 'Do any of you know a man who fits the description?'

The guards muttered among themselves for a while, and Rollo heard various Haralds being discussed, most of them dismissed as unlikely because they came from a different place, or were the wrong age. Finally, Ottar turned to him and said, 'I'll ask around among some of the men who aren't here just now. Maybe someone will be able to help.'

'Thank you,' Rollo replied, adding politely, 'I hope you won't go to too much trouble.'

'Ah, it'll be no trouble,' Ottar assured him. 'We always enjoy contact with our homes.' He leaned closer to Rollo, lowering one eyelid in a suggestive wink. 'And you did say your friend was pretty. Perhaps she'll reward you with a kiss if you can return home with word of her great-uncle.'

On cue, the others chimed in with other likely rewards, many of them verging on the obscene. Smiling, Rollo stood up and, promising he'd come back, slipped away.

Ribald joking and laughter with gate guards was all very well, he thought as he closed the guardroom door behind him. But if he was going to find a way to the emperor's ear, he needed to speak to someone higher up the chain of command. Emerging on to the wide yard that spread out inside the encircling walls, he turned away from the gates and headed for the imposing entrance to what appeared to be the main building.

He felt a momentary apprehension. He ought to be used to operating alone; it was the only way that a man doing his job *could* operate. At times, however, his vulnerability threatened to undermine him. Here he was, a stranger and an outsider, hundreds of miles from anyone he knew or loved, with nobody to speak for him or watch his back. Yet he was proposing to demand access to whatever charmed inner circle ruled here, with no greater explanation for the outlandish request than that he had been travelling in the lands of the enemy and had information which the emperor might like to hear.

For a split second, his step faltered. What would his own king do, he wondered wildly, faced with such an impudent and presumptuous visitor? He felt his heart hammering in his chest, making the sweat break out on his skin. And it seemed to him that a quiet voice inside his head said, *There is danger here.*

He stopped dead. For the space of a heartbeat, he was paralysed by fear.

But then the moment of weakness passed. As he walked on, released from whatever enchantment had held him and confident once more, he realized that it was the thought of King William's reaction that had reassured him. William, he reflected with a secret grin, lapped up information like a thirsty hound laps water. As long as the intelligence was accurate, and something the king did not already know, then the source was unimportant.

Rollo's information was without doubt accurate: he had gathered it himself. As to whether it would come as news to Alexius Comnenus, well, only time would tell.

He had reached the long flight of stone steps leading up to the main building's door. His confidence and his belief in himself restored, he leapt up them two at a time and went inside.

SEVEN

The hammering at the door came just as I'd finally managed to get back to sleep. Or so I thought as I struggled to wake up, although it was fully light, so I must have slept for longer than I'd imagined.

Edild was fully dressed and already hurrying to open the door. We are quite used to such urgent summons, and I did not think anything of it, merely getting up and going into the small still room to wash my hands and face, put on my overgown, braid my hair and arrange a clean white coif over it.

I had got as far as washing and putting on my gown when I realized who had come banging on Edild's door. Forcing myself to ignore my reaction, I hurried the rest of my preparations and went back into the main room.

'. . . found some four or five miles north of here, stuck under a bridge,' Jack Chevestrier was saying. He was standing on the doorstep – one look at his filthy, mud-caked boots explained his reluctance to come into the house – and he broke off to give me a quick smile. Then, resuming, he said, 'The full moon and the strong wind combined to make an exceptionally high tide, and the sea has flooded in up several of the fenland rivers, including the Ouse.' For a town dweller, he knew the local geography pretty well. 'The man who came to report the discovery of the body –' *body?* – 'reports that there was wreckage floating around it, so it's possible some vessel foundered, and both its planking and one of its crew or passengers ended up together. The man who found it said—'

I stopped listening. I shuddered. It wasn't that I was cold; it was the thought of some poor soul having been out on that wild, ferocious sea last night, and suffering the terror of his ship breaking up beneath him. Falling into the relentless waters, being swept, helpless, up a river swollen out of recognition. Fighting to breathe; to keep his nose and mouth above the torrent. Giving up, drowning, his poor body hurled against a bridge . . .

Edild gave me quite a hard nudge. 'Lord Gilbert has sent for us,' she hissed. Had Jack said so? If so, I'd missed it.

'What about our patients?' I asked. 'Shouldn't one of us stay here?' I was still feeling very strange, and, oddly, frightened; as if the fierce sea would leap up to drown me the moment I put my head outside the door.

'They will just have to wait. It is an order, Lassair, from the lord of our manor. We *do not* refuse,' Edild said firmly. Then, since I must have gone on looking stupid, she leaned close to me and said quietly, 'The flooding is extensive. No doubt Lord Gilbert fears there will be more bodies and many wounded. People swept into the water in the dark are all too likely to be hit by floating objects.'

There was nothing more to say. I picked up my satchel, slung the strap over my shoulder and followed Jack and my aunt out of the door.

Outside, conditions were dire. Not as bad as my fearful imaginings had suggested – no huge wave rose up to engulf us – but nevertheless, it was hard going. The furious, howling gale that

had screamed all through the night had lessened, although it
still produced occasional spiteful blasts that almost knocked us
off our feet. Reaching the track, we turned left in the direction of
Lakehall, the sodden ground tacky beneath our feet so that every
step was an effort. Glancing over to the right, I was shocked to
see that the waters had encroached at least two-thirds of the way
across the low-lying land between the fen and the village. Thank
God our homes lay on higher ground. It was, I reflected as we
struggled along, probably why the wise ancestors had sited
the settlement there in the first place. This wasn't the first time the
region had flooded, and it wouldn't be the last.

After what seemed an age, at last we reached the short track
that led up to Lakehall. I wondered if we would encounter Lady
Rosaria. I hoped not; I wasn't eager to see her again. Hurrying
to draw level with Jack, I asked, 'Was Lady Rosaria present in
Lord Gilbert's hall when you left?'

'No,' he replied. 'I asked after her, and I was told that she's
keeping to her room.' He turned to Edild. 'The wet-nurse who
you found has brought the baby up to Lakehall, and the three of
them have shut themselves away together.'

I was relieved to hear it. It sounded as if Lady Rosaria was
starting to act like a mother at last. I should have been more
charitable towards her, I thought. I'd suspected from the first that
she'd suffered some awful experience, and was still in a state of
shock. That could easily account for her apparent indifference
towards Leafric. She was safely ensconced now with people
of her own station; people who had promised to do their best to
help her find her kinsmen. It was only natural she'd begin to feel
better. To remember, perhaps, that she had a child who needed her.

Cheered by the thought – I'd become very fond of Leafric – I
hurried after Jack and Edild.

We went in through Lakehall's open gates, and Jack strode on
across the yard and up the steps to the great door. Edild's and
my boots, I noticed with horror, were now as muddy as Jack's,
although we'd had the foresight to tuck up our gowns and keep
them relatively clean. I turned in dismay to my aunt. 'We're
going to make the hall filthy!' I whispered. 'Should we not take
our boots off?'

Jack overheard. Turning, he said, 'You are here at Lord Gilbert's request, because he has need of you. Don't worry about dirtying his floor.' There was, I reflected, not for the first time, something very fair-minded about Jack Chevestrier. Then, with a grin, he added, 'Besides, the damage has already been done.'

I followed Edild up the steps.

Lord Gilbert and Lady Emma were waiting for us. There was no sign of their children, and I guessed they'd been packed off somewhere with their nursemaid, well out of earshot. What we were about to discuss wasn't really fit for young ears.

Lord Gilbert greeted Edild and me, murmuring his thanks for our prompt arrival, and Edild acknowledged him with a graceful inclination of her head. Then he turned to Jack, instantly engaging him in conversation, and, from the way he addressed him, I realized something.

I hadn't been present the previous day, when the two men first met; Leafric's abrupt onset of yelling had seen to that. I had therefore missed the chance of observing Lord Gilbert's reaction to having Jack Chevestrier turn up in his hall. Now, as I could plainly see, it must have been a favourable one. From the way Lord Gilbert was treating him, it was clear he both knew of his reputation and, on meeting him, had liked him. Also, there was little in Lord Gilbert's manner to suggest Jack was some lowly underling well below his notice. On the contrary, Lord Gilbert was listening to him attentively, giving him the respect that only a senior lawman would warrant.

Lord Gilbert, as I've said before, is fat and indolent, content to leave much of the running of his manor to his intelligent and capable wife and his efficient reeve. However, he is still a lord; if he judges a man worthy of respect, then that is something to bear in mind.

'We have, as you suggested, Jack, dispatched four men with a cart to collect the body,' Lord Gilbert was saying. He glanced towards the door. 'They should be back soon, although conditions will probably mean the journey takes longer than normal.'

'We must prepare a cool place to receive the body,' Edild said calmly.

'Cool?' For a moment Lord Gilbert looked puzzled, then, with a grimace, he nodded. 'Yes, I see.' He turned to Lady Emma, his expression suggesting he was at a loss.

'The undercroft, I think,' she said, exchanging a glance with Edild. 'We should be able to avoid going down there for a few days, and the door is stout.'

'Thank you, my lady,' Edild said. 'I have brought sweet herbs to burn. Perhaps Lassair and I might make a start now?'

'Of course.' I had half-expected Lady Emma to summon a servant, but instead, pausing only to pick up a lighted lantern, she took us herself. We went back down into the yard, then, walking round to the side of the building, she unlocked and opened a low, heavy oak door. Steep steps led down into the ground, and we found ourselves in a low-ceilinged, vaulted space apparently as broad and as wide as the hall above. There was a strong smell of lavender; all to the good, I thought. Perhaps we wouldn't need our sweet herbs. Lady Emma lit half a dozen rush lamps, and the shadows danced back to the far end of the crypt. Indicating a trestle table set up in the middle of the floor, she said, 'Only last week I was sitting there preparing lavender to refill the little bags we use in the linen store.' She sighed, as if the table's abrupt change of use saddened her.

Edild put down her bag. 'Thank you, my lady. Lassair and I can manage now.'

It sounded rather like a dismissal, and, risking a quick glance at Lady Emma, I wondered if she thought so too. But, as hurriedly she turned and went back up the steps, the only expression I saw on her face was relief.

Laying out the dead is not to everyone's taste.

When at last we heard sounds of commotion above, we were ready for the corpse. A length of worn but clean cloth was spread on the trestle, wide enough to wrap around the body, and Edild had set bunches of her herbs smouldering in the corners of the cellar. Combined with Lady Emma's lavender, the effect was almost overpowering. The tools of our trade had been neatly laid out on an upturned chest: pots of ointment, skins of water for washing out wounds, and Edild's own leather-wrapped set of sharp knives and probes.

I wasn't looking forward to witnessing their use, and was hoping fervently that a detailed examination of the body wouldn't prove necessary. We were, I assumed, here to determine how the dead man had met his end, and, in all probability, he'd drowned.

There was quite a lot of shuffling and one or two muttered curses, and then two men appeared at the foot of the steps, carrying one end of a hazel hurdle. Two more men followed, and the four of them carried their burden over to the trestle and laid it down. The corpse had been covered with a thin, much-mended cloak.

'Thank you.' Edild turned to the men. 'You may go now.'

I've rarely seen four people move so fast. Not that you could blame them: despite the herbs and the lavender, I could already smell the corpse. I was used to the smell of death – well, becoming used to it – and even I felt like retching.

'Come along,' Edild said briskly. 'The sooner we complete our task, the sooner we can leave.'

She picked up the cloak at what appeared to be the head end of the body. Just as she began to fold it back, once more we heard feet on the stairs. Jumping the last few steps, as if he couldn't wait to join us, Jack emerged into the undercroft.

Edild raised her eyebrows in query. He indicated the cloak she held in her hands. 'I'd like it back, when you're done,' he said. 'The man it belongs to won't be able to afford another one.'

'You can take it now and go. I have cloth with which to cover the body.' She indicated the fabric folded to the side of the trestle.

Jack held her gaze. 'I'll stay, if it's all the same to you.'

She smiled at him. 'You are welcome, of course, although it will not be pleasant.'

'Nevertheless, I'll stay,' he said shortly.

Edild turned back to the body. She arranged the cloak so that the head and face were exposed, and all three of us stepped forward to take our first look at the victim.

He was young, about my age, which made his death more poignant. I couldn't help thinking of the years he'd been denied. His hair was worn long, and it was dirty from his immersion in the wild water. Edild picked at the filth, getting a fingernail under a big flake of caked mud, and a strand of bright blond emerged. His face was well-shaped, the cheekbones high and proud, and the wide mouth looked as if it would have readily spread in a smile.

The eyes were half-closed. I took one glance at them, then hastily looked away. I'd believed I had conquered my revulsion, but, at the sight of those eyeballs, the nausea threatened to return. Edild's quiet voice brought me back from the brink. 'Enough remains to determine that the eyes were blue,' she said, her tone devoid of any emotion. *We are here to do a job*, she seemed to be reminding me.

She folded the cloak back another turn, exposing the shoulders and upper arms. So far, the flesh was unbroken, although here and there angry bruises darkened its whiteness.

'Is there any sign yet to suggest he did not die by drowning?' Jack said softly.

Edild paused, apparently thinking, then reached under the cloak and brought out the corpse's right hand. It was long-fingered and quite small. She turned it over, revealing the palm and the under-sides of the fingers, all of which were deeply wrinkled. 'He had obviously been in the water a long time,' she said, 'and I noticed a crust around his mouth and a small amount of foam in the nostrils, which can indicate death by drowning.' Tucking the hand away once more, she went on, 'I am, I confess, puzzled by some aspects of the markings on the skin, and I think it is time to study the body in its entirety.' She looked up at me, nodded, and, taking this as my cue, I went round to the far side of the trestle and took hold of the cloak. Together we drew it right back to the feet of the corpse.

Then, as all three of us stared down at the naked body we had just revealed, our mistake shouted out at us.

The body was that of a woman.

She had been tall and strongly built; it was easy to see how, covered as she had been when brought into the hall, she had been taken for a man. Presumably it had not occurred to those who found her to reveal her sex, reasoning, perhaps, that it would be obvious as soon as the cloak was removed.

She was long-limbed and slim-hipped, but, as soon as the eye moved up to her chest, all resemblance to a man ended, for her breasts must have been round and generous. Not that we could have said for certain, for much of the soft flesh had gone. In part, this might have been due to the battering she had received as the furious waters drove her upriver. In part, also, it was the work of the marine creatures which had fed on her. An image came into my mind of the eels my father catches, with their wide, voracious mouths and sharp little teeth. Eels, it is well known, are partial to decaying animal remains.

For the second time, nausea threatened. I swallowed a couple of times, took a deep breath, and it receded.

With a soft sigh, Edild picked up her cloth sheet and draped it over that poor, ruined body. She drew it up over the head, then combed out the tangled hair with her fingers. I looked at Jack, and saw that his face was twisted in compassion. Edild stepped away from the woman's body, and for a while the three of us simply stood, heads lowered, to pay our respects.

The silence was broken by the sound of some small object falling on the stone floor. Jack bent down to retrieve it, moving closer to one of the lamps to inspect it. He studied it for a while, then murmured, 'It's a crab. Quite dead –' he tapped a fingernail against its dry, brittle shell to demonstrate – 'and I imagine it fell out of her hair.'

'We don't normally find crabs this far inland,' I said. 'The water's not salty enough.'

'It probably is just now,' Jack replied. 'There will still be a lot of sea out in the rivers and the marshes. But this little thing's been dead quite a while.' He went on looking at it for a moment, then closed his hand on it.

'We should report our findings to Lord Gilbert,' Edild said. She gave the sheet a final adjustment, and I thought that it was only with reluctance that she stepped away from the trestle.

'And what are those findings?' Jack's voice, I thought, had an edge of urgency.

'That, as far as I can tell, this woman drowned,' Edild replied, 'but, in the absence of any garment, article of jewellery or any other possession, we are quite unable to establish her identity.'

He nodded, then, with a gesture of one hand, invited Edild and me to precede him up the steps. Before I left the undercroft, I blew out the rush lamps. It seemed kinder, somehow, to leave the dead woman in darkness.

*   *   *

'I suppose,' Lord Gilbert said heavily, 'we'll have to set about discovering who she is.' He spun round to Jack. 'Was there any clue from the three men who found her? Anything at the scene that might have belonged to her?'

'I asked them, my lord,' Jack replied, 'and they said no. It may be, however,' he added thoughtfully, 'that the shock of discovering a naked body drove all thoughts of having a thorough search out of their minds. It would perhaps be worth having another look.'

'The waters may have gone down a little by now,' Lord Gilbert said, 'so I think, Jack, that the idea is a good one.' He paused. 'And then what?'

'Then I'll go on downriver, north towards the coast,' Jack said promptly, 'and try to discover if any family is missing a tall, strongly built, fair-haired young woman.'

'Thank you,' Lord Gilbert said. I was sure there was relief in his voice. He'd probably been thinking that the painstaking and laborious task of discovering the dead woman's name would fall to him, and, since he's not renowned for being painstaking, and certainly never takes on an arduous task if anyone else will do it for him, his relief was understandable.

Edild suddenly spoke. 'He should take Lassair with him.'

If I hadn't happened to be looking at Jack as she said the words, I'd have missed the quick, appraising glance he gave me.

'Why do you suggest that, Edild?' Lady Emma asked.

Edild turned to her. 'For two reasons, my lady. First, because Lassair is a dowser, and has a talent for finding things that are lost.' Well, I couldn't argue with that, although it embarrassed me to hear it mentioned in such company. 'Second, because she is skilled at finding the safe ways over marshland that are usually hidden from our eyes.'

That, too, was true. Once, I had led two people – one of them Rollo – across the deadly, waterlogged land surrounding the island of Ely. Edild knew about it; in some strange way, she had predicted that I would do it. I was surprised, however, that she should bring such a private matter to the attention of anyone outside my own family.

'What do you say, Lassair?' Lord Gilbert was saying.

I felt four pairs of eyes intent on me, and my first instinct was to turn tail and run. But, resting my gaze on Jack, I saw his mouth briefly twitch in a smile.

I realized that he wasn't at all dismayed at the prospect of my company.

'Very well,' I heard myself saying. 'I'll do it.'

We set off only a short time later. Edild had bade me a swift farewell, squeezing my arm briefly by way of encouragement. I had checked my satchel to make sure I had everything I was likely to need, and Jack had gone out to prepare the horses. The prospect of riding the beautiful Isis again was, I had to admit, one of my main reasons for agreeing to the mission. Lady Emma, meanwhile, had sent to the kitchens for food and drink for us to take with us.

Lord Gilbert and Lady Emma stood at the top of the steps, Bermund just behind them, watching as we rode out of the courtyard. Lady Emma raised a hand in farewell. We rode down the track leading to the road, and I went to turn to my right, through the village.

Jack stopped me. 'I think,' he said, 'we'll avoid the village.' Putting heels to his grey, he trotted off to the left, then urged his horse up the bank and on to the higher ground. We cut across the neck of the bulge that forms Aelf Fen, past the ancient, solitary oak that stands behind Edild's house and, very soon afterwards, descended on to the road leading north. Turning to me, Jack said, 'How quickly do you think we can cover four miles?'

Never one to refuse a challenge, I tightened my knees against Isis's flanks and we leapt forward.

We followed the track that runs along the fen edge, although occasionally, where the flood waters had overrun it, we had to veer up to the higher ground to the east. Over to the left, the great basin of the fens looked like one solid sheet of water. I could see that not many hours ago, the extent of the flooding had been even wider. My heart went out to all the fen dwellers that morning. I know, from bitter experience, what it's like to try to clean a house that has been inundated with black fenland mud. And I was quite sure there would have been deaths: our long-limbed woman was surely not the only casualty of the night.

Jack and I kept up a good pace, and quite soon we came to
the place we sought. Jack had taken directions from the man
who had come to report the body, who had said that we really
couldn't miss the spot because it was the first bridge we would
come to after leaving Aelf Fen. I had wondered if the man and
his companions would still be lurking about, but there was no
sign of them, or, indeed, of anyone else. This was odd, because
more than once I had the distinct sensation that someone was
watching us.

Jack and I drew rein above the flood water, and we stared
down at the scene. The bridge was a simple affair of wooden
planks lashed together, and it spanned two distinct rises in the
surrounding ground. I knew the place; the banks there are a
good spot for comfrey, which we use to knit wounds and broken
bones. Now, the little bridge had a collection of debris caught
up against it, so that it was acting like a dam. A large pool
had spread out downstream, and the slowly circling current
carried bolts of wood, planks, broken branches and part of a
smashed barrel.

Jack said, 'I imagine we're only seeing the bits that nobody
could reach.' He pointed towards a long, thin branch, stripped
of its side shoots, which had been left on the bank. He was
undoubtedly right, and I had a mind picture of a group of people
doing their utmost to collect the bounty that the flood had unexpectedly provided.

I couldn't blame them – I'd have done the same thing myself
– but, all the same, my heart sank. 'They'll have probably taken
the very objects we're hoping to find,' I said dolefully.

But Jack had seen something. He jumped down from his horse,
and, eager not to miss anything, I dismounted too. He didn't bother
with tethering our mounts; he must have known they wouldn't
stray far. He made his way cautiously down from the track to the
waterside, holding out a hand to me. I took it; the ground was
incredibly slippery, and I didn't want to spend the rest of the day
with a wet bottom.

Once we were on the level ground of the water's edge, he ran
over to fetch the discarded stick. I took the opportunity to wind
up my long skirts, twisting the gathered fabric into a loose knot
and thrusting it under my belt. Turning back to me, the stick in

his hand, I watched as he took in my altered appearance. 'It's wet down here,' I said lamely.

He stopped looking at my legs and grinned. 'Very sensible,' he remarked. Then once again he thrust out a hand in my direction. 'Hold on to me, will you?'

I went to stand behind him, dug in my heels and did as he said, taking his left hand in mine, with my other hand round his arm. His wrist felt like steel. With the stick in his right hand, he leaned forward, right out over the water, and began swirling it gently just under the surface.

'What are you doing?' I whispered. I had no idea why I was whispering.

'Well, I'm not fishing,' he muttered. Then, with a soft exclamation, he leaned out even further, and hastily I threw my weight backwards to counterbalance his. He crouched low, stretched out one more time, then said, 'I've got it!'

I held on tight as he straightened up, waiting till I was sure he'd got his balance before releasing him. He gave me a quick smile. 'Thanks. Now, let's see what we've found.'

Carefully, he drew in the stick, just as if he was pulling in a fishing line. Its tip remained under the water, but I could see there was something snagged on it. When it was close enough for Jack to reach, he put his hand down into the water and took hold of it, dragging it to the surface and laying it on the bank.

At first it looked like a nondescript rag. Then, as Jack untangled it and smoothed it out, I saw that it was a woman's under-shift. It was made of a pale, soft, smooth fabric which I didn't recognize; it wasn't linen or wool. It was well-made but unadorned, and it wasn't new. There was a darn on the front of the skirt, and the seams had been mended at least once.

'Was it hers, do you think?' Jack asked quietly.

I rubbed the material between finger and thumb. 'It's likely, isn't it? It's a shift, so she'd have worn it next to her skin. As such, it would have been the last garment to be shed.'

'And you're thinking it would be too much of a coincidence to find it here if it didn't belong to her,' he finished.

I nodded. I gathered the shift up, rolling it and wringing it to remove the water. I was finding it quite emotional to handle something the dead woman had worn.

Jack seemed to pick up my mood. He stood up, rested his hand on my shoulder briefly, then said, 'I'm going to see if I can find anything else. The water's falling quite fast now –' I'd been so preoccupied with my thoughts that I hadn't noticed – 'so I suggest we wait here for a while, to see if anything turns up, then continue downriver.'

I nodded again. I was still clutching the shift, and now I held it up to my face, rubbing my cheek against the smooth, wet fabric. I didn't understand it, but there was something about the dead woman that seemed to be reaching out to me; reaching right into my heart.

I knew Jack was right, and we must continue with our task. But it was hard, when the greater part of me just wanted to run away home.

EIGHT

The slowly receding water revealed a mass of flattened vegetation caked with mud and assorted rubbish. Jack and I realized that it was only by an unlikely stroke of luck that we would come across anything else belonging to our dead woman. After standing silently for some moments staring out over the ruined landscape, Jack turned to me.

'Did I not hear your aunt mention that you were good at finding things?'

'It has happened, on rare occasions, that I've managed to locate lost items –' a vision of an ancient crown* flashed through my head; there and gone in a blink – 'but, for it to work, it seems that I have to have a pretty good idea of what I'm looking for.'

He nodded his understanding. 'Perhaps you have to visualize the item?'

'Er – well, sort of,' I agreed. It wasn't exactly that – I'd had no idea what that crown would look like – but it was hard to explain.

---

* See *Out of the Dawn Light*

He stared at me a while longer, and I saw interest in his eyes. He had a way of looking at you very directly, as if you held every bit of his attention. He would, I guessed, have loved to pursue the matter. I was surprised. If anyone had asked me, I'd have said that a Norman lawman, with quite an important position in a place like Cambridge, would have been down to earth, pragmatic and totally lacking imagination; a man, in short, to be utterly dismissive of anything he could not detect by sight, smell, hearing or touch.

Again, I began to understand that there was more to Jack Chevestrier than met the eye.

His quiet scrutiny was making me uncomfortable. Carefully I stowed the shift in my satchel, then said, 'I'll have a go, though. Just give me a moment.'

He knew exactly what to do. He turned his back and walked away along the bank, catching up with the horses. They were taking advantage of the halt to graze, and I could hear the soft sound of their big teeth ripping through the grass.

I stood quite still, closing my eyes. Normally, when I'm searching for a specific item, I hold out my hands palms down and focus on it, and, with any luck, when I'm near it I feel a sort of tingling in my hands. I think that I must be open to strange forces at such times, because once – it was when I found the crown – I'd been assailed by the most terrifying feeling that invisible lines of power were attacking me, and I'd seen a vision from the past that still haunts me.

I hoped very much that wasn't about to happen again.

I stretched out my hands. I waited. Nothing happened. I turned in a slow circle. Again, my palms gave no response. Now I was back where I had started, facing out over the swollen river.

It happened so suddenly that there was no time to feel afraid. I saw a huge wall of water, sweeping up the river towards where I stood. It went past me, and I should have been right inside it, helpless as it swept me away; but this was not reality, it was vision, something intangible that originated within my mind, and although I saw myself within a deadly swirl of furious water, in fact I stood, perfectly safe, on firm ground.

I saw a body, its long pale limbs turned over and over in the wild current. A garment still clung to it but, as I watched, it detached, sinking down into the water. Suddenly I was face to face with her, and I could see the devastated eyes, the half-eaten breasts. Nausea rose up, and I heard myself groan as sweat broke out on my forehead. I made myself go on looking, and, as I'd known I would, I saw the poor body thrown against the underside of the bridge. It – she – was battered to and fro by the force of the flow, and then, as the ferocity of the current slowly eased, finally the body came to rest.

The vision faded. I was about to open my eyes when, totally unexpectedly, something else happened: out of nowhere, I was hit with a sense of fear so overpoweringly strong that I gasped. Somebody was watching me from a place of concealment, but in my trance state – if that was what it was – I saw eyes, glittering with malice, narrowed with intent. I felt a surge of malevolence which seemed to roar towards me and break against me like a wave. There was a flash of silver, a whistle as if something was flying through the air, and then I was on the ground, flat on my face, winded from the force with which I'd thrown myself down.

As soon as I could breathe again, I sat up, then got to my feet. Jack was standing a respectful distance away, but with the anxiety easily readable in his expression. Suddenly I wanted to laugh: did he imagine that every attempt at dowsing ended with me flinging myself on the ground?

I didn't really appreciate it until later, but his first question was actually rather revealing. He must have been desperate with impatience to find out if I'd discovered anything relevant to the woman's death, but what he said was, 'Are you all right?'

I started to say yes, but then, as I made to move towards him, I stumbled. He was by my side in an instant, strong hands supporting me. Feeling stupid, hastily I straightened up. 'I'm fine!' I said with an embarrassed laugh. 'And I didn't sense anything other than the shift, which you've already found. Oh, except that she was dead some time before she got here.' My voice didn't sound quite normal. 'I saw her poor body, with the eyes so badly damaged and those wounds to her breasts, and she was in that state when the surge drove her here.'

He gave a soft exclamation of sympathy and put his arms round me. He felt as tough as he looked; it was a bit like being

hugged by a barrel. When he spoke, the tenderness in his tone
came as an odd contrast to his physical toughness. 'She is at
peace now,' he said. 'The fear and the pain are all over, and she
lies quiet, warmly wrapped in your aunt's clean cloth.'

In normal circumstances, I'd have treated that remark with a
derisive snort. I deal with death pretty frequently, and I know
full well that corpses have no feelings, and can't possibly be
aware of being snug in their winding sheets. But these were far
from being normal circumstances. For some reason – I had no
idea what it was – I had formed a bond with the dead woman.
Her awful death had touched me, and her fate affected me deeply.
To hear Jack speak those consoling words was like balm to my
sore heart.

He went on holding me. He was very close, and his clear
green eyes looked straight into mine.

'There's something else, isn't there?'

'Yes,' I whispered. Could I tell him? What had I seen, after
all? I'd sensed danger, imminent and strong, but I was almost
sure it was simply an overactive imagination. We were standing
where a woman had just died, and I'd already had a jittery sense
of eyes on me on the way here. 'I'm sure it's nothing,' I added.

'Tell me anyway,' Jack said.

I drew a breath. 'I thought I saw – or sensed – that someone
was watching us. He meant us harm, and I heard the sound of
a weapon as it whistled towards me.'

'Is that the sort of thing you often pick up when you're
dowsing?' he asked.

I smiled. 'No, not really, although there was a time when I
felt as scared as I did just now.'

'And did the danger—' But he must have felt how violently
I was shuddering, and, tactfully, stopped asking penetrating
questions.

After a few moments, I said in a small voice, 'What if she
was murdered, Jack? What if whoever did it is still here, watching
to see what we discover?'

He was quiet for quite a while, and I guessed he was thinking.
'Your aunt seemed to be fairly sure that our victim drowned,' he
said eventually, 'but it need not necessarily have been an
accidental drowning.'

'You mean, somebody could have held her under till she died?' I said in a whisper.

'They *could*,' Jack agreed, 'but that's not to say they did.'

It took me some time to pull myself together. I needed to show him I was all right, and that he could let me go without fearing I'd instantly collapse on him. Gently I disengaged myself, gave him a grin and said, 'We can go on now.'

Then I bent down to pick up my satchel and, with as much determination as I could muster, strode over to the horses.

We rode on through the day, stopping wherever we saw a village, a hamlet, a collection of houses and even a gaggle of people, to ask if a tall, fair young woman had gone missing in the floods. The going was hard, and at times we had to make long detours to get round inundated ground. My knowledge of the area helped, and once I even tried my hand at finding the safe path across a stretch of marsh, as I'd done at Ely. Jack was impressed at my success, and I felt compelled to admit that I'd been all but sure the hidden path was there, since it was one I use at least twice a year going to and from a place where marsh mallows grow.

It seems to be a factor in our dealings with others, this compulsion to be straight and honest with those who are straight and honest with us.

Nobody we spoke to was looking for a young, fair, blue-eyed woman. They were searching for plenty of other things: missing livestock, doors, bits of fencing, household items; and some, indeed, were frantically hunting for people. Heartbreakingly, one wild-eyed man was trying to find his six-year-old son.

We helped where we could. Jack used his muscle to assist a group of men heave a cart out of the ditch into which the water had flung it. We both joined an old woman trying single-handedly to round up a flock of geese, and, while she and I shut them up temporarily inside her own tiny hovel of a house, Jack repaired their pen. He was, I noticed, well used to dealing with geese. I used quite a lot of the supplies in my satchel patching up various wounds and dispensing remedies for the many aches, pains, sniffles and coughs caused by people having spent far too long out of doors up to their knees or waists in cold water and soaked to the skin.

We found the little boy. Out in the open ground beyond the village with the geese we heard frantic sobbing, and found the child sitting in the lower branches of a hazel tree. It took quite a long time to coax him down, encourage him to get on my horse and take him back to his father, but the man's inarticulate joy at being reunited with his son was more than adequate reward.

I don't think either Jack or I had noticed how late it was until darkness began to fall. We were miles away from Aelf Fen, and we'd had no luck at all in trying to find where our dead woman had come from. Turning to me with a rueful expression, Jack said, 'It looks as though we'll have to find somewhere to spend the night, and then continue with the search in the morning.' I nodded. 'I'm sorry,' he added, 'I hadn't expected to be away so long. Do you mind?'

Not really being used to people asking if I mind things, I was taken aback. Then – for he was clearly waiting for me to answer – I said, 'No, I don't. In any case, I'm here because Lord Gilbert sent me with you to try to help you, so whether I mind or not isn't really important.

I thought he said, *It is to me*, but I was probably wrong.

We found a lonely, run-down and desolate little monastery, although *monastery* implies something far grander than the meagre set of ramshackle buildings and the half-dozen monks in residence. Jack's status as a man of the law guaranteed their cooperation, such as it was, although I'd like to think that they would have honoured their Christian duty to take us in, whoever we were. The guest accommodation was a draughty barn full of old, musty hay, but at least it was dry. The food was indescribably bad, but, happily, we had plenty of Lady Emma's supplies left. As we wrapped ourselves in our blankets and settled in the hay for the night, I was extremely glad to be safe under cover, and, hopefully, in a place where those haunting, threatening dark eyes could not spy on me.

We set out again at first light. It quickly became clear that the day would follow yesterday's pattern. Again, we found plenty of folk needing our assistance, but nobody missing our dead woman.

By noon, we were only a few miles south of Lynn. We stopped

at the top of a gentle rise whose summit was crowned with pine trees, and as we ate the last of Lady Emma's food, Jack broke the silence – I guessed he'd been thinking hard – and said, 'I have a proposition to put to you.'

'Oh, yes?' The shiver of excited anticipation took me by surprise.

He finished his mouthful, swallowed and said, 'We could be in Lynn this afternoon. Since it's the first settlement of any size we've come to, and since it must have suffered the full force of the tidal surge, it's quite possible that we may at last trace the kin of our dead woman.'

'True.' I knew, even before he drew breath to go on, that there was more.

'We will, of course, do our utmost to do so, since it is why we're here. But there is something else we could look into.'

'*The Maid of the Marsh* came from here,' I said. He met my eyes, and he was smiling. 'She left from Lynn to sail down to Cambridge,' I went on. 'This was where Lady Rosaria went aboard.'

'Indeed it was,' he agreed. 'Sheriff Picot told me, you'll recall, to help her, and I suppose finding out how she came to be separated from her companions could be described as simply following orders.'

'Also,' I said, 'Lord Gilbert would be delighted if we find out something that enables him to locate her kinsfolk, so, in a way, we'd be following his orders, too.' In a burst of confidence, I added, 'I don't like Lady Rosaria. I know she's making an attempt to look after her child, and I do realize she's probably suffered some bad experience that's still affecting her, but—' I didn't really know how to put it into words. 'There's just something about her,' I finished lamely.

Jack was busy packing away the remains of our food. I heard him repeat softly, 'Just something about her.'

There wasn't really any more to say.

The industrious inhabitants of the small settlement of Lynn had set about clearing up with great energy, and already the place was getting back to normal. A great muddy, sandy, salty swathe had cut through on either side of the river, and there was a very distinctive high-water mark all along the seaward-facing side of the town. Everywhere there was bustle and noise, and the endless sound of dozens of brooms energetically sweeping out water, mud and assorted debris.

The prospect of being among a crowd of busy people was more attractive than I liked to admit. Although I'd been trying to tell myself it was all in my imagination, still the sense that unfriendly eyes were on me – on us – persisted. Several times that day, the certainty of somebody behind me, careful to stay out of sight, had become so strong that I'd whipped round, trying to catch him, or, I suppose, her, before they had a chance to slip back into hiding.

I approached Lynn with a relieved smile. But, just as we entered the first of its little streets, it suddenly occurred to me that if this was where the drowned woman came from and if, indeed, she had been murdered, then the killer might easily be a local too. Just biding his time for the right moment to get rid of the inquisitive pair who'd come to investigate her death . . .

But there was a job to do. Ruthlessly I put my fears aside.

Jack found stabling for the horses, then we split up, each taking a different segment of the settlement. I worked my way to and fro, up the narrow tracks leading away from the water and back down again. People had died, I learned; not many, but one fatality would have been more than enough. A few were missing, but none of their descriptions matched our dead woman. After what seemed hours, I met up with Jack once more. He reported much the same story.

'We may yet find out that she came from Lynn, although the population is small and most people seem to have been accounted for,' Jack said. 'Apparently they're still getting word of the damage in outlying places, and reports of missing people. I'll ask around again in the morning. I've been told about a place we can put up overnight.' He smiled briefly. 'It sounds all right; better, anyway, than the monastery.'

I was barely listening. I was seeing that image again, of the body in the water. Briefly I shut my eyes, and I was suddenly very sure of something I'd previously only suspected. 'She isn't from here.'

His voice seemed to reach me from a distance. 'How do you know?'

'She was a very long way from home,' I whispered. 'She—'

But the strange moment had passed. I opened my eyes, feeling awkward. 'Sorry,' I muttered.

He shook his head. 'I don't think you need to be sorry. What happened?'

I sighed. 'It was nothing – just a strong feeling that we're not going to succeed.'

'We still have to try,' he said. 'But, for now, I think we should turn our attention to that other matter. Come on – there are still several hours of daylight.'

He spun round and strode away, and I hurried after him. Quite soon, we emerged from a narrow and extremely smelly little alley out on to the quayside. Here, down at the waterfront, the area had received the full force of the encroaching sea. There was damage everywhere, and the air echoed with the sounds of industry as small groups of people went about repairs. Several smaller craft had been hurled up on to the land and as we stood taking in the scene, a gang of some dozen men gave a ragged cheer as one such vessel was finally shoved back into the water.

Larger boats were at moorings along the quay, and, again, it was clear that few had escaped unscathed. There were quite a lot of vessels; no doubt, alerted to approaching danger, their masters had made for the nearest port, many of them ending up here at Lynn. The captain of *The Maid of the Marsh* had mentioned a boat out of Yarmouth, *The Good Shepherd*, which had transported Lady Rosaria to Lynn; thinking that it was too much to hope for that her master would have been one of those who had made a run for this particular port, nevertheless I crossed my fingers surreptitiously behind my back as Jack and I set out along the quay.

I've never really had any faith in crossed fingers. This time, the ruse worked. *The Good Shepherd* was second to last in the line.

She was a much bigger vessel than *The Maid of the Marsh*; she was a seagoing ship, considerably longer and broader in the beam. Few people were visible on her deck. At the stern, a group of five men stood close together, apparently deep in conversation, and a couple of youngsters lounged on the foredeck, close to where a narrow plank ran up to give access from the quay. Her master, it seemed, had already effected whatever repairs might have been necessary, and the ship looked as if she had just received a thorough clean.

Jack called out to the lads, who jumped to their feet and stood stiffly in response to the authority in his voice. They both looked guilty, and I suspected their master was a hard taskmaster who would not encourage his crew to stand about idle.

'We're looking for your master or your mate,' Jack said. 'If either is aboard and willing to see us, we'd be grateful.'

The two boys put their heads together and muttered for a while, then the taller one said warily, 'Captain's gone ashore. But the mate's here, only he's busy, see.'

'I'm sure he is,' Jack said politely. 'All the same, we wish a few moments of his time.'

The boy, perhaps recognizing that Jack wasn't going to give up, dipped his head in a sort of bow, and hurried off down the deck towards the five men. Waiting until one of them deigned to notice him, he spoke some urgent words, pointing back at Jack and me. The man who had addressed him – he was short and wiry, with a soft cap pulled down over curly dark hair – studied us for a few moments. Then, muttering something to his companions, he detached himself, strode up the deck and ran nimbly down the plank.

'Thomas Gournay,' he said. 'You wanted to talk to me?'

He was looking intently at us, the deep-set brown eyes flashing from one to the other. But his expression was pleasant; he seemed more curious than hostile.

Jack introduced us – Thomas Gournay gave me a courteous nod as Jack spoke my name – and said, 'I understand from the master of *The Maid of the Marsh* that you recently carried a passenger here from Yarmouth? She was a noblewoman, dark-eyed, well-dressed and—'

'She had a baby with her – a little boy,' I interrupted. It was the most distinguishing feature about Lady Rosaria.

Thomas Gournay was shaking his head slowly, his expression puzzled. 'We didn't pick up anyone in Yarmouth,' he said. 'We only stopped to unload some cargo. Wine,' he added, 'from Spain, for the lords and ladies up at Norwich Castle.'

'You've come up from Spain?' I asked. Maybe that was where Lady Rosaria came from! Gurdyman had told me a lot about Spain, and its dark-eyed, olive-skinned inhabitants.

'Oh, no!' Thomas said with a short laugh. 'We don't venture

much further away than northern France, and it's only very rarely we go down to Bordeaux, although that's where we've just been. We picked up our cargo of wine, as well as a party of pilgrims on their way back from Santiago. But, like I said, no passengers came aboard at Yarmouth.'

I remembered something that the master of *The Maid of the Marsh* had told us. *She'd underpaid the cost of her passage, and one of the crew came after her to collect what she owed.* 'She didn't pay her full fare,' I said. 'One of your crew had to follow her to *The Maid of the Marsh* and ask her to settle with you.'

Thomas Gournay's eyes widened in understanding. '*Her!*' he exclaimed. 'Oh, yes, I remember her, all right.' He frowned. 'She maintained it was a mistake, apparently. Said she didn't understand the coinage. A likely tale,' he added in a mutter.

'Where did she board your ship?' Jack asked. Although you couldn't have detected it from his voice, I sensed that he was suddenly very tense.

'She was with the pilgrims waiting at Bordeaux,' Thomas replied promptly. 'There was quite a party of them, all glowing with the joys of Saint James's shrine, and eager to get back home and tell everyone all about it. And that showed just how impressive the place must be,' he added thoughtfully, 'when you consider they had bad weather all the way from Corunna.'

'Do you recall the lady's name?' Jack went on.

Thomas grinned. 'We don't usually bother to ask,' he said. 'It's all the same to us as long as they pay, and when people do volunteer a name, very often it's not the one they were given when they came into this world.'

'Did she have servants with her?' I demanded.

But Thomas was shaking his head. 'Now that I can't tell you,' he said. 'They all came pushing on board, and it was pelting down with rain, so they were shoving each other out of the way so as to get to the best spots. Not that there's much to choose one place from another,' he added, glancing up at the exposed deck, 'especially when there's a south-west wind blowing hard. You don't notice the rain so much once the spray hits you!' He laughed. 'And then most of them started being sick, which added to the confusion. You'd be amazed how many folk don't know not to vomit into the wind.'

'You didn't notice if—' Jack began.

But Thomas Gournay, evidently, had just experienced a flash of memory. 'Seasickness!' he cried. 'Now then, that does recall something to mind. She *did* have a maid with her, that haughty woman, and the maid was poorly. She'd been fine on the run up from Corunna, apparently – and usually, if you can survive those conditions without losing your breakfast, you can survive anything – but she started being sick maybe half a day after we left port, and the lady rigged up some sort of a shelter for the pair of them and the baby. Folk quite often do that; anything that keeps even a part of the wet off them is welcome. It wasn't much, just a heavy cloak and a bit of blanket fastened to the rail above them and stretched out to the deck so as to make a little private space underneath. Now you're likely to find rough seas anywhere in the Bay of Biscay, even hugging the shore, and normally the sickness eases once you find calmer water. That poor maid, however, went right on suffering, and her lady was forced to roll up her sleeves and look after her.'

He paused to draw breath. I saw Lady Rosaria in my imagination, all alone with her infant son in an alien world except for one single maid so ravaged by seasickness that she had become a liability rather than a help. I began to feel very sorry for her, and I experienced a sharp stab of guilt at the way I'd judged her so harshly. She—

Jack's quiet voice broke into my thoughts: 'What happened to the maid?'

I understood the importance of his question even as my mind raced to catch up. The maid had gone aboard at Bordeaux with Lady Rosaria, but by the time the veiled lady and her baby reached Cambridge, she had been alone. We knew the servant hadn't boarded *The Maid of the Marsh*; had she actually left *The Good Shepherd*, or had something happened to her on the journey up from Bordeaux?

Thomas Gournay was screwing up his face in his efforts to remember. 'We'd been disembarking passengers all along the coast, and we dropped off a handful here,' he said, 'and then there was only a couple left who sailed on with us to Boston, and that was the end of our run. I wouldn't swear to it, but, as far as I can recall, the lady enlisted the help of two of the other pilgrims to get her maid ashore. Well, I can tell you that two men carried *someone* on to the quay, and I'm guessing it was the maid, because the lady was fussing about and giving orders. It was raining again, like it had been in Bordeaux, and they all had their hoods up.'

'Do you recall what the maid looked like?' Jack asked.

Thomas frowned. 'I'm trying to remember if I ever noticed,' he admitted. There was what seemed like a very long silence. 'Yes,' he said eventually. 'She approached me at the start of the run, soon after they'd all boarded and had finished elbowing each other out of the way. She said her lady needed fresh water, and complained because all that was available in the barrel was brackish. I told her it was the best they were going to get, and she sniffed and turned on her heel.'

'And?' Jack prompted.

'And, what?'

Jack gave an almost inaudible sigh, which I thought was remarkably restrained of him. Personally, I felt like screaming with frustration. 'What did the maid look like?' he asked again.

Was she fair-haired and blue-eyed? I wanted to shout. *Was she tall and strongly built?* Surely she must have been; suffering terribly, exhausted from prolonged seasickness, our poor dead woman had been carried off the ship that had brought her so far, only to succumb to death once she was back on dry land. Had she fallen into the water? Had her body lain somewhere in the complex system of river estuaries here at Lynn, to be dislodged and swept far inland with the flood? Oh, it *must* be so! At last we would be able to establish who she was, even if not her name, and we could go back to Lord Gilbert and—

Thomas Gournay, after another pause to assemble his recollections, was speaking. 'Like I say, they were cloaked and hooded most of the time, both of them, lady and maid,' he said slowly. 'Muffled up with veils and scarves, too, like the other passengers. But I noticed the way the maid moved – she was nimble, and quick on her feet. She wasn't very tall, and I remember thinking that people like her seem to do better on a rolling deck than tall folk.' He smiled sadly. 'Shows how much I know, when the poor lass ended up being sick all the way home.'

She wasn't very tall. Oh, no . . .

'Do you remember anything else?' Jack asked, although I could tell from his expression that he was as disappointed as I was. 'Was she fair and light-eyed, like a northern woman?'

'No, oh, no,' Thomas Gournay said, shattering the last of my hopes. 'I reckon she was probably a Spaniard, or some such. She was dark as they come.'

Something was niggling at me, and I couldn't seem to pick it out from the tangle of my thoughts. It was something to do with what the mate of *The Good Shepherd* had just told us. As Jack led the way up into the settlement and towards our lodging for the night, I almost had it. But then abruptly the rain began again, and the problem of trying to keep at least a bit of me dry in the downpour drove everything else from my mind.

NINE

Rollo was on the run. He had almost been caught, and the knife wound on his left upper arm, inflicted as he slipped from his would-be captor's grasp, was bleeding, throbbing with pain. That had been late yesterday, and he had spent a sleepless night down among the stinking alleyways that wound their way behind the quays along the Golden Horn. Before dawn this morning, in an attempt to change his appearance, he had crept through a tunnel lined with unspeakable filth and eventually emerged into a tiny square, off which was a wash house where the women of the neighbourhood did their laundry. He had stripped, sluiced off the dirt and then rummaged through his pack and found a reasonably clean faded tunic to put on, winding a length of cloth around his head.

He had hardly dared look at the cut on his arm. He had bathed it thoroughly, then filled it with several drops of lavender oil. Lassair had given him the oil. He pictured her as he treated his wound. Strangely, he could not see her as clearly as he usually did. It was almost as if she stood behind a veil of mist.

As the day broke, he gathered his strength. The chase was

about to begin again, and his pursuers must not be permitted to catch him.

He was skilled at trailing people, and at observing men but not allowing them to realize it. Had he not been, he would already be dead; or, perhaps, worse than dead. It was said that there were dark, dank dungeons below the emperor's palace, where his gaolers had honed their talent for extracting the truth out of reluctant prisoners. Nobody held out for long, for the promise of ending the agony outweighed just about everything.

The men following Rollo were good, but he was better. He had noticed a particular man who appeared in his vicinity a little too frequently for coincidence, and, once his suspicion was aroused, swiftly he saw other tell-tale signs. A man, unremarkable to the casual eye, who, having observed Rollo for some time, slipped away like a shadow. To make his report to whoever had sent him? Another man, less professional, had noticed that Rollo had seen him and instantly fled.

Then Rollo had been faced with the terrible decision: *Do I run and demonstrate that their interest in me is justified; or do I continue about my business, in the hope that they will realize I am no threat?*

He had inclined to the latter. He *was* no threat to Alexius Comnenus; he had attempted to speak to someone who had the emperor's ear for no more sinister purpose than an honest and open exchange of information. Rollo had seen much in the lands under the power of the Seljuk Turks, storing his observations in his well-trained mind. He had tried to seek out Alexius to lay them before him, asking in exchange that the emperor hint at his next course of action and how it would affect the lords of the west: would he, as King William believed, appeal to Rome for the arms and the men to help him in the great mission to repel the Turks from Constantinople and drive them out of Eastern Christendom?

Rollo had his own view of what would happen if Alexius did so. He had witnessed a vision, if that was what it was; a scene from hell that still haunted him. He had seen not a well-drilled professional army, focused and tightly disciplined, but a great mass of ordinary people, men, women and children, hungry, barefoot, sickening, dying, but driven on by the faith that burned within them.

It was something that Rollo prayed would never come about.

The irony was that if he could only have managed to speak to the emperor, he was prepared to pass on the crucial discovery he had made in the south; the discovery which might have prompted Alexius to act sooner rather than later, and perhaps avoid the scenario of Rollo's vision.

He had found out that the Seljuk Turks were not the invulnerable force the outside world believed them to be. Their conversion to Islam in 1071 had filled them with the fierce zeal of all new converts, and they had been unstoppable, meeting little resistance as they persecuted Christians, desecrated churches and overran city after city, culminating in the biggest prize of all: Jerusalem. But back then they had been led by an extraordinary man. Nizam al-Mulk had been Malik Shah's vizier, but it was he who had held power, and it was said that his assassination the previous year had been at the hands of a man in the pay of the sultan, who had tired at last of his underling's supremacy over him. Not that Malik Shah had enjoyed his liberation for long; he had been murdered later that year, killed, many believed, by someone loyal to the dead vizier.

With both vizier and sultan gone, a desperate struggle had begun between the men competing for the throne, and they were forced to fend off local men, grown too powerful already and intent only on increasing their kingdoms. The new sultan, Mahmud, had a fist of iron, but even he seemed unable to bring all the disparate, quarrelsome elements into a whole.

Rollo's conclusion was that the power of the Seljuks was gravely weakened. If a strike against them could be made soon, before Mahmud had a chance to organize himself, it might meet with success.

This was what Rollo had been prepared to share with Alexius Comnenus. But he hadn't had the chance. He didn't know why the officials he saw had become suspicious of him, and he was unlikely ever to find out. At first they had seemed welcoming enough, treating him courteously, speaking openly of the emperor's views, more than willing to listen to what Rollo had to say. It was likely that men like him were not unusual; in those troubled times, surely many men came to Alexius with intelligence to barter.

One of the officials had been called away. Perhaps whoever had summoned him had told him that Rollo wasn't to be trusted.

They had gone on being polite and interested, and it was only Rollo's well-developed instincts – and equally well-developed sense of self-preservation – that had alerted him. He had nerved himself to go on chatting, desperate not to reveal that he knew they no longer trusted him. Then, eventually, he had made his excuses and left.

From the moment he left the palace, he knew he was running for his life.

Panting, soaked in sweat, Rollo peered out from his hiding place. His face twisted briefly in a hard smile as he recalled the moment of fear as he approached the emperor's stronghold. *I should have heeded that warning voice*, he thought. *It told me there was danger, and I didn't listen.*

He knew he couldn't get out of Constantinople without help. With at least three men on his trail and, undoubtedly, many more on the lookout for him, he wasn't going to walk out through one of the city's gates. Constantinople was built on a promontory, roughly triangular, and the north-western side was heavily defended by double walls, the inner ones rising high in the sky and reinforced with well-manned watch towers. Beyond the outer walls was a moat, which could only be crossed by drawbridges let down from the small number of gates; these, too, were heavily defended. The fortifications were to keep invaders out, but they served also to check those trying to leave the city. A fugitive stood no chance of getting away by that route. The better option was to escape by sea. If Rollo could make his way to an out-of-the-way harbour, perhaps further up the Golden Horn where traffic was lighter, he'd try to find a ship to take him away.

He was feeling sick. His wound was throbbing and his head ached. He didn't seem to be able to think as quickly and decisively as usual.

He tried to think who, in all that great city, might help him. *Those guards were friendly*, he thought. He put a hand to his forehead, and, although he was shivering, it felt burning hot. *One of them was going to try to find someone for me. Yes* – the memory slowly surfaced as if through thick soup – *he was going to find Harald.*

He couldn't remember who Harald was, or why he wanted to see him. As if his feet had a life of their own, he found himself heading back towards the Bucoleon Palace.

He had no idea how long he'd been walking, or if he was going the right way. He passed a vast, magnificent building whose brilliant gold decorations hurt his aching eyes. The interior looked cool and inviting, and he slipped inside. In his fevered and bemused state, he wondered if he had died and was in heaven, for above him rose a vast dome, apparently floating in the air and illuminated by bright sunlight that turned a riot of colour into a living, moving rainbow . . . Blue; everywhere, blue predominated. Turquoise, lapis, azure, violet, indigo, aquamarine, the clear warm shade of the sky. He slumped down beside a pillar, his hot skin shivering from the chill of the marble, and slipped into a doze.

Someone kicked him awake, and he left. Now, wandering with no specific goal, he had found his way into a maze of tiny narrow streets, most of them so overhung by the buildings huddling on either side that the bright daylight barely penetrated. The sea was near – he could hear and smell it – and he sensed that the street he was in would lead him out into the open area before the palace. He took a step, faltered, then, nerving himself, another. A brilliant sunlit space spread itself out before him, and, with a smile that cracked his dry lips, he moved towards it.

An arm like a hawser took him round the throat, and he was pulled against a body that felt tall, big and rigid. Steely fingers grabbed him round the wrist as, instinctively, his hand went down to grab his knife. The springy hairs of a thick beard tickled his cheek, and a voice in his ear said, very softly, 'I shouldn't go out there, if I were you.'

Rollo struggled, and the arm around his throat tightened. He began to gasp for breath, and bright lights swam through the blackness before his eyes. *I'm dying*, he thought. Sick, aching, weak with fever, it seemed almost a relief.

*   *   *

Jack and I set out for Aelf Fen at first light the next day. The
rain had eased off but the ground was still sodden, the water
level several feet above normal. We climbed on to the higher
ground to the east, and the flooded basin of the Wash spread out
below us on the right. Up there, the ground was firmer, although
even so the track had been churned into a muddy morass by the
passage of many feet and hooves. I was glad to be riding and
not walking.

We had both felt deep frustration when the neat solution to
our search for the dead woman's identity slipped through our
hands. She wasn't Lady Rosaria's maid, and no careful manipula-
tion of the facts could make her be. I was beginning to wonder
if we were even correct in the assumption that she must have
ended up where she had as a result of being swept inland along
the Ouse; the whole area had suffered from the surge, and every
river, stream and rill had burst its banks.

The same thought occurred to Jack. As we stopped to eat at
midday, he said, 'She could have come from anywhere.' I looked
up into his clear green eyes. I knew he saw the same truth that
I did: we had failed in our mission, and we were not going to
discover who our drowned woman was.

I hoped very much that our unseen watcher realized we were
no longer a threat.

For the rest of the journey back to Aelf Fen, it felt as if we
had been given leave to abandon our responsibilities and simply
enjoy ourselves. It was a beautiful day; the best that early autumn
provides, with the sun shining out of a deep blue sky and sending
dancing, twinkling points of light dappling on the flooded fen.
The bright sunshine turned the dying leaves of copses and
spinneys to rich shades of gold and russet.

Jack was good company, and once we had overcome our
diffidence the conversation flowed. I sensed that, for that brief
afternoon, I was seeing the man behind the office. He was, I realized, a man who did not often talk about himself, and I guessed
what he told me on that ride home had been shared with few
others. He asked me about my background – there wasn't much
to tell that he didn't already seem to know – and he spoke of his
family. His grandfather had provided horses for the dukes of
Normandy – a particular breed that was a cross between the

region's native heavy horses and the lighter, faster animals introduced by the Arabs – and his father had joined Duke William's army and been with him as he set about conquering England.

We both knew that if we were to judge by the actions and opinions of our forebears and what had happened in the past, he and I would be enemies. But I found myself putting that aside. Jack Chevestrier came from Norman stock, but it didn't alter the fact that he was a decent man.

His father had been a carpenter, and the Conqueror, sufficiently astute and practical to ensure that each of the men under him was put to work best suited to his skills, had despatched him to the huge team building the wooden castles that sprang up across England as, following the victory in 1066, William the Bastard stormed his way through the rest of the land, ruthlessly quelling rebellions and imposing his iron rule. In 1068, Jack's father had come to Cambridge, where he had met a woman and fallen for her.

'And they married, and you were the result.' I finished the story for him, for he had lapsed into silence.

He glanced across at me, and I saw the echo of some profound thought in his eyes. 'Yes,' he said, after a moment. 'That's right.' There was a pause and then he said, 'My father died when I was a boy, but I was big and strong, more than capable of being the man of the family, and I was ready to work.' Again, he paused. 'I became a soldier,' he said softly, as if it were a confession. 'My father talked of life in the king's army, and it was the only job I knew about.'

Yes, I thought, *I might have guessed.* There was something military both in his bearing and in the air of command that radiated from him. Something I'd noticed, it dawned on me, right from that first moment, on the quay in Cambridge.

He spoke of his life in Cambridge. He told an entertaining tale, but the one thing he did not mention shouted out to me so loudly that it was hard to believe he hadn't actually uttered it. Honest himself, he was surrounded by unscrupulous men, and the rot began with Sheriff Picot himself, who had instigated and encouraged the prevailing and deep-rooted climate of coercion, cheating, dishonesty and bribery. Jack did not believe that was any way to run a town, and probably made that fact clear. But being the one lone honest voice that insisted on speaking the truth, when everyone else around you took the easier path of fawning obedience to the man at the top, was a hard road, and it did not win you any friends.

Jack Chevestrier, I understood, was a very lonely man.

We reached Aelf Fen in the early evening. I wanted more than anything just to go home to Edild's house, warm my hands and feet – the day had grown chilly as the sun fell down the sky – and rest. I wasn't used to riding, and my thighs were stiff and sore. I longed for warm water to bathe in, and for Edild's special liniment that eases aching muscles. But when Jack led the way along the track behind the village along which we had ridden out two days ago, I realized I wasn't going to be indulging in that sweet relief just yet.

'I must report to Lord Gilbert,' Jack said, turning in the saddle to look at me. 'I'd like it if you came too, as there will undoubtedly be things you observed that I missed.'

When he phrased it like that, I could hardly refuse.

Lord Gilbert had clearly been expecting our return, for when Bermund heard the sound of hooves in the courtyard and came to the door to investigate, he nodded curtly and called out, 'Make haste. Lord Gilbert awaits you.'

Jack, however, wasn't going to be chivvied out of following his normal routine. He dismounted and, before obeying Bermund's curt command, he spoke for some moments to the groom who had come out to take the horses. I did wonder if he was making a point – we had, after all, just returned from a thankless and tiring task, and surely deserved better than being ordered about by Bermund – for I was sure every last one of Lord Gilbert's stable lads knew full well how to tend tired, dirty, hungry horses.

I did my best to tidy myself as we crossed the yard and went up the steps, tucking my hair beneath my coif and brushing mud from my heavy skirts. Behind me, Jack muttered, 'You look fine, Lassair.' It was decidedly heartening.

Bermund announced us, and we stepped into Lord Gilbert's hall. He and Lady Emma had been sitting on a bench drawn up to the hearth – its lively blaze was a welcome sight – and both got up to greet us. Jack said without preamble, 'We have found no trace of the drowned woman, my lord. We have travelled to Lynn and back, asking everyone we met, but it seems she was a stranger, and hailed from further afield.'

Lady Emma sank back on to her bench, a frown of dismay creasing her smooth brow. 'Ah, but I am disappointed!' she exclaimed. 'I am sure you have done your best –' she looked from one to the other of us – 'but I had so hoped we would have been able to return that poor soul to her kin. I—'

There was a sudden small sound from the shadows over on the far side of the hearth, at the spot where a low doorway gives on to a passage leading to other parts of the house. Turning, I caught movement. As my eyes adjusted to the low light over there, I made out a still, silent figure.

She must have realized she'd been seen. Slowly, elegantly, Lady Rosaria came into the hall. Above the concealing veil, her slanting dark eyes roamed over us, and then, like a queen seating herself on a majestic throne, she spread her wide skirts and sank down on to the bench opposite Lady Emma.

'My lady Rosaria, I did not appreciate that you would be joining us.' Lord Gilbert spoke courteously, giving her a brief bow, but I sensed there was a mild accusation behind the polite words: *What are you up to, lurking unseen in doorways and listening to us?*

I wondered just how tricky a house guest Lady Rosaria was proving to be.

Jack had other concerns. Turning to Lord Gilbert, he jerked his head in Lady Rosaria's direction and raised his eyebrows, asking permission to address her. Lord Gilbert, looking perplexed, nodded.

'My lady,' Jack said, going to stand before her, 'we have been to Lynn, as perhaps you already know?' She made no answer, either by word or gesture. 'We have spoken to the mate of *The Good Shepherd*, on which you arrived from Bordeaux.'

I was watching Lady Rosaria very closely, and I would swear that her face betrayed no reaction to Jack's words. Of course, being veiled as she was, only her eyes were visible, but they went right on staring at him.

'According to the mate, you—'

But Lord Gilbert intervened. 'Jack, Lady Rosaria is a guest

in my house,' he said quietly. 'I was not aware that you had gone
to Lynn to enquire about *her* doings.' There was a slight note of
reproof in his tone.

'My lord, I understood that Lady Rosaria seeks her late
husband's kinsmen,' Jack replied, 'and—'

Again, Lord Gilbert didn't let him finish. 'Yes, indeed she
does, and precious little progress we seem to be making.' He
glared at Bermund, lurking in the shadows beyond the hearth.
His irritation seemed to swell up and burst out of him – Lady
Rosaria really must have been upsetting his normal, easy routine
– for, spinning round to face her, he said with deceptive smoothness, 'The lady has provided a little more for us to go on, which
perhaps, Lady Rosaria, you will share?'

I thought she was going to refuse. But then, with one of those
sighs of hers that accused the entire world of being against her
and persisting in making unreasonable demands, she said, in her
low, husky, heavily accented voice, 'You already know my name,
and that I was the wife of Hugo Guillaume Fensmanson. His
father came from a noble family possessed of a fine house and
extensive lands hereabouts, and, richly endowed, he set off overseas to forge his own estates and augment his fortune.'

She stopped. We all waited, and then Lord Gilbert said, 'This
much you have told Lady Emma and me. Will you now say more,
my lady?'

For some time, she did not speak. Then she said, 'In May, my
husband and I were blessed with the birth of a son, but Hugo
did not live to enjoy his child for long. Both he and his father
died.' She paused, bowing her head, and then, with an evident
effort, resumed. 'They perished in an outbreak of fever, both
dead in a matter of hours.'

I had heard of such fevers. Gurdyman had described to me
the way a quarter, a third, of a town's population could be lost,
almost before anyone knew what was happening. It must have
been a terrifying time, and this poor woman had been caught up
in it. No wonder she'd been reluctant to talk about her past.

Lady Emma was clearly moved. I heard her whisper a prayer
and murmur soft words of dismay.

'My late father-in-law survived his son long enough to tell me
what to do,' Lady Rosaria went on. She sat erect, as if keeping

a steel-straight backbone would give her the strength and resolve to tell her dreadful tale. 'He gave me money – a bag of gold coins – and he told me to take my child and flee, before we too succumbed. We left that same day, taking ship and sailing away from the pestilence and the grief we had left behind.'

The echo of her voice faded and died. For a while, everyone else in the hall was shocked into silence. Then Lord Gilbert cleared his throat and said, 'And your father-in-law told you to come here.'

She turned to him. 'This is where he came from. Now that both he and my husband are dead, it is his family's duty to take in my son and me, for we are the last of that line.'

She was right. No well-to-do family would turn away the widow of one of their own, particularly when she had borne that family a son.

'And now,' Lord Gilbert said heavily, 'it only remains for us to locate this family.' It was his turn to sigh, although I dare say he had more cause than Lady Rosaria.

'My lady,' Jack said, again approaching Lady Rosaria. 'May I speak to you?'

Lord Gilbert intervened. 'Lady Rosaria needs to retire, Jack,' he said. 'We have just made her endure the retelling of her story, and it has obviously caused her deep distress.' I glanced across at her. She was sitting with lowered head, a tiny, lacy handkerchief pressed to her eyes. 'Talk to me instead.'

He gave the ladies a bow, then strode towards the door, hurrying down the steps and into the courtyard as if he couldn't wait to get away. Jack and I followed.

'Now, what is it?' Lord Gilbert demanded, his frown deepening to a scowl and his tone angry.

Jack was probably used to dealing with more threatening men than Lord Gilbert. Quite undismayed, standing relaxed and easy with one hand on his sword hilt, he said, 'Lady Rosaria sailed into Lynn on *The Good Shepherd*, as I said. She boarded in Bordeaux, accompanied by a maid.'

'So?' snapped Lord Gilbert. 'Presumably that's where this fenland lord went to make his fortune. And what's strange about her having a maid with her? She'd have been the wet-nurse, no doubt, and—' He stopped suddenly, looking puzzled. 'You'd think her father-in-law would have sent other servants to care for her and her son, wouldn't you?' he mused. But then, answering his own question, he went on, 'Perhaps the maid was the only member of the household staff not to sicken and die.'

'She's dead now, or so we surmise,' Jack said bluntly. 'The mate of *The Good Shepherd* said the woman was unwell, and had to be helped off the ship at Lynn by two other passengers. When Lady Rosaria took passage on *The Maid of the Marsh* from Lynn to Cambridge, she and her baby were alone.'

Lord Gilbert was silent for so long that I was beginning to think his mind had slid away to seek refuge from the whole business. He is not a great one for doggedly teasing problems to a conclusion.

But he was still thinking about what Jack had just said, as, eventually, his words revealed. 'She has endured a dreadful time,' he said. 'She witnessed a terrifying sickness, which robbed her of her husband and father-in-law, and then, before she could even begin to grieve, she had to flee for her life, travelling in uncertainty towards the only hope left to her: that her husband's kin would take pity on her and give her a home. It is surely not to be wondered at if she is not in her right mind.'

'She should still be—' Jack began.

But Lord Gilbert held up an imperious hand. 'I appreciate, Jack, that you are doing your job, and I applaud you for it,' he said. 'You have unearthed what seems to be a small mystery – what happened to this wretched maid – but I will not permit you to question Lady Rosaria.'

Jack opened his mouth to protest, as well he might. I wasn't sure that Lord Gilbert had any right to give him such an order, and I imagine Jack was of the same opinion. And even from where I was standing a couple of paces away, I could sense his furious indignation at the idea of a maid's disappearance and likely death being so casually dismissed.

I wondered what he was going to do.

But then, his expression softening, Lord Gilbert patted Jack's arm and added, 'Give her a few days. She is grieving, she is lost and lonely, and her situation must seem to her very precarious.' He sighed again. 'We will fulfil our duty, and go on looking after her here –' his doleful tone revealed how reluctant he was to do that duty – 'and we shall redouble our efforts to locate the whereabouts of this Harald Fensman's manor and estate, so that she may be taken to her rightful place as soon as possible.' He eyed us both in turn. 'And that,' he said firmly, 'is my final word.'

TEN

It was a great relief to reach the sanctuary of my aunt's house. I closed the door behind me, pushing into place along its base the fat, narrow, straw-stuffed sack that keeps out the worst of the wind. Straightening up to greet my aunt, I noticed she wasn't alone. Facing her across the hearth sat Hrype.

The events of the past three days had driven all other preoccupations right to the back of my mind. I was tired, dispirited and quietly grieving for the drowned woman whom nobody had claimed. I knew why Hrype was there, and while it was certainly not my place even to *think* that he was unwelcome in my aunt's house, never mind say it aloud, he was the last person I wanted to see just then.

He wanted me to make another attempt with the shining stone. Such was his power that I would do it.

As if he could see my thoughts as they flashed in quick succession through my mind, he said softly, 'It is necessary, Lassair. I appreciate that you are weary, but I would not ask this if I did not have to.'

Without a word, I went over to where my bedding was rolled up, reaching behind it into the recess. My hand closed on the bag, and I drew it out. I sat down cross-legged beside the hearth, and extracted the stone.

Edild gave a soft gasp. 'Won't you eat first, Lassair?' She sounded anxious, and, in a quick glance, I saw her look doubtfully at Hrype.

'I'm not hungry,' I said shortly.

'But you've been—'

'I said I'm not hungry.' It was rude, and I'm never rude to Edild. I hold her in far too much respect; awe, even. But I believed, rightly or wrongly, that if I'd pleaded fatigue or weariness of spirit – from both of which I was indeed suffering – as reasons to put the shining stone away again, she'd have sided with Hrype and added her persuasive will to his.

I was angry.

Deliberately controlling my movements so that they were smooth and unhurried – also, so that Hrype would not see my anger – I laid the stone, wrapped in its soft sheep's wool, into the hollow made by my skirts stretched across my crossed legs. Then, still taking my time, I peeled back the wool and took the shining stone in my hands. I rested it in my open palms, delighting in its smooth weightiness. Each time I hold it, I am taken aback at how heavy it is; as if it contains a huge mass of matter, crushed down into an impossibly small, dense sphere.

Then, focusing my mind on it to the exclusion of all else, I looked into its dark depths.

I swear that it picked up my fury.

In that first instant, it felt as if some power within it was looking straight into my mind, detecting my already strong emotions and magnifying them, hurling them back at me so that they throbbed with power. It seemed to force me to look at what I was feeling, and why, and suddenly I wanted to shout out, to rail against a world where so often I do what others want of me, and not what I want for myself.

I was, I realized, seeing the truth.

We were communicating, the stone and I, and for an unknown time, I simply revelled in the feeling it roused in me. I felt that my mind was slowly and inexorably being expanded. All sorts of images came roaring up out of memory, many of them unpleasant. Over and over again, I observed myself folding my lips as meekly I hurried to obey some command. I saw myself with Rollo, or, more accurately, yearning for him when I desperately wanted him, yet knowing that he was far away and would not come. A thought rang out in my head, clear as a cry on a still morning: *What use is a strong, resourceful lover if he isn't here when I need him?* The same thought had burst in my mind earlier in the year, when I was in terrible danger. Strange, that the stone had picked it out and now threw it up, along with other uncomfortable truths, for my consideration.

I didn't want to think about those truths. I stared deep into the stone, concentrating on one of the mysterious bands of green light that swirl through its blackness, and instantly other images – emotions – flew up. I felt comforted; I felt as if someone, or something, understood me, right to my core. Understood, and was there by my side. In a heartbeat of clarity, I thought, *The stone is giving me its support.* It was; I had no doubt. It was helping me to be strong, giving me the resolve to turn away from my negative thoughts.

As if it, too, was revelling in our new closeness, I saw a series of scenes, flash, flash, flash, one after the other in rapid succession. I saw a conical hill, or perhaps it was a mountain, and its top had been blasted off in a great convulsion of rock and earth. I saw a wide river of molten glass. I heard a sepulchral voice in my head: *Behold, the Hill of the Knives*, and I saw dark men with feathers in their long black hair, dancing in the flames as if possessed.

I was, I believe, seeing my stone's birth.

I saw my own ancestor, the man who had first brought the shining stone so far across the wide seas. In another vivid series of images, I saw its recent history, and somewhere within me I knew that the past hundred years were nothing to it; that it was unbelievably ancient, as old as the very fabric of the earth.

I cradled it in my hands, and an odd feeling of pity for it swept through me. So old, so alone.

Perhaps it understood. Perhaps it wasn't used to feeble mortals expressing sympathy. I'm sure I was imagining it, but, just for an instant, I felt it was allying itself to me.

An intense sense of well-being flooded through me, and I heard myself laugh. Hrype must have been watching me intently, and he said urgently, 'Skuli! Can you see Skuli?'

At least, I thought he spoke the words. Perhaps, after all, he just thought them, and in my heightened state of awareness I picked them up.

Skuli. Miklagard. A long, lean ship. She was very like the vessel called *Malice-striker*, the vessel which had come to me in her prime in a vision and whose skeletal ghost I had seen on a beach in Iceland. This, though, was Skuli's ship, and, although he had lost crew members on the long and perilous journey down through the centre of the vast land mass – I *knew* this; the stone told me – yet there he was, in the Great City.

And, just as I had concluded the last time I'd been persuaded to look into the stone, his mission was not yet fulfilled.

I was right! I sang inside my head. *I knew it!*

For a moment my concentration wavered. I looked up, staring about me, surprised, somehow, to see Edild's and Hrype's anxious, intent faces so close. But then the shining stone called me back.

I watched as scenes were played out in the flashes of golden light. I did not understand, but I appreciated that it didn't matter. *Others will know*, I thought.

I simply sat and observed. At one point, what I saw touched my heart, and I felt a tear roll down my face.

After what seemed a very long time, the stone went quiescent. I thought I felt it grow cool in my hands. I wrapped the wool around it, then pushed it gently inside the leather bag, drawing up the strings that held it closed. I got up – my legs felt shaky – and put the bag back into its recess.

I sat down again. I was shivering despite the warmth, and drew my shawl closely around me. Because my sister Elfritha made it for me, before she went away to be a nun, wrapping it round me is a bit like having her hug me.

Hrype gave me a moment. Then he said, 'What did you see?'

Some things – those deeply personal to me – were not for sharing. They had been thrown up purely for me; truths, perhaps, originating within myself, presented for my consideration. Besides, I guessed they were not what Hrype wanted so keenly to hear about. I drew a deep breath.

'Skuli lost crewmen on the journey south,' I began, 'but that did not hold him back. There are new names carved in runes on the big stone beyond the rapids, so those men will not be forgotten.' I heard Edild make a small sound of distress, but in that moment she was not my concern.

I turned to Hrype, and, for the first time ever, I felt able to meet the power in his eyes without flinching. 'You have all been lying to me,' I said calmly. 'I suspected it before, and now I know for sure. If not lying, you've been careful with how much you revealed. My—' *No.* I stopped myself. I must not call Thorfinn my grandfather. Granny Cordeilla had told nobody but Hrype, and it was not for me to break the confidence and tell Edild. 'Thorfinn said, and you let me believe,' I pressed on, not allowing him to interrupt, 'that Skuli's sole mission was to reach Miklagard. Thorfinn told me that Skuli was driven to succeed where his father failed, and that he was convinced he would only complete the journey if he possessed the stone. That, however, is not true.'

I paused. I was watching Hrype closely – as closely as he frequently watches me – and I sensed that he was deliberately masking his thoughts. 'Really?' he asked mildly. 'What, then, *is* the truth?'

'I do not yet know,' I admitted. 'But Miklagard is not an end in itself, nor was it ever. Skuli is going on, driven towards some goal that is hidden from me, yet which I know to be perilous.' The stone had revealed a little to me, and I had been very afraid. I'd heard those two galloping horses again, and the ravens had flown out towards me. The stone had whispered reassurance – *They do not come for you* – and that had given me the resolve not to turn away in abject terror.

I went on staring at Hrype. 'You know where he is going, don't you?' I said softly.

He didn't answer at first. He glanced at Edild, then lowered his eyes so that he was staring into the fire. 'I suspect,' he said eventually. 'We – I believe there is a destination for which he may be bound.'

We. Before he corrected himself, he'd said *we*. Did he mean him and Edild? No. I knew for sure he didn't. Who, then?

The answer seemed to be leaping up through the layers of my mind. But just then, before I could grasp it, Hrype began speaking again. Well, not exactly speaking; his voice was a soft hum, like the background noise of insects when you stand in woodland on a warm summer's afternoon. The note rose and fell, apparently at random, and the sound was sweet and hypnotic. I felt my eyelids grow heavy, and the urge to sleep was all but irresistible . . .

Then, some time later, there was Edild, kneeling before me, pushing a bowl of hot, fragrant gruel into my hands. 'Eat this, Lassair, then go to bed,' she commanded. 'Hrype's just going.' She shot him a look, and I had the impression she was displeased with him.

Hrype got to his feet, drawing his cloak round him and putting up the hood. He stared down at me, a strange expression on his face. He was obviously pleased with what I had achieved; self-satisfied, perhaps, in that he had made me do what he wanted and, apparently, achieved the desired result. In addition, there was, I believed – although I could very well have been fooling myself – a very tiny amount of respect.

'There you are,' he said quietly. 'The lapis lazuli did its job, didn't it? You kept it close, like I told you, and it helped you to draw the spirits to you.'

I met his silvery eyes. I experienced a moment of triumph: powerful, joyous. I jerked my head towards my rolled-up bedding. He frowned, then turned to look.

My precious little piece of lapis was on the floor beside my blanket. Whatever had just happened between the shining stone and me, I had achieved it all by myself.

It was late when Hrype left Edild's house, but he did not go home. He hastened his steps, for he had some way to go. He crossed the neck of high ground behind the village, taking the same path by which Lassair and the sheriff's man had arrived earlier. To divert himself from the damp and the cold, Hrype turned his mind to the Cambridge lawman. Hrype had not met him, but Edild had spent some time in his company, on the morning when the drowned woman had been found.

Hrype wouldn't have given the fellow a thought, except that Edild appeared to be preoccupied with him. She believed there was a connection of some sort between him and Lassair; an affection? Friendship? Hrype didn't know, and Edild had not said. *So what if there is?* Hrype had said when Edild had voiced her suspicions. *He's a Norman and a man of the law*, Edild replied. Instantly Hrype had thought – although just about refrained from saying – that there was little to choose between this new man and Lassair's other Norman, except this one was *here*.

He grinned in the darkness. Had he said as much, Edild would undoubtedly have told him bluntly that he didn't under-stand women.

She'd have been right.

He strode on, long legs eating up the distance. He passed the wooden bridge where the dead woman had been found, pausing a moment to honour her spirit, whose presence he could feel. Then he hurried on, for she was not his concern tonight.

Presently he turned away from the fen edge, following the course of a narrow, winding little river running in from the east. It twisted this way and that, and for much of the time the water was hidden behind stands of hazel, alder and willow. The boat, small and lying low in the water, was well-concealed, and it was doubtful anyone who did not know where to look would have happened upon it.

Hrype stood on the bank and called out, keeping the pitch of his voice low. A heavy covering, supported by a line running from posts at the bows and stern, had been draped across the boat's sides; briefly it was pushed aside, allowing the soft light of an oil lamp to spill out. A voice said softly, 'Hrype?' and he said, 'Yes.'

The covering was drawn further back, revealing a big, hairy, bearded man hunched inside a thick fur-trimmed cloak. 'Come aboard, quick, then I can shut out the night again,' he said brusquely.

Hrype did as he ordered, tucking the covering back into place as he sat down beside the man. He had to be careful where he placed his feet, for the boat was crammed with provisions, and two barrels stood in the prow. It was a small craft, of the sort used to row to shore from a larger vessel. The golden lamplight gave an illusion of cosiness, but in fact, Hrype soon realized, it was warmer inside the shelter than he'd imagined.

The man settled towards the stern, smiling as Hrype sat down beside him, looked around with interested eyes. He patted the sacks padding the narrow bench on which they sat. 'Stuffed with down and feathers,' he remarked. 'They keep our northern geese warm in the bitterest weather, and they perform the same service for me. Now, what news?'

Hrype stared into the old face, feeling the keen eyes bore into him. 'She has just tried again. She – there is something different about her. Some new experience has marked her, although I do not know what it is.'

'She has been off trying to trace the kin of the drowned woman, you said.'

'Yes. She met with no success, yet I believe some other matter concerns her; one which she has not shared with her aunt or me.'

'Why should she?' the old man countered. 'She is a woman grown, Hrype. She does not need your approbation over everything she does or thinks.'

There was pride in his voice; the pride of kinship, Hrype reflected. As well there might be, given that this was Lassair's grandfather.

'She is still under tuition,' he said. 'Both Edild and Gurdyman have a great deal to teach her yet. It is far too soon for her to think of acting independently.'

'But she has succeeded with the shining stone, has she not?' Thorfinn said silkily. 'Come on, Hrype, do not deny it. I know by your presence here that something has happened. Besides –' he heaved a sigh – 'do not forget that the shining stone was once in my guardianship. Although I had to part from it, still there is a bond.' He passed a hand over his face as if he were in pain.

Hrype watched him in concern. 'Are you all right?'

'Yes,' Thorfinn said shortly. 'Now, tell me what happened.'

Hrype closed his eyes, replaying the scene in his mind. Then, succinctly, he described it to Thorfinn.

When he stopped speaking, there was a long silence. Finally breaking it, Thorfinn said, 'Then it is true. What I so feared is indeed about to be enacted.' His heavy brows contracted in a fierce scowl, and he thumped one huge fist into the palm of his other hand. 'I should have sent Einar after him,' he muttered. 'He would have gone! He and his crew were itching to test themselves on the route from the Varyani to the Greeks.'

'Your son would have risked his ship, his crew and himself had they done so,' Hrype said, 'for once they had caught up with Skuli, they would have pursued him on to his final destination. And if you are right—'

'I *am* right.'

'*If* you are right, then your Einar, the son who follows most closely in your footsteps, would have been lost to you.'

'He is a skilled sailor and a brave fighter!' Thorfinn shouted. 'He could have fought shoulder to shoulder with Skuli, and together they might have stood a chance!'

'*No*,' Hrype said, the single syllable ringing like the chime of a bell through the turbulent mood. 'You say you know where Skuli is bound, and what he plans to attempt there. Thorfinn, what he attempts is surely beyond him; beyond any man, for he believes he can walk with powers that are not of this world, yet come out unscathed.'

Thorfinn's anger seemed all at once to die, and he sank into the warm folds of his cloak. 'But to be there, Hrype, while Skuli makes the attempt!' he breathed. 'Would you not give a great deal – all that you have, perhaps – to be a witness to that moment?'

'Perhaps,' Hrype muttered. Then, more honestly, 'Yes, I would. Of course I would, for what Skuli aims to do will, if he succeeds, alter the very way in which we perceive our world and its relationship to that of the spirits.' His mind flew away, and for a moment he was lost in his imagination. Then, as if the rational side of him was summoning him back, he added, 'If you believe it is true, of course.'

'You forget, Hrype, who I am,' Thorfinn said softly. 'I was brought up with the old stories, legends and myths. They are in my blood.' He glanced at Hrype, his eyes glittering in the lamplight. 'In yours too, I think, Northman,' he murmured.

Hrype grimaced, but made no reply.

After a while, Thorfinn said, 'So, my granddaughter begins to forge her link with the stone.' He spoke lightly, but Hrype was not deceived. 'And does she, I wonder, sense its danger?'

'She is not you, Thorfinn,' Hrype said gently, 'and her experience will not be as yours was. She—' He smiled suddenly, seeing in his mind's eye Lassair's mutinous expression when he had bent her will to his and made her look into the stone. 'She does not like being forced to use it on behalf of another,' he said wryly. 'She wants to explore it all by herself.'

'Good for her,' Thorfinn said forcefully. 'What else have you observed?'

Hrype paused, collecting his thoughts. 'She does not, I believe, view it as a tool that will help her achieve what she desires.' He shot a quick look at the old man. 'I do not mean to accuse; merely to observe. From all that you have told me, it would appear that you and your forefather saw your possession of the stone in terms of what it could do for you. It was your talisman; it would keep you safe while you pushed harder and harder

against the boundaries as you sailed further into the unknown.'
He paused, waiting to see if Thorfinn would comment.

'That is fair, as far as it goes,' the old man muttered. 'And
what of Lassair? You have lately witnessed her with the shining
stone. How, in your opinion, does her attitude to it differ from
mine?'

A brief sentence flashed into Hrype's head. How very strange!
His eyes widened in astonishment, but then, as he considered it,
he began to appreciate that it was absolutely right.

With a smile, he turned to Thorfinn and said, 'She treats it
like a friend.'

ELEVEN

I woke grumpy and out of sorts, and my head ached. I was still
feeling cross; with Hrype for bullying me into looking into
the shining stone, with Edild for letting him, and, most of all,
with myself for being too feeble to say no. It wasn't that I didn't
want to get to know the stone; far from it. It fascinated me, and
I think I was already beginning to fall under its spell. But I
wanted my explorations to be on my own terms, preferably
conducted when I was by myself.

Edild seemed to read my mood and she left me alone. After
we had cleared up our simple breakfast and tidied away our
bedding in preparation for the day, I announced I would go out
to the little still room and catch up with the never-ending task
of washing out empty jars, pots and the many vessels we
constantly use in our preparations. She agreed, a little too readily.
Presumably she preferred my absence to my company, and I
couldn't say I blamed her.

I took out my ill temper on giving the little room the sort of
extremely thorough tidy and clean that only a woman taking out
her anger on inanimate objects can achieve. I managed not to
break anything, which was quite a triumph. I opened the low
door that gave on to the rear of the house and Edild's herb garden,
for the morning was mild and sunny and the warmth would, I

hoped, help to dry the freshly scrubbed room. I was just finishing off, putting all the gleaming pots and vessels back on the immaculate shelves, when a shadow fell across the sunlit floor and I turned to see Jack standing in the doorway.

'Your aunt is busy with a white-faced man clutching his belly as if his bowels are about to burst,' he remarked, 'so, since I didn't think either of them would welcome a witness, I came round the back.'

I pushed my hair back under my cap and wiped my hands on my apron. 'I'm sure both patient and healer appreciate your tact.'

'It's you I wanted to see, anyway,' he went on, his clear eyes roaming around the shelves that lined the room. 'I've been talking to . . .' But his interest in the surroundings overtook his need to explain his visit. 'You prepare all these things? All these ointments, medicines, remedies and potions?' His hand was reaching up to the high shelf where we keep the poisons.

'My aunt and I do, yes. I shouldn't touch that,' I added as his hand closed round a tall, slim bottle.

'Why?'

'It's thung, but you may know it as monkshood or wolf's bane.' From the way he instantly withdrew his hand as if it had been scalded, I guessed he did. 'It's one of the fiercest poisons.'

'Why do you keep it, then?' He sounded genuinely interested.

'If you greatly dilute it, it's a very good pain reliever.'

He nodded. 'Anything else potentially fatal up there?'

'Hemlock, which calms and sedates; savin, which is a sort of juniper and used externally to treat warts; deadly nightshade, which induces sleep, and woody nightshade for coughs and shortness of breath; yew, to treat snake bite; buckthorn, useful as a purgative and to ease chronic constipation—'

I was only halfway along the shelf, but he put up his hands to stop me. 'Enough!' He grinned. 'Do you ever make mistakes?'

'Not so far.' I crossed my fingers behind my back, sending up a quick, silent prayer. 'I've only started using the dangerous preparations recently. That's why they're on the top shelf. You're not allowed to use anything you can't reach.'

He nodded again. 'So an undersized healer will never handle anything poisonous?'

It was my turn to smile. 'You wanted to see me,' I reminded him.

'Yes,' he agreed. His expression suddenly grave, he said, 'Lord Gilbert still refuses to let me ask Lady Rosaria about her maid. In fact, he won't let me speak to her at all today – he says she's ill. A headache, sickness; I wasn't permitted to hear any more details.'

'You think he's making it up as an excuse to keep you away?'

'He doesn't need an excuse,' Jack said bluntly. 'He's the lord, she's his guest and a lady. I'm the sheriff's officer.'

'But you have good reason to think her maid may be very sick, or even dead,' I persisted, indignant on his behalf.

'Lord Gilbert, if I had the temerity to press the point, would no doubt inform me that Lady Rosaria's servants are her responsibility and nothing to do with anyone else, particularly me,' he said. 'He would probably add that, after all, the woman we want to know about is only a maid.'

Only a maid, and therefore not important. I wondered if that was fair to Lord Gilbert. Probably, I decided, although the same did not apply to Lady Emma, who was a decent and humane woman.

'So, what do you want me to do?' I asked. Anticipating his reply, I added, 'I can't go crashing in offering to treat Lady Rosaria if she hasn't sent for me. Besides, it's usually Edild who is summoned to treat the nobles of Lakehall.'

'No, that's not what I was going to ask. The important thing is to locate Lady Rosaria's kin because, once she's safely in the bosom of her family, she'll relax, stop being so prickly and defensive, and be more prepared to explain what happened to her maid.' He was staring down at the floor – the immaculate floor – and seemed a little abashed.

'What *do* you want from me, then?' I prompted.

He looked up. 'Lord Gilbert's lot are having no success in trying to find Lady Rosaria's father-in-law's kin, which is, I imagine, because they have little idea how to go about it, other than visiting the grand households suggested by their lord and asking if anyone knows the name Harald Fensman. If it were left to me, I'd suggest widening the search and asking some of the ordinary people.' He paused, then went on, 'I've mentioned to you before, I believe, the value of observation in my sort of work. The importance of using the evidence of your eyes and ears, and making a considered picture. I also pointed out –' now he was studying the floor again – 'that you have a talent for it.'

'You want *me* to come and help you look for this Fensman clan?' I regretted the words instantly. I was going to look and feel such a fool when he said, *No, that wasn't what I meant at all.*

But he didn't. He just said, 'Yes.'

He had anticipated that I wouldn't be able to refuse. He'd left Isis and his beautiful grey gelding tethered to a stumpy hazel close to where the path up to Edild's house branches off the main track through the village. I went up to Isis, patting her graceful neck and putting my face close to hers, and she nuzzled her soft nose into my hand. The gelding, his dark eyes wide with interest, pushed up against me, and I reached out a tentative hand to stroke his long mane. 'Pegasus,' I whispered to him.

I'd have had no idea how to go about our search, but fortunately Jack did. The plan was to ride to the many villages and settlements dotted around the fen edge, locate some central figure such as the smith or the priest, and simply ask after the name Fensman. *Harald* alone was just too vague; it's a far from uncommon name.

We kept to the high ground as much as we could. There were a few hamlets out on the marshy ground, in places where small areas of raised land permitted people to live without the constant fear of the encroaching water, but just now the prospect of finding a way to them was daunting. The flood was subsiding slowly, but in many areas the paths and tracks were still under water. In any case, there were enough places to visit without wasting time plunging up to our necks in mud.

We enquired at one village, and another. A couple of hamlets; a settlement of half a dozen hovels. A big village, almost substantial enough to be called a town. To my embarrassed gratification, I was recognized in quite a few of the places. I hadn't realized how far people travelled to come to consult my aunt and me. I'd imagined, if I'd thought about it at all, that most of our patients were relatively local, and that other people usually either treated themselves or discussed their ailments with their own village healer. Coming across familiar faces ten or twelve miles away was something of an eye-opener.

The down side of being recognized, of course, was that quite a few people suddenly discovered that their bad back had flared up again, or their piles were itching, or their wife had been moaning about a rash on her neck for more than a week now and would I have a quick look, seeing as how I was in the vicinity? I didn't really mind. I always carry my healer's satchel, well supplied with the things I use most, and handing out some remedies and a bit of advice didn't take up much time. As it happened, dealing with complaints gave me the perfect opportunity to ask people about Harald Fensman, since, to a man or woman, they all asked me what I was doing so far from home.

The beautiful evening, with the daylight slowly fading and a clear, still twilight approaching, found us on our way back to Aelf Fen. We had come across any number of Haralds – I did say it was a popular name – but nobody seemed to have heard of any family who had adopted the name of Fensman, with or without a son who had left the area.

I was turning over something in my mind, and had been quiet for some time, when Jack said, 'What are you thinking?'

'Er – it's probably nothing.'

He grinned. 'When people say that, what they mean is, *I'm pretty sure I've come up with something important but I don't want to admit it in case I'm wrong.*'

I laughed. 'I don't think it's important, exactly, but it may be relevant. It's bothering me, anyway.'

Jack looked enquiringly at me. When I didn't respond, he said, 'Speak up, then!'

'It's the name, Fensman. What occurred to me is that everyone here could call themselves that. All of us are fensmen, or fenswomen, and for someone to use the name as a way of distinguishing himself just wouldn't work.'

He nodded. 'Go on.'

'We know from Lady Rosaria that her father-in-law Harald left his fenland home to make his fortune overseas somewhere, and we know she began her voyage back to England in northern Spain.'

'Corunna,' Jack put in.

'So, what *I* think is that he only adopted the Fensman name once he settled in Spain, and he left here as plain Harald.'

'In which case, you and I have wasted a day asking for someone called Fensman,' Jack concluded, with understandable frustration.

'I'm sorry,' I said, 'I didn't mean to—'

'You have nothing to apologize for,' he said swiftly. He turned to me and smiled. 'And even if today was a waste as far as we're concerned,' he added, his mouth twisting in a grin, 'I'm sure the old woman with the phlegmy cough and the man with piles are most grateful we, or rather you, happened by.'

I felt myself blush. I've grown used to the more intimate and personal ailments people present to me, and take them all in my stride. I wasn't, however, quite capable of hearing someone outside my profession speak of them without feeling embarrassed.

'We must think, Lassair,' Jack said after a moment, 'what else we know about Lady Rosaria's husband's family. Did she tell us anything else that might help discover where they originated? Was there *any* hint as to a specific location? Any mention of other kinsmen?'

I was thinking very hard, trying to remember everything that the veiled woman had ever said. Since she was one of the most rigidly reserved women I'd ever come across, nothing much came to mind. 'I can't recall anything,' I confessed after quite a long silence. 'What about you?'

'No, I can't either,' he agreed. 'But I do have the advantage, in that I'm going to be staying under the same roof as our mysterious foreign lady tonight. I'll try to speak to her. I'll leave her in no doubt that we'd find her family a lot more quickly if she'd tell us a bit more about them.'

'Rather you than me,' I said.

He grinned. 'No, I don't relish the prospect, I must say.'

We reached the place on the track where the path leads up to Edild's house; the spot from where we'd set out that morning. I dismounted, feeling the long day of riding in my sore thighs and backside. Sensing his eyes on me, I looked up.

'You have several shelves of remedies in that little room,' he

said. His eyes were bright with laughter. 'Don't try to tell me
there isn't some wonderfully effective liniment which your aunt
can rub on for you.'

'I wouldn't dream of it,' I said with dignity. 'By the time I go
to bed, every ache will have been eased. And,' I added with a
grin, 'it's not me who'll be trying to gouge information out of
Lady Rosaria.'

I handed Isis's reins to him then, with a wave, set off up the
path. After a moment, I heard him mutter a few words to his
grey, and two sets of hoofbeats pounded the ground as they
cantered away.

As evening fell, the veiled woman in the comfortable guest
chamber at Lakehall went over to the narrow window and looked
out on to the gilded landscape. The long rays of the setting sun
made the scene quite beautiful, but Rosaria was in no mood to
appreciate it.

She had tried praying, hoping for relief from her torment. She
had imposed solitude upon herself, and her hosts were too courteous to intrude. The local woman was taking adequate care of
the infant, leaving Rosaria with little to do except worry.

She had thought it would be easy.

My family in the fens, Harald had said countless times, *are
numerous and mighty; we are people to be reckoned with!* He
used to speak proudly and lovingly of his home: of wide acres
spread under a huge sky; of waterways – streams and little rivers
– so rich in fish that you had but to put your hand in and grab
hold of your supper. He spoke of warm hearths where kinsmen
gathered, of hospitality, of sheltering walls and a stout roof. And
as they had listened wide-eyed, hanging on his every word as he
described that faraway land, he had elaborated, describing the
long, low hall, the fires that always burned, the stacked sheepskins
and furs in which to snuggle on a cold night, the feasting, the
conviviality, the open-handedness of a secure, wealthy family
willing and able to offer hospitality to friend and kinsman.

Rosaria's soul had responded, and she had longed to be a part
of that rich, comfortable, safe life which Harald described so
well.

Now she was here, in Harald's own land, and it ought to have been easy. She had imagined, in her innocence and ignorance, that *Fen* was a place; that, once delivered to the nearest port, it would simply be a matter of locating the homestead of Harald Fensman's family and announcing, *Here I am.*

But *Fen* wasn't a place. It was a huge watery, marshy, confusing and half-flooded wilderness, and she had no idea how to find the household she sought. Oh, yes, this Lord Gilbert was trying to help, although Rosaria was certain it was only because he wished to be rid of her. What did that matter, though, as long as the right result was achieved? If – no, *when* – the day came that they brought her the wonderful tidings that the Fensman clan were ready to welcome her and the child with open arms, and one of them was indeed standing in the hall with a smile on his face ready to take her away, she would thank Lord Gilbert with a pretty little speech, take herself off and he would never have to bother with her again.

That day will come, she told herself firmly. *It will. It must. It is only a matter of waiting.*

But, oh, how tired she was of the wait; of the constant effort of being a guest in a household that had neither expected nor invited her. How she longed for a place to call her own. A household where, as a daughter-in-law of one kinsman and mother of another, they would welcome her, make much of her, sympathize with her and tend her . . .

She allowed her mind to slide off into a happy daydream. It was the only comfort she had.

After a time, shivering suddenly as the temperature began to drop, she moved away from the window, allowing the heavy hanging that covered it at night to swing into place. She paced up and down the room, eyes roaming over the luxurious bed, the heavy, colourful tapestries lining the walls and the fresh rushes on the clean flags of the floor. Would her new home be like this? Harald had implied as much, and her impression had always been that his home in the country of his birth had been sumptuously luxurious.

Oh, she thought, *oh, how I long to be there.*

She had paid a price: a huge price. Allowing herself just for an instant to think the unthinkable, she wondered what would become of her if that price proved to be all for nothing.

But straight away her mind screamed out in protest. *Stop!*

She could hear voices in the great hall. The servants were starting on the preparations for the evening. There would be the meal – they ate well here – and perhaps an entertainment. One evening, there had been singing. Another time, someone had told stories. A polite invitation was always issued to Rosaria to join the household, but usually she declined. Food was brought to her room, and she would listen to the sounds of merriment which she could not share.

She wandered across to a large wooden chest that stood against the far wall. A lamp stood on it, and, stooping, she lit a spill from the glowing fire in the little hearth and set it to the lamp's wick. A pool of brilliance spread out, and a ray of light struck the shiny surface of the mirror that had been put down beside the lamp.

It had been kind of Lady Emma to supply it. Rosaria never carried a mirror, and would have refused the offer if she'd dared. It was a handsome object. The reflecting surface was a plate of brass, highly polished, in size perhaps the width of a hand with the fingers widely spread. This plate was set into a piece of beautifully carved cherry wood, which formed the handle. It was a costly, luxurious item. Rosaria recognized and loved fine quality.

She stood quite still, staring down at the mirror. In the short time that she had been a guest at Lakehall, she had stood like that many times before, for the mirror was always on her mind and she could not forget it.

It was a constant, agonizing temptation.

You must not look, they had told her.

She knew they were right; she understood the consequences of disobedience. They meant it for her own good, for she would suffer if she yielded.

She watched as her hand stretched out towards the mirror's handle. She saw her long fingers close around it, and her eyes widened in alarm.

Her free hand was clutching at her veil, unfastening the ties that held it so firmly and permanently in place. She never removed it when there was even the remotest chance that anyone could see her face. When she took it off as she went to bed, she replaced it with a close-fitting cap which merged into a high-necked collar, and the collar included a fold of the same soft fabric that could be drawn up over her mouth and nose.

Do not let them see you.

The mantra was so deeply entrenched in her that it had become a part of her.

Her fingers were on the veil, slowly, gradually drawing it away from her face, pulling at the ties so that the veil inched slowly downwards. Now it was under the bridge of her nose. Now it was halfway down, and in the lamplight she could clearly make out the curve at the top of a deeply etched nostril. She gave a little gasp.

She felt as if something outside herself was forcing her hand. Making her act, when everything in her cried out *Stop!* The veil had caught on the tip of her nose, and, in a sudden, violent movement, she tore it away.

She stared into her own deep, dark eyes. She watched as the tip of her pink tongue wet her full, beautifully shaped lips.

She took a deep breath and looked herself full in the face.

Then she began to weep.

TWELVE

For perhaps the fourth or fifth time, Thorfinn eased aside the heavy awning that turned a small boat into a reasonably comfortable refuge and stared into the deepening darkness. Then, climbing up on to the bank, he stood and breathed in the night air. He realized he might well be looking out for somebody who wouldn't turn up; there was no certainty, and his expected guest had only said *maybe*. He had a long way to come, and timing could never be precise when it depended on currents, tides and winds.

Nevertheless, Thorfinn kept on looking.

Eventually, when night had fallen and bright stars were beginning to appear in the black sky, he heard the sound he had been listening out for. With a smile, he jumped up on the bank once more, and, bending over the small brazier that stood on the bank, poked up the fire and put water on to heat. His visitor would undoubtedly be cold, hungry and thirsty. Thorfinn knew which of those needs would be the most urgent. As he heard soft footfalls on the narrow track that led to where the little boat was concealed, he drew out from under his cloak a silver flask of mead.

He smiled again. It was very fine mead, made by his own kinswomen back at home, and he kept a barrel of it stowed away in the prow of the boat. It would warm his guest better than the little fire and the hot food.

'It's me,' a deep voice said softly.

Thorfinn hurried forward and took him in his arms in a bear hug. Then, as the two men broke apart, he thrust the silver flask into his visitor's hand. 'Drink, son,' he said. 'I will prepare food. Then, when you are restored, we will talk.'

And Einar, with a swift grin at the wisdom of his father's priorities, stepped on to the boat, sank down on to the narrow bench that ran around its sides and proceeded to drain the flask.

Quite a short time later, when Einar had wolfed down the savoury porridge and gnawed his way through the strips of dry cured meat, he wiped a large hand across his beard and moustache, turned to Thorfinn and said, 'Is there more of the mead? It's particularly good.'

'It is, isn't it?' Thorfinn reached over to the barrel, deftly filling the flask from it. He watched Einar take another couple of mouthfuls, then, unable to restrain his impatience any longer, said, 'You have news?'

Einar nodded. 'Yes. I waited, just where you suggested, anchoring at Gotland, close to Visby. You reasoned that the returning crew we sought would put in there, and you were right. For many days and weeks, there was no word of them. Others arrived, but few from the right place.' He grinned ruefully. 'My crew began to complain that we were wasting our time and because I could not tell them the true reason for our mission, I was at times hard put to explain why we must not yet leave. But, in the end, Yngvar came.' He gave his father a rueful look. 'You judged your old friend and confidant astutely, Father.'

'And he had news of Skuli?'

'Yes. He told me Skuli had reached Miklagard, making

amazing time. He must have driven his men to the limits of endurance, and, in addition, had extraordinarily good fortune with the winds and tides. They say he managed to cover the many miles of portage in record time – not much over a week, although I find that hard to believe. Apparently he paid out very generously for the strongest ox teams and the toughest men.'

'What of the rapids?' Thorfinn demanded. 'Those seven cataracts are no place for reckless speed; not if you want to reach the far end with your ship and your crew intact.'

'He didn't,' Einar said shortly. 'He lost three crewmen. They say he was reluctant to leave the water and waste time carrying the ship around the obstacles and only did so at the waterfalls, where there was no alternative. He took that fine ship of his straight down the rapids, and it was only because he is such a fine mariner – or maybe because he was so desperate – that he did not come entirely to grief.' He was watching his father intently. With a soft exclamation, he leaned closer, studying the fine old features in the gentle light of the oil lamp. 'This is not news to you,' he breathed. 'Is it?'

'I suspected, but I needed confirmation,' Thorfinn replied.

'Why did you suspect?'

Thorfinn turned away. Then, keeping his face averted, he said, 'Because of the shining stone.'

Einar grabbed at Thorfinn's sleeve, turning him round so that once more they were face to face. 'She's mastered it? *Already?*'

'No, oh, no. That would be far too much to expect. She has a long way to go.' Thorfinn paused. 'She begins to have glimpses, it seems. She can—'

Einar shook his head impatiently, and the small coins braided into the two long plaits either side of his face clinked together. 'I don't care what she can and can't do. Just tell me what she saw.'

'She knew, somehow, that Skuli had reached Miklagard. She also knew he had lost men.'

Einar gave an impatient snort. 'That much she could have guessed. She is not stupid.'

'She is very far from stupid,' Thorfinn countered swiftly. He raised his eyes, studying his son. *Still you do not welcome her, this new kinswoman of ours*, he thought. He had been about to reveal what else Lassair had seen in the stone, but something held him back. 'There was more news of Skuli?' he asked instead.

Einar shrugged. 'He is a driven man, they say, but we already know that. Yngvar reported that he would have to contain his impatience, however, for he would have had to remain in Miklagard for some time. His recklessness at the rapids damaged his ship and, although they managed to patch it up enough to complete the journey south, even Skuli would not risk going on without a fully sound vessel. And he would have needed more hands to replace those lost.' He shook his head. 'It's amazing, given all that has happened, that his crew remain loyal to him. Were they not, they'd surely have slipped away on reaching Miklagard and left him to his madness.'

'Perhaps they share his dream,' Thorfinn murmured.

Einar shot him a glance. 'What dream?'

Still Thorfinn was not ready to share his deepest thought. 'How is the situation in Miklagard?' he asked. 'The city's enemies are close, I believe, and I imagine the emperor is anxious for the safety of his city.'

'Yes, there is much unrest, apparently,' Einar said. 'It's the Seljuks, they say. Miklagard used to be a city where it didn't matter what a man believed or what faith he practised. Its main purpose was trade, and it has always been one of the great meeting places of merchants from east and west, north and south. Now, though, those newly converted Turks want everyone to share their fervour, which makes men of different beliefs anxious. There was an attack on the Jewish quarter in the spring of this year, and many were killed. Then, early in the summer, a series of ferocious conflicts between Christians and Muslims began, from which the city hasn't yet recovered, or, at least, hadn't when Yngvar left.'

Thorfinn sighed. 'It was, I suppose, only to be expected,' he said heavily. 'The presence of an enemy on the doorstep cannot make life easy. And the heat of a southern summer shortens tolerance, so that a man may pick a quarrel with a neighbour over some matter he would usually ignore.'

'That is true,' Einar agreed. 'Although the worst riot was sparked off by a specific act of brutality: the murder of a much-loved local character.'

'Did Yngvar have the whole story?'

'Most of it. The inhabitants were deeply shocked by what happened to the man – he was a Muslim doctor – and the city was still reeling. According to Yngvar, it was still the main talking point several weeks later.'

'This doctor must indeed have been popular,' Thorfinn observed.

'He was a good man, who treated rich and poor alike and only asked in payment what a patient could afford,' Einar said. 'Moreover, he was totally impartial, reasoning that someone who was sick or in pain needed help, no matter in which way he chose to worship God.'

'He sounds like a saint,' Thorfinn said wryly. 'I wonder if he was really as pure and godly as the talk made out, or whether his demise has elevated his reputation.'

Einar shrugged. 'I have no idea,' he said. He glanced at his father. 'Being more concerned with finding out about Skuli, which was what you told me to do, I didn't think to ask Yngvar what he thought about this dead doctor.'

'No, of course not,' Thorfinn said, his tone placating. 'And please do not think I am unappreciative. You have done just what I asked, and I am glad to see you safely returned.'

Einar snorted. 'I was hardly going into danger, sailing into the Baltic and back.'

Thorfinn reached out a hand and lightly touched his son's thick upper arm. 'I know you wanted to pursue Skuli all the way to Miklagard. I had my reasons for commanding you otherwise, and I stand by them.'

'But you're still not going to tell me what they are,' Einar said bitterly, pulling his arm away.

'I—'

Suddenly Einar stood up, although, in the confined head room under the sheltering awning, he could only manage a half crouch. 'Don't worry, I won't ask you again,' he said coldly. Then, pushing aside the heavy fabric, he jumped out on to the bank. 'I'm going back to my ship,' he said. His face was full of anger.

Thorfinn struggled to his feet. But his old bones had stiffened from sitting so long in the confines of the boat, and it was several moments before he was up on the bank and staring after his son. 'Einar!' he called. 'Please, come back.'

He waited a long time. Einar did not return.

Thorfinn retreated back beneath the awning. Moving slowly and deliberately, his distress at his son's abrupt departure echoed in his lethargy, he made his preparations for the night. When he was snug in his bed roll, he extinguished the lamp.

In the darkness, he forced his mind away from thoughts of Einar. He knew he would not sleep otherwise. Instead, he thought about Lassair. Hrype had said she was reluctant to look into the shining stone when she believed she was doing so at another's behest. She wanted to make her own relationship with it; *She treats it like a friend*, Hrype had said.

Thorfinn was filled with conflicting emotions. He was over-joyed that what he had so hoped had turned out to be true, and that the granddaughter of his blood had inherited her forebears' ability with the precious object. But he was also concerned. He of all people knew what the stone could do once it had weaved its way into your mind.

He turned over, trying to get more comfortable. He worried at the problem for a while, realizing that it was just as capable of keeping him awake as thinking about Einar. Frowning in the darkness, he focused his mind and concentrated hard until, even-tually, he saw what he should do next.

With a smile, he closed his eyes and drifted into sleep.

Rollo woke up to find himself in a narrow, hard but clean bed in a shady room that felt pleasantly cool. He turned his head slightly – even the careful movement sent a wave of vertiginous nausea through him – and looked towards the source of the light. Heavy shutters had been closed across the one little window, deeply set high up in the whitewashed stone wall, but a few rays of the brilliant sunshine filtered in through gaps in the slats. He could hear sounds of everyday activity from outside, although they were faint and possibly quite distant.

The room was small and sparsely furnished. Apart from the bed he lay on, there was a low table on which was a lacquered tray of small jars and bottles; a tall blue jug; a cup and a bowl of water, on the rim of which was a piece of wrung-out cloth, neatly folded. Beyond the table was a stout wooden door. There was a large keyhole beneath the door latch, but no sign of the key. Without a doubt, the key was on the other side, and he was locked in. He tried to get off the bed to go and check, but instantly felt so dizzy and weak that he had to give up. A wave of heat ran through him, and he felt sweat break out on his skin. Not fully well yet, then.

He lay back, his thoughts racing. Sunshine . . . It was daytime, then. But which day? How long had he been there? And then, urgently, *Why am I still alive?*

He tried to reason himself out of the terrible anxiety. His last memory had been of someone strangling him, and, thinking back, he thought he could feel again that iron-hard arm thrust around his throat. The voice in his ear had muttered, *I shouldn't go out there if I were you.* Blackness had come down, and he had fallen. He had been trying desperately to get somewhere, and he had an important task to do. He remembered that much, but, try as he might, there was nothing more.

They had caught up with him. Someone, perhaps one of the emperor's officials or one of the spies who would constantly feed information, had received word of him. A stranger acting as he had done – making his sly way into the company of the Varangian guards, asking questions, moving on to search out other members of the emperor's household – was always likely to arouse suspicion. He'd had a very good reason for trying to find someone who had the ear of the emperor, and what he had to impart to Alexius would have been welcome; Rollo was certain of that. But he appreciated now that he had underestimated the climate of suspicion and fear within the city. It was really not the moment to try to creep in unannounced.

So, one of the shadowy men sent to follow and apprehend him had succeeded. He wondered again why he wasn't dead: they'd found their spy, so wouldn't the next step have been to execute him at once, before he had the opportunity to pass on whatever he had discovered?

Then a horrible realization dawned.

They hadn't killed him yet because they wanted to find out what he knew. When he'd been caught, he'd been sick with fever and delirious, and presumably they had decided there was no point in trying to interrogate him until he was in his right mind. To that end, they had cleaned him up, mended his wound – he put experimental fingers up to the cut on his upper arm, feeling the rough edges of several stitches – and nursed him while the fever slowly burned itself out.

Once he was well, they would come for him.

The weakness of illness was still upon him, and for a moment he despaired. What would he do when they began to question him? When they demanded to know why he had been creeping around the Bucoleon Palace, sneaking into the guards' room and asking them questions about some old man called Harald? Trying to find someone in authority who would liaise between him and the emperor? Who would, perhaps, have been persuaded to take him into Alexius's very presence, where, the accusing voices would insist, he planned to pull out a hidden knife and plunge it into the emperor's heart?

That would be difficult to deny once they'd discovered the thin blade he kept hidden inside his boot.

What would happen when they refused to believe that his intentions had been honest? When they laughed in his face as he tried to tell them that his aim all along had been to bring valuable intelligence to the emperor and discuss it, to their mutual benefit?

They would not believe him. And, attempting to get what they thought were more likely answers out of him, they would torture him. He wouldn't be able to give any better answers, since none existed, and so they would not stop. They would carry on, down there in some dark, stinking dungeon from which no prisoner ever emerged, and the world would forget that Rollo Guiscard had ever existed.

Gradually the heat rose up through his body. He thought he saw shapes coming at him out of the shadowy corners of the little room. Nightmare shapes; distorted, unnatural shapes. Then hard on their heels came men with chains, manacles, whips, sharp knives, pincers, long iron spikes whose ends glowed red-hot. As delirium claimed him again, he moaned aloud. Falling deep into hallucination, he raised his hands, feebly trying to push the brutal men and the devilish creatures away.

'Stop that,' a firm male voice said somewhere above him.

Rollo batted his hands against a thick forearm, but his gesture was as feeble as a child's. Whoever it was pushed him back against his pillows, muttering steadily, and, from somewhere very close, there was the sound of trickling water. Then the blessed coolness of a cold, wet cloth across his forehead.

'There's steam coming off you, you're that hot,' said the same voice. Rollo tried to peer through the mists of his fever and make out the man's face, but the cloth was over his eyes, blinding him. 'Rest easy, now,' the man went on, his tone soothing. Rollo heard him move away from the bedside. Then the sound of water again, this time being poured, and presently he felt an arm slide beneath his neck, raising his head slightly. 'Drink,' said the man.

Should I? Rollo wondered wildly. *What if it's poison?*

As if the man read his thoughts, he chuckled. 'It's intended to help you,' he said. 'It's good medicine. You're in the best place for a sick man.'

Helplessly Rollo felt the liquid pour slowly into his mouth. He swallowed, once, twice, again. The taste was odd: very bitter, with an unusual tang, and over everything the sweetness of honey.

'Good, very good,' the man murmured. 'Now, you'll soon feel sleepy again, and I suggest you yield to it. When you wake up, we'll see if you feel like eating, since the sooner you do, the sooner you'll start to get your strength back, which is what we want.'

So you can begin the interrogation, Rollo thought.

He raised a hand and pushed the cloth up, wanting to look on the face of his enemy. But his sense of timing was awry; he'd have sworn the man had only just finished speaking, but already he was in the doorway, about to close the door. The area was deep in shadow, and Rollo caught barely a glimpse. He was left with just an impression of a big, tall, broad-shouldered man; a bulky shape that filled the low doorway.

As the door shut, Rollo waited for his fear to escalate. *I am feeble with fever, helpless, and they wish to make me well purely so that they can torture me into telling them things that aren't true*, he thought wildly.

But the fear didn't come.

After a time, he fell asleep.

* * *

When next he woke, it was deep night. No sound came in from the street outside, and the sky through the partly opened shutters was deepest black. The room was lit by a single candle, set in a metal holder on the little table.

Someone moved in the shadows. The big man loomed over him. 'You've slept long,' he remarked. He put a hand on Rollo's forehead, nodding in satisfaction. 'Fever's down. How do you feel?'

Rollo thought about it. Slowly he did an inventory of his body, inspecting all the places where he had been suffering. 'Better,' he said cautiously. His voice croaked, and instantly the big man poured water in the cup and held it for him while he drank. The water was cool, very refreshing and, as far as he could tell, just that: water.

'You're right,' the man said as he gulped it down, draining the mug. 'It's plain, honest water. No medicine this time.'

'My arm hurts,' Rollo said. He tried to crane round to see the cut. He remembered the feel of the ragged stitches beneath his fingers.

'I'm sorry for the needlework,' said the man. 'It was the best I could do, and I'm not skilled at stitching wounds. The person you really needed isn't here.' His face fell into sadness.

'Thank you, anyway,' Rollo said. 'You did your best.'

'You'll have an interesting scar,' the man remarked. He smiled, although it seemed to Rollo that it took an effort. 'Can you eat, do you think?'

'I'll try.'

Now the man's smile was more genuine. '*Good.* I have prepared simple food. Nothing fancy – bread, cheese, figs, honey.'

At the mention of the items, Rollo's mouth filled with saliva. The man helped him to sit higher in the bed, propping him with more pillows, and then turned away, hurrying out of the room. He returned swiftly, carrying a tray on which there were more candles and platters of food. He unfolded a clean white napkin, spread it out on Rollo's chest and then handed him a piece of bread soaked in olive oil, seasoned with a small sprinkling of salt. Rollo chewed, and the tastes filled his mouth. It was quite possibly the best thing he had ever eaten.

The man perched on the side of the bed, feeding more food

as fast as Rollo consumed it. He was intent on the task, and didn't notice that Rollo was studying him closely.

He was no longer young: perhaps in his fifth decade. His hair was still long, thick and bushy, its reddish-blond colour streaked with wide bands of silver that spread back from the temples. He was large, although not fat; he looked as if he had worked at maintaining his muscular strength, even as age advanced. He was dressed in a simple light robe, belted at the waist with a cord, and his feet were bare. Finally sensing Rollo's intense regard, he looked up from the tray of food and met Rollo's stare. His eyes were large, and light greenish-grey in colour, the rims of the irises circled in deep indigo.

He is a northerner, Rollo thought. *No one whose blood was purely of the south has eyes that colour.*

There was something about him . . .

For some reason Rollo trusted this man, although he could not have said why: in that first instant, it was pure instinct. Pushing that aside, he made himself think logically. *He has tended me to the best of his ability. He is alone, and there has been no indication that this room is guarded. It is not a dark, hidden cellar; we are above the ground, and the street outside is close.*

Something else was niggling at him, and, still eating, he picked away until he found it.

He did not lock me in.

And, following on the heels of that, *I am therefore not his prisoner.*

He proceeded to demolish a plate of figs, dipping them in runny golden honey. The man poured out more water, and he drank it. Then, wiping his fingers on the napkin, he held up his hands to indicate he had eaten enough.

He looked up at the big man. 'Was it you who held me back when I was about to head out into the square before the Bucoleon Palace?' he asked. Memory was galloping back now.

'It was,' the man acknowledged.

'I think you saved me from an act of extreme folly.'

The man grinned. 'I agree.'

'Why were you following me? To protect me?'

'You don't know how this city works,' the man said. 'Few do

who don't live here. Little remains secret for long, and when a stranger starts asking questions, people's ears prick up.'

Which questions? Rollo wondered. The ones he had asked of the Varangians in their guardroom, or the ones he'd posed to the senior official?

'I heard tell they're on the lookout for a man answering your description,' the man continued, 'and I didn't think you'd want to go falling into their hands.'

'Why are you helping me?' Rollo demanded.

The man eyed him cagily. 'First, tell me why you are here in the city. And, come to that, why men of the emperor's most secret and deadly force are after you.'

The moment extended. Rollo, thinking furiously, weighed up his options. They were few, and, on balance, the truth seemed the best. Or, at least, some of it.

'I've been journeying in the south,' he said in the end. 'Syria, Palestine; the lands overrun by the Seljuks.'

'Why?'

'To assess the strengths and weaknesses of the region.' He paused, working out how to give this astute, alert man enough to make his actions credible while keeping back the most intimate details, such as the identity of the man who had sent him and exactly what he had been commanded to discover.

'Again, why?'

'The Turks have advanced spectacularly in a short time,' he said, not answering the question directly, 'but just now they are weak. There is much squabbling and fighting between the many men who would rise up and take the dead sultan's place, and they take their eyes off their borders.' He paused, then said, 'I wanted to speak to someone who had the ear of the emperor, for I wished to know if he too has observed this present frailty. If so, what will he do about it?'

The big man whistled softly. 'You don't want much, do you?' he muttered. 'The ear of the emperor, indeed.'

'I—'

But the man stopped him, holding up a hand. 'You've not told me everything,' he said softly. 'There's something else, and you've decided to keep it to yourself. You're someone's spy, or I'm a Saracen.'

Rollo did not speak.

'Well,' the man sighed, 'I dare say I'd keep that to myself too, in your place. So, you got as far as the inner guard?'

'Yes. They seemed eager to hear what I had to tell them at first. Then – it changed.' He held the other man's eyes. 'I don't suppose you know why?'

'I can provide a pretty good guess,' the big man said. 'They keep watch on comings and goings. Well, you can hardly blame them. They have informants everywhere, and especially on the gates. It seems someone saw you arrive, dressed as a Turk.'

'I'd been travelling in the Turks' lands, for God's sake. Is it any wonder?'

'Don't be so touchy. You asked, I'm telling you.'

'Sorry.'

'Hmm. Anyway, you weren't as discreet as you thought you were. You were seen going into one of the communal bath houses in one guise and emerging in quite another.'

Rollo was impressed. 'Someone's got sharp eyes.'

'Of course,' the big man said wearily. 'What else did you expect? Alexius Comnenus is besieged here, along with all the rest of us. Is it any wonder he keeps a very good lookout for anything out of the ordinary? They think,' he added, almost as a throwaway, 'you're a Turkish spy.'

'I'm not.'

The big man smiled. 'No, I don't believe you are. Like I just said, I reckon you're *someone*'s spy, but, unless you've turned away from your faith, your kin and your own past, it's a lot more likely that it's someone on the other side.'

'You know nothing about me,' Rollo countered quickly. The big man's conclusion was dangerously near the truth.

'Oh, you'd be surprised how much someone reveals about himself when he's in the grip of fever,' the man replied. 'And I have been nursing you for quite some time.'

'Again, why?' Rollo demanded. 'I asked you before, but you merely said you'd heard I was being hunted and you didn't want me to be caught. But why? What am I to you?'

Even watching the big man as closely as he was, he only just spotted the split second of reaction, covered up almost before it had happened. Resuming his bland expression, the big man said,

'I still have many friends and former colleagues among the Varangian Guard. One of them sought me out and said you'd been asking after someone. A man called Harald?'

Instantly Rollo's senses quickened. 'I was,' he agreed.

'My name's Harald, as it happens,' the big man remarked, 'although I'm only one of many. The way I heard it,' he went on, 'this man you're after left England after the Conquest, and you reckon he ended up here in Miklagard.'

'That's what I believe, yes. It's logical, for a man such as him. His family have had no word of him in twenty-five years, and are at a loss to know where he is or what happened to him.'

The big man was watching him closely. 'Many who serve with the Varangians could tell a similar tale,' he remarked.

'He—' Rollo began.

But the big man interrupted. 'England was once my home, too,' he said, 'and, for that reason, and because you are hurt, and far from home, and because I rescued you from your own folly, I feel responsible for you.'

Was that a good thing or a bad one? Rollo didn't speak.

For some time, there was silence in the little room. The big man appeared deep in thought. Rollo guessed he was weighing up the implications of helping a man suspected of spying for the enemy.

Eventually, straightening his shoulders with a firmness that suggested the gesture was intended to restore the backbone in him, the big man said, 'I am all but certain you're a Norman, and by rights I should hate you because you're my former enemy. But I've lived too long to allow an old fight to affect what my heart tells me I should do. You have travelled far from home, on a mission, I'm guessing, for some Norman or Frankish lord who fancies his chances of carving out a bit of the eastern Mediterranean as his own personal fiefdom, and, accordingly, wishes to know the strengths, the weaknesses and, most of all, how the emperor Alexius views the situation.'

His summation was so close to the truth that Rollo did not dare reply. He struggled to keep his expression neutral.

The big man grinned. 'No, I didn't expect you to confirm or deny it,' he said lightly. He fixed Rollo's eyes with his own. 'I do not see you as a threat to this wonderful city that has become my adopted home,' he went on, 'and, I tell you now, if I'm proved wrong, and my actions bring harm to the place and the people I love, then I shall seek you out and kill you with my own two hands. Do we understand one another?'

'We do,' Rollo said.

'Good.' The big man nodded. Then, standing up, he said, 'In that case, I'm going to help you.'

THIRTEEN

I was awake early the next morning. I'd been dreaming about Granny Cordeilla. She had a skillet in her hand and she said, *Use whatever weapon is to hand!* As the image receded, I smiled. She'd been a feisty little woman, my Granny Cordeilla, but, in the way of dreams, reality had been altered slightly. It was my mother, not my grandmother, who had once utilized a cooking implement to lay someone out.

Granny's presence stayed with me as Edild and I began our day. Edild saw a series of patients, and she gave me a long list of tasks. Around noon, she was called to attend the birth of the carpenter's wife's first child. I stopped for a bite to eat, then went back to my chores. Now that I was alone, the sense of Granny's presence intensified.

Whatever weapon is to hand . . . The more I thought about it, the surer I was that my granny hadn't been referring to skillets or frying pans. I *did* have a weapon, of a sort; and it was very closely associated with Granny Cordeilla. Was that what she had meant?

Abandoning my chores, I took the shining stone in its bag out from its hiding place. Then I wrapped myself up in my shawl and, using the rear door, let myself out of the house.

There was really only one place to go. Closely associated as it was with both my grandmother and the shining stone – for the stone had lain hidden with her out there for many years – I struck off across the sodden ground towards the little island where my ancestors lie buried. I knew it was going to be hard going, but the flood waters had receded further overnight and at no point did I get wet higher than my knees. There was, however, no possibility of actually going across to the island; apart from the deep water all around it, only its summit broke the surface.

I made my way to a low rise on which stood a group of willows. Their branches grew thickly, sweeping down close to the ground, and once I had pushed my way within their circle, I was hidden from the casual glance. I found a reasonably dry spot among the roots of the largest tree, sat down and took out the shining stone.

I'd been anticipating the moment when I had a proper look into its depths purely because *I* wanted to, rather than at another's request. I'd been both excited and curious, and I'd also been apprehensive. Now that the time had come, apprehension was the dominant emotion, swiftly escalating to fear.

I held the heavy stone in my palms, staring down into it. It was black; shiny, unrelieved black. It was dormant, inert. Nothing was going to happen; I'd—

But then it changed.

I'm not entirely sure what I saw in its depths. I saw vision after vision, one scene succeeding another in the blink of an eye. I saw myself, as I understood myself to be. I saw another me, and it felt as if the shining stone was drawing out of me aspects of myself that had always been there, had I but troubled to look. I had no idea how it was happening – it was as if the stone's presence in my hands was somehow allowing me to see with far clearer eyes.

It seemed to be aware of my present concerns. It *told* me things; or, perhaps, it helped me to use my own knowledge, reason and wits to understand what had previously been hidden. It could be that, sensing I had a new and very powerful entity very firmly on my side – there was absolutely no doubting that – I had, for the first time in my life, the confidence truly to be myself; to trust my own judgement.

I leaned back, stretching my neck, shoulders and back, making myself relax, about to wrap the stone in its wool and put it safely away. But it hadn't finished with me.

Out of nowhere, I saw those narrow eyes again. Now the fierce intent glittered out of them, and the features of the face clarified into an unreadable mask. This was a man intent on violence – of the most brutal, irrevocable sort – yet he was detached; whatever terrible act he was about to do, it would not be performed out of any deep emotion.

Who is he? I asked the question inside my head, praying the stone would answer. I saw a swift succession of images – the track leading out of the village; the drowned woman; Jack and me by the pool where she'd been found; the derelict monastery where we'd slept in the hay. Was this man her murderer? Had I been right when I'd felt his eyes on me, heard the whistle of the knife flying towards me to take my life?

I couldn't bear any more. Swiftly I covered the stone with my hands, blocking it from my sight. I didn't know what to do: should I stay where I was, hidden among the bare willows? Should I break cover and run as fast as I could back to the village? But the ground was waterlogged, and fast running all but impossible. He'd spot me instantly, and even my best speed would be no match for that silver blade . . .

Then I realized something. It might have been the stone, communicating with me; it might have been my own common sense, fighting to be heard, but, when I made myself stop to think, I noticed that I wasn't afraid. Whoever it was, watching and waiting his moment, just then he was no threat to me. *I* was safe; but I wasn't the only one who mattered.

I had to go . . .

I looked down at the stone. Did I trust it? Did I trust myself?

As if I was watching someone else, I saw myself put the stone back in its bag and stand up. I brushed down my skirts, wrapped my shawl around me and strode out from under the willows, setting off for the village at a steady pace that was nowhere near a panicky run.

I had my answer.

It was late afternoon when I reached the village. I'd been out for hours; far longer than I'd thought. I wondered if the shining stone somehow altered the perception of time. It seemed quite possible. I let myself into Edild's house, and saw straight away that she was not back. I poked up the fire, building it up until I had a cheery blaze, then set water on to boil in order to prepare food. I was ravenous, and Edild would need to eat when she came in.

Presently there was a knock on the door. I got up, opened it and saw Jack standing outside. I felt a huge wave of relief. I'd known it would be him. 'Come in,' I said.

He did so, settling on the floor beside the fire and holding out his hands to the flames. 'That feels good,' he murmured. Then, raising his eyes to look at me, he said, 'I came looking for you earlier. Nobody was at home.'

'No,' I agreed. 'Why did you want to see me?'

'I thought you might have come with me again to help me look for Harald Fensman's clan,' he said. 'I wanted—' But then he stopped, and whatever he'd been about to add remained unsaid.

'Did you have any luck?'

He shook his head. 'No.'

'And you were going to talk to Lady Rosaria last night – did you?'

'Not for long,' he replied. 'Lord Gilbert is very protective. A sheriff's officer is not permitted to interrogate a lady.' His tone was carefully neutral.

'Do you think she's recovering?'

He shrugged. 'I'm not sure I can say, since I've never known what's wrong with her. What do you think, healer woman?'

I made myself concentrate. It wasn't easy, when other things were batting about in my head, clamouring to be said. *All in good time*, I told myself. 'Undoubtedly she's had some very bad experience,' I said. 'She, her baby son and her maid took ship from their home in northern Spain to Bordeaux, where they changed vessels and came up to Lynn aboard *The Good Shepherd*. The maid was very sick, and had to be helped ashore at Lynn. Lady Rosaria and her son then went on to Cambridge alone.' I looked at Jack. 'Can it be that the maid falling ill and perhaps dying was enough to cause Lady Rosaria's state of deep shock?'

He shrugged. 'What else is there?'

I thought for a moment. 'Did she speak of her circumstances back in Spain? She mentioned her husband's father, but was there anyone else?'

'There was *his* old father, who was called Leafric – she did reveal that last night – but he died years ago,' Jack said. 'If there

were other family members, she'd surely have turned to them
rather than set out for England.'

'She told you her husband's grandfather was called Leafric?'

'That's right.'

'Yes, that tallies. She told me her son is named after a forebear
of her husband's.'

'Is that relevant?'

Slowly I shook my head. 'I'm not sure.' Funny things were
happening inside my mind. I had the feeling that we'd just
stumbled on something important.

I said, 'We too have a Harald whose father was called Leafric.'

There was quite a long silence. Then he said, 'Are you sure?'

I smiled. 'I'm the family bard.' I remembered all those endless
hours with Granny Cordeilla, and how she would test me over
and over again until I stopped making mistakes. 'My father's
mother was called Cordeilla, and it was her youngest brother
who was called Harald. Along with his two elder brothers, he
fought at the great battle, and he was the only one who survived.
The family never saw him again, and my granny always said
he'd left his homeland rather than bend his neck before the
conquerors.' As soon as the words were out of my mouth, I
wished I'd been more diplomatic, since the son of one of those
conquerors was sitting beside me. 'Harald and Cordeilla's father
was called Leafric.'

After a pause, Jack said, 'So your family has a missing
relative called Harald, who left England and might well have
ended up in Spain. His father's name was Leafric. Now here we
are, with a woman who claims her father-in-law was called Harald
Fensman, and *his* father was called Leafric. Do you think it's
possible we're referring to the same man?'

'Possible, yes,' I agreed, 'but highly unlikely. For one thing,
nobody in the family heard from Harald after he disappeared.
There's nothing whatsoever to suggest he went to Spain, and, as
far as we know, he didn't. Why would he?'

'As far as you know,' Jack repeated softly. 'But what *do* you
know?'

I was stumped. 'I'm not sure.' Had there ever been any hint
of what had happened to Harald? If he had contacted anyone in
the family, then the most likely person was his sister Cordeilla,

my grandmother. She'd always said they were close. It was too late to ask her, but I could do the next best thing: I could speak to her two favourite children, my aunt Edild and my own father. 'I'll ask,' I said, 'and—'

'What's the other thing?'

'Huh?'

'You said, for one thing, and that usually suggests there's going to be at least one more.'

'Oh, yes. The other thing is that my great-uncle really couldn't be Lady Rosaria's father-in-law, because he wasn't rich and his kin didn't have wide estates and luxurious houses. He came from kin just like mine.'

I hoped he would nod his head in agreement, and we'd finally abandon the idea of Lady Rosaria having anything to do with me and my family.

He didn't.

'Harald Fensman became a man of position and status, that's for sure,' he said instead. 'But how do we know what his circumstances were when he first arrived in Spain?'

I had a horrible feeling that I knew what he was going to say. 'Don't,' I muttered.

He must have picked up my distress. He leaned closer to me, and I felt my hand being enclosed in his. 'Does it upset you so much?' he said gently.

'The thought that Lady Rosaria's late father-in-law was my Granny Cordeilla's youngest brother, which means she is related by marriage to my family, and we'll have to look after her when all the time she'll be looking down that long nose of hers, dismissing my poor mother's cooking and housekeeping, despising my beloved father's lowly occupation and treating the rest of us like slaves? Oh yes, it distresses me, all right!'

To my shame, I found I was crying; great sobs were bursting out of me. Jack gave a soft sound of sympathy, put his arms round me and drew me tightly against him.

He felt so strong.

After a while, I sat up and dried my eyes. 'I'm better now,' I said.

He smiled, and I tried to respond, but failed. Then he said, his mouth quirking as if trying not to laugh, 'You don't know she's got a long nose.'

'*What?*' I was already grinning.

'None of us have seen her without that veil,' he pointed out. 'For all you know, she may have the most pert and lovely little nose.'

If his intention had been to cheer me up, he had succeeded. He had released me from the hug, but now he took hold of my hand again. 'I'm not belittling how you feel,' he said. 'If I were in your position, I'd feel just the same. The thought of Lady bloody Rosaria as a permanent house guest is abhorrent.'

'And you don't even know how small my parents' house is,' I put in.

'Oh, I expect I do,' he replied. 'But, dear Lassair, I think you may be overlooking something.'

'What?'

He paused, then: 'It's not only Lady Rosaria who's looking for a kind, loving family to take her in, is it?'

I knew what he meant. Instantly the outlook became a lot better. 'No,' I said. 'There's the baby, too.'

'And you've developed quite an affection for Leafric.' He squeezed my hand. 'Wouldn't it make her more tolerable, if he was also part of the arrangement?'

I nodded. 'Yes, I suppose so. Whatever has happened, and whatever she has become, he's not to blame.'

'Indeed he's not,' Jack agreed, and I was surprised at the vehemence in his voice. 'The innocent never are, yet so often it's they who suffer most.'

I looked at him. Something had sparked off a memory, and it clearly wasn't a happy one.

It was my turn to squeeze his hand. I went on holding it, even after the need for a kind touch was past, for the moment seemed right to speak. 'Jack, there's something I must tell you.'

'Hm?' He didn't sound very interested; perhaps his mind was still on his memories.

'It's important,' I went on. 'We're in danger.'

Now I had his attention. His green eyes fixed on mine and he said urgently, 'What makes you think that?'

I don't think, I know, I said silently. *The shining stone doesn't deal in uncertainties.* 'Remember, beside the pool where the drowned woman was found, we speculated that her killer might be watching us?'

'Yes,' he said.

'That wasn't the only time I've sensed eyes on me. Today, I felt his presence again –' it hadn't been quite like that, but I wasn't ready to explain about the stone – 'and I am certain he means to harm us.' I met Jack's intent stare. 'To be precise, he means to harm *you*.' Before he could interrupt, I hurried on. 'It makes sense, doesn't it? If he's worried because he thinks we've found out something that incriminates him, then it's you, as the lawman, he'll want to get rid of.'

I'm not sure what I expected; it certainly hadn't been that Jack would smile. 'I appreciate your concern,' he said, 'and I'm grateful.' He was getting up, preparing to leave.

'But—'

He looked down at me, staring right into my eyes. 'Lassair, if I took account of all the men who wish me harm – who wish to kill me, no doubt – I'd never leave the safety of my house.'

I stood up too, and stood face to face with him. 'I really do believe your life is at risk.' I hesitated. 'I can't tell you why, but please don't dismiss it.'

'I'm not dismissing it!' The denial came so swiftly that I knew it was sincere. 'And I'll be careful. I promise.'

Something in his direct gaze was disturbing me; I turned away. 'I'll walk with you some of the way,' I muttered.

He went as if to stop me, but then, with a shrug, nodded.

There was rain in the air; it was not yet falling, but it would very soon. We were passing the church when I felt eyes on me. I spun round, my heart thumping in alarm, but then I saw who it was. 'Just a minute,' I said to Jack. I ran across the track.

Standing deep in the shadow beneath the ancient yew tree in the churchyard was Hrype, cloaked and hooded, his face concealed and his silvery eyes glinting in the fading light.

'Why are you hiding?' I whispered.

'I have my reasons,' he said gruffly. Then, glancing out to where Jack stood waiting, he said acidly, 'I won't keep you from your *friend*.' Only he could imbue that pleasant, inoffensive word with such dark meaning. 'You're to come out with me tonight. There's a task you must perform.'

'*Must?*' I repeated, instantly angry. 'On your orders, Hrype?'

He gave a sound expressing his impatience. 'No. The prime concern isn't mine.' He hesitated. 'There is someone else; someone who—'

'Lassair?' Jack called. 'Are you all right?'

'Get rid of him!' Hrype hissed.

'No!' I hissed back.

Hrype muttered a curse, and then, as both of us stepped out from the shadows, I witnessed the extraordinary thing I'd seen once or twice before: Hrype changed his appearance. Somehow, using no more than adjustments in how he stood, his attitude and how he held his head, he turned from a tall, straight and proud man in vigorous middle age to a cringing, crippled peasant, worn down to decrepitude by decades of toil. In a thin, reedy voice quite unlike his own, he looked up at Jack, bowed and said, 'Good evening to you, sir.' Pulling his hood forward to conceal his face, he slipped away.

I knew why he had stopped me. He wanted me to look into the shining stone; to attempt once more to extract what he so badly wanted to know. My first reaction was to feel distressed and afraid.

Then, as I stood staring after Hrype, another emotion stirred. The shining stone was rightfully in my keeping; my own grandfather had told me so. It had been in his possession and he had given it to my Granny Cordeilla, trusting her to keep it safe until the right hands were ready to receive it.

Those hands were mine.

I wanted to be left alone with the stone. To form my own links with it; to explore it slowly, waiting to see what it offered in return. Discovery promised to be an exciting, seductive and mysterious path, and, that very afternoon, I had made my first solo steps on it.

I was no longer prepared to use the stone at someone else's bidding, even that of a man as powerful and persuasive as Hrype. I raised my chin, squared my shoulders and gave a nod.

Beside me, Jack gave a soft laugh and said, 'Have you finished?'

I spun round, to see that he was studying me closely. 'What?' I demanded sharply.

'You've just been going through some personal crisis, I'd say,' he replied, his tone mild. He jerked his head in the direction in which Hrype had melted away. 'That man asked you to do something, and you don't want to. At first you looked cowed, and you started chewing on your thumbnail in the way you always do when you're worried. Then you made up your mind you were going to be strong – I saw it in your face – and refuse him.'

Chewing on my thumbnail? *Really?* Surreptitiously I glanced down at my hand: four decent nails on the fingers, and the one on the thumb nibbled down to its limit.

I looked up, straight into Jack's clear, honest eyes. He said softly, 'Lassair, you can tell me it's nothing to do with me, but I'd like to help you.'

I didn't answer. I just went on looking at him.

'I'm trying to tell you that you can trust me, which isn't really fair when you know next to nothing about me,' he said. 'You know where I live and what my work is. As I said, I was once a soldier, and the change from fighting man to lawman was an obvious and relatively easy step.' He hesitated, weighing his words. 'I dislike and distrust the man who gives me my orders – Picot is a crook and a rogue, out to make his own fortune – but I believe it is right to have laws, and that those laws must be upheld and defended. The alternative is every man for himself, and, under that regime, the strong prosper and the weak are trampled in the dust.'

I nodded. Rollo had once said something very similar.

My thoughts veered away from Rollo as if I'd been burned.

Jack shrugged, and I sensed his passionate explanation of himself had made him uneasy.

Then, thinking back, I remembered something he had said earlier: *the innocent are never to blame, yet so often it's they who suffer most.*

I looked at him. As if he was prepared for my scrutiny and wanted to stand firm before it, he stared right back at me. He stood easily, yet, even at rest, his broad shoulders and chest revealed his solid strength. What had he been through to be such a champion of the weak, the innocent and the powerless? Had he been a Saxon, I could have understood, for you didn't have to walk many miles to find people who had suffered appallingly when the Normans came; people whose lives had been changed in a flash from comfort and security to wretched poverty and brutal violence. In the red-hot mood of conquest, William the Bastard, his lords and his soldiers had had neither the time nor the inclination to be merciful.

But Jack Chevestrier hadn't even been born back in 1066. No blame could attach to him personally for William the Conqueror's barbarities.

Still he did not speak. He was waiting, I thought, to see what I would do. Whether I would trust him or keep my secrets to myself.

After what seemed a long time, I said, 'I *have* made up my mind about something.' I paused, for I wanted this to sound right. 'I do believe you wish to help me, and I'm grateful.' He began to speak, but I stopped him. 'I'm not ready to tell you what it's about,' I hurried on, 'but please understand that it's not because I don't trust you. I do.'

His eyes widened.

'I'm honoured,' he said after a moment, his voice low. 'I respect your right to privacy, but, if you change your mind, I'll be there.'

For no very clear reason, suddenly I felt moved almost to tears. I sensed that Jack rarely made such offers, and that he had just presented me with a very precious gift.

He looked at me, his face solemn. 'Lassair, sometimes the hardest thing is standing up for yourself, especially when you're accustomed to doing what others tell you.' He paused. 'For all of us, there's a moment when we have the chance to assert ourselves, and if we fail to take it, that moment sets the pattern for the rest of our lives.' He paused, his clear green eyes holding mine. 'I just wanted to say,' he concluded, 'that, if this is your moment, make the most of it.'

He smiled briefly, then turned and walked away.

Just then, the first drops of rain began to fall: heavy, insistent. Jack broke into a run, haring off up the track towards the shelter of Lakehall as if the god of thunder were after him. I pulled my shawl over my head and hurried off to Edild's house before I was soaked through.

As I flung the door open and burst inside, desperate to be out of the increasingly awful weather, I could still hear Jack's parting words inside my head. Despite being drenched, I felt as warm as if I'd been sitting snug beside the fire.

Edild came in late, tired but satisfied; the carpenter's wife had been delivered of a healthy girl. She fell on the food I'd prepared, and, while she ate, I remembered my resolve to ask if she knew anything about the disappearance of Granny Cordeilla's brother Harald.

'Edild,' I began, 'did Granny Cordeilla speak much about her three brothers?'

'She had four,' Edild corrected. 'One of them, Sihtric, became a monk.'

I had forgotten about Granny's cloistered brother; it tended to happen when a family member shut themselves away within an enclosed order. But Sihtric the monk wasn't the man I was interested in. 'Tell me about Harald,' I said

'He was a likeable man,' my aunt said, her expression softening. 'He was big and brawny, like so many of the men of the family, but kind-hearted beneath the tough, bluff exterior. Cordeilla took his loss hard,' she added quietly, 'and missed him sorely. It troubled her greatly, not knowing his fate.'

'Could he have died at Hastings, like the other two?' I asked. I felt very guilty about the rush of hope that rose up in me. I might have preferred Harald dead in battle to Harald as the father-in-law of Lady Rosaria, but that wasn't very fair on him.

But Edild was shaking her head. 'No, he survived the fighting.' She paused. 'He was seen running away.'

It sounded as though Edild thought that was something to be ashamed of. 'Running for his life, surely?' I protested. 'His king was defeated and lay dead, and his brothers Sagar and Sigbehrt had perished defending him.' Edild did not answer. 'Was he not right, to try to save himself?' I asked in a small voice.

'Perhaps, but Cordeilla believed he should have brought their bodies home to the island to be buried among our kin, and she was deeply upset.' Edild closed her eyes, as if the memories pained her.

'And she had no idea where he went or what became of him?' It seemed unkind to press her, but I really needed to know.

Edild shrugged. 'She was convinced he'd left England,' she said. 'Otherwise, she believed, he would have found some way to send word to her of his fortunes. Or lack of them,' she added grimly.

'Could he have gone to Spain?' I asked timidly.

'Spain?' She shot me a look. 'Why would he have gone to Spain?'

'To make his fortune?' I suggested.

She gave a short laugh. 'And just how do you imagine he'd have gone about it, in a strange, foreign land where he had no kin, no friends, no contacts and, other than his abilities as a fighter, no skills?'

I nodded, accepting the wisdom of her words. Then – for she had folded her lips in a tight line, as if to indicate that the conversation was over – I started to clear away the supper.

Afterwards, tired out by my long day, I dozed by the hearth. When I'd drifted off, it had still been raining hard, the wind howling like a savage animal, and I'd thought that not even Hrype's urgency would yield before such a violent storm. But the rain must have stopped, for when there was a soft tap on the door and Hrype came into the room, he was quite dry.

'Are you ready?' he demanded, glaring at me. 'Fetch the stone,' he added, not waiting for my reply, 'and we'll be on our way.'

I stayed where I was. Edild, on the opposite side of the fire, watched each of us in turn. Noticing her interest, Hrype made a low exclamation, then, grabbing hold of me, ushered me outside. The sky had cleared, I noticed, and it was a fine night, the moon just rising and shedding a pale light on the damp ground.

Hrype looked down at me, half-frowning, half-smiling. 'I thought you'd be ready and eager to go,' he remarked. 'Especially after I told you who we'd be visiting tonight.'

'You didn't tell me anything of the sort!' I flashed back.

'Yes I did – I said there was someone else!'

'But you didn't say who it was,' I said with exaggerated patience.

He studied me. 'I didn't think that was necessary.'

'But—'

He sighed. 'Think, Lassair. You know what it is I want you to try to decipher from within the shining stone.'

'Yes, of course. You want to know what Skuli's doing and where he's going.'

'Yes?' He looked at me enquiringly.

Then I knew. It was obvious, and Hrype had been right to assume I'd have worked it out for myself. There was only one person who was intimately connected with both the stone and Skuli, and I'd been thinking about him only that afternoon. I'd had no idea he was anywhere near, and the thought that he was, and that, moreover, I seemed to be on my way to go and see him, made my heart sing for joy.

I grinned at Hrype. 'I'll fetch the stone,' I said.

I slipped back inside and removed the stone from its place of concealment. Edild watched me, but made no comment. I felt guilty but if Hrype had chosen not to enlighten her, it wasn't up to me to do so. With an apologetic smile, I wrapped myself in my shawl, went outside again and closed the door.

Then, hurrying to keep up with his long strides, I set off behind Hrype to go and find my grandfather.

FOURTEEN

'If I try to get you out via the gates in the land walls,' the big man said, 'we won't stand a chance, and both of us will fetch up in the emperor's dungeons in neighbouring shackles while they decide how best to wrest the truth out of us. Yes, *I* know you're no threat and have no terrible secrets to reveal.' He spoke over Rollo's interruption. 'But if they are convinced you're a spy, then that's how you'll be treated, and, believe me, you don't want that fate.'

'And you think they'd deal with you the same way?' Rollo asked.

'There's no *think* about it,' Harald replied grimly. 'If and when they finally decide we're telling them the truth, there won't be much left of us that's still in one piece, and we'll wish we were dead.'

Rollo didn't want to dwell on that. 'So, we'll get away by sea.'

'*You* will,' Harald corrected. 'I'm not going anywhere.' His expression saddened. 'This is my home, for better or worse, and I'll live out my days here.' He gave a deep sigh, as if the prospect pained him. Then, with a visible effort, he looked up at Rollo and said, 'As it happens, I know someone who's sailing west in the very near future.'

'Sailing *west*?' Rollo echoed. What did that mean? He needed to get back to England; if he couldn't share the intelligence he'd gathered so laboriously with Alexius in exchange for some hint as to the emperor's intentions, then he must return to King William and reveal the discoveries to him.

Harald smiled briefly. 'Just a turn of phrase. Everything's west, to us out here in the east. This man is going to England.'

'You're sure?' Rollo persisted.

'Yes, yes,' Harald replied impatiently, waving a hand as if to brush away the question. 'That's where he came from, so that's where he'll return.' He paused. 'It's odd, because, now I come to think of it, you're not the first man I've encountered recently who claims kinship or acquaintance with people in the east of England. This man I'm thinking of—' But he stopped, shaking his head. 'It's not surprising, I suppose, when we still get so many arrivals who have sailed down the old route.'

Rollo was hardly listening. The prospect of a saviour, ready and waiting to take him away and out of danger, was all-absorbing. 'What sort of vessel?' he demanded. 'Merchantman?'

Harald gave him a sly glance. 'Not exactly.' Before Rollo could ask more, Harald said, 'First things first. You only got up out of your sick bed yesterday, so you ought to test yourself to see if your strength is returning. It's not going to be easy getting you down to the harbour, and I don't want you collapsing on me.'

For the rest of that day, Rollo alternated spells of increasingly demanding activity – Harald seemed to know a lot about putting a man through a strict drill – with periods of lying, panting, sweating and spent, on his bed. His appetite increased, and Harald fed him well. By evening, he felt he was starting to return to his usual form. The wound in his arm was healing, and his fever had not returned. He reckoned he was ready.

Harald agreed. 'We'll spend tomorrow as we spent today,' he said, as Rollo prepared, with great relief, to turn in for the night. 'Then, once darkness falls, I'll get you down to the quay.'

'Will this man be expecting me?' Rollo asked. 'And is he willing to take an extra passenger?'

'He is,' Harald said. 'I saw him this morning when I went out for provisions. He was reluctant, but finally saw the benefits.'

Instantly Rollo was suspicious. 'What do you mean, *benefits*?'

'Never you mind,' Harald said. 'Get some sleep.'

The next day tested Rollo's nerves to the limit. Knowing he was about to get away made him desperate with impatience, and the hours crept by with unbelievable sloth. He was also apprehensive: he and Harald would be out after curfew, and the prospect of evading the watch as the two of them made their stealthy way down to the shore was little short of terrifying. At one point, unable to restrain himself, he asked why they didn't go in the daytime, but Harald merely said, 'Leave it to me. I know what I'm doing.'

Harald had cleaned the blood off Rollo's tunic and mended the rent in his shirt where the knife had cut, and Rollo was touched to see that the old man had also polished his boots. Not that the small kindnesses came as a surprise; in the many hours they had spent in each other's company, Rollo had learned a great deal about Harald.

As Rollo lay on his bed in the late afternoon, trying to obey Harald's injunction to rest while he could, he thought about the man who had so readily cast himself in the role of Rollo's saviour. Harald was a generous man, and he had opened his heart to his unexpected guest. Rollo had learned many things: some that had shocked him, some that had moved him to deep pity; some that, when he came to reflect, he sensed he had known all along. And in the end, when the two men who had so recently been strangers had finally finished the last of their long, soul-baring conversations, Harald had made a request, and Rollo had promised to do his utmost to fulfil it.

What Harald had asked explained, in part, why he was prepared to lay his neck on the block to help Rollo get away.

Harald prepared a good, sustaining evening meal, but now, his tension rapidly increasing, Rollo had little appetite. The daylight faded and darkness deepened. Finally, Harald looked at him and said, 'Ready?'

'Yes.'

Harald handed him a heavy cloak made of grey wool, its hood bordered with braid. 'The watch wear similar garments on chilly nights,' he said. He didn't elaborate.

Rollo's apprehension deepened.

They stepped out into the night. For the first time, Rollo saw the outside of the house where his life had been saved. It was built of small reddish bricks, some courses of which had been laid in decorative patterns. He spotted a series of chevrons and a herringbone design. The house was modest in size, but no expense appeared to have been spared. As in the interior, the best materials and craftsmen had been used. It was situated up on one of the city's hills, high above the tumultuous tangle of streets far below, and soaring over the towers and domes of the glorious imperial buildings and the many churches.

For a few moments, Rollo simply stood and drank in the beauty of the Queen of Cities spread out beneath him, her stonework glimmering pale and silver in the moonlight against the backdrop of the deep navy sky. Then Harald gave him a nudge, and muttered, 'Come on. We should keep moving.'

The street descended steeply, in places turning into a flight of stone steps. Rollo wondered how Harald had managed to carry him up to his house; perhaps he'd had help. He should have asked . . .

Harald was moving swiftly but with great caution, darting from one patch of shadow to the next, his eyes everywhere, staring ahead, behind, and to the side in a repetitive pattern. He seemed to be leading them down on the opposite side from the Golden Horn. Wherever the ship awaiting Rollo lay at anchor – unless Harald planned to double back on himself – it must be on the Sea of Marmara side. *So much the better*, Rollo thought. *Less far to sail under the watchful eyes of those up on the sea walls.*

Presently he caught sight of those sea walls. They were battle-
mented, and along their city-facing side ran a long parapet from
which defenders would fire down on attackers. He was about to
make some comment to Harald when suddenly, breaking the
night's stillness, came the sound of boots on stone: five, maybe
six, marching men.

Quick as a snake, Harald stepped into a narrow, dark alley,
dragging Rollo in behind him. Already the light of the watchmen's
flaring torches was splashing against the walls rising on either
side of the street. With a violent gesture, Harald dragged Rollo's
hood over his face, pushing his head down into his chest.

Rollo could hardly believe he had forgotten his training.
Usually it was automatic to cover his head, knowing as he did
that the pale oval of a face glowed in the dark, and the bright,
liquid surface of a pair of eyes caught and reflected the light like
a sheet of glass.

Once again, it seemed, Harald had saved him from disaster.

The watch passed – far too close – and Harald held Rollo
back for a long time after they had gone. 'Varangians,' he said
very softly, right in Rollo's ear. 'Three of them I know very well.'

When at last they stepped out on to the street once more,
Rollo's sense of vulnerability had greatly increased. He could
make out the sea walls quite clearly now, and they were a
formidable obstacle. He had no idea how Harald proposed to
get him past them: through one of the gates? But surely there
would be sentries, primed to be on the lookout for a man
answering Rollo's description.

They edged down a wider street, then branched off down a
very steep, narrow alley; little more than a crack between two
tall buildings rising high on either side. The alley's sides seemed
to be closing in, and Rollo feared they would not be able to
get through. Then, abruptly, Harald turned to his right, bending
double to crawl beneath a low archway, its sides and top faced
with bricks. In pitch darkness, he led the way onwards for
perhaps a dozen paces, then stopped again. It was too dark for
Rollo to see but, from the sounds, it seemed Harald was feeling
along the brickwork that formed the sides of the tunnel,
searching for something.

With a grunt of satisfaction, he found it. There was a series of metallic sounds – Rollo caught the chink of keys – and a scratching sound as Harald thrust open a heavy wooden door, slightly lower than the arch through which they had entered the passage. He pushed Rollo inside, then crawled in after him, turning to close and re-lock the door. Having no idea where he was, nor on what he was standing – it could have been the edge of a precipice, or the top of a flight of steps – Rollo stayed very still. There was the rasp of a flint, and then a light flared, very bright in the utter darkness.

'Now we can risk a flame,' Harald said, satisfaction in his voice. 'It won't be spotted in here.' He held up the torch, and Rollo stared round in amazement.

They were indeed at the top of a flight of steps. Carved out of stone and perilously steep, they descended into the darkness below. 'Where are we?' he whispered.

Harald grinned, pale teeth flashing amid the heavy beard. 'This joins up with a passage leading from beneath the palace,' he replied. 'The palace is that way –' he pointed ahead – 'and we need to turn south and a little west. There's a series of these passages,' he added, 'running from the walls back into the heart of the city.'

'How did you know that door was there?'

'Privileged information.' Harald tapped the side of his nose. 'I was a Varangian guard, remember. We who defend the emperor need to know how to get him out of danger, in any and every way we can devise.'

'You just said the passage runs *from* the walls,' Rollo said as they began the long descent. 'It's not going to help us if we emerge on the city side, is it?'

Harald sighed. 'Use your head,' he said. 'Do you imagine I'd be bringing you down here in the subterranean dankness and darkness if I didn't know a way to get you out safely? On the *other* side of the sea walls?'

'But such a route, evading the walls, surely makes the defences vulnerable?' Rollo protested.

With exaggerated patience, Harald said, 'Not if nobody knows about it except the emperor's personal bodyguard.'

That made sense, Rollo thought. Very good sense: if ever an enemy succeeded in bursting through Constantinople's formidable defences and breaking into the palace, then it was wise indeed to have a secret way of getting the emperor out to safety.

'You Varangians appear to have thought of everything,' he remarked.

'We try,' said Harald modestly.

There followed a long time of slipping and sliding down endless steps, scrambling over unseen obstacles and crawling through impossibly tight tunnels lined with cold, damp stone. At one point they emerged into a vast open space, in which a series of deep stone-lined cisterns extended under a vaulted roof. 'Emergency water supply in case of siege,' Harald said. 'The Romans built them.'

At last they reached the end of the passage. For the final hundred paces or so, they had hurried down a long incline to a lower depth – Harald said they were going under the sea walls – and, just as abruptly, steep steps had risen up again. Rollo had been aware of passing through a succession of strong iron grilles, one at the start of the tunnel under the walls, one in the middle and one at the far end. Each had opened with a clang and a clatter as Harald wielded his keys and removed the chains that bound them shut.

Now they stood close together in a small, cramped space, the opening of the tunnel behind them and, before them, a wall made of huge blocks of stone. Harald slapped it with the palm of his hand. 'The outer skin of the sea wall,' he said. 'Hundreds of years old, and as impregnable as the day it was built.'

Turning away, he bent low, and again there came the sound of jingling keys. Then, perhaps half a man's height from the base of the wall, a small round aperture appeared, about the size of the top of a barrel. There was a sudden and very welcome inflow of fresh air. It was cool, and scented with the salt of the sea and the tang of seaweed. Rollo filled his lungs, once, then again. Looking up at him with a grin, Harald said, 'There's plenty more of that outside. Give me your pack – I'll throw it out after you. Off you go,' and indicated the hole.

Rollo folded his shoulders forward and thrust himself through the gap. But Harald grabbed his arm, holding him back. 'Best go feet first,' he advised. 'There's a bit of a drop.'

That, Rollo thought as he landed hard, instinctively bent his knees and landed in a heap on his side, was an understatement. He struggled to his knees, then fell back again, suppressing a cry of pain, as his pack landed on his head. A short time later, Harald jumped down beside him.

Rollo stared up at the vast walls soaring up behind them. There was no sign of the hole through which they'd just emerged. 'Where's it gone?' he whispered.

'I shut it up again,' Harald replied.

'But – but I can't even see it!'

'That's the general idea,' Harald remarked. Then, suddenly serious, he added, 'Don't imagine the possibility of enemies gaining access that way didn't occur to the men who made that tunnel. At the landward end, there are great tanks of sea water, and if ever an invader managed to discover that opening –' he jerked a thumb up at the sea wall – 'the tunnel would instantly be flooded.'

An image filled Rollo's head: men struggling through that dark, rough, narrow gap; single file, hampered by the weapons they bore; shouts and curses. Then a sound from hell: water, broiling and rushing down to engulf them. Panic as those in the front desperately tried to turn, to push back against the men crowding behind them. The first overwhelming attack of the water . . .

'The tanks are always kept full,' Harald said. 'But, fortunately for you and me, they are very well maintained and they don't leak.'

Rollo shook the pictures of horror out of his mind. Then, firmly turning his back on the sea walls, he took his first proper look at the scene before him.

They were right at the south-western end of the long shore that faced the Sea of Marmara, and the city rising up on its hills seemed already distant. Spinning round, he stared back along the quays and the many harbours, and the impression was of a stretch of water full of seagoing vessels of every kind. Many of the quays were well-lit and guarded, but the spot where he and Harald stood was in deep shadow. It was very still and quiet. Rollo could hear the sound of small waves splashing as they broke on the shore, and a soft rasp of pebbles as the water receded again.

'You've brought me to a beach!' he said in an angry whisper, turning to glare at Harald. 'No ship can tie up here.'

Harald grinned. 'Not *just* a beach.' He pointed, and, stretching out into the smooth water, Rollo saw the dark silhouette of a wooden jetty. 'See?' he added quietly. 'I told them exactly where to meet us.'

Hurrying forward, Rollo peered out into the darkness, hardly able to credit what lay alongside the jetty.

It was a sinuous, graceful shape, perhaps twenty paces long, riding low in the water. The end nearest to the shore rose up in a narrow curve, tapering into a curl. The front end soared higher, and was topped with the long, slim, stylized head of a fearsome creature . . . a serpent? Rollo narrowed his eyes. No: a boar, its cruel tusks extending in sharp points that glistened in the starlight. Halfway along the vessel was a tall mast, the lines of its rigging stretching fore and aft to prow and stern, and from these lines hung down sheets of canvas, presumably sheltering those on board.

'The *Gullinbursti*,' Harald said beside him. Totally absorbed by the incredible beauty of the ship – and by the miracle of its presence out there on the water, waiting for him – Rollo had momentarily forgotten about Harald. 'The name means Golden Bristler,' Harald went on, 'which was what they called the famous boar made by the dwarves Brokk and Eitri out of pigskin and golden wire, and given to Freya. Gullinbursti was fastest of all creatures, both over water and in the air, and the light that shone from him was like the sun's rays.'

It was hardly the time for myth-telling, Rollo thought. As his initial wonder had faded, it had been replaced with dismay. 'This boat is so small,' he said. 'I can't believe its master means to sail it all the way to England. You must be mistaken, Harald.'

But fiercely Harald shook his head. 'I don't make mistakes like that,' he said indignantly. '*Gullinbursti* may have arrived here in Miklagard via ways other than the open seas, but there is nowhere she cannot sail, and she will go wherever her master directs her.'

With a sick feeling of dread, Rollo remembered the storm that had blown his ship so far off course when he had tried to sail to Constantinople from Sicily. That had been a merchantman, and huge in comparison to the sleek and slender craft that now lay on the calm sea before him.

'It looks so frail,' he murmured. But, even as he spoke, something about the small craft seemed to be reaching out to him . . .

'Don't be deceived by the size,' Harald replied. 'In the hands of an expert mariner and a loyal, stalwart crew, such ships have travelled the known world.'

'But—' Rollo was quite sure he had other objections; sensible, practical comments to do with his great need to hurry urgently back to England, and his serious doubts as to this diminutive vessel's ability to get him there. But, somehow, as he stood drinking in its beautiful lines, the objections seemed to fade from his mind.

'You don't have much choice, to be honest.' Harald's down-to-earth tone brought him out of his reverie. 'Most of the other quays and harbours are manned, and the watch regularly patrols the most important ones. To buy your passage on a merchant ship sailing your way, I'd have had to pay for so many men's silence that it'd have required you to sell your soul. Even then, one small slip and you'd have been discovered.'

Slowly, Rollo nodded. Harald was right. 'So what must I pay for my passage on this ship?' he asked. He still had plenty of coins; the master who had sent him on this mission expected the best and was prepared to pay for it. Nevertheless, Rollo had been travelling for a long time, and his purse was not bottomless.

'Ah,' Harald said. Rollo spun round to stare at him, and saw that, for the first time, the old man looked discomfited. 'Didn't I explain?'

'You've said virtually nothing about my voyage,' Rollo said coldly. 'When I asked if you'd found me passage on board a merchantman, you said, as far as I recall, *not exactly*.'

'Well, that was true!' Harald protested. Then, in a rush, as if he was reluctant to say what he must and wanted to get it over with: 'You're not travelling as a passenger, but as one of the crew. The master lost men on the way here, and can't sail on until he makes up the complement.'

Rollo made himself take a couple of deep breaths. Then he said, 'So I'm going to have to row myself back to England?'

'Not all the way!' Harald protested. 'There's a sail – see the mast? – and, whenever the conditions are favourable, you can all have a rest and let the wind do the work.'

Rollo was beginning to accept the inevitable, but, before he gave in, he said, 'Is there really no alternative?'

'No,' Harald said firmly. 'And you're only being taken on as one of *Gullinbursti*'s crew because the master has no choice. He's desperate to start the voyage, and is prepared to do you a favour in return for one from you. It suits you both – you need each other!' he said, his voice rising in frustration. 'Can't you *see*?'

Rollo turned to him, aware suddenly that he was being very ungrateful. 'Of course I can,' he said. 'And thank you, Harald, from the bottom of my heart, for this and all that you have done for me.' He put out his right hand, and Harald clasped it, gripping tightly.

'No need for thanks,' Harald said gruffly. Then, meeting Rollo's eyes: 'You'll do it, then? You'll sail with the dawn aboard *Gullinbursti*?'

'I will, and gladly.'

Harald let out a sigh of relief. After a moment, he said quietly, 'And once you are safely back in England, you'll do what I ask of you?'

'Yes. You have my word.'

Harald nodded. 'Thank you.'

Both men fell silent. The air between them was full of many emotions, and Rollo could think of nothing to say. Eventually Harald muttered, 'I should leave you. I'm not proposing to return the same way we got here. Most of the watch know me, and I'll have no trouble entering the city through the gates. All the same, I'd like to be safe back within my own four walls by daybreak.'

'Yes, I understand.' Rollo glanced into the east, where the indigo sky was beginning to lighten. 'You'll have to hurry.' He picked up his pack, then followed Harald along the stony path that ran along behind the strip of beach, down to where the jetty angled out into the water.

'They're expecting you,' Harald said quietly, 'and, indeed, the lookout will undoubtedly already know we're here.'

They were on the jetty now, both walking soft-footed to keep the noise to a minimum. As they approached *Gullinbursti*'s high stern, the canvas awning was twitched aside and a face appeared in the narrow gap.

'Is that you, Harald?' a low, deep voice called.

'Yes. I've brought your new crewman.'

In the swiftly waxing light, Rollo stared at the man. The man stared right back, his intent blue eyes alive, as if fire burned within them. From what Rollo could see, he was a very big man; broad in the shoulder, barrel-chested, his bare arms thick with muscle. He had abundant, flowing hair and a long, bushy beard, and both were light coppery red.

'You take the watch yourself, master?' Harald said lightly.

'I take my turn with my men,' the man replied brusquely. 'This morning, I was awake anyway. I have tarried here far too long, and I am eager to set sail and leave.' He turned the hot blue eyes to Rollo, as if the delay had been his fault.

'If I may step aboard,' Rollo said courteously, 'then I will detain you no longer.'

The man gave a curt nod, pushing the awning back further to allow Rollo access. Rollo turned to Harald, and, in the moment of parting, put his arms round the old man in a hug. Harald returned it, then, disengaging himself, gave Rollo a light shove. 'Go on, then,' he said. 'And may God go with you.'

Rollo stepped down on to *Gullinbursti*'s wooden planking, Harald's last words echoing in his head. He'd spoken softly, and Rollo wasn't entirely sure what he'd said: it might, he reflected, have actually been, *May the gods go with you.*

'Stow your gear there,' the master said shortly, pointing to where a wooden chest stood beside an oar hole, presently covered by its wooden flap. 'Not superstitious about taking a dead man's place, are you?'

'No,' Rollo replied. He opened the box, putting his pack inside. The box, presumably, doubled as a seat for when the ship was under oars.

The big man was heading back to the stern of the ship, rummaging in another, larger chest. 'I'm going to rouse them,' he said, nodding towards the shapes lying well-wrapped along the sides of the ship. 'We'll take a quick bite, then be on our way.'

Rollo was relieved to hear it. 'What should I do?' he asked.

'For now, nothing. Sit and watch, and see how *we* do it. Then you can join in, and, with any luck, do so without getting in anyone's way.'

It made sense. Rollo sat down on his chest, staring along the length of the ship as the crewmen were wakened from sleep. As the copper-haired man passed beside him, he said, 'What do I call you, master?'

The blue-eyed stare flashed down on him. 'Skuli.'

FIFTEEN

Hrype and I walked through the darkness for a long time. I was wondering how much further we were going to have to go when a big, broad shape loomed up out of the shadows ahead.

'I decided to walk to meet you,' a deep and well-remembered voice said.

With a gasp, I broke into a run. My grandfather opened his arms to receive me, and I fell against him. For some moments I just stood there, breathing in his scent. It was just as I remembered it; the essence of him. When he had first embraced me, long before I knew of our close relationship, something deep within me had recognized him. Perhaps, I've subsequently thought, it was his blood calling out to mine.

Gently he disengaged himself, keeping hold of my hand, then, nodding ahead down the narrow track that wound through the reed bed, he said, 'Come with me. I have made camp down there, and we will be more comfortable under cover.'

We followed the little waterway for perhaps thirty or forty paces, then, as the track rounded a gentle bend, I saw a small wooden boat tied up to the bank. Thorfinn had rigged up lengths of skins and oiled cloth, giving the impression that a low tent rose up over the boat.

Thorfinn let go of my hand and, striding ahead, opened a gap in the awning, indicating that Hrype and I should go aboard. I eased myself down the bank and stepped inside. Instantly the little craft rocked beneath me, and hurriedly I sat down on the bench that ran around the boat's sides, reaching out to steady the single lamp that Thorfinn had left alight.

Hrype settled beside me, and Thorfinn took what I guessed was his accustomed place at the back of the boat, wrapping his thick cloak around him. He lit another lantern, and as the flame flared up, I looked around. Thorfinn's stores of food and drink were neatly stowed in the bows, and he had padded the seating area with well-stuffed sacks to keep out the cold. Rolled-up blankets were stored under the bench. I smiled. I might have known an experienced mariner such as he would know how to make life on a small boat adequately comfortable.

My grandfather looked at me. 'Have you brought the shining stone?' he asked softly.

'I have.' I placed the stone, still inside its leather bag, on my lap.

'Will you look into it and tell me what you see?' Thorfinn's expression was hungry.

I made myself stare into his eyes. His gaze was steady and penetrating, and, although I knew he meant me no harm, I was unnerved by the power I sensed in him.

I eased the bag open and drew out the stone. I pushed aside the sheep's wool and spread both my hands around its cool, hard smoothness. Then, surely too fast to have been as a result of my touch, the stone began to feel first warm, and then hot.

I tore my eyes away from my grandfather's and looked down. The rivers of gold and green that ran deep within the stone were already beginning to shine, and, even as I watched, they became incandescent, their light rivalling and then eclipsing that of the two lamps. I heard someone gasp – my grandfather? Hrype? – but it was as if the sound was from far away and nothing to do with me.

Perhaps as a result of my experiment that afternoon, the shining stone was responding to me. To the warmth of my blood pulsing through my veins; to my soul, maybe, which the stone had begun to recognize. Out of somewhere in the recent past, I heard Gurdyman's voice, speaking of the stone: *It needs to stay close to you.*

As if the shining stone had a will of its own.

Well, if that was right – and still the reasoning, logical part of my mind was struggling to accept the evidence I could see with my own eyes, and feel in my own hands – it suggested that Gurdyman had been absolutely right. The stone was as curious about me as I was about it, and it was setting about satisfying that curiosity by sending its essence out to meet mine.

But that, a rational and steadily diminishing part of me responded, was nonsense. It was just a *stone* . . .

I stared into the shining stone, now living up to its epithet with such a glorious display of light that my eyes had instinctively narrowed. Those fascinating strands of green and gold drew my gaze, and I had the sense that I was falling more deeply into the dark depths. But I was not afraid: I knew the stone was not my enemy but my ally.

And then from somewhere came understanding so firm, so certain that there was no arguing with it: the time when others could command and control my interaction with the shining stone was over.

For some time I just sat there, my hands clasped around the stone, my eyes half-closed as I stared at the movements I could see within it; the shapes, images, pictures, ideas, even, that formed, melted and reformed as I watched.

Thorfinn and Hrype were very patient; I'll give them that.

Finally, I believed I was ready for them. Carefully I moved my hands so that my palms and interlinked fingers covered the stone's surface. The light instantly dimmed and, once more, the scene was illuminated solely by Thorfinn's two lanterns. Then I raised my eyes and looked straight at my grandfather.

'You wanted me to see what Skuli was doing, and I've done so. I'm not referring to what I've just seen,' I added swiftly, as he opened his mouth to speak. 'I'm referring to the last time I looked into the stone, when I was with you, Hrype.' I gave him a quick glance, then turned back to Thorfinn. 'I won't repeat the information, since I'm quite sure Hrype will already have told you every last detail, but, to summarize, we know that Skuli reached Miklagard after a headlong rush that lost him crewmen.' I paused, steadying myself. Despite the new-found confidence which the shining stone seemed to have bestowed on me, it was still nerve-racking to confront two such powerful men. 'We also know,' I went on softly, 'that Miklagard was not Skuli's final destination.'

In the sudden, utter silence, I heard the hoot of a hunting owl, somewhere out on the fens.

Now I had to grab my chance. I was about to do something I'd never attempted before, and I knew that my slender courage would fail if I gave myself time to think.

'Before I describe what the stone has just revealed to me,' I went on, trying to keep my voice steady, 'you must tell me where he's going, and what he intends to do there.'

Thorfinn's expression smoothed into bland indifference, but not quickly enough; I had caught a glimpse of his anguish. Clearly, he didn't want to share whatever he knew, or suspected, with me. He met Hrype's eyes, and I thought Hrype gave a small shake of the head. So that was how it would be . . .

With a smile, my grandfather said, 'I can't tell you, child, because I don't know for certain. He—' A pause. 'Skuli has a warped soul. He believes life has treated him very unfairly, and that the shining stone should be his. If it were, he is convinced that he would have led the hero's life he so desperately wants. With its help, he would have made voyages and discoveries of the sort that become legends, to be told and retold by the bards until the end of our line.' Briefly he closed his eyes. 'For better or worse, actions were taken to ensure Skuli never got his hands on the shining stone. But, in the end, it made no difference; he has gone to pursue his dream anyway.'

I waited, but it seemed he had finished.

I could scarcely believe it.

'But *what* dream?' I cried, my voice loud in the enclosed space.

Now Thorfinn's distress was written all over his face. He leaned close to me. 'Child, child, it is perilous even to speak of it!' he said, his voice almost a moan of pain. 'You must trust to older and wiser heads, and accept that some things it is truly better not to know.'

Once more, silence fell. I said, wondering at my nerve even as I spoke, 'Then you're not going to hear what the stone just imparted to me.'

Thorfinn's mouth fell open. 'You saw?' he hissed, and anger flared in his eyes. 'You saw the place? Those ancient, wondrous halls, and the ravens which—'

'Enough.' Hrype spat out the single word with the force of an arrow hitting the butt. I twisted round to him, my fury about to erupt, but he forestalled me. 'She's fooling you, Thorfinn! She saw nothing – she's leading you on, in the hope that you'll tell her what she wants to know.'

Hrype was right. In that moment, I hated him for his perception. He knew me far too well and he hadn't hesitated to use that knowledge against me, stepping in to stop Thorfinn just as he was about to speak.

Ravens. He'd said *ravens*.

I'd seen them.

Thorfinn was looking at me. 'Is this true, child? You were trying to mislead me?'

I met his eyes. Gathering the remnants of my courage, I said, 'Yes, Grandfather, I was.' Making myself ignore the disappointment in his face, I hurried on. 'You have asked too much of me. You would have me use the shining stone – which *you* put into my hands – for your own purposes.' I stopped, my response to his pain making my eyes fill with tears. Then, anger rising again, I said, 'If you have a use for the stone, you should have held on to it.'

He went white. I knew I had gone too far, but whatever was driving me wouldn't let me apologize. Instead, I said coldly, 'Please don't ask me again to use the shining stone to do your bidding. It doesn't work like that any more.' I paused, for this was important. 'It's mine now, and it's concerned only with my preoccupations. Nobody else's,' I added for emphasis, 'even yours.'

Thorfinn didn't reply. I think he was shocked into silence. Hrype made no comment either, although I could feel his furious disapproval coming at me like a wave. I risked a glance in his direction. His silvery eyes were narrowed to slits.

I busied myself wrapping the stone in its soft wool and stowing it back inside the leather bag. Then I got up from the bench, pushing aside the heavy awning.

'You're going?' Thorfinn's voice cut into the silence.

'Yes.'

'But you can't go alone! It's dark, and the waters still run high. You should—'

I cut him off. 'I've lived in the fens all my life and I'm perfectly capable of finding my way home,' I said. I stepped up on to the bank.

'Hrype, stop her!' Thorfinn commanded.

'She knows her own mind,' Hrype replied coldly. 'Let her go.'

He spoke as if he hated me. It was too much. Sticking my head and shoulders back in through the gap in the awning, I let all the anger, hurt and resentment fuse into a weapon as sharp as a sword. Unfortunately, I aimed it at the wrong target.

Glaring at Thorfinn, I said, 'One more thing: you need to explain to my father who you are. It's not right or fair that I know and he doesn't. Apart from anything else, you're forcing me to enact a lie with someone I really love, and it's very, *very* painful.' I paused for breath, fighting not to let the sight of Thorfinn's expression affect me. 'My father's a grown man, and he's tough,' I finished. 'The news won't break him. Compared to everyone and everything he holds dear, it's just not important enough.'

I flung the awning back into place and strode away along the narrow track.

Hrype studied the old man. He sat with bent head, the broad shoulders sagging, one hand covering his face.

She has hurt him, Hrype thought. *So far he has only known one face of his granddaughter, and now he has seen another. She is a lot tougher than he had suspected.*

He watched Thorfinn struggle to overcome his distress. Finally, the old man lowered the concealing hand and turned to Hrype. 'She is quite right,' he said quietly. 'What she said pained me, but in both matters – her right to use the shining stone as she wishes, and my need to confess the truth to my son – she tells me what my conscience already knows.'

Hrype considered, his head on one side. 'In essence, yes,' he agreed. He paused. There was something he knew he should add, but it was not strictly necessary, and he was impatient to discuss what he and Thorfinn should do next. But, somewhat to his amazement – he prided himself on being above emotion – the old man's distress had affected him.

'You should not be surprised at her strength,' he heard himself say. 'She is of your own blood, old man, and you do not breed weaklings. Her mother, too, is formidable.' He smiled, a swift expression there and gone in a moment. 'Threaten those she loves and she'll use an iron cooking pot on you as if it were a battle axe,' he murmured.

Thorfinn looked up at him. 'Really?'

'So they say,' Hrype confirmed. There was more; he made himself go on. 'Thorfinn, I sense that already she is regretting her cruel words to you,' he said. 'It was me she wished to hurt, but you, being more vulnerable, were the easier target.'

'Why should she wish to hurt you?'

Because she grows in strength and will one day rival me, and because I cannot let myself admit it, I suppress her, was the honest answer. Hrype wasn't going to share that with Thorfinn. He shook his head. 'Explanations would take too long. The important thing is that what has just happened will not come between you.'

Thorfinn's face lightened. 'You are sure?'

'I am.' All at once weary of the discussion, Hrype hardened his tone and said, 'Now, what are we to do about Skuli?'

Next morning, I was heavy-eyed after my night's excitement. I was also sore at heart and guilty; I had shouted at my grandfather and hurt him, and he really hadn't deserved it.

I didn't try to justify to myself why I sought out Jack. I needed to be with him: that was all.

He was in the Lakehall stables, tending his horses. He seemed to find conversation as awkward as I did, and, for want of anything better, I said, 'I asked my aunt if my Granny Cordeilla revealed anything useful concerning her missing brother, but she said not.'

He didn't reply straight away. Then, just when I was thinking I ought to go and leave him to his work, he said, 'The missing one was the youngest brother, you said. What of the others?'

'He and the two who fell at Hastings were the final three. There were two older sisters, but they died years ago.' I paused. 'Oh, and one entered a monastery. His name was Sihtric.'

'Is this monk still alive?'

'Yes, as far as I know. He's in an enclosed community out to the south-east of Cambridge, at Little Barton.'

'Quite an easy ride, now that the flood waters are receding,' Jack observed. He reached out for the grey gelding's bridle, deftly buckling the straps.

'But he won't know what happened to Harald!' I protested. 'He may not even be still alive.'

'Wouldn't his monastery have notified his family if he'd died?' Jack asked.

'Yes, I suppose so.'

His own horse was now tacked up. Gently pushing me out of the way, he turned his attention to Isis. 'We'll go and find out.'

We reached Little Barton in the late morning. Jack had been right about the flood water, and there had only been one place where we'd had to make a detour. The village was tiny: a collection of lowly dwellings, a run-down smithy, a church with holes in its roof. Jack asked a man waiting for the smith to finish replacing a shoe on his horse's hind foot if he knew of a monastery in the area. He removed the straw from his mouth, spat, then silently pointed down the narrow track leading off behind the church.

We headed out of the village. Several small boys emerged from a line of hovels, and one of them said a dirty word. For a few awkward moments, we were the centre of attention, and several pairs of round eyes in snotty-nosed faces watched as we rode by. Perhaps they didn't get many visitors.

The monastery was about a mile out of the village. It consisted of a small group of wattle-and-daub buildings up on a slight rise, and the largest of them had a wooden cross on its roof. The buildings were enclosed by a high paling fence, and the tops of the palings were sharpened into points. On three sides, the fence merged into thick undergrowth from which stands of willow, hazel and alder rose up, effectively concealing the monastery. In the fence facing us as we approached there was a gate, firmly closed.

'Do you think they're trying to keep the world out or the monks in?' Jack wondered, staring at the wretched enclosure before us.

'A bit of both,' I replied.

'What do they do all day?' Jack went on. 'They obviously don't spend their time tending the poor and the needy.'

'They'll have to support themselves,' I said, 'so presumably they farm their land.' In a field to our right there was a small herd of skinny cows. 'And most of their time is probably spent in prayer.'

'Praying for a better world,' Jack muttered. 'I can't help but think they'd do more good trying to heal the sick and feed the hungry, but I suppose it's a matter of belief.'

'Granny Cordeilla said Sihtric was always a dreamer, even as a boy,' I said. 'He got out of a lot of distasteful chores by saying he had to go and communicate with God.'

'It looks as if he's still doing the same,' Jack observed. 'Let's see if they'll open the gate and admit us.'

We rode up to the fence and dismounted. I held our horses' reins, and Jack banged on the gate. It was some time before anyone came to see what we wanted. Finally, a tiny gap appeared between the stout wood of the gate and the frame in which it was set, and a cowled face peered out. 'What do you want?' hissed a reedy voice.

'We wish to speak to Brother Sihtric,' Jack said firmly. 'This young woman is his great-niece, and needs to consult him urgently on a family matter.'

'We abandon our families when we enter St Botolph's,' the monk said reprovingly.

'But perhaps your families do not abandon you,' Jack replied gently. 'Is Brother Sihtric here?'

'Of course he is,' the monk snapped. He opened the gate a fraction more, glaring out at me from faded, rheumy eyes narrowed into suspicious slits. 'You can't come in, you're a *woman*,' he accused. 'No women allowed!'

He went to slam the gate shut, but Jack had put his foot in the gap. Wincing slightly – the stringy old monk must have been tougher than he looked – he said reasonably, 'Well, if we can't come in, perhaps Brother Sihtric could come and speak to us here?'

The monk frowned, furiously working empty jaws together as if chewing on invisible meat. Then he said, 'Wait,' and slammed the gate shut.

We waited. There was the sound of a brief muttered conversation, and within the enclosure a door creaked open and closed.

Footsteps approached, and the gate opened again – a little wider this time – to reveal an even smaller and more wizened monk dressed in a patched and fraying habit.

I knew he was my great-uncle even before he spoke. He had a look of Granny Cordeilla in his very stance, and the deep, dark eyes, bright as a robin's despite his advanced years, were hers exactly.

'You wish to speak to me?' he asked, his voice cracked and rusty with disuse. He cleared his throat of accumulated phlegm and spat a glistening, yellowish gobbet on to the ground.

'I'm Cordeilla's granddaughter,' I said before he could change his mind and shut himself away again. 'Her son Wymond's child.'

'Cordeilla.' His lined old face softened. 'How is she?'

'She died,' I admitted. 'Two years and more ago.'

He nodded, as if it was only to be expected. 'I shall pray for her,' he said. 'Was that what you came to tell me?'

I hesitated, but, with those eyes so like my Granny Cordeilla's burning into mine, I could only tell the truth. 'No,' I said. 'I'm sorry that nobody thought to inform you before, but that isn't why I'm here.' I drew a breath. 'I wanted to ask you if you ever heard word from Harald. Do you know where he is?'

Sihtric watched me. 'Harald fled,' he said. 'Didn't want to stay here, once the fight was lost.'

'I know,' I said gently. 'I'm not judging him. I just want to know if he ever sent you any communication, any message, that might reveal where he went.' Sihtric didn't answer. In desperation, I said urgently, 'He didn't go to Spain, did he?' I prayed he wouldn't say yes.

Perhaps prayers said right outside a monastery stand a better chance of being heard and answered; I don't know. But, with a smile, Sihtric said, 'Spain? No, no, Harald didn't go to Spain.' He chuckled, as if to say, why on earth would anyone wish to go *there*?

'Where, then?' I whispered, hardly daring to breathe.

'He was a fighter, child,' Sihtric said kindly. 'It was the only thing he was good at, and, even then, Sagar was a better shot and Sigbehrt a far better warrior. Where would a warrior go, d'you imagine?'

I didn't know. I shook my head.

But Jack knew. 'He'd make his way to where warriors of his race and size were known to be welcomed,' he said softly. 'Like so many of his Saxon comrades, he'd have gone south.'

'South, aye, south,' Sihtric agreed, shifting his gaze to Jack and nodding his approval. 'He went to serve the emperor in Miklagard, as one of his Varangian Guard. As far as I know, he's still there.'

As the initial shock began to wear off, I said, 'How do you know? How could he possibly have *told* you?'

Sihtric looked at me, my Granny Cordeilla's smile brightening his face. 'Many of our race travel to Miklagard,' he said. 'It is not so unusual a voyage.' He was speaking more easily now, and I had the sense that he was enjoying this rare chance to converse with someone other than his fellow monks. 'Many come back again, since, unlike Harald and the Varangians, they go not to make a new life but to trade. Harald sent word to me via one such trader returning to these shores. It was –' he screwed up his face in concentration – 'perhaps ten or a dozen years after he disappeared? I cannot recall exactly, for time passes slowly in this place and one year is very much like another.'

'What did the message say?' I asked, trying to speak calmly.

'He wished me to know that he was married,' Sihtric replied with a gentle smile. 'Crusty old bachelor that he was, he had fallen in love with the daughter of a Frankish merchant, and she, it appeared, reciprocated the sentiment. Her name was Gabrièla de Valéry, and, according to Harald, she was tall, blonde-haired, blue-eyed, very beautiful and utterly perfect.' The smile widened into a reminiscent grin. 'Mind you,' he added, 'there was never anyone like Harald for building up a tale, and we always took everything he said with a pinch of salt.'

Harald had married! And this Sihtric, this sibling who had shut himself away from the world, had known, yet my beloved Granny Cordeilla hadn't.

'Why did he tell you when he didn't tell Cordeilla?' I demanded, the pain and hurt I was feeling on her behalf making me angry. In my distress, I felt her presence acutely. I could *see* her, a vague, misty shape on the edge of my vision. She was fuming. 'She was his last surviving sister, and she *loved* him!' I yelled.

Sihtric looked at me, compassion in his face. 'I cannot say for sure,' he said, 'although I can guess. Harald thought, I imagine, that Cordeilla hated him. He believed she could not forgive him for not having brought the bodies of Sagar and Sigbehrt back to Aelf Fen. I would guess that, in addition, he thought she would rather one of the other two had been spared instead of him. Perhaps he was right.' He sighed, his dark eyes softening. 'When we were children, it was always Cordeilla and Harald who picked the most frequent and violent fights with each other.'

'That might suggest that they were the closest and the most alike,' Jack said quietly. 'It is often the way, that the siblings who most resemble each other find so much more to disagree about.'

'You are right,' Sihtric said, turning to him with a smile. His eyes seemed to stare out over our heads, as if he were focusing on the distant past. 'How long ago it all seems. And now, you say, Cordeilla is dead, and I am the only one left.'

'Harald may still be alive!' I protested. For some reason, I very much wanted to believe it was true.

Sihtric returned his attention to me. 'Perhaps so, child,' he said kindly. 'But he was a fighter, and that is a dangerous profession. He would be an old man by now, nearly as old as me.' He sighed. 'I cannot hold out much hope that he still walks this earth.' He nodded, already turning to retreat back inside his monastery. 'I shall pray for him too,' he added, stepping inside and beginning to close the gate, 'and for all my brothers and sisters, gone before me to the paradise that we hope awaits us. Farewell, child.'

And, very firmly and finally, the gate was shut. There was the sound of heavy bolts being shot across. The monks of St Botolph's, it seemed, had finished with us.

Jack did not speak as we rode away. I was grateful. My mind was in turmoil, and I needed time to sort out my emotions. Harald had gone to Miklagard! He had married, made his home and lived the remainder of his life in that impossibly distant city. Oh, why had none of us known? Why, in God's name, had the only member of the family Harald had seen fit to inform been a monk

who didn't communicate with the rest of us from one year's end
to the next?

Poor Granny Cordeilla! How hurt she would have been, that
he had sent no word to her. She would have—

I'm all right, child. I could hear her, inside my head. *Sihtric
spoke wisely; Harald and I did fight more than the others, and
we were two of a kind.*

'I'm sorry he never contacted you,' I whispered very quietly.

Don't you fret, she replied robustly. *Typical Harald, to send
his information to the one sibling who didn't talk to any of the
others! Two of a kind we might have been, but that doesn't mean
I liked him much.*

It was so typical of Granny Cordeilla that I had to laugh.

The day was warm, and we stopped at a ford to water the horses.
I felt like singing: relief that our Harald had gone to Miklagard,
not Spain, and therefore couldn't possibly be Lady Rosaria's
father-in-law, was bubbling up into happiness. I flung myself
down on the grass beside Jack, leant back against his tree and
accepted a drink from his water bag.

He seemed preoccupied, barely responding to my remarks.
After quite a long silence, he said, 'Lassair, I've been thinking.'

'Oh?'

He got to his feet, then held out his hand to me and helped
me up. 'Yes. I—'

I heard the whistle. I saw the glint of sunshine on a bright blade.
I knew what it was: part of me had been expecting it. Instinctively
I flung my arms round Jack's neck and, using my full weight,
dragged him down so that we fell in a heap on the ground.

The knife plunged deep into the trunk of the tree, precisely
where our heads had just been.

He had fallen on top of me, and I could hardly breathe. He
rolled off me, already up in a crouch, eyes everywhere as he sought
for the thrower of the knife. With a shout he was on his feet,
sprinting across the grass and plunging through the stream.

'*Be careful!*' I screamed. 'He'll have other weapons!'

I don't think Jack heard. Moving with unbelievable speed, he
thrust his way into a thicket on the far bank, and a cry of pain
rent the air.

I raced after him, down the slope, across the stream, up the bank on the far side. I launched myself into the thicket, my small blade in my hand, tripped over an outstretched pair of legs and landed on a supine body.

It wasn't Jack's. In that first moment, that was all I could take in.

Jack had turned the assailant on to his belly, the face pressed into the earth, and he was tying the man's wrists behind his back with a leather thong.

'I punched him and knocked him out,' Jack panted, 'but he's not hurt otherwise.'

I stared down at the still form. I noticed that my hands were empty, and that a pool of blood was welling up in the middle of the man's back, staining the cloth of his tunic. In the centre of the red patch, the handle of my knife stuck up.

'Yes, he is,' I said softly.

I began to shake, covering my face with my hands. Jack gave an exclamation, and I heard the sound of ripping material. Then he said, 'Lassair, you need to look at this.'

'I *can't*!' I whispered. 'Oh, God, what have I done?'

Then Jack was beside me, holding me by the shoulders. 'He just threw a knife at us,' he said harshly. 'You acted in self-defence and to protect me. That is no crime. Now, tend his wound.'

I did as he told me.

When I pulled out my blade, the blood flowed so fast that I was afraid the man would die. Then I became purely a healer, instructing Jack where to apply pressure while I prepared a length of gut, and then how to hold the man still while I closed the wound. He was coming round, and screaming in agony.

'Untie his wrists,' I said to Jack.

'No.' He sounded implacably stern; quite unlike the man I was starting to know. 'He threw a knife at us, Lassair. He's dangerous and skilful – had you not pulled me down, one of us would now be dead.'

He was right.

Jack turned the man over and forced him to sit up. Then he slapped his face once, hard. 'Why did you drown her?' he demanded. 'Did someone order you not to leave any witnesses alive?'

The man stared up at him, his face full of hate. He spat out a mouthful of bloody spittle, then said, 'I don't know what you're talking about.'

Jack gave him a shake. 'You've been following us. You tried to kill us. You won't leave here alive unless you tell me why.'

Suddenly I heard something. 'Jack, there's someone else out there,' I said urgently.

Jack shoved the man back down on the ground and got to his feet. Swiftly he pushed his way through the undergrowth on the far side from where we'd entered the thicket, and through the tangle of branches I saw him circle round. I guessed he was going to jump whoever was out there from behind.

I waited.

Then Jack came crashing back, pushing before him a tall shaven-headed man with dark close-set eyes. I'd seen him before, but in that moment of fear and danger, I couldn't place him.

But Jack knew exactly who he was. He had twisted the bald man's arms behind his back, and from the expression on the man's face, he was causing considerable pain.

'So you thought to take your chance while I was out in the wilds, did you?' Jack said with icy fury. He wrenched the man's arms again, and he suppressed a cry. 'You sent your killer to throw his knife and pin me to a tree in the depths of the fens, where nobody would find me?' Another wrench and this time the bald man yelled in pain. 'I should kill you right now, *and* the dregs you paid to do your work for you.' He gave the wounded man at his feet a savage kick.

'Jack,' I said warningly.

He'd forgotten I was there. Now, he turned his head fractionally to look at me. 'Don't waste your pity on the likes of these two,' he said coldly. 'One of them is a hired murderer –' he kicked the wounded man again – 'and the other –' he twisted the bald man's arms so violently that he was lifted off his feet, his mouth wide in a silent scream of agony – 'is Gaspard Picot.'

Picot . . . Then I knew who the bald man was: the sheriff's nephew. He'd argued with Jack as we were leaving Cambridge with the veiled lady.

A lifetime ago.

The silence extended, broken only by Gaspard Picot's ragged

breathing and the harsh panting of the man on the ground. I said,
'Are you going to kill them?'

With an exclamation of disgust, Jack extracted another length
of leather from inside his tunic and bound the bald man's hands
behind him. Then he kicked his legs from under him, so that he
collapsed against the man he'd hired to kill for him.

'No,' he said shortly.

Then he strode out from the thicket, waded back across the
stream and, gathering the grey's reins, mounted. I hurried after
him, struggling to get on to Isis's back and kicking her into a
canter; Jack had already ridden away.

I caught him up. 'You're not – surely you're not just going to
leave them there?' He said nothing. 'Jack, they could *die!*'

He turned to me, his eyes alive with fury. 'That'd be two less
enemies, then.'

I didn't know how to respond. I was out of my depth, for Jack
was dealing with something with which I had no experience.

I reined Isis back, slipped in behind Jack's grey and we rode
back to Aelf Fen.

SIXTEEN

Rollo enjoyed being on board *Gullinbursti*. The weather
was fine and sunny, and a good store of provisions had
been laid in before leaving Miklagard. The crew did not
stint themselves when water and food rations were handed round.

Rollo understood why Skuli had needed another crewman. The
ship had been designed for twenty-four oarsmen, twelve on each
side. The rigours of the outward journey had led to the loss of
three men, leaving twenty-one; an odd number. Now the eleven
pairs rowed with two empty places, but Skuli, impassive at the
tiller, seemed content.

The voyage south-west across the Sea of Marmara was not
taxing. The water remained calm, and, for much of the time, the
wind blew from the north, enabling the use of sail. The crew,
aware that Rollo was convalescing, did not push him. At times

when they were required to row, however, he was determined to show himself ready to labour as hard as any of them. For a couple of hours during the first day of sailing, he sat at his oar, watching, learning and putting his new skill into practice. It had been the right thing to do; having shown that he was willing to work, and did not intend to play on the fact that he was recovering from injury, the crew responded by treating him with consideration.

He discovered that he could converse with them readily enough. Brought up in an environment where many tongues were spoken, he had developed early on an ability with languages. The speech of his new companions resembled the tongue in which he conversed with Lassair and her countrymen. Rollo began to learn his fellow crewmen's names: Eric, big and brawny, the ready laugh and the beer belly that spread out over his wide leather belt disguising the fact that he was as hard as iron; Tostig, tall and wiry, who sang to himself as he worked; Hakon, who loved to observe the seabirds and the fish, and who stared into the night sky seeking patterns and portents; the brothers Torben and Anders, who spoke almost exclusively to each other.

They tied up early that first day. They had set out at dawn, and everyone was ready to rest. They had stayed close to the northern shore, and now, as the afternoon shadows grew long, the master directed them to a stretch of pebbly beach, backed by grassland and a band of pine trees. There was no sign of any village, hamlet or even an isolated habitation.

Gullinbursti was hauled up the beach, and, once secured to the master's satisfaction, the crew could relax. Rollo, hot and soaked with sweat, watched as, to a man, they stripped off to their bare skins and plunged into the water. They called out to him, encouraging him to join them. He didn't need to be asked twice.

As night fell, the master and his crew gathered round the fire that had been lit within a circle of stones, both fuel and hearth stones scavenged from the shore. The red-faced man named Brand, the ship's cook, was busy over an iron pot that bubbled over the flames, and, looking inside, Rollo could make out chunks of salt fish and vegetables; the latter were undoubtedly fresh, since the ship had so recently been in port. He was filled with admiration for the crew's efficiency. There they were, on an unknown beach hundreds of miles from home and the men's known world, yet the well-practised routine meant that within a very short space of time, they were sitting round a fire with hot food to eat and a mug of good, heartening drink to hand.

He found himself sitting next to one of the youngest members of the crew, a slim, fair-haired man named Sven. They had exchanged several remarks during the long day at sea, Sven's post being just behind Rollo. Now, as the other crewmen chattered and ribbed each other, and good-natured squabbles broke out over the best pieces of stew, once again Sven started a conversation with him. Perhaps, Rollo reflected, the young man was pleased to have a new shipmate who was nearer to his own age. The majority of the crew were seasoned sailors with many years' experience behind them.

'Tomorrow will be easier than today,' Sven said, picking a flake of fish out of his front teeth.

'Today wasn't too bad,' Rollo observed.

Sven glanced at him. 'You did all right,' he acknowledged. 'The master said he wouldn't sail without one more crewman, which means you're a bit of a godsend, since most of us were getting pretty impatient to get away and set off for home.' He grinned.

'Glad to be of service,' Rollo said, smiling. But, even as he spoke the mild response, part of his mind had gone on the alert. *Most of us were impatient*, Sven had just said. Who, he wondered, was the exception?

Sven leaned closer. 'Reckon he thought it'd have been unlucky, sailing with an odd number of rowers,' he said very quietly, jerking his head towards the master.

'Really?' Rollo had never heard that superstition before.

Sven was slowly shaking his head, his light eyes still on the master. 'Well, I don't know,' he confessed. 'There's been *something* up with him, that's for sure.' He leaned closer. 'We had a terrible journey down to Miklagard,' he whispered. 'I probably shouldn't tell you, but the whole bloody lot of us almost came to grief on the rapids. That was where we lost our men,' he added, his face falling.

'I'm sorry,' Rollo said gravely. 'I can't imagine how terrible that must have been.'

'They were good men,' Sven said very quietly. His youthful face showed his emotion. 'We carved their names on the stone,' he added in a whisper. 'They won't be forgotten.'

Rollo wanted to hear more about the master's strange mood. 'Losing crewmen would be enough, I'd guess, to rob a man of his peace of mind,' he observed.

Sven flashed him an anxious glance. 'What do you mean?'

'You just said there was something up with the master,' Rollo replied softly.

'Yes, that's right,' Sven said. He glanced round the circle of faces, lit by the dancing flames. Everyone else was busy eating and talking, and the occasional loud burst of laughter echoed in the stillness. Apparently reassured, Sven leaned closer and said, 'For all the haste to get down to Miklagard, once we were there, that's where we stayed, for week after week.' Again, he glanced nervously around. 'It looked as if he was afraid of what lay ahead, although we knew that couldn't be, not when he'd brought us all that way.' He paused, frowning as if the matter still perplexed him. 'None the less, we couldn't help but conclude that the master was reluctant to go on.'

'Go on?'

Sven raised the hand holding his eating knife and waved it around. 'With the journey,' he muttered. 'Miklagard was never our goal. We're going on to—' Abruptly he stopped. Looking up, Rollo noticed the master's cold, unblinking eyes on them.

It was the moment for improvisation. 'Put that knife down!' he said, pushing Sven's hand away and forcing a laugh. 'Go ahead and stab another piece of fish, but let me get out of the way first!'

Several of the crew joined in. It sounded as if the teasing, ribald remarks were part of a well-rehearsed and frequently repeated litany. Risking a quick glance at Skuli, Rollo saw that even he was smiling. Hoping that the master's suspicions hadn't been alerted, he helped himself to more stew.

They made good, steady progress the following day. In the mid-morning of the day after that, Skuli steered *Gullinbursti* out into the deep, strong current flowing down the Dardanelles, and, with minimal effort on the crew's behalf, the ship's pace increased until it felt as if they were flying over the wave-tops. The huge volume of water pouring steadily and constantly out of the Black Sea towards the Mediterranean swept them along, and there was little to do except steer. At the helm, however, Skuli was constantly on the alert, and quick to shout at any man who didn't keep his eyes open.

Watching the master as closely as he was, Rollo could have pinpointed the moment when his mood began to alter. From the start, he had given the impression of a man with something on his mind. Other than the regular, tersely given commands, he spoke little. He never smiled, and, as the days passed, Rollo noticed that his brooding presence was gradually darkening the mood of the crew.

The change began when, as the narrow Dardanelles strait began to widen into the Mediterranean, abruptly Skuli left his place in the stern and paced the length of the ship up into the bows. He stayed there for some moments, gazing at the southern shore far away to his left, down into the water, then back at the shore. It was as if he was looking for something; a marker, perhaps, by which to determine their progress. He went back to his accustomed place at the tiller, only to repeat the exercise a little while later.

His actions had allowed Rollo to catch a glimpse of his expression. The inward-looking, grave-faced man seemed to have vanished. In his place was a man who appeared to be barely containing his excitement.

Rollo looked around at the crew, expecting his surprise to be reflected in other faces. It wasn't. One or two looked fearful; Sven was muttering under his breath, and Rollo thought he was praying. The rest were all staring out to the south, as if some invisible force drew their gaze and they could not look away. On the faces of many was the same expression: awe.

Skuli was once again standing in the ship's prow, one hand on the great, soaring figurehead. His back had been turned to his crew, but now he spun round. The sun was beginning to set, and for an instant he was silhouetted against its golden light, so that a shining halo seemed to encircle his head. He was transformed; a smile of sheer joy had altered his appearance almost beyond recognition.

What was happening? Rollo, apprehension making him suddenly cold, waited.

'Now we are close, my friends!' Skuli said softly. Then, raising his arms as if to embrace both ship and crew, he cried, 'The great challenge is before us! The goal for which we have strived so hard, risked so much and lost precious lives, is now within our grasp.' His light eyes, wide as if he were seeing far beyond the range of normal human vision, roamed over the faces of his crew, smiling, nodding. Then he raised his head and shouted out into the evening sky, 'Will we go on, my friends? Will we achieve our purpose, here in this place so far from our homes?'

And, to a man, the crew shouted back, '*YES!*'

The ship was suddenly busy with bustling activity, as men ran to what were clearly pre-arranged places. Skuli leapt nimbly back to the tiller, leaning heavily against it, and *Gullinbursti*, instantly responsive, heeled over hard and turned in a steep, graceful circle so that her bows and her proud figurehead were sailing due south. Tostig raised his mighty voice in song, and the crew picked it up, singing with him, harmonizing, until the air seemed to thrum with the noise.

Now they were racing along, the vast sail filled with a strong, steady breeze that came from the north. A shudder of superstitious dread ran through Rollo; the notion had leapt into his head that the singing had raised that perfect wind, and he had to fight very hard to force his reason to dispel it.

The southern shore was in sight now, coming towards them alarmingly fast. Struggling to concentrate, Rollo tried to recall what he knew of the local geography. The coastline ahead of them formed a plain, built up over the centuries from the silt washed down the Scamander River as it flowed into the Dardanelles. The waters were shallow and treacherous, and not fit for ships. The nearest port was around the bulge of the coast, away to the south.

Yet, in the fast-approaching twilight, Skuli was steering *Gullinbursti* straight for that perilous shore.

Rollo stared at him. Didn't he know the danger? He opened his mouth to speak, but Skuli forestalled him. 'You fear for our safety, Norman?' he said, a wide grin creasing his face. 'You forget what ship this is! *Gullinbursti*, like all her kind, is shallow-drafted, and she can proceed in confidence where no other vessel dare venture.'

Then he threw back his head and laughed.

Rollo hoped he was wrong, but he was sure he detected a note of madness.

They sailed on, and only at the very last moment, when Rollo had convinced himself that the ship would run straight into the shore, smash to pieces and throw them all to their deaths, did Skuli order the sail to be lowered.

Gullinbursti, quickly losing way, floated through the shallows and finally grounded gently on the long, flat shore.

The crew leapt into action, jumping out of the ship and hurrying to pull her further up the beach, where they hammered in wooden stakes to which they secured her with ropes. Then, following Skuli's lead, they headed inland, stopping at his signal after only a few paces.

Skuli stood perfectly still. He seemed to be watching, and perhaps also listening, for something. Rollo tried to make out the details of this mysterious, alarming place. The low-lying, sandy ground was criss-crossed by streamlets and what looked like a dry river bed, and the whole shore was broken up with marshy thickets. Further inland a plateau rose up, and a spur of higher ground stretched out towards where they now stood. On top of the spur there seemed to be the ruins of buildings: part of a wall, and huge tumbled stones that might have once formed a vast temple or fortress.

Where on God's earth *were* they?

Why had Skuli brought them here?

Rollo had no idea.

Daylight was fading fast now, and, standing on that alien shore, with no sign of human habitation and the crew the only company for maybe dozens of miles, Rollo felt fear creep up his spine. He began to see things on the edge of vision; things which, when he spun his head to look, were not there. And he could *hear* things: the long-drawn-out, eerie howl of a wolf; a whisper, a buzz, the clink of metal; then a steady hum which grew until it sounded as if a great army of men were encamped somewhere nearby.

Rollo twisted this way and that, eyes frantically searching, but, even as he did so, he already knew: there was nobody there.

A sudden coarse sound split the darkening sky; a raucous bird cry. Speeding straight towards them like arrows flew a pair of ravens.

And, very close at hand, came the sound of horses: two horses, ridden hard. It *sounded* like two horses, for there were more than four feet pounding the ground, yet when Rollo strained to see, he made out just the one vague, shadowy shape, looming huge in the dim light. A horse with *eight legs*, its hooves thundering on the earth so that it seemed to shake.

I am hallucinating, Rollo told himself.

The ground *was* shaking. Rollo's cry of alarm was echoed by others, and, for a few terrifying moments, the men on the shore quavered before the fury of the earthquake.

It stopped as abruptly as it had begun. Skuli, acting like a good captain should, instantly encouraged his crew. 'Do not be afraid!' he cried. 'These signs are *good*, for they tell us that the gods recognize our presence, and are bidding us welcome!'

Then Rollo was assailed with a horrible thought. *No*, he told himself frantically, *it cannot be.*

He had to be wrong: the alternative was just too frightening. Here he was – here they all were – at one man's bidding, and that man was the master of the ship which had brought them here.

The dread suspicion was growing, and Rollo was faced with the awful fact that he'd stumbled on the truth: it was the only explanation. Yet still he fought to accept it. No rational man, he thought, could still believe the old myths!

Perhaps Skuli was not rational.

Skuli was marching ahead. Fear making his very blood feel chill, Rollo joined the rest of the crew and marched after him.

Jack and I were almost back at Aelf Fen. Jack had barely spoken. Although I longed for reassurance that the men we had left bound and helpless in the thicket would not die there, I dared not ask.

This was a different Jack. Ruthless, brutal, unforgiving. We had been attacked, and it was only by sheer luck that neither of us was dead; if I'd asked, he'd have said Gaspard Picot and his hired killer deserved all they'd got.

I called it *luck* to myself. I wasn't ready to think about the way in which the shining stone had forewarned me. It was just too frightening.

Breaking the long silence, Jack said, in a surprisingly normal tone, 'I've been going over your great-uncle Sihtric's revelations.'

'*What?*' It came out in a squeak. Then, swiftly trying to overcome my astonishment that he seemed to have put our encounter with violent death behind him – perhaps such things happened regularly to him – I gathered my ragged thoughts together. It proved quite hard to remember what had gone on back at Little Barton, but finally I succeeded.

'Harald went to Miklagard,' I said. 'It proves he wasn't Rosaria's father-in-law because she came from Spain.'

But Jack was keeping ominously quiet.

'He can't have been!' I cried.

Still Jack didn't speak. I pulled Isis to a halt. We'd been riding side by side and, instantly noticing I'd stopped, he did too.

'Go on, then,' I said sharply. 'Tell me.'

'Tell you what?' Jack replied.

'Why have you got that *look*,' I demanded, 'as if you know something terrible and don't want to tell me?'

He smiled very briefly. 'I'm afraid I might have,' he said. 'It's something I've had on my mind for days.'

'Tell me,' I said.

He looked at me, and I couldn't read his expression. Then, dismounting, he said, 'Come and talk to me. There are things I should tell you before we go on into the village.'

I felt a horrible sense of doom, as if something was heading straight for me and I wouldn't be able to avoid it or run away. I did as he asked, and he looped the horses' reins around the branch of a willow tree. I went to stand beside him and he took my hand, looked into my eyes and said, 'Do you recall how, as you, Lady Rosaria and I approached Aelf Fen on the day we brought her here, I said I must know her name, in order to present her to Lord Gilbert and Lady Emma?'

'Yes. What of it?'

'She said she was Hugo Guillaume Fensmanson's widow, and her name was Rosaria Dalassena.'

'Yes, that sounds right.'

He paused, as if reluctant to continue. Then he said, 'Lassair, *Dalassena* reveals that she belongs to a well-known family. I knew I'd heard it before, and eventually I remembered: Anna Dalassena Comnena is the mother of Alexius Comnenus.'

I stared right back at him. 'And who might he be?'

Jack sighed. 'He's the Byzantine emperor.' In case I was still missing the point, he added, 'Lady Rosaria bears the family name of the emperor in Constantinople.'

My mind was casting frantically round for an answer; one that would allow me to go on believing that Lady Rosaria wasn't my great-uncle's daughter-in-law. But if her illustrious name really did mean she came from Constantinople, I was on shaky ground.

'She might have left her home and settled in Spain!' I protested. 'She might be one of the Dalassena kin who doesn't live in Constantinople. She might . . .'

I was out of ideas. I had to accept that it now seemed more than likely Lady Rosaria did come from Constantinople. We knew that before she went aboard *The Good Shepherd* she had sailed from Corunna to Bordeaux, but there was absolutely nothing to say that her journey had originated in Spain.

If Lady Rosaria had set out from Constantinople in search of her father-in-law's kin, and if her father-in-law was my Granny Cordeilla's youngest brother, then it was my family she sought and we could not turn her away. I knew it was our duty, but the thought of *her* as a kinswoman was abhorrent to me.

Jack seemed to understand how I was feeling. He didn't speak, but simply drew me very close, and waited until my harsh breathing calmed. Then he held me at arm's length and said firmly, 'There's only one way we can be sure.'

I nodded. 'I know.'

'I'm going to ask her, right now.'

I grinned. 'I know that, too. Can I come with you?'

He returned my smile. 'Under the circumstances,' he said, 'I think it would be unreasonable if you didn't.'

We rode up the track to Lakehall, where we handed our horses over to a stable boy's care. We went up the steps, and Bermund admitted us into the hall. He announced us to Lord Gilbert and

Lady Emma, seated either side of the hearth. Lord Gilbert rose to his feet, his eyebrows raised in query.

'You have news?' he demanded. 'You have located Lady Rosaria's kinsmen?'

Jack didn't answer. Instead he said, 'We need to see her, my lord.'

'You can't. She is unwell, and has taken to her room to rest,' Lord Gilbert said firmly.

'Nevertheless, I must speak to her,' Jack insisted.

Perhaps something about his resolute manner suggested to Lord Gilbert that he wasn't going to take no for an answer. 'You can't just—' Lord Gilbert began. Then, with a shrug, he seemed to give up. Frowning, he turned to Bermund. 'Fetch her,' he said curtly.

We waited. After quite some time, Lady Rosaria glided out into the hall. Her veil was in place but her eyes were red-rimmed and puffy, as if she hadn't been sleeping. Or, perhaps, had been weeping . . .

Lord Gilbert made to step towards her, but Lady Emma put out her hand and held him back. I heard her murmur, surprisingly firmly, 'Leave it to Jack.'

Jack had turned to face Lady Rosaria. As she stopped a few paces away, he gave her a low bow. 'Once again, I have come to ask you to answer my questions, my lady,' he said courteously.

Lady Rosaria, who had been staring at Lord Gilbert, turned her great dark eyes to Jack, but did not speak. Lord Gilbert, shaking off Lady Emma's hand and going to stand beside her, said, 'Chevestrier, do not trouble her! She is unwell, as surely you can see?'

'Lassair is a healer,' Jack said. 'I am sure she would be happy to help, if you wish it, my lady?'

Lady Rosaria shot one quick look in my direction, then tossed her head, dismissing me. 'I do not need help,' she said.

'Then please answer my questions,' Jack said. He stepped closer to her, ignoring Lord Gilbert's thunderous frown. 'If you are sick, my lady, we offer you the services of a healer to make you better before we continue. If you say you do not need them, then I conclude that you are well. It is for you to tell us –' Lord

Gilbert tried to interrupt, but Jack, raising his voice, spoke over him – 'but I *will have* your answers.'

It was too much for Lord Gilbert. 'You do not address a lady in this manner!' he spluttered, his round, jowly face scarlet with furious indignation. 'Were my guest already in her rightful place with her kinsman and his noble family, you would not dare, and I will not have it here in my own hall!'

Jack, his patience apparently at an end, spun round to face Lord Gilbert. 'You, my lord, should join me in demanding Lady Rosaria's answers, for matters may not be as you believe.'

Lady Rosaria gave a gasp, quickly muffled as she put a long, be-ringed hand to her mouth. Turning back to her, Jack said, 'Where did you come from, Lady Rosaria? You arrived in Cambridge on a boat out of Lynn, and you reached there on a ship which you boarded in Bordeaux, having sailed there from Corunna.' He paused, staring intently at her as if gauging her reaction to hearing all that he – and I – had discovered. 'I do not believe,' he added softly, 'that your long voyage began in Spain.'

Slowly she shook her head. 'I did not say that it did,' she said in a low voice.

'Where, then?' Jack pressed on. 'Where was your home?'

There was utter silence in the hall. Then she lifted her chin, stared Jack in the eyes and said, 'Constantinople.'

Oh, dear Lord, I thought, *Jack was right.*

'You gave your name before marriage as Dalassena,' he said. 'Do you claim kinship with the emperor's mother?'

She made no response for a moment, then, almost reluctantly, she nodded.

Jack was relentless. 'And tell us again why you fled your home.'

She waved a hand in a gesture of frustration. 'My husband died of fever, and my father-in-law also became sick.' Her voice gathered strength as she spoke, and in her strange accent I caught intonations that my own people use. Had she picked them up from her husband and his father, even as she learned their language?

With a terrible sense of foreboding, I began, at last, to accept the truth.

'Disease is sweeping through the city,' Lady Rosaria went on, 'my husband dies, and Harald, he fears for the safety of me and of my child, last of his line. He gives me money, he gives me a maidservant, he commands me to take passage to England to find his kin so that they can take me in and so that the boy will be raised in the right manner for someone of his status.' Again, she raised her chin, the heavy veil floating in soft ripples across the lower part of her face and her throat. I caught a hint of her perfume; sweet, smelling of roses.

'Harald Fensman was a great lord, then?' Jack asked.

'Yes! He came from a fine manor with many acres, many slaves, big family with wealth and position!'

'This was what he told you?'

'Yes, yes! Always the tales of his home in *Fen*, of his rich kinsmen who prospered and thrived!'

'Why, then, if they were so wealthy, did he need to go abroad to make his fortune?' Jack asked.

'Because – because—' She shrugged. 'I cannot say,' she said angrily. 'I do not know these things; such matters are not discussed with me. I can only repeat what my father-in-law told me.'

'My lady, I believe that I can now tell you who Harald Fensman really was,' Jack said. His voice, I noticed, was suddenly gentle.

'You have found the home of my kinsmen?' Her eyes lit up. 'I go there, now?'

Jack turned to look briefly at me, and there was something in his expression . . . it was compassion. I realized he didn't like what he was doing. As if he sought some final proof before he revealed what we had discovered, he said, 'Your late husband's mother was called Gabrièla de Valéry, wasn't she?'

Lady Rosaria looked flustered. 'I – yes, I believe she was. I did not meet her,' she hurried on, 'for she had died before I entered – before I was wed to my husband.' Rallying, she straightened her spine and glared at Jack. 'What of it?' she demanded haughtily.

'My lady, there is no noble family,' Jack said gravely. 'No great house and no rich estates.'

'There is!' she cried. Then, her eyes holding growing horror, 'There *must* be!'

'Lassair and I have discovered the truth,' Jack went on, 'and we can reveal that Harald, son of Leafric, was born into a family of fenland fishermen and fowlers, who had lived here in this place for generations and whose descendants still do.' Again, he turned to me, holding out a hand to draw me forward. 'Lassair is Harald's great-niece, for her grandmother was his sister.'

Lady Rosaria was staring at me, her eyes wide with anguish. '*No*,' she whispered.

Lord Gilbert, I noticed, had taken quite a large step away from his guest, his action saying more plainly than words that, now the truth was emerging, he wished to distance himself from her. His face reddening, he snapped out at Jack, 'Is this true, Chevestrier?'

'We believe so, yes, my lord,' Jack said calmly.

Lord Gilbert backed further away, going to stand close beside Lady Emma. She, good woman that she is, frowned at him disapprovingly, murmuring something under her breath which I assumed was a reproof. 'Woman's an impostor,' he muttered back, his flabby cheeks shuddering with the force of his anger.

'I think, my lady,' Jack said, watching Lady Rosaria very closely, 'that Harald lied to you. He wished to impress you, I imagine, for to have a woman of your blood marry his son was a great honour, and he probably wanted to elevate his own kin so that their status stood a little closer to yours.'

Lady Rosaria seemed to have been struck dumb. She stood very still, swaying slightly, and I thought I could hear her whispering.

I remembered the state she'd been in when I first met her. She was in shock, for something had recently happened – in all likelihood, as we now surmised, the sickness and death of her maid – and she had been on the brink of despair.

I knew she wouldn't welcome me – my family and I were a far cry from what she'd believed she was coming to England to find – but, nevertheless, I wanted to stand by her. What we were to each other was irrelevant just then; she was in dire need, and I was a healer.

I moved to her side, reached down and took her icy hand in mine. 'Let me take you to your room, my lady,' I said, keeping my voice soft and low. 'You should lie down, I think, for you are all alone and have suffered a grave disappointment.'

She turned to me, panic in the huge eyes. 'We will support you,' I went on. 'Your baby son is part of my family, and we will not desert him. You are his mother, and you too will have our help.'

Quite how we were going to help her, I had no idea.

I moved forward, one small step at a time, and she came with me. She was sufficiently aware to remember where to go, and led me down a long passage, up a short flight of steps and into the guest chamber where Lord Gilbert had housed her.

She sank down on the wide bed, and I swung her legs up, pushing her gently back on the heaped pillows. 'Shall I remove your veil, my lady?' I asked. 'There is only me to see you, and—'

'*No.*' The one, brief word came out in a tone as hard and cold as ice. I had raised my hand towards her face, about to unfasten the veil, and she caught my wrist, holding it in a fist like a steel bracelet.

I bowed, backing away. 'Very well. You should try to sleep, Lady Rosaria. I will prepare a draught for you.'

But she turned her face away and did not answer.

The door closed softly behind the healer girl. Rosaria was alone. At first, she just lay there on the sumptuously comfortable bed, barely conscious, barely thinking.

Then slow tears began to fall from her eyes, soaking into the rich fabric of her veil.

She reached out her fingers and stroked the smooth silk of her gown. She touched the pearls around her throat, then moved her hand to the coverlet on which she lay. It was fur: smooth, glossy, warm.

I thought I would be going to a home like this, she thought, still hardly able to absorb the devastating disappointment. *I thought I would be kept in comfort, security and warmth for the rest of my days, fed with good, abundant food and given fine wine in a silver goblet.*

Deliberately she conjured up all the little luxuries of Lord Gilbert's house, accepted so casually by the lord and lady, given willingly to her, their guest, with the generosity of those who had plenty.

She curled her hands into fists, the knuckles showing white

against the taut skin. 'You lied, Harald,' she whispered. 'You *bastard*.'

For a disorienting instant, she thought she saw Harald in the room, standing straight and tall. He was pointing his finger at her.

And then, welling up from deep inside her, terrifying in its intensity and quite unstoppable, came the bitterest emotion of all.

Much later, when the raised voices in the hall had long ceased, the hurrying footsteps had stopped and the house was quiet, she got up. On silent feet she left her room, then, keeping to the shadows and out of sight, she made her way out of the great house where for the past days she had lived the life of which she had dreamed. They had treated her like a lady. She had worn beautiful garments, slept in a luxuriously soft bed, with sheets of clean, fine linen, soft blankets of finest wool, and, when night fell cold and chill, she had been comforted by a merry fire in the hearth.

She slipped out through the gates. Night was drawing on, and people were busy with the final outdoor tasks of the day. She huddled into her cloak, drawing the hood up. She did not want anyone to identify and stop her, to ask where she was going at such a late hour, to offer to come with her to make sure she returned safely.

She listened for the sound of water. It was close; here in this bleak marshy land, it was always close. She shivered. It was so different from the home she had left so far behind. No sun, no brilliant colours, no deep blue sky.

Oh!

Her grief, her pain and her guilt rose up in a devastating flood.

She walked on, the pretty, unsuitable indoor slippers sliding in the muddy ground. She hoped she could find the place. She had listened carefully when they described it, on that terrible day when the news came. It had been the beginning of the end: somehow she had known it, even then, some time before today's devastating discovery of the true nature of Harald's kin. *There is no rosy future for me*, she thought, the words running through her head again and again as she hurried on. *I have struggled so hard, and it has all been for nothing.*

Remorse hit her like a fist to the heart.

She walked on. One of the little shoes came off, and cold mud oozed between her toes. She bent down to put the slipper on again.

Then, after quite a long time, suddenly, she was there. She had found the right spot, and she stood for a moment staring down at the meandering little waterway. Torn branches and bits of dead vegetation clung to the steep sides of the banks, and she saw that the water level was lower now as the flood receded.

She came to the bridge.

Debris brought upstream by the flood still partially blocked its arch, forming a wide pool on the far side.

Perfect.

She walked into the water. There was no grip for her feet in the silly little slippers, and her legs went from under her. It was so cold. Her veil floated for an instant as the water closed over her head. Weighed by her heavy cloak, she sank quickly. The pool was very deep, and her feet, the toes pointed, found no firm ground.

There was only the water.

Presently, the rush of bubbles coming up to the surface ceased, and all was still.

She hadn't even struggled.

SEVENTEEN

S kuli stood staring up at the ancient ruins soaring above. Rollo had worked his way through the crewmen crowding around their captain, and now he was at Skuli's side. Standing so close, he was able to pick up every nuance of Skuli's mood.

What he observed horrified him.

Skuli had metamorphosed from a taciturn, driven, silent and brooding figure into a being who seemed lit from within. His expression was radiant, and his light eyes shone as if reflecting brilliant starlight. Somehow he was giving off energy. Rollo, glancing down at his own bare forearm, noticed that the hairs were on end.

They had been standing below the ruins for some time. Breaking abruptly from his enchanted stillness, Skuli turned to his crew and said, 'At last, my faithful friends, we have reached our goal! At the almost unbearable cost of the loss of our three honoured companions, we stand at the very spot we have dreamed of and yearned for over so many long months.'

He opened his mouth in a great cry of joy, stretching out his arms as if to embrace the whole place. 'Asgard, my friends! Here we stand on the very edge of the blessed realm, and soon we shall find Valhalla, and Bifrost that links Asgard to heaven!'

He paused, breathing hard. Then, more calmly, he went on. 'Since we were children crouched wide-eyed round our fathers' hearths, we have heard the old tales, learned of the deeds of the great heroes who fought a mighty war before these very walls, their chariots raising the sand in vast clouds and the fine dust soaking up the brilliant blood of the wounded and the glorious dead. And the blood of legendary men bred with the Aesir, who dwelled in Asgard, and from their loins sprang our own honoured gods, Thor, Odin, Freyr, Freya, Tyr, and even the evil Loki and his wolf-son, Fenrir.'

With a shiver of dread, Rollo recalled that haunting wolf's howl . . .

'Our beloved Odin travelled into the north, as the poets tell us,' Skuli hurried on, his voice getting steadily louder, 'and there he took many wives and populated our world. Now, at long last after the endless millennia, we have returned to pay homage.' He paused, his eyes roaming around his enthralled crewmen. 'And,' he added, swooping down to a whisper that was even more frightening than the loud proclamations, 'to tell them that the men of the north do not forget.'

Filled with disbelief, horror and dread, Rollo found he couldn't move.

Solemnly Skuli turned to face the ancient ruins up on their plateau. Raising his voice again, he began to sing a hymn of praise, and after only a moment the crew joined in.

Rollo thought he had drifted into a dream world.

His reason battling with the evidence of his senses, his mind working frantically, he felt the deep shudder of the soul that affects a man when he comes face to face with madness.

For surely Skuli was mad; a sane man did not travel halfway across the known world in search of his gods.

Did he?

And why? What purpose did it serve, other than to bow down in worship? Could that not be done *anywhere* on the good earth that the gods had created? That, anyway, was what good Christians believed. But then, his rational mind pointed out, Christians in their droves went on pilgrimages, undertaking arduous, dangerous and expensive journeys purely to visit a shrine, a holy site, or even the place where a sacred relic was housed.

Skuli's hymn was continuing, its intensity growing in pace with its volume. The air was thrumming and humming with the sound, which was being magnified as it rebounded from the great ruin-topped mound soaring up before them.

Rollo was in turmoil, the noise and the disturbed air seeming to crowd in on him, beating him down, spurring him to respond and fight back so that he could barely organize his thoughts.

But something was emerging . . . An idea, sparked off by something he had just been trying to work out . . .

Yes! He had it.

He knew suddenly, and without a doubt, why Skuli had come here; why he had risked so much, striven so hard and paid such a terrible price.

His gods had had their day; the world had changed, and a new deity was in the ascendant. The Christians had spread their faith all over the places where Skuli's gods had once reigned unchallenged.

And Skuli had come here, to this place from which he believed they had once sprung, to reawaken them.

The singing had worked the men up into a state of ecstasy. Some were on their knees; some were weeping, sobbing, tearing at their hair and their beards. Skuli stood before them all, staring up at the soaring ruins, singing in a voice that seemed to shake the earth.

Shake the earth . . .

The wolf howled, close at hand; it was Fenrir, Loki's wolf-son, evil in his heart. In a tumult of fear, Rollo heard the eight-legged horse again; Sleipnir, with Odin on his back, was thundering across the plain and racing into battle. Overhead flew Odin's ravens, Huginn and Muninn, Thought and Memory, their sharp black eyes piercing any who dared to look, and—

With superhuman effort, Rollo pulled himself back. *NO!* There was no eight-legged horse; no evil wolf; no cruel-eyed, magical ravens! Such things did not exist; they belonged to the realm of legend and myth.

The earth shook again, and a deep, resonant rumble sounded from somewhere far beneath them.

Earthquake.

Grabbing Skuli, Rollo yelled, right in his ear, 'We have to move! We must get the men away from the mound and from what stands on top of it, before the whole lot falls on us and crushes us to death!'

Skuli twisted round to face him, trying to shake him off. The mania that had him in its grip made his eyes blaze. '*We stay where we are!*' he shouted. 'This is what we have come for!'

Rollo tightened both hands on Skuli's arm, dragging at him, only his desperation driving him to tackle a man so much taller, broader, stronger and heavier. 'You cannot do this!' he yelled. 'These men are your responsibility! They have followed you loyally all this way, endured everything you have asked of them – you must not abuse their loyalty by endangering their lives!'

For an instant, Skuli stopped struggling. Rollo had time for one fleeting moment of relief – *he's seen reason!* – and he eased his fierce grip.

It was a huge mistake.

Released, Skuli swung back his massive right arm and punched Rollo very hard on the side of the head. Blackness flooded Rollo's vision even as he fell.

Lady Rosaria's body was brought back to Lakehall on a hurdle. Someone had covered her with a beautiful velvet cloak, its rich purple shimmering in the soft autumn sunshine.

Lord Gilbert and Lady Emma stood side by side at the foot of the steps leading to the great door of the hall, heads bowed. Edild and I, summoned to Lakehall as soon as Lord Gilbert had learned what had happened, stood behind them, a couple of steps up. Looking down on them, I saw Lady Emma straighten her back. I thought she was disguising her emotions well, but then, revealing a more human side, I saw her reach out for her husband's hand. He turned to her briefly, giving her a quick smile.

In the mood of distress and shock, it was comforting, somehow.

The four men carrying the body came slowly up to the steps, and one of the pair at the front looked up at Lord Gilbert. 'Where shall we take the lady, my lord?' he asked.

Lord Gilbert looked at Lady Emma, who turned round to us. 'Where do you think, Edild?' she asked quietly.

'Again, the undercroft is suitable, my lady,' my aunt replied. 'Lassair and I will tend her there.' She hesitated, looking at Lady Emma with raised brows.

Lady Emma understood the unasked question. 'The other body has been removed,' she said, her voice quite steady despite her shocked pallor. 'It is now in the crypt beneath the church. Lord Gilbert and Father Augustine have decided to postpone the burial, in the hope that someone may yet turn up to claim her.'

It was, I thought sadly, an increasingly faint hope.

Lady Emma murmured to the men with the hurdle, and they bore their burden away around the side of the house, to the door that opened on to the undercroft. Hitching my satchel on my shoulder, I followed Edild in their wake.

The wide vaulted ceiling of the huge undercroft spread out above us as we bent over the trestle on which Lady Rosaria had been laid. Lord Gilbert's house servants had provided many candles, set in tall brass holders and spaced around the trestle. Our little area of the crypt was brightly lit but the shadows gathered in the corners, and the bulky shapes of whatever was stored there loomed over us as if they drew close to watch us at our work.

Water from Lady Rosaria's garments dripped steadily on to the stone floor. We removed her little silk slippers – her feet were tiny – and rolled her over on to her side so that we could unlace her gorgeous gown. Edild slid it down off the cold, pale body, then handed it to me. I was touched to see that the hem was coming down; in her flight, she must have caught her heel. I had a sudden, painful image of her, sitting sewing in that tavern room in Cambridge. As I inspected her work, I thought, *Poor Rosaria; you weren't very good with your needle, were you?*

Edild was now stripping off the undergarments: there were

several underskirts. Now she handed me a chemise made of some fine, smooth fabric . . .

I had seen a garment made of this material before.

'Edild, I—'

My aunt gave a *tsk!* of impatience. 'Not now, Lassair. Help me with her – I must attempt to detect if there's water in her lungs.'

Together we gently turned the body so that it was face-down, and Edild applied steady pressure on the upper back. Water came out in a lazy stream, seeping through the veil and out from beneath it.

'I think we can tell your lawman that she did indeed drown,' Edild said.

We rolled Lady Rosaria on to her back once more.

Edild had covered her with a length of linen, and now, respectful of the dead woman's modesty, she examined the body, uncovering it a bit at a time. Shoulders, chest and breasts, then waist and belly. Feet, ankles, legs, thighs, groin.

Edild stood back from the table, a frown of perplexity on her face.

'What is it?' I felt apprehensive; afraid, almost.

Slowly my aunt beckoned. 'Come and see. I may be wrong – I must be wrong – but I'd like to hear what you think.'

'What must I look at?'

'Her breasts, then her private parts.'

I did as I was ordered. The breasts were small; I remembered the gown that had been too big in the bust, and how I'd imagined Lady Rosaria had lost the fullness as her milk dried up. The nipples were pink and dainty, like a girl's. Carefully I drew up the sheet to cover her chest, then, raising it from its lower end, looked down on her belly and thighs.

It felt wrong to be examining her. She had been so proud, so haughty, and her stiff, erect posture had informed you, all the time that you were in her presence, that she was a fine lady. But I had a job to do, and I could not afford scruples.

I looked at her slim, smooth thighs, at the narrow hips, the flat, almost concave, belly. She must have padded out her underskirts for, naked, she had a much slighter, more boyish figure than she'd appeared to have when clothed.

Finally, aware of Edild's eyes watching me, I gently parted the thighs and stared at the genitalia.

After a moment of utter stillness, I covered the body, tucking the sheet in around it. Then I met my aunt's eyes.

'She has never borne a child,' I said.

'No,' Edild agreed.

We went on looking at each other.

'So whose baby is Leafric?' I whispered. 'Is he an adopted child, do you think?' My thoughts were racing ahead. 'Perhaps Lady Rosaria was barren – she does look quite immature – or perhaps her husband was infertile? As members of a great family, they'd have definitely wanted a child to inherit and to carry on the name, so maybe . . .'

I trailed to a stop. Lady Rosaria bore an illustrious name, or so Jack had informed me, but her late husband – her Hugo Guillaume Fensmanson – hadn't belonged to a prominent, important family. He and his father had been my own kinsmen.

Edild was looking down at the dead woman's head, encased in the elaborately wound headdress with its jewels and its fringe of tiny bells, and at the dead face, still shrouded in the heavy veil. Drenched, like every other garment she had been wearing, the veil clung to her features.

'I think we must remove this,' she said, delicately touching its bottom hem with her forefinger. 'The headdress first; she should be allowed to go on concealing her face until the very last moment.'

She began to unwind the headdress, the cloth coming away from the head in a long stream of gorgeous fabric. Lady Rosaria's hair had been dark, long and wavy, and she had braided it into two heavy plaits.

Then, at last, Edild took off the veil.

And we stared, aghast, at what had happened to Lady Rosaria's face.

We made sure that she was decently covered from her chin to her toes before I was sent to summon Jack. We had already drawn our conclusions concerning her body, and there was no need for any eyes other than ours to look upon her.

Her face, though, was a different matter.

Now Jack stood between Edild and me, and, from his expression, I guessed he was as horrified as we had been.

Lady Rosaria's left nostril had been slit. The cut had gone right into the whorl that joins the nose to the cheek, slicing up so that the nostril was open, and the cartilage inside revealed.

Below this horror, her mouth was now slack and blueish, but it was clear to see it had been generous and well-shaped.

Eyes and mouth, then, were beautiful; before her mutilation, she must have been wonderful to look at.

Unless the wound had been a terrible accident, or a healer's attempt to excise diseased flesh, it looked as if someone had inflicted the cut as some barbaric punishment. I could scarcely make myself believe it. 'Was this the result of some frightful sickness?' I whispered, looking at Edild.

'No, I do not believe so,' she replied. 'It looks, from the neatness of the wound and from the healthy flesh surrounding it, that it was done deliberately.'

'*Why?*' I cried.

Beside me, Jack stirred. He hadn't spoken since he had come down into the crypt, but now he did, and his voice was vibrant with emotion. 'I believe this is the mark of a slave,' he said. 'In just such a way, or so I have heard, do men of the southern lands mark the men and women who are their property. If they try to run away, they are easily identified, and can be recaptured and returned to their masters for punishment.'

I tried to absorb that. I knew such things existed; that, in many parts of the world, men did not think it wrong to own another human being. Serfdom, indeed, was only a little removed from slavery.

But to mutilate someone in this way! To mutilate a woman like Lady Rosaria; to take away her beauty, so that she was driven to cover herself up every second of every day. It was beyond barbarous.

Then I thought, *If she was a slave, how can she be Lady Rosaria?*

And a slave, surely, can't be a member of the family of the Byzantine emperor . . .

I said, 'Who was she?'

And, with a sigh, Jack replied, 'Well, we know who she wasn't.'

He must have sensed my frustration at the inadequacy of the response. Catching my eye, he said with a faint smile, 'It's a start.' Then, turning to Edild, he said, 'Can she now go to her grave, or is there more that you can learn from the body?'

Slowly Edild shook her head. 'I think we have seen all we need to.' She touched the dead woman's shoulder with a gentle hand. 'I will prepare her for burial.'

'Need we tell Lord Gilbert and Lady Emma about her nose?' I burst out. 'It seems so – disloyal.'

Jack looked at me, compassion softening his features. 'We have to tell them, I think,' he said gently. 'But let's wait until we have a few more answers.'

I nodded. It was the best Lady Rosaria was going to get.

We left Edild to her task. She said she didn't need my assistance, and I was glad to get away. Jack went back up into the hall to tell Lord Gilbert what the corpse had revealed, but, again, I wasn't needed. At the top of the steps, however, he turned and said, 'Don't go away.'

He was gone for some time. I guessed Lord Gilbert's outrage at having been fooled by a slave girl into believing she was a great lady, and entertaining her accordingly for a whole week, was forcing him to demand answers which Jack wasn't able to give. *Yet*: a brighter man would have hurried Jack away to get on with his investigations, but Lord Gilbert, as I have often observed, does not have the sort of mind that flashes and fizzes with intelligence.

In the end, it seemed to be Lady Emma who extracted Jack from Lord Gilbert's angry indignation; she it was, at least, who ushered him to the door of the hall and wished him good luck.

He came flying down the steps, grabbed hold of my hand and, pulling me along, ran across the yard and down the track. 'We need to talk, but not here,' he panted. He glanced back at the hall. 'If that fat fool asks me *once more* who she is, I'll punch him.'

I grinned. 'It might shake his brains up a bit, but I don't believe it'd make him any brighter.'

Jack laughed shortly. I joined in, but then suddenly I had an image of what he'd done to Gaspard Picot and his man. Jack, I realized with a shiver, was more than capable of punching even a man of Lord Gilbert's status, and I should not fool myself otherwise.

It was frightening.

We hurried on, and, reaching the main track, turned away from the village. A man and a woman passed, then an ox cart rumbled in the opposite direction. Jack looked around. 'Where can we go where we can speak in private?'

'Follow me.' I led the way up the sloping ground to the left, heading past the fields and the pastures until, at the summit of the higher ground, we reached the ancient oak tree that stands its solitary watch over Aelf Fen.

Jack and I were alone.

He leaned back against the oak's massive trunk, closed his eyes and let out a long breath. 'That's better,' he said after a while. 'Now I can think.'

Deducing from his words and his actions that he wanted to be left in peace, I moved away, round to the other side of the oak. I hitched up my skirts and climbed up to the convenient cleft between two of the huge lower branches. It's a spot I've been hiding in since I was a child, and very good for quiet contemplation.

I copied Jack's example, leaning back and closing my eyes. Immediately I saw Lady Rosaria's ruined face. *No; don't think about that.* I made myself relax, and very soon, out there in the peace and the silence, I appreciated the good sense of getting right away from the clamouring, demanding voices and the unanswerable questions.

Unhurriedly, I went through everything I'd noticed about Lady Rosaria's corpse. After a while, one thing floated to the surface of my mind: the chemise. It was made of a fabric with which I wasn't familiar, yet, as soon as I handled it, I knew I'd recently seen something similar: the shift which Jack had found in the pool where the first drowned body had ended up, and which we'd surmised had belonged to our tall, fair-haired woman.

Although that had been a cheaper, poorer-quality garment, I'd have been ready to swear that both were made of the same fabric.

Clothing . . . I had a sudden vision of Lady Rosaria back at the inn in Cambridge, sewing up her hem. Then I saw that same hem as I'd seen it just that morning, the stitches already coming undone. I'd thought it meant she hadn't been much of a seam-stress. But another reason for making a botch of a sewing task is that you're in a hurry.

The bodice of the gown had been loose.

She was tall, blonde-haired, blue-eyed, very beautiful and utterly perfect.

Facts and snippets of conversation were flowing freely around my head, and I was beginning – just beginning – to see a picture. The urge to leap down and run to lay it before Jack was almost irresistible, but I kept calm, stayed where I was and thought some more.

Was it too much to construe, when all there really was to go on was two undergarments made of the same, unfamiliar, *foreign* material?

No.

Slowly I descended from my perch and walked round to where Jack was still leaning against the tree.

'They swapped clothes,' I said.

His eyes flew open. 'What?'

'Lady Rosaria and the woman who was found in the flood pool. They both had undershifts of the same fabric, only one was a far more costly item; a lady's garment as opposed to a maid's. And Lady Rosaria – the woman we knew as Lady Rosaria – had altered her gown. I know she did,' I insisted, 'I caught her sewing when I visited her in the Cambridge inn. And the bodice was too loose.'

He was staring at me intently, the green eyes slightly narrowed in fierce concentration. 'You're saying Lady Rosaria and the drowned woman travelled to England together?'

'Yes.'

He shook his head. 'But the drowned woman didn't match the description of the maid which the mate of *The Good Shepherd* gave us – he said the maid was small, nimble and dark, and he'd have sworn she was a Spaniard – *oh!*'

I almost heard the blinkers fall off his eyes. For a moment we just stood grinning at each other. Then he said, very softly, 'Lady Rosaria was the maid, and the drowned woman was her mistress.' He pursed his lips in a silent whistle. Then, frowning, he said urgently 'Does it stand up to scrutiny? Does everything fit?'

'*Yes!*' I shouted, although the response was inspired more by instinct than reason. Forcing my flying thoughts to slow down, I said, 'The real daughter-in-law – the tall, fair woman who drowned – was heading to England, to Harald's only living kin. She became ill, and her maid – Rosaria – realized she couldn't save her. So she took her place, in the expectation that she was exchanging the life of a servant, or even a slave, for that of a lady.'

Jack nodded slowly. 'It's easy to understand why,' he said. 'Rosaria must have been a slave, and probably had already tried once to run away to a better life. It was that attempt which earned her the mutilating mark that would henceforth always identify her status.'

'If the real daughter-in-law was dead,' I went on – thinking even as I did how strange it was that both Jack and I were trying so hard to defend Rosaria, given that neither of us had liked her – 'then she must have asked herself, where was the harm?'

'Had she reported her mistress's death,' Jack said, 'she wouldn't have been able to carry out the deception.' He looked at me steadily. 'And it wouldn't have altered the fact that the mistress was dead.'

'She could have—' I began. Then a new thought struck me; perhaps the most powerful consideration of all. 'Leafric,' I whispered. 'No wonder Lady Rosaria wasn't much of a mother to him – she *wasn't* his mother.'

I realized I hadn't told him what Edild and I had discovered. 'Rosaria had never given birth,' I said. 'I'd wondered if Leafric had been adopted, but that's not right, is it?'

I think Jack and I both had the same impulse at the same moment. As we started to run, winding through the fields and jumping the ditches, I was thinking, over and over again, *There's one way to prove it! There's one way to prove it!*

We arrived, hot and panting, in the churchyard. 'What's the priest's name?' Jack demanded.

'Father Augustine.'

'I'll find him and explain – you go and check.'

Trying to calm my gasping breathing, I went into the cool, dark church. I approached the simple altar, pausing to bow my head. In common with so many of the people of our region, my family still remember the old gods. However, I had come to recognize much to love in the merciful, compassionate God of the Christian faith. He was, I had discovered, a good, true friend in times of severe trial. I whispered to him now, praying that what I was about to do was the right thing. That, somehow, it would help the innocent, helpless infant who had lost so much.

I went over to the low door that opens on to the steps down to the crypt. The sweet herbs and incense helped to disguise the smell, but only a little. I told myself to ignore it.

The body of the drowned woman lay in its winding sheets, ready for burial. There was no need to look at her upper body; I remembered what her face had been like when first she'd been brought to Lakehall, and didn't want to see the damage done by the passage of another week. And there was no point in inspecting her breasts; what remained of them had indicated she had been full-chested.

Slowly I unwound the fabric covering her lower limbs, folding it back until the belly and pubis were revealed. Forcing myself on, I looked at what I had come to see.

Compared to my aunt, I was still a novice midwife. But I knew enough to judge. There were stretch marks over the lower belly, extending out towards the hips. And, when I further violated the dead woman's privacy, there was no more room for doubt.

She had borne a child.

I covered her up again. I knew I should hasten away – Jack was waiting to hear what I'd found out – but I couldn't tear myself away from her. I reached out my hand and laid it over hers, clasped on her breast.

This woman, I knew without any doubt, was Leafric's mother. She had given birth to him, loved him, played with him, nursed him. I knew she had; it *must* have been her breasts he'd fed at, for Rosaria had been no wet-nurse. And there could be no doubt that this woman had cared constantly and devotedly for her baby son; why else would he have missed her so very much when she disappeared?

He's sad, Mattie had said, back in Cambridge. *He just lies there, staring around, for all the world as if he's looking for something.*

Not some*thing*; some*one*. His mother. She had become ill, and she had died. Someone else had tried to take her place, but her poor little son hadn't understood why that someone else didn't smell right. Didn't taste, feel or sound right. Didn't hold him as he needed to be held.

He just wanted his mother.

Tears were splashing down on our hands; mine and the dead woman's. I hadn't realized I was weeping. Now, staring down at her long shape, wrapped all ready for burial, I wanted to gather her up and take her in my arms, devastated and ruined though her poor body was. I leaned down over her so that my lips were close to her ear.

'I'll see he's all right,' I whispered. 'I promise.'

It was time to leave her. I kissed the smoothly wrapped fore-head, and now there was no revulsion.

As I mounted the steps back up to the church and hurried outside, I wondered if I had just been touched with the great love which they say is the gift of the Christian lord. Kissing a body dead for well over a week wasn't something I'd ever done before, yet it had been too strong an impulse to resist.

Love.

Yes, the gesture had been prompted by love.

I dried my eyes and hurried to find Jack.

EIGHTEEN

Jack and Father Augustine were standing, deep in conversation, by the gate into the churchyard. Hearing my running footsteps, both turned towards me.

Father Augustine's lean face was creased with concern. Bending his long, thin frame so that he could peer into my face, he said, 'Are you all right, child?'

'Yes!' I was taken aback at the question.

'It is hard to accept the death of a kinswoman, even one who you did not know in life,' he went on.

'But—' I'd been about to protest that she was only a relative by marriage, but just then I experienced another surge of that strange, unearthly love for her, and somehow our exact relationship didn't seem important.

'Now that we know who she is,' the priest went on, 'I will make arrangements for her burial service, if you and your family are ready?'

He was treating me with such kindness. Until quite recently, I'd thought him a chilly, self-contained man without much compassion. I'd been wrong. 'Thank you, Father,' I said. 'We will discuss it and let you know.'

He bowed. 'Of course.' Then, almost hesitantly, he added, 'I shall pray for her, and for you all.'

As if his offer had embarrassed him, he dipped his head again, turned and hurried away towards his church.

Jack grabbed my hand and led me down on to the track, turning left towards Lakehall. 'Come on,' he urged, hastening the pace.

We were going back to find Edild, I surmised, to tell her what we had just discovered. I said breathlessly, 'We must make it clear to Father Augustine that the drowned woman was Harald's daughter-in-law, not his daughter.'

Jack glanced at me, slowing his pace and drawing to a halt. 'Describe her,' he commanded.

'What? We can't waste time on—'

'*Yes we can.* Describe the drowned woman.'

'Strongly built, tall, blonde, blue eyed.'

'Now describe her child, as you did when you first examined him.'

Responding to his urgency, frantically I tried to think back. 'I said he had his mother's olive skin, his hair was fair and his eyes light blue, and—'

'And from that you concluded his father was a northerner,' Jack interrupted. He was looking at me expectantly.

Then I understood. 'It was his *mother* who was the northerner,' I whispered. 'Harald's daughter?' I couldn't help making it a question.

'I believe so,' Jack agreed. 'Remember how your great-uncle Sihtric told us Harald described his wife?'

'"Her name was Gabrièla de Valéry, and she was tall, blonde-haired, blue-eyed, very beautiful and utterly perfect."' One of the benefits of being the family bard is learning how to memorize words after only one hearing.

'Which could equally well describe the woman lying up there.' Jack jerked his head in the direction of the church.

Slowly, inexorably – joyfully – the truth dawned. 'She's my kinswoman,' I whispered. 'My father's cousin.'

I had felt love for her; perhaps it had been the link of our common blood, calling out as it recognized its own.

There was no time to dwell on that now, although I had the feeling I would do in the future. Already we were hastening on again, and all too soon we'd be confronting Lord Gilbert. And my aunt . . .

Something else occurred to me. 'I've been thinking,' I said.

Jack gave a swift grin, quickly suppressed. 'Go on, then.'

'It's probably not important, but I can't quite work it out. Lady Rosaria and the blonde woman exchanged clothes *before* they disembarked at Lynn – they must have done, because the mate of *The Good Shepherd* said it was the maid who had to be helped ashore, not the lady. But we now know it was the blonde woman, not Lady Rosaria, who was dying.' I paused, trying to work it out. 'I suppose Rosaria recognized that her mistress was already very sick and would probably die, and so swapped their roles while she had the chance.'

Jack gave me a strange look. I'd expected him to dismiss my unease, but instead I was left with the feeling that he shared it.

We got as far as telling Lord Gilbert that it had been the blonde woman, not Lady Rosaria, who was the infant's mother, but he seemed to be unable to take it in. He asked the same questions over and over again, and I think we'd have gone on all day had Lady Emma not intervened, summing up our discoveries with admirable brevity and clarity. Holding my eyes, she inclined her head subtly towards her husband, as if to say, *Don't worry about him, I'll explain it later.*

Addressing my remarks to her and to Edild, who had been in the hall talking quietly to Lady Emma when we got back, I said, 'The fact that Lady Rosaria wasn't his mother explains his sadness, since he was pining for his real mother, and also why the bodice of Lady Rosaria's gown was too loose, and why she'd taken up the hem. It wasn't her gown.'

'*Please*,' Lord Gilbert said plaintively, 'can we all stop calling her *Lady* Rosaria?'

I hid a smile. It was going to take Lord Gilbert some time to get over having been so thoroughly taken in.

'I cannot but feel sorry for L— for Rosaria,' Lady Emma said. 'And for the mistress whose place she usurped. To have come all that way, surviving the perils of the rough seas, only for both of them to die on reaching the longed-for goal.'

'Yes, my lady,' I agreed. 'And the poor blonde woman was sick almost all the way; certainly, from Bordeaux to Lynn . . .'

Three curious, intent pairs of eyes stared at me; four, if you counted Lord Gilbert's, but he still only seemed to have a vague idea of what we were talking about.

My aunt said softly, 'What is it, Lassair?'

'Something has been worrying me for some time, and I've just realized what it is,' I said, the words tumbling out. 'It was odd, surely, that, according to the mate of the ship on which they sailed, the "maid" wasn't sick on the voyage from Corunna to Bordeaux – perhaps the worst bit of the Bay of Biscay – yet, as soon as they sailed north from Bordeaux, she was vomiting continuously. Because—'

But all at once I found I didn't want to go on.

Jack turned to Lady Emma. 'Have we your permission to search through Rosaria's belongings?'

She nodded, clearly understanding. 'Of course. This way.'

She and Lord Gilbert stood in the doorway while Edild and I inspected the many items that Lady Rosaria had spread out. Beautiful robes and underclothing; fine shoes; rich jewellery. And then, in a small leather bag tied with a drawstring, a little glass pot containing a mysterious dark substance.

Edild removed the lid and inspected the contents. After quite a long time, she said, 'This is kohl. It is a cosmetic, used to outline and enhance the eyes.' I wondered if the others were having the same thought: having suffered the terrible mutilation of her nose, it was hardly surprising that she wished to make her other features as beautiful as possible. And, out of memory, once again those magnificent dark eyes stared at me.

'Kohl is made from finely powdered stibium, otherwise called antimony,' Edild went on, 'mixed up with soot and blended with olive oil to make a paste.' She was already searching through the remainder of the objects Rosaria had left spread around the room. 'We must try to find the raw ingredients,' she muttered. Then she raised her head, looking at each of us in turn. 'Stibium is a poison, producing headaches, dizziness, sickness. It is used as an emetic, but in ruthless hands, it is the tool of a murderer. Fed in regular small amounts over many days, the resulting continual vomiting weakens the victim, until finally they become so debilitated that they can no longer hold off death.'

Edild was still searching, her movements increasingly desperate. Gently Jack caught hold of her hands. 'If you are right,' he said, 'and I am sure you are, she will have got rid of the poison long since.'

Edild stopped, then stood perfectly still. 'Of course,' she said neutrally.

'So – so Rosaria, who was originally the maid, poisoned the blonde woman, who was originally her mistress, by putting this stuff in her food all the way home?' Lord Gilbert's fury seemed about to choke him, and I couldn't help wondering if he would have been as indignant had it been the lady who had poisoned the maid.

'It seems likely,' Jack said.

'Can this theory be put to the test?' Lord Gilbert demanded. 'The drowned woman is still in the crypt beneath the church. You!' He spun round to Edild. 'Can you tell for sure if she had taken poison?'

'I will try,' Edild said calmly, 'although it must now be almost a fortnight since her death.'

'I'll come with you,' I said firmly. I was desperate to get her alone, for she needed to know the whole story.

My aunt and I stood over the body of the blonde woman, and Edild frowned in concentration. After some time, she said, 'To establish with certainty whether or not she was given antimony, I'll have to open her stomach and inspect the contents.' Already she was pulling at the winding sheet.

I caught hold of her wrist. 'Don't,' I said softly. I'd once seen

Gurdyman perform the procedure on a corpse, and I didn't want it to happen to this woman.

Edild shot me a look. 'Explain.'

I paused, gathering my thoughts. Then I said, 'As we surmise, Rosaria was a slave. She wasn't Harald's daughter-in-law, but one of his servants, sent by the dying Harald to accompany the tall, blonde woman and her little boy on her long voyage to find her English kin. Rosaria wasn't married to any son of Harald; perhaps he never even *had* a son.' Again, I paused. 'But he did have a daughter, and his daughter married a man of the south, dark-haired and olive-skinned. When he died and Harald was dying, Harald's daughter and her baby were the last of his line, for had there been other family in Constantinople, then there would have been no need to send them so far away. He had to save them,' I went on, 'and getting them away to his kindred in the north was the best he could do.'

Edild was touching the dead woman's shoulder with delicate fingers. I saw a tear on her cheek.

Very softly I said, 'This is Harald's daughter. She's your cousin.'

I heard Edild sharply draw in her breath.

There was silence for a long time. Then Edild put her hand down to where the sheet covered the dead woman's heart, resting it lightly above the smooth linen. 'We would have welcomed you, cousin,' she said gently. 'We are not rich, and have no fine houses such as Rosaria was hoping to find, but what we have we would have shared with you.'

I waited until Edild raised her head, then, my eyes holding hers, I said, 'Rosaria killed her. She poisoned her, bit by bit, making her sick for days on end, and she took her identity. Then, when she finally succumbed and died, Rosaria pushed her body into the water. The storm surge and the flood that came immediately afterwards dislodged the corpse from wherever it was hidden, and washed it so far inland up the river that, when it was found, Aelf Fen was the nearest place to which to go for help.'

Slowly Edild nodded. 'Yes,' she whispered. 'Yes, that is how it must have been.' Then, frowning, she said, 'But why, when Harald sent his daughter away to England, did he let her and her maidservant believe they were going to find a noble, rich house-hold where they would live in luxury? He knew they wouldn't. He knew they'd only find us.'

I thought about what Sihtric the monk had said: *There was never anyone like Harald for building up a tale, and we always took everything he said with a pinch of salt.* 'He exaggerated,' I said softly. 'So far from home, who was to know if he made his family out to be richer and more powerful than they really were? In time, no doubt, like many braggarts, he came to believe his own boasting. I don't think,' I concluded, 'that he'd deliberately have misled his beloved daughter.'

For some time, neither of us spoke. Then, taking a breath and squaring her shoulders, Edild bestowed a last gentle pat on the dead woman and turned away. 'I shall leave her be. The kohl we found among Rosaria's belongings is sufficient to suggest she could have poisoned her mistress; whether or not she did, it hardly makes any difference now.' She met my eyes. 'God will judge her,' she murmured.

Then she led the way across the crypt to the steps, and we left our dead kinswoman to the peace of death.

The earthquake that hit the north-western tip of the Anatolian plateau that September morning brought down a long section of the ruined walls of ancient Troy. The group of twenty-three northerners who had been standing at the foot of the plateau when disaster struck got off lightly; only two of them died.

The remainder, leaderless, terrified almost to madness, at first tried with frantic hands to extract their fallen comrades from the huge heap of earth and stones. But it was hopeless. The ground was still shuddering, and, pausing only to scratch a few hasty runes on to a block of fallen masonry, they fled.

As they hastened back to *Gullinbursti*, carrying the unconscious and helping the injured and dazed, a pair of ravens soared overhead.

Rollo came to himself two days later. His head ached so badly that he groaned aloud. Exploring his skull with nervous fingers, he found a lump the size of an egg on his forehead and a long ragged cut running up into his hairline. His left leg hurt, too.

Risking a glance at it, he saw that his ankle had been put in splints and bandaged.

He dared not even start to think what sort of injury those wrappings concealed.

But I am alive, he thought.

He thought back to the moment of disaster. He had seen the high cliff that formed the edge of the plateau begin to quiver, and then, as it had *melted* before his horrified eyes, he had dashed forward to try to pull Skuli back.

Now, as he gazed around the deck, slowly counting heads, he understood that he had failed. Skuli was gone; so was Tostig the singer, who had been at Skuli's side as they approached the place Skuli had convinced his crew was Asgard, home of the gods. Fat Eric now held the tiller, but he wasn't laughing any more.

Gullinbursti was under sail, and a stiff breeze from out of the south-east sped them along. It was a blessing, for the depleted crew, shocked and grieving, were as yet in no state for the hard physical work of rowing. Perhaps, Rollo thought vaguely, the gods, having punched Skuli and his men very hard in the face for their audacity, were now feeling a little remorse, and sending them a favourable wind.

Conversation was limited to everyday matters. Nobody seemed ready to talk about what had happened. Brand the cook, apparently having made up his mind that good food was the best cure, spoiled them every evening with meals that were irresistible, and, whenever supplies of fresh foods ran low, he insisted on putting in to shore to replenish his stores.

And so *Gullinbursti* made her way home. As they rounded the southern tip of the Peloponnese, Rollo took his first stumbling steps unaided along the ship. As they headed west for Sicily, he won the argument with Brand – who as the oldest and most experienced mariner had taken the role of master – and finally took his place as a working member of the crew. His broken ankle prevented him from rowing, so Brand set out to teach him how to steer.

The days passed. Sometimes the wind failed, and then the hours of daylight were sheer hard slog. At the tiller, Rollo began to learn his craft, and now found he no longer had to concentrate to the exclusion of everything else. With time to think, he went back in his mind over the preceding, extraordinary weeks.

It was too painful to dwell on what had happened on the plateau, and Skuli's madness still had the power to shock. Instead, Rollo turned his thoughts to Harald.

What a tale he had told! With his inner eye, Rollo saw once again the old man's face as he had described his marriage to his beautiful wife, and his boundless joy when the baby girl born to them grew up in her mother's image. His happiness when the daughter – her name was Agathe – made a good marriage to an intelligent and perceptive Saracen doctor; the summit of all his hopes when her baby, Harald's grandchild, was a boy.

But then violence had spread through Miklagard. Frightened into panic by the rumours of the Turks at the door, the people had turned on each other, seeking out, as mankind will always do, those who worshipped God in a different way and using them as a focus for the angry attacks they could not make on the real enemy. And Ismail Adil Adnan, Agathe's gentle, courageous, compassionate husband, had been brutally slain; attacked and cut to pieces by the blood-hungry, mindless mob.

Then, with tears in his eyes, Harald had told Rollo how he had made the great sacrifice: fearing that the baby, as a child of mixed blood, would also be a target for the mob's fury, he had made his beloved daughter and her son flee the overheated, dangerous city, sending them, with only a servant woman for company, far away to the only kin he had.

You saved my life, old man, Rollo thought. *And as you nursed me back to health and strength, you opened your heart and shared your soul with me.*

He'd had little to offer in return, but what he did have was probably the best possible gift. The memory of that was good, and Rollo gave it free rein.

He had said to the old man, 'Be comforted. Agathe's long voyage won't be in vain.'

As he had heard the words, Harald's face lit up. 'Members of my family survive?' he whispered tentatively, as if it were almost too much to hope for.

'Indeed they do, and they are thriving,' Rollo said gently. He described Lassair and her family, striving to remember all the names. 'Your sister Cordeilla is dead –' he heard the big man gasp, the small sound quickly suppressed – 'but she lived to a good age, revered and loved by her family.'

'When did she die?' Harald asked, his voice shaking.

Rollo searched his memory for the detail. 'Two years ago. She's buried on the secret island.'

There was a long silence. Rollo, reluctant to break it, gave the man the time he seemed to need, and, eventually, he raised his head and looked straight at Rollo. His eyes were full of tears.

'She'd have had two of her brothers there to keep her company, if I'd tried harder,' he said. 'But it was all such a mess after the king fell. The men had flocked to him, protecting him, driving forward with him, and the heaps of corpses were thickest around him.' He bowed his head, his face working with emotion. 'I know Sigbehrt was right beside him,' he said quietly, 'because I heard him shout that great cry he always gave when his blood was up, and I saw him standing, so tall and proud – they used to call him the Mighty Oak – just before he was cut down. And, wherever Sigbehrt was, Sagar wouldn't be far away. He was an archer, really,' he went on, some of the life returning to his face as he became swept up in his memories, 'and his nickname was Sureshot. But when it came to close fighting, he was pretty handy at that, too, and anyway, since he was older than Sigbehrt – the oldest of the three of us – he reckoned it was his job to look after Sigbehrt and me.' He chuckled. 'It always looked so comical, seeing Sagar fussing round Sigbehrt, when Sigbehrt was a head and a half taller and twice as broad.'

As if his thoughts threatened to overcome him, he got up, paced to and fro across the little room, and then came back to sink down on to the end of the bed where Rollo lay. He said simply, 'I couldn't find them. There were so many of us, all searching for our own dead, and, in truth, given the injuries, it was no easy task. Then the rumours started – William the Bastard's men were coming back and they were going to finish off anyone they found still lurking around. That cleared away most of the living, I can tell you, and I took my chance and made one final attempt. I must have stared into a hundred dead faces, but I didn't find either of my brothers.' He gave a shaky sigh. 'They lie buried with all the others now, on the field where they sacrificed themselves for the way of life they wanted to see endure. All in vain.'

His head dropped. Respecting his mood, Rollo waited, not speaking. After quite some time, Harald got up again and went over to the table. He picked up an object and, turning back to the bed, held it out to Rollo.

It was a small knife, the fine, sharp blade set into a handle carved in a pattern of curls and swirls which, when Rollo looked closely, resolved into extraordinarily shaped birds and beasts. 'It's beautiful,' he said. 'Which one did it belong to?'

Harald smiled; a soft expression of happy reminiscence. 'Sagar. I found it not six paces from where the king fell.'

Rollo gave the knife back, and Harald, after clutching it briefly in his right hand, laid it back on the table. He coughed a couple of times, then said, 'So, you tell me I have a very pretty niece.'

'She's actually a great-niece, the granddaughter of your sister Cordeilla, but she is most certainly pretty.' Rollo was staring into Harald's eyes, understanding why their shape and colour had sparked off memories. 'She has your eyes,' he added.

Harald nodded, although he didn't speak. It seemed to Rollo that, for a few moments, speech was probably beyond him.

As *Gullinbursti* covered the miles – sometimes flying over the waves as fleet as a swan; sometimes, when the wind failed or blew from the wrong direction, moving laboriously under oars rowed by increasingly exhausted men – Rollo's mind roamed on. He thought often of Lassair; it was inevitable, given the depth of his sudden and intense friendship with the man who turned out to be her great-uncle. He wondered what she was doing, and if she was thinking of him.

He found himself almost hoping she wasn't. If he could make himself believe that, what he was about to do wouldn't make him feel so bad . . .

He would make his report to King William. He would be very well paid, for what he had to tell his king would please the man greatly, falling in as it did so neatly with how William judged events in the land beyond the seas would develop.

The Eastern Mediterranean was going to explode. The Seljuk Turks were disorganized; their great advances had ground to a standstill while men fought over which heir should succeed the sultan, and powerful lords throughout the territory quietly got on with creating their own small fiefdoms.

But the threat which the Seljuks posed to the Christians of Constantinople wasn't going to go away. The Turks held the Holy Places; they were more than capable of arranging matters so that no Christian pilgrim ever again walked where Jesus Christ was born, where he ministered, where he died, where he was resurrected. Sooner or later, the Turks would regain all their former strength and probably more, and then the assault would begin anew.

Alexius Comnenus would have no alternative but to appeal to the Church in the west for help. The Church would no doubt raise its powerful voice and call out for strong men, men of wealth and position, demanding their compliance, telling them in no uncertain terms that it was their duty as Christians. And kings and lords would answer: the draw of the fabled wealth of the east would be just too great.

King William of England would resist; he had already made that clear to Rollo, his trusted spy. William had his own scheme, however. His brother Robert, he was convinced, would race to answer the summons, and he would need money. In all likelihood he would beg a loan from William – nobody but a king would be able to provide the sort of funds such a venture would require – and William, after all, was family. William would agree, and Normandy would stand surety.

Rollo's retentive memory was full of the Holy Land. He had information to sell which would be of inestimable value to a man bent on recapturing the lands of the Turks. It would be of no use to King William, but there were others who would pay.

And why, Rollo mused, *should I not sell my hard-won intelligence twice over?* To King William first, for it was he who had sent Rollo on the mission and to whom he owed first loyalty.

But, once he had divulged to his king every last fact and figure, extrapolation and opinion that could possibly be of interest, then what was to stop him slipping away, adopting a different guise and finding another paymaster? One who, if Rollo was any judge, would lap up the precious information even more eagerly?

Robert, Duke of Normandy.

NINETEEN

Lord Gilbert saw to the removal and interment of Rosaria's body. I admired him for putting aside his angry resentment at how she'd fooled him, and doing the right thing. If I'm honest, it was a relief to see the last of her.

Although my aunt and I were in no doubt that Rosaria had poisoned her mistress in order to adopt her identity and take her place in what she believed would be Harald's wealthy, influential family, we did not tell Lord Gilbert. Edild reported to him that the corpse of Harald's daughter showed no obvious signs of poisoning, which I suppose was true. We would have had to look a lot deeper to discover the remnants of the substance that killed her. Without the label of murderess, Rosaria went quietly to her last resting place in the Aelf Fen graveyard.

I'd been very cross at first. I wanted her to face recrimination and punishment for what she'd done, even if only posthumously. But, as Edild pointed out, what was the point, when Rosaria would have to explain herself to the sternest judge of all? And, her voice unusually gentle, she reminded me that Rosaria's life hadn't been easy. 'To what lengths might you have been driven,' she asked me, 'had you been mutilated as she was?'

We might not have revealed the truth to Lord Gilbert, but I had to tell Jack. He and I had been involved right from the start, when we met Rosaria on the quay at Cambridge, and it was only right to explain what had happened in the church crypt. I sought him out later on the day we finally knew how Harald's daughter had met her death, meeting him coming out of Lakehall as I approached. When I explained how Edild and I had held back from checking the dead woman's stomach for poison because, as our kinswoman, we could not bring ourselves to do so, he nodded in understanding. 'For what it's worth,' he said, 'I couldn't have done it either.'

We buried Harald's daughter in the Aelf Fen graveyard, too. My family, once they all knew who she was, would have liked to have put her to rest her with her kin out on the little island, but Father Augustine seemed to have taken a personal responsibility for her, and her funeral and burial had been arranged before we could protest. Maybe the priest was right; she might have been deeply devout, and lying in hallowed ground the best place for her.

We didn't know her name. She was buried as the daughter of Harald of Aelf Fen and mother of Leafric.

I hope it was good enough.

The question that worried all of us was what was to become of the infant Leafric. He was the child of my great-uncle Harald's daughter; my Granny Cordeilla was his great-aunt. His mother was a first cousin to my father and Edild, he was a more distant cousin to me and my siblings, and I don't think any of us could have borne the idea of abandoning him. Yet we were poor people, and at times we had barely enough to feed ourselves and our close kin. My parents, I knew, were reluctant to take on the burden. Their youngest child – my little brother Leir – was six now, and there would be no more born to them. I knew that my mother had greeted the end of fertility with some relief. It would be cruel to play on her conscience and persuade her to take on yet another baby. I wondered if Edild would be prepared to adopt Leafric, and I dare say she thought the same about me. Both of us were, after all, single women with no dependants, and strong and healthy. But she had her work and, over and above that, I was pretty sure that she wasn't very maternal. The only child she would really have welcomed would have been Hrype's, and that was forbidden her.

In the end, it was my dear father who came up with the right solution.

He has a brother, Alwyn, the second eldest of Granny Cordeilla's children. When I say *brother*, I really mean half-brother, my father having been sired by Thorfinn and not by Cordeilla's quiet, reserved husband, Haward. It would be stretching the truth to say that my father and his two eldest siblings were close, but they cared for one another, were aware of how each other's lives progressed, and, to an extent, shared in each other's joys and griefs.

Alwyn was a fisherman and a fowler, living close to his

creatures and the land which they shared. He had always been
a self-contained man; my father and Granny Cordeilla always
said he closely resembled Haward. Apparently the family had all
decided he would live out his life in self-sufficient solitude, apart
from the fish and the water birds, but, when he was heading into
middle age, he surprised everyone by marrying a very pretty but
extremely shy woman named Edith. She, too, was on the cusp
of middle age, but nevertheless their union was just in time for
her to conceive and bear a child: a daughter who they named
Gytha.

Gytha was perhaps a couple of years older than my eldest
sibling, Goda, and she had married the year before my sister. (I
had only met her on a handful of occasions, but I could see that
she was much nicer than Goda; that, however, applied to most
people.) Gytha's husband was a very pleasant, nice-looking man
named Eddius, and I knew him rather better than I did Gytha
because he, like my father, was an eel-fisher, and quite often they
worked together.

You would have thought life was good for Gytha and Eddius.
They clearly loved each other. They had a tiny but immaculately
kept house close to a little-known waterway which was a fine
source of eels. They were young and strong. Yet they had a great
sorrow, for, despite seven years of marriage, they had no children.
I believe both of them had consulted Edild, and apparently there
was no obvious reason why the joys of parenthood had not been
forthcoming. I was well aware that the barrenness of the marriage
pained both of them, especially Gytha. On the rare occasions
since the wedding that I had seen the pair – often at some gathering to welcome the newest member of the family – it had
obviously taken a huge effort for Gytha to smile, congratulate
the new parents and dandle the proffered baby on her knee.

I learned afterwards that, as concerned as the rest of us over
Leafric's heartbreaking circumstances, my father had had a private
word with Edild, and she had quietly slipped away to see Gytha
and Eddius, and asked them if they would consider adopting a
six-month-old orphaned baby boy, adding, as if the proposal were
not tempting enough for a child-hungry couple, that the baby
was in fact kin to Gytha, her father and the baby's dead mother
having been first cousins.

It's rare in life that what is a highly satisfactory outcome for one party in an arrangement is equally good for the other, but the adoption of Leafric by Gytha and Eddius quite definitely qualified. Of course, I never met Harald's daughter alive; I only wish I had. But, from the moment I set eyes on Leafric, I had felt some sort of bond with him. It had affected me deeply to see him look so lost and sad, staring round him in puzzled misery as he tried to find the loving mother who wasn't coming back. Gytha wasn't the woman who bore him, but she made a very, very good substitute. Seeing her with her newly adopted son in her arms, smiling down into his little face, her eyes full of love and her hands as gentle as an angel's, it was hard not to be moved to tears. Had Harald's daughter been able to watch, too, I think she would have thanked her fenland cousin from the bottom of her heart.

Gytha and Eddius, knowing so little about their new son, decided to ask their priest to baptize him. The priest, a rotund, cheery, affectionate old man called Father Henry, readily agreed. As he said, better twice than not at all, and he was quite sure God wouldn't mind a repetition.

To my surprise and delight, Gytha asked if I would stand as their son's godmother. As I stood beside the font watching Father Henry pour the holy water over Leafric's firm little head, his wide blue eyes looked straight into mine and he smiled.

Jack returned to Cambridge. With both his official and his unofficial business concluded – trying to locate Lady Rosaria's kin, and identifying the woman whose body was found in the flooded pond – there was no reason for him to remain in Aelf Fen. He sought me out in the little back room at my aunt's, and, staring down at the floor, told me he was leaving. I thought he sounded detached – cold, even – but then he raised his head and I saw his expression.

'Will you be all right?' I said. I wanted to reach out for his hand, but I didn't know if he'd have welcomed such a gesture.

He grinned. 'All right?' he echoed.

I leaned closer, lowering my voice. 'Your sheriff's nephew sent a man to kill you. Unless he died out there where you left him –' the thought still haunted me – 'he'll undoubtedly try again.'

'Gaspard Picot was already among my many enemies,' Jack

said with a shrug. 'Admittedly, I now have another, in the form of Gaspard's hired killer, but one more won't make a lot of difference.'

I didn't understand how he could take it so calmly. 'But you—'

'How did you know?' he asked, interrupting. His eyes were intent, his expression hard to read. 'You knew the knife was aimed at us, and it was only because you threw yourself on me that it failed to find its target.'

I looked at him for some moments. I very nearly told him, but in the end I held back. 'I said to you before that there was something I'd tell you one day, but I wasn't yet ready,' I said. 'Do you remember?'

'Of course,' he said quietly.

'This – how I knew we were in danger – is connected to it.' That was an understatement, if ever there was one, and, feeling panicky, I hoped the shining stone wasn't somehow able to pick up my words.

He waited, but, when I didn't go on, he seemed to understand that I had said all I was going to. He smiled briefly. 'I can wait,' he murmured.

I didn't know how to respond. Very aware of Edild in the next room, I muttered something about returning to Cambridge myself soon and no doubt we'd bump into each other.

I think he felt as confused as I did. He gave me a sort of bow, backed out of Edild's little still room, struck his broad shoulders quite hard on the door frame, muttered something inaudible and then, turning so fast he almost tripped, hurried away.

I gave him a few moments, then slipped out after him. Crouching behind the low trees and bushes which conceal Edild's house from the track, I watched him mount the grey gelding and, with my beautiful Isis following behind on a long rein, break into a trot, and then a canter.

An uninformed observer would have thought he couldn't get away fast enough.

With a private smile, I went back inside and got on with my work.

I went back to Cambridge two weeks later.

I *had* to go back. I was in the middle of a course of

instruction. When I'd left, Gurdyman was in the middle of revealing to me the mysteries and intricacies of the Nine Herbs Charm, and I knew he had many more such charms to teach me before I return to Aelf Fen for the dead time that is the middle of winter.

There was something else for which I needed Gurdyman's wisdom; something whose importance, to me, exceeded every-thing else.

The shining stone.

I hadn't seen Thorfinn since the awful night I'd shouted at him and told him the stone wasn't his any more, and he could no longer use me to look into it for him. I had wished ever since that I had bitten back that parting shot, when I hurled at him that he ought to tell my father the truth.

I wasn't very proud of myself for that.

I'd hoped to see Hrype, for then I could have asked him to act as intermediary. But Hrype was away from the village, and, when I asked my aunt when he'd be back, she merely shrugged. Finally I went back to the little inlet where Thorfinn's boat had been moored, but, as I had feared, he was no longer there.

'Did you find out what you were so desperate to know, Grandfather?' I asked softly, gazing out over the marshy, treach-erous ground and the numerous small waterways threading through it. 'When I shut you out of using the shining stone, did you get Hrype to read the runes for you?'

I was still deeply curious about what he'd wanted me to see. What was the dreadful mission that Skuli had embarked upon? Had he succeeded? Was he even now on his way home, or had he and his crew perished? And – the question wouldn't leave me alone – why had that image of Rollo intruded?

I had no answers.

Bending down, I gathered a handful of dry grasses and the last of the autumn wildflowers, weaving them into a little wreath. I threw it in the water where Thorfinn had moored his boat. 'Be safe, Grandfather,' I said. 'And please come back soon.'

Then I turned and walked home.

I looked into the stone again that night. I cleared my mind, deliberately banishing thoughts of my grandfather and Skuli. I tried to let the stone speak to me. For a long time, I saw nothing but a sort of dark mist, with the ribbons of green and gold weaving through it. I was on the point of stopping when, just for an instant, I saw a long, beautifully shaped ship, flying on dark blue water under a huge square sail.

Then, in a flash so brief I couldn't be sure if I'd really seen it, I saw Rollo. For an instant, he looked straight at me. Then he turned away.

The stone withdrew into darkness. With shaking hands, I wrapped it and put it back in its leather bag, then I stowed it away.

I would not look into it again, I vowed, until I had Gurdyman to guide me.

I walked back to Cambridge singing.

The resumption of my studies and the request for Gurdyman's help with the shining stone were good enough motives for returning; both were true enough, after all.

But the real reason I wanted to be in Cambridge was because that's where I'd find Jack Chevestrier.